THE ZEALOTS

G.K. JOHNSON

Publisher's Cataloging-In-Publication Data
(Prepared by The Donohue Group, Inc.)

Names: Johnson, G. K., 1985- author. | Dawson, James, 1993- illustrator.
Title: The Zealots / G.K. Johnson ; [illustrated graphics: James Dawson].
Description: Littleton, Colorado : Capture Books, imprint G.K. Johnson, [2021] |
    Interest age level: 13 and up. | Includes glossary of Hebrew and Jewish terms. |
    Summary: "Comradery goes awry. Restless young men are separated in the
    political angst of Roman rule over Judea. One seeks vengeance to satiate his
    demons. The other is taken into the underbelly of the Holy City, Jerusalem"--
    Provided by publisher.
Identifiers: ISBN 9781951084264 (hardcover) | ISBN 9781951084271 (paperback) |
    ISBN 9781951084288 (mobi) | ISBN 9781951084301 (ePub)
Subjects: LCSH: Simon, Apostle, Saint--Juvenile fiction. | Zealots (Jewish party)--
    Juvenile fiction. | Jesus Christ--Passion--Juvenile fiction. | Revenge--Juvenile
    fiction. | Judaea (Region)--Politics and government--Juvenile fiction. | CYAC:
    Simon, Apostle, Saint--Fiction. | Zealots (Jewish party)--Fiction. | Jesus Christ--
    Passion--Fiction. | Revenge--Fiction. | Judaea (Region)--Politics and
    government--Fiction. | LCGFT: Historical fiction.
Classification: LCC PZ7.1.J613 Ze 2021 (print) | LCC PZ7.1.J613 (ebook) | DDC
    [Fic]--dc23

Preface

The Zealots is the product of standing on ancient soil and seeing, tasting, and smelling history coming to life around me. I learned about context. The depth and texture of lives I had only known on a surface level developed new acuity as my imagination soared. I began putting myself in the shoes of those I had read about.

For many of us, these images have been shaped by books we've read or teachers' lectures. A few of us have talked to people who have been there. But some of us have visited or lived in the places where these historical moments happened. How we experience history can drastically impact our view of the world.

For a large portion of my life, I viewed history through the lens of pictures in textbooks and PBS documentaries. But all of that changed when I had the privilege of actually visiting, in person, some of the places where history happened. Doing so changed my life.

I began to think differently about those whose names are only briefly mentioned in history. What were their stories, beyond what landed them in a textbook or historical document? I let my mind wander, and this is the story that revealed itself. I hope you enjoy it.

For David, the love of my life.
Thank you for showing me
what grace and true love look like.

Y e s h u a

I

Yeshua reached down and scooped up a handful of dark, rich soil. Standing, he allowed the warm earth to sift between his fingers. An east wind distracted him, whispering through the sagebrush. It carried the sweet scents of lavender and sage, and it ruffled his linen tunic against his legs.

A rabbit darted past, and then another, weaving an erratic path through the bushes. Yeshua watched them until they disappeared over a nearby hill.

Before him lay the freshwater Sea of Galilee, reflecting the oranges, pinks, and reds of the descending sun that was dropping slowly behind its surface. No fishing boats were left bobbing on the sea's surface tonight as *Shabbat*, the day of rest, would soon begin. Already Yeshua could see one star twinkling in the dusky sky, and he knew that when three appeared, the *shofar* would trumpet the start of Shabbat.

"Yeshua!" He turned at the sound of his friend running toward him, out of breath.

"We have to hurry! Did you find it?"

"No," Yeshua shook his head. The errant arrow shot from twenty-five yards away seemed to have disappeared.

"Maybe you hit it?" Shim'on suggested.

"Maybe." Yeshua shrugged, "I don't see any blood, so I'm not sure."

1

Once again. he scanned the foliage and ground around him for signs of blood or rabbit fur but saw neither.

"It's almost time for the shofar to be blown. We need to get back." Shim'on paused for a moment, then flashed a mischievous grin. He turned and ran, his words caught in the wind, "Race you home!"

Yeshua set off after Shim'on, their course undulating in the hilly terrain. Puffs of brown dust rose from their sandaled footfalls. Breathing hard, Yeshua tried to keep Shim'on in view. He knew it would take all his energy simply to keep up with the other boy's pace.

While fifteen-year-old Shim'on was tall and lanky and built for running, fourteen-year-old Yeshua was shorter and more muscular. His frame and additional weight did not aid in speed. The differences between the boys did not end with physical appearance. Whereas Shim'on was loud and passionate to the point of being hot-headed at times, Yeshua had a steady and quiet demeanor, which gave him an unspoken air of wisdom beyond his years. Despite their differences, they were like brothers to one another.

The sun was ducking below the horizon as Yeshua descended the final hill. He could see the town of nearly fifteen hundred residents in the dusk. Although it was evening, the village of Capernaum still showed vigorous signs of life. Through open doors and windows, he could see women lighting the customary Shabbat candles. Soldiers stood at their posts or walked through the town in cadres, mixing with travelers and residents of Capernaum.

Shim'on halted his run just before the entrance to the village and stood cockily, hands on his hips. Laughing breathlessly,

Yeshua knew his friend was teasing. He threw up his arms in false protest and Shim'on laughed.

Running past him into the village, Yeshua jibed, "Now you're tired? You may be faster, but it's obvious who has more endurance."

Two soldiers who were standing nearby watched them with disinterest, clearly bored and ready for their evening meal.

Shim'on grinned back, "I didn't want you to feel too outpaced brother."

A group of families on their way to the synagogue approached, and Yeshua watched as Shim'on suddenly flushed. Yeshua knew the reason for his friend's reaction was the pretty brunctte who smiled at him shyly.

"Shim'on?" Yeshua teasingly prodded Shim'on. When his friend failed to respond he jabbed him with his elbow.

"Ow!" Shim'on glared at him and flushed again as the girl passed by.

Yeshua laughed, "I'll see you at the synagogue."

With the sky growing darker and the heat in the air refusing to relent, he wiped the sweat trickling down his forehead. Per Hebrew law, he needed to perform his ritual *mikvah* bath before the start of Shabbat. There were mikvahs available in town, but the best source for cleansing was the Sea of Galilee. Yeshua hurried to the shore and disrobed.

The cold water refreshed as he submerged himself once, twice, and three times reciting the customary blessing:

"Blessed are You, O Lord, our Adonai, King of the universe, who has sanctified us with Your commandments and commanded us concerning the immersion."

Ceremonially clean, Yeshua hastened to the black basalt dwellings of Capernaum.

"Yeshua!" *immah* clucked her tongue as he entered the u-shaped compound of dwellings where he and his parents, siblings, and extended family lived. "We've been waiting. Where have you been?"

"We need to leave now, Son." A*bba* looked him over sternly, yet Yeshua noticed a twinkle of relief in his eye.

The shofar rang the customary notice that no further labor could be done until the end of Shabbat, tomorrow evening.

Yeshua fell into step beside his abba as they left home for the synagogue, trailed by his immah and two younger siblings.

"Did you get anything tonight?" Bin-yamin asked.

"I may have hit a rabbit, but I couldn't find it," Yeshua answered.

"Well then, it's good your immah already has dinner prepared," his abba winked at him, then smiled as he nodded his head in greeting to a neighbor. Everyone in Capernaum knew Bin-yamin Bar Joicha. He was the rabbi of the town's synagogue school and was respected by most who knew him.

Bin-yamin was also a *tekton,* skilled at working with wood and stone. As customary, Bin-yamin was teaching Yeshua to be a similar craftsman, just as his own abba had taught him.

Many in Capernaum and towns nearby lived in the homes Bin-yamin and Yeshua had helped to construct.

Yeshua's abba was a lover of peace and encouraged those under his teaching to fight with words if necessary, but never weapons. His perspective stood in sharp contrast to the members of the violent Roman resistance movement, the Zealots.

Men, women, and children stood in groups outside the synagogue and many greeted Bin-yamin and Yeshua with respect as they entered the courtyard. The rabbi and his family were considered among those most righteous in town, and Yeshua couldn't help but enjoy the attention.

Glancing around the courtyard, Yeshua saw Shim'on standing beside his abba and brother. Bin-yamin good-naturedly joked that the family of fishermen were never hard to find because of their height and volume. It was true. Many times, Yeshua could hear Shim'on before seeing him. Yitzchak, Shim'on, and Hanoch were cut from the same cloth. Passionate, loud, and fiercely loyal, Yitzchak was liked and respected by most who knew him. Though simple fishermen, Yitzchak and his family were religiously devout, and kept the law nearly as adamantly as Bin-yamin and his family. While Bin-yamin adhered to maintaining a peaceful coexistence with the Romans, however, Yitzchak tended to be rebellious, refusing to pay taxes to Rome. He showed no respect to their oppressors, holding fast to the belief that doing so would mean breaking Adonai's law. Shim'on shared his abba's passionate beliefs.

Not surprisingly, Yitzchak's deep voice could be heard across the courtyard as Yeshua's family drew near, but Yeshua couldn't quite make out his words. When Yeshua caught a glimpse of Shim'on's face, it was flushed with anger.

What's going on with him? he wondered as he climbed the steps to the synagogue. But there wasn't time to find out before the assembly began. The building, which Bin-yamin and Yeshua had helped to construct, was made of black basalt like the rest of the structures in town and was neither beautiful nor pretentious. Bin-yamin often said that no one could judge the value of what lay within a man's heart simply from looking at the exterior, and the same was true of the synagogue. While the outside of the building was unassuming, what happened inside had eternal value to those who worshipped there.

The doorway opened into a large area. Columns on either side of the room were spaced approximately ten feet apart and supported the roof.

The design lent the interior an air of understated grandeur. Four windows were cut from each of the synagogue's walls and allowed light and airflow into the space. Three large black stone steps descended from one of the walls. During the week, students sat on these steps during school, listening, discussing, and memorizing whatever the rabbi, his abba, taught.

On Shabbat, these steps were reserved for upper-class Hebrews, and commoners sat on mats on the floor. In the center of the room was a small platform where those leading the assembly stood, and a chest containing numerous parchments sat nearby. Bin-yamin Bar Joicha was the teacher of the synagogue during the week, but other religious elders in Capernaum took turns leading the community spiritually on Shabbat. Yeshua and the rest of the family stood and recited the opening *Shema* with the other worshippers gathered.

The words poured out beautifully, each unique voice lending depth and passion to the verses.

"Hear, Israel, the Lord is our Adonai, the Lord is One. Blessed is the name of His glorious kingdom forever and ever.

"You shall love the Lord your Adonai with all your heart and with all your soul and with all your might. Take to heart these instructions with which I charge you this day. Impress them upon your children. Recite them when you stay at home and when you are away, when you lie down and when you get up. Bind them as a sign on your hand

and let them serve as a symbol on your forehead, inscribe them on the doorposts of your house and on your gates."

The prayer was handed down from the time of their ancient leader, Moses, and reminded them of all Adonai had promised and commanded during their escape from Egypt hundreds of years prior. After reading from a portion of the *Torah*, specifically from a teaching given by Adonai to Moses, and passed to the *Nevi'im*, the elder blessed them and the villagers dispersed to their homes.

From the top of the synagogue steps, Yeshua could see Shim'on's curly head in the street, surrounded by his family. The evening air was still hot, and Yeshua slapped at a mosquito.

"Shim'on!"

His friend glanced his way, but shook his head and mouthed the word, "later". Bin-yamin passed him on the stairs and Yeshua watched as he spoke with Shim'on's abba, Yitzchak, who still looked upset. It was odd. Just hours ago, Shim'on was fine. What had happened since then to merit such bad temper? Yeshua wondered if Yitzchak's uncompromising beliefs had caused another altercation with the Romans.

Bin-yamin soon rejoined the family and they turned toward home. As they walked, they passed six Roman soldiers marching toward the barracks. They walked in formation, their red capes slung over one shoulder and their iron armor glinting with the reflection of the fiery torches they carried for light. Their swords clanked by their sides and the gravel crunched loudly beneath their feet, exuding fierce pride and arrogance. The soldiers posted in Capernaum were a mix of Romans and mercenaries from nearby areas, and had been hired by Herod, Tetrarch of Galilee.

After they passed, Yeshua listened as his abba spoke softly to his immah.

"Yitzchak was visited by a group of soldiers collecting taxes this afternoon. He refused to pay. Miriam was afraid and finally brought them the money, but by then they were demanding more than the standard tax. A penalty, they said. Of course, Yitzchak doesn't have that amount." Bin-yamin's voice was grim. "They forced them to give up their donkey and made them promise to fulfill the tax with interest."

Sarai murmured softly.

Yeshua now understood the anger on Shim'on's face. His abba was extorted while they were at target practice. He felt a flash of anger for his friend.

Bin-yamin continued, "I pray Yitzchak will quickly realize the danger he puts his family in." He turned to Sarai. "Let Miriam know they can have use of our donkey whenever they need him. Adonai has given us what we have to share."

They reached home and Sarai nodded in agreement as Bin-yamin closed the door behind them. Turning away from the rest of the family, his abba lowered his voice so that only Yeshua and Sarai could hear him, "Also, I am afraid that Yitzchak may be meeting with the Zealots."

"Oh no," Sarai sounded concerned. "I wish he would realize that violence is not the way of Adonai."

Bin-yamin shook his head, "Amen, but even the Torah says a tooth for a tooth, an eye for an eye. There are those who use those words to justify vengeance on our enemies. I believe Yitzchak is beginning to feel that way as well." He looked sad. "Although I don't take their side, I can understand their anger. Adonai knows this Roman oppression is taking its toll on our people."

"Adonai help us," Immah said softly.

Signaling that it was time to end the conversation, Bin-yamin walked across the room with a smile, "Let's pray and eat!"

Parents, children, aunts, uncles, cousins, and grandparents prepared for the customary Shabbat meal, reclining on mats around the meal. The ground in the center of the group was soon filled with platters of food previously prepared by the women in Yeshua's family so as not to break Shabbat law. Bin-yamin held up a clay cup of red wine and the rest of the family lifted their cups of wine for the adults and grape juice for the children as he recited the *Kiddush,* for sanctification.

"Praise to You, Adonai our Adonai, Sovereign of the universe, Creator of the fruit of the vine. Praise to You, Adonai our Adonai, Sovereign of the universe who, finding favor with us, sanctified us with mitzvot. In love and favor, You made the Holy Shabbat our heritage as a reminder of the work of Creation. As first among our sacred days, it recalls the Exodus from Egypt. You chose us and set us apart from the peoples. In love and favor, you have given us Your Holy Shabbat as an inheritance."

The family drank from their cups as they celebrated Adonai's gift of a day of rest, and the table grew cheery and loud as they talked and served themselves from the dishes of warm challah, sweet and eggy, the hearty kugel, and savory lamb. Normally, Yeshua enjoyed the relaxed dinner and time with his family, but tonight his mind was on other things. He needed to talk to Shim'on. Did he know that his abba was meeting with the Zealots? An idea came to him.

Once everyone was asleep, he would sneak out to Shim'on's home and talk to him about all of this. If Bin-yamin found out he would discourage the idea, but Yeshua knew that he would not be breaking Shabbat law.

After the meal was finished and everyone was in bed, Yeshua rolled off his mat. He walked carefully toward the door. His home was simply a series of rooms with dirt floors, and a hearth in the corner of the largest communal space. When the day came that Yeshua found a bride, his abba would help him add another room to the home.

The fire that Yeshua's immah had added logs to before going to bed cracked suddenly, a pocket of sap popping in the heat. Yeshua paused, hoping no one would wake up and see him at the door. The orange light that flickered on the faces of his sleeping parents, sister, and brother showed no signs of wakefulness.

He breathed a sigh of relief as he simultaneously pulled the door open noiselessly and closed it behind him in one quick movement. There! He was out and on the street.

The full moon bathed the dirt around and the stone dwellings on either side in a pale bluish light. Yeshua walked briskly in the direction of Shim'on's home. He hoped that no soldiers were out in the area at this time of night. It would be unpleasant to try to explain why a Hebrew boy was out this late, especially on Shabbat. The crunching of gravel under his feet sounded loud in the stillness and he started at the sudden bark of a dog. Yeshua was slightly nervous, aware of the foolhardiness of this plan. Of course, he had snuck out before and for much less serious reasons.

One time several years ago, he and Shim'on had met in the late hours of the night to observe a regiment of Roman soldiers from the hills above. They had pretended they were David of old, spying on King Saul and his troops. But he was a foolish youth then, unaware of the real risks of being caught by soldiers.

Tonight was different. He and Shim'on were young men now, and the Roman occupation had been in effect their entire lives and beyond, over five decades ago. They were no longer children who were unable to grasp the reality of their life circumstances.

Yeshua reached Shim'on's home and knelt in the darkness beside it. He knew Shim'on would still be awake after the events of the day, and he knew the mat that he shared with his brother was against this wall. He lightly tapped on the mud and stone with his knuckles and then waited.

After several minutes Shim'on emerged and gestured to Yeshua to follow him. The young men moved quietly down the street, and Yeshua was relieved not to hear any more dogs barking. The homes dwindled and they came to a short rock wall.

Finally, they reached the sea and Yeshua breathed a sigh of relief. There would be no soldiers here at this time of night. Together, the young men walked to Shim'on's family boat.

The vessel was pulled part way onto the sandy shore, and they climbed over the railing, their nostrils enveloped in the scent of brackish water mingled with the pungent smell of fish. They wouldn't push out tonight as it was Shabbat, and the action of effort was not allowed.

Enjoying the warm air, Yeshua could hear the gentle lapping of the Sea of Galilee against the shore. The stars, bright-white needle pricks against the blue-black sky, reflected off the surface of the water which gently nudged the boat back and forth. A night under the star-studded sky was a fisherman's busiest time. Except for Shabbat when the fishermen and the rest of Capernaum's Hebrew population rested.

"Hard to believe that there could be such evil in our land when I'm on the water." Shim'on said, looking out on the sea. A stiff wind blew across the water's surface, flattening his tunic against his legs and kicking up whitecaps that rocked the boat. "If only we could live out here, away from them."

Yeshua knew that his friend meant the Romans and those who served them. He nodded and Shim'on glanced at him darkly.

"You heard, then?"

"Yes. I'm so sorry, Shim'on. I wish that we weren't in the hills when they came."

"I feel the same way, but really, what difference would that have made?" Shim'on sat heavily on a pile of fishing nets. "It's not as though I could have stopped them from taking our donkey. But I wish I could have kept Immah from giving in to them."

"But if your immah hadn't given them the money, it could have been even worse for your family." Yeshua reasoned.

A flash of anger crossed Shim'on's face and then departed, leaving behind a look of defeat.

"I suppose." The look of anger reappeared. "It just feels as though our lives are not our own anymore! Is this my future? Spending my days fishing just so I can pay all that I earn to Herod? I would rather die!"

Shim'on stopped talking and sat, clenching, and unclenching his fists and looking at the wooden decking beneath his feet.

"I don't like them either," Yeshua said.

"Don't *like* them?" Shim'on snorted. "You're just like your abba."

"What does that mean?" Yeshua asked defensively.

"Don't you see, Yeshua?" Shim'on threw his hands up. "They demand the place and honor that rightfully belongs to Adonai! They demand that we worship Rome! You *don't like* them. Well, I and my family *hate* them. And we refuse to give them what they want, unlike your abba."

Shim'on's words hurt, but Yeshua struggled to formulate a response. It was true; Bin-yamin taught tolerance of their enemies. But that didn't mean he worshipped Rome. He didn't know how to communicate this to Shim'on, though.

"If you hate them so much, why aren't you doing something about it, then?" Yeshua asked angrily.

"I am." Shim'on said, lifting his head and looking at him.

"What?"

"My abba has been meeting with the Zealots, and I'm going to too."

So Shim'on did know. "How? Where do they meet?" Yeshua asked. The Zealots were well known for their passionate hatred of the Romans and the violence they used to strike back against them, but who the members were and where they met was not common knowledge.

"Probably in the hills late at night." Shim'on shrugged, "There's lots of places to hide out there."

Yeshua let out a long breath. "How does he keep the other fishermen from noticing when he's gone?"

"He told Hanoch and I, but we're the only ones who know. Well, except for you now. We have to tell lies to the others," Shim'on answered, an edge of defensiveness in his voice.

Yeshua shook his head, "This is dangerous, Brother. If he were caught by the Romans, they'd likely kill him. You, Hanoch, and the hired men are in danger too." He felt safer playing this role of friend. "Do not murder" was one of the ten commandments handed down by Moses. A man could only justifiably kill another if commanded by Adonai.

Shim'on surprised him by looking up from the planking beneath his feet and uttering a short laugh, "Yeshua, don't you see? What does your abba teach every day? That Adonai hears us, that He sees all, that He is going to send the *Mashiach*. We've all waited for the Anointed One to save us one day soon! But where is this Mashiach? How could Adonai allow these Romans to treat us this way? They rob us at best and destroy us at worst!" He flung his head up proudly. "What if Adonai's will means that we defend ourselves and strike back at Rome? What if the Zealots are the means that Adonai uses to bring about His restoration of our people? The Creator has given us arms as well as eyes. He has chosen us, not them."

Yeshua sucked in his breath. He was grateful that they were alone on the vessel. Such talk was dangerous, and both boys knew it.

"Just think of our forefathers," Shim'on continued, clearly passionate. "King David, or even Saul before him. They fought anyone who stood against them. They killed thousands in the name of Adonai. And what happened? Adonai blessed them with authority over the land and abundance."

"Yes, but they did those things because Adonai specifically told them to. He spoke through the Nevi'im," Yeshua replied, "but there are no Nevi'im telling us to revolt against the Romans. There is only the prophesied Mashiach."

"Yes," Shim'on nodded, "And what if the purpose of the Zealots is to demonstrate our trust in Adonai's promise of a Mashiach by preparing the way for him? It is prophesied that he will lead us to conquer our enemies and restore the glory of our people. We can begin that effort!"

"What do you plan to do?" Yeshua asked.

"I'm not sure yet," Shim'on replied, "I just know that I am done doing nothing. I'm going to follow Abba to a meeting of the Zealots and find out what they're planning."

A tingling energy tightened in Yeshua's chest. Despite his conflicted thoughts he said slowly, "Let me know when you go, I may go with you."

"Go with me to a meeting of the Zealots?" Shim'on echoed his surprise, "Why? What if your abba found out?"

"Do you think that I am not also weary of Roman rule? What happened with your abba today has made me angry also. What's the harm in finding out what the Zealots are planning to do?" He didn't say the other reason he wanted to go; that he was intrigued by the idea of being in control of their freedom.

"All right," Shim'on said skeptically, "But I would think carefully about it, Yeshua. You're not like us. At least my abba is already going to their meetings. Your abba would never approve." He glanced up at the sky trying to determine the time, "I should be going."

"You don't have a right to tell me what I can or can't do." Yeshua felt an uncharacteristic flash of anger.

Shim'on turned to face him. "Yeshua. You're my best friend, but you know that we're different. You may not be a rabbi, but your father is. My family follows the law, but we're willing to fight and die for it. Your abba teaches peace. I just don't think that you could kill another man."

As if mirroring his feelings, a gust of wind whipped at Yeshua's shoulder-length hair. He felt like shouting. Who was Shim'on to tell him what he could or could not do? Both of their families were passionate for Adonai and His law, but they had each come to different conclusions as to what Adonai wanted of them. His family believed Adonai's will was to follow the law

15

and comply with their enemies' demands, doing their best to live a life of peace. Yitzchak's family, however, believed that serving Adonai meant defying any other power that set itself up as their authority. And they were willing to shed blood over their beliefs. Despite knowing their differences, Yeshua resented Shim'on's judgment that he didn't have what was required to be a Zealot.

He simmered as Shim'on jumped from the boat. The boys walked back up the hill to town and separated to their homes without speaking.

Yeshua closed the door softly and went to his mat, sliding under the blanket. He wasn't tired though. His heart thumped quickly in his chest and his mind was fully awake.

The more he thought of spying on a meeting of the Zealots with Shim'on, the more uncertain he felt. The excitement and danger of it intrigued him, yet he felt guilty even considering it. His anger toward Shim'on lessened, but he felt disoriented by his friend's words regarding their differences. It was the first time that he felt distant from Shim'on.

Yeshua lay awake for what seemed a long time considering the distinct directions awaiting his future and that of Shim'on's. Finally, moments before dawn, he fell asleep.

II

A rooster's incessant crowing woke Yeshua on Sunday morning, but he lay with his eyes closed resisting the urge to prepare for the day. In the lingering darkness, he reviewed his conversation with Shim'on on the boat a couple of days prior, allowing his sleepy body to catch up to his mind. Murmurs of his abba speaking quietly to his immah filled the background. Sleepy embers of the fire crunched softly as Sarai prodded them back to life with a stick.

Yeshua pictured his sister kneading and rolling *lehem*, and heard the corresponding thump each time she turned the dough over on the clay board. Once the fire was sufficiently hot, she would lay today's loaf over the coals to bake.

Yeshua sat up on his mat and murmured aloud the *Modeh Ani*. "I offer thanks to You, living and eternal King, for You have mercifully restored my soul within me; Your faithfulness is great." He then rose and walked over to the basin in the corner of the room.

He cleaned his hands to as sanctify them also for the day ahead as the household code dictated. Using the pitcher nearby, he poured cold water over his left hand, and then his right, performing the morning *netilat yedayim,* and reciting the accompanying prayer,

"Blessed are You, Lord our Adonai, King of the universe, who has sanctified us with Your commandments, and commanded us concerning the washing of the hands."

The familiar rituals comforted him as he was reminded of his sole purpose: to obey Adonai. To be righteous. Yeshua had spent the previous day mulling over his conversation with Shim'on. After a while, intense guilt had set in over even considering going to a meeting of the Zealots. Yeshua had pondered what the Torah and Nevi'im said about Adonai fighting for them. He longed for assurance that the Hebrews were Adonai's chosen people, and that they need not defend themselves against Rome.

He questioned Bin-yamin. "Abba, why do the Zealots pursue a path of violence when Adonai tells us not to kill?"

His abba thoughtfully responded, "Sometimes a man finds it easier to pretend that he can control his life and the outcome of a situation. Sometimes, he is impatient and does not want to depend on Adonai. But what he truly fears is that Adonai may not see his situation and that He does not care." His abba looked sad, "The man feels alone and afraid and wants to make his enemies feel as he does. He tries to justify his violence by saying that he is bringing about Adonai's justice. And this is what the Zealots do. But Adonai does see. He tells us that He does and that we are not forgotten. And that He is sending His Mashiach soon. We must wait for the Mashiach to bring justice against our enemies."

Bin-yamin's face took on the joyful look of peace that it always did when he spoke of the Mashiach's coming. Hundreds of years earlier, the Nevi'im spoke concerning the Anointed One, who would make Judea the epicenter of the known world. He would bring about the destruction of their enemies and restore the Hebrews' wealth and success. He would rebuild the temple in Jerusalem, which was damaged and only a shadow of its former glory. Many believed that the Mashiach would be a descendant of King David himself.

The Zealots

As always, his reading and conversation with his abba encouraged Yeshua. He felt peace this morning that the way of the Zealots was not the answer. They must wait for the coming of the Mashiach. He could understand Shim'on's anger, of course. But when Yeshua told him of the peace that he had found in Adonai's promises in the Torah, surely Shim'on would agree with him and see the truth. In the meantime, he tried to press Shim'on's words concerning their differences to the back of his mind.

After washing, Yeshua took the food his immah gave him and set off for the synagogue with his abba and his younger brother, Tobias. Yeshua's sister had attended school until she was ten, the age at which girls then stayed home, learning, and preparing to be a wife and immah.

Tobias was five, which meant he was in *Beth Sefer*, for elementary learners. Yeshua attended *Beth Midrash*, a special learning privilege for those gifted in the Torah and learning to interpret it orally for others. Only two other young men studied Torah alongside him learning to faithfully divide the *Mishnah*.

All ages were taught by his abba at the synagogue. After the midday meal the students were dismissed, and Yeshua and his abba worked as tektons for the remainder of the day. Currently they were among a group commissioned by Herod to add to the Roman garrison. The job provided for their needs, but Yeshua would have preferred any other work to that of aiding the Romans. It was far from joy to be forced to help the military presence in their city grow stronger.

Yeshua breathed in the crisp air, enjoying the sounds of birds chirping mixed with the soft lapping of the Sea of Galilee. Before he saw the sea, he could hear the fishermen speaking to one another, their voices echoing off the water between the surrounding hills. Soon the sea came into view, and their steps slowed as they enjoyed the beauty before them. The sun was beginning to edge over the mountains, the light shattering over the water.

Fishing boats bobbed along the shore as the fishermen unloaded their catches. Their wives and young children helped to sort the fish, preparing them to sell at the market.

Yeshua knew that the fishermen's day was far from over, however. They would spend the next several hours cleaning and mending their nets in preparation to go out on the water again that night. It was the life of a fisherman.

Fish jumped to catch the insects humming over the water's surface. Gulls circled in the air above them, keeping a sharp eye out for any opportunity of food. Shim'on was out there, Yeshua knew, helping his abba and brother with their catch.

As they passed a soldier on the street, Bin-yamin smiled at the man, blessing him with "*Shalom*". Yeshua, always impressed by Abba's kindness, even to their enemies, had asked him about it once.

"How else will they know that we are different?" His abba told Yeshua, "If our actions and words are no different than the Gentiles?" By Gentiles, Bin-yamin meant those who were not Adonai's chosen people.

The soldiers were initially surprised by his greetings until they came to expect them from the rabbi. Those who knew Bin-yamin greeted him on the street, drawing a critical eye from those surrounding them.

For his part, Yeshua ignored the soldiers. Capernaum belonged to the Hebrews, not the scum who served Rome.

"We had best get ready," Bin-yamin said as he turned to climb the stairs to the synagogue's entrance.

Yeshua sighed. Some days he longed to be outside and wished he wasn't in Beth Midrash so that he could join Shim'on on his abba's boat. He turned to follow Bin-yamin and settled himself and the sack containing his meal on one of the black basalt steps inside the synagogue.

He watched as his abba pulled several parchments from an urn and unfurled them on the table at the front of the room. Parchment and writing utensils were precious and rare, so while his father taught from the scrolls, the students were expected to memorize all the Torah and the teachings they discussed. In several years, he would cease attending Beth Midrash altogether, and commit to the trade he would invest his life in. Only those who were exceptionally gifted would be called to follow in the rabbi's footsteps.

By now, most of the village's young children sat around Yeshua on the steps. Bin-yamin stepped to the front of the table and cleared his throat, causing conversation to quiet.

"So," Bin-yamin said, directing his words to Shim'on and the two young men who sat beside him, "Why do we wear the *tallit*?" He touched the prayer shawl draped over his shoulders. The tassels of his tallit hung bright blue against Bin-yamin's tunic. Yeshua also wore a tallit, as did all Jewish men, but why? Marcus, who sat beside Yeshua, raised his hand, "To remember, Rabbi."

"Yes," Bin-yamin nodded, "but what is it that we are remembering?"

Marcus responded, "The Torah tells us that the *tekhelet* ought to remind us to live holy lives. Adonai tells Moses, "'You shall have the tassel, that you may look upon it and remember all the commandments of the Lord and act faithfully on them being holy for Adonai.'"

"Yes, well spoken," Bin-yamin praised Marcus, "and why," he looked at Yeshua, fingering the fringe on his tallit, "are the tassels blue?"

Yeshua raised his hand, "Rabbi, because blue indicates royalty and kingship. Adonai wants his people to be set apart from all others."

"Exactly," Bin-yamin responded. "And this is why we must obey all of Adonai's commandments. So that in doing so, we may be saved by Adonai and set apart from the Gentiles who surround us."

Just then, Yeshua heard rapid footfalls on the outside stairs. Breathing heavily, Shim'on burst into the room. Panic filled his eyes and he glanced around before taking a step toward Bin-yamin.

"Please, Rabbi, you have to help me! He's bleeding— so much! I tried to find Hanoch, but soldiers are all over the shore and I couldn't—he's badly hurt!"

III

The suddenness of Shim'on's appearance surprised everyone and, except for his raspy breaths, the room was completely silent. Shim'on's cream-colored linen tunic hung wet with sweat, and his pants and sandals were slick with dark brown mud, leaving gritty prints on the synagogue floor. Dark crimson blood covered the front of his tunic, and a streak of blood stretched across his forehead where he had wiped sweat away.

Trying to maintain calm despite Shim'on's disturbing appearance, Bin-yamin spoke, "All of you are dismissed. Please return to your families. I will see you tomorrow." He waited until all the children, aside from his sons, exited the synagogue before turning back to Shim'on.

"Now, who is hurt, Son?"

"My abba!" Shim'on said, his voice unsteady.

Bin-yamin's face filled with concern. "Where is he?"

"Come with me!" Shim'on said in a half yell, half sob. He turned and stumbled toward the synagogue door.

"Shim'on, wait." Picking up his sack, Bin-yamin gestured to Yeshua, who woke from his surprise and leapt from his seat, nudging Tobias ahead of him. Bin-yamin insisted that they stop at their home to leave Tobias with Sarai, and for Shim'on to get a fresh tunic. Yeshua knew what his abba was thinking. The soldiers would be suspicious if they saw Shim'on in his blood-soaked clothes. It was a miracle that he hadn't already been stopped and questioned, especially considering that he had come to the synagogue to find them.

Yeshua knew his friend was not thinking clearly. Sarai looked up in bewilderment as they entered the house, and Bin-yamin quickly explained the situation to her.

They left the home again minutes later with Shim'on in the lead. The streets brimmed full as usual. Capernaum was a hub city near the *Via Maris,* the Way of the Sea. The road ran from Galilee to Samaria and cut through the lush Jezreel Valley. Traveling with the daily commotion blanketing the Via Marias route to and from Capernaum, Shim'on and his companions were simply faces in the crowd. The trio finally left the city and entered the hills. The sun hung high in the sky and beat down upon them.

Yeshua saw no rabbits today; they were all in their burrows hiding from the heat. He could tell Shim'on was exhausted. But the young man still ran, up and down the green and brown hills and through the sagebrush. Unlike their last run, it was not difficult for Yeshua to keep pace with him.

Twice, Shim'on tripped over undulations in the soil. Once, Bin-yamin reached out to steady him, otherwise he would have fallen. Yeshua saw his abba's tunic grow dark with sweat against his back and then realized his own hands were wet with it, the sweat dripping off his fingers and falling like raindrops onto the dry earth. Approaching another hill, Shim'on stumbled up it, propelled by sheer momentum. They finally reached a plateau at the top of the incline, and Shim'on led them to a copse of olive trees that provided a small patch of shade.

Yeshua slowed, trying to catch his breath. He glanced around for any signs of life but saw none. Ahead, he saw Shim'on fall to his knees at the base of one of the olive trees and quickened his gait to a jog. Reaching the tree, he joined his abba, then took a step back at what he saw.

Shim'on's abba, Yitzchak, lay on the ground before them. Yeshua could now discern the reason for the bloodstains on his friend's tunic. This was not due to a fall. Yitzchak's chest and head were bloody, and he looked to be barely conscious. His olive-hued skin was pale and every so often a shiver passed through his body. It was clear he had lost much blood.

The wounded man groaned, a strange noise to Yeshua's ears. Yitzchak was a strong bear of a man and seeing him so helpless seemed wrong to Yeshua.

Bin-yamin knelt on the ground beside Yitzchak and reached out to touch the man's arm. Yitzchak stirred and his eyelids fluttered but did not open.

"Shim'on, how did this happen?" he asked quietly, as he began to tear cloth from the hem of his tunic to bandage Yitzchak's wounds.

Following his abba's lead, Yeshua ripped a strip of material from his own tunic and handed it to Bin-yamin. His abba pulled away the tattered remains of Yitzchak's tunic and poured water from a flask onto the bloody wounds.

The man moaned incoherently and Shim'on cleared his throat, his eyes red and bloodshot. "Roman soldiers," he replied. "Last night he went to a meeting of the Zealots." He glanced at Bin-yamin, trying to gauge his reaction.

Bin-yamin's eyes focused on the work at hand, and he nodded.

Yeshua wished he could tell Shim'on that his abba already knew about Yitzchak meeting with the Zealots and did not harbor any judgment toward him, but now was not the time. Shim'on continued, "I followed him. I made sure to leave enough distance between us that he wouldn't hear me. I know that he wouldn't have wanted me to come."

Shim'on coughed, trying to compose himself. "We hiked east into the hills for close to three miles. I saw Abba join a group of maybe fifty men. There was only a half-moon and no other light, so it was hard to tell exactly in the dark. I stayed in the shadows near a hill. It was so quiet that it wasn't difficult to hear them speak."

Yitzchak shuddered uncontrollably on the ground. Blood leaked out of his mouth.

Shim'on paused as Bin-yamin worked to wrap the cloth from their tunics around Yitzchak's chest and head. He winced as spots of the material instantly grew bloody. Shim'on shifted his legs under him.

Yeshua was curious to know what the group talked about, but Shim'on continued, "They met for an hour or so, then separated. It looked like most left with companions, but Abba was alone. He passed me, and I stayed in the shadows until he was ahead, then I followed.

"We had walked maybe a mile when I heard the sound of horses over one of the hills. I stopped and so did Abba. I hid behind some brush, but Abba was in a more open place with less cover."

Shim'on couldn't keep the shakiness out of his voice. "Four centurions on horseback came over the hill. They circled him so that he couldn't run and then they questioned him, asking why he was out here alone."

Yeshua pictured the scene, horses rushing down the embankment carrying soldiers clad in red tunics, iron armor, and helmets, with swords hanging from their waists. Circling Yitzchak before he knew what was happening and leaving no way out. He would have been terrified.

"I heard him say that he was returning from Bethsaida and had left the city later than he planned. But they kept saying that he was lying and that they knew he was a Zealot."

Shim'on looked down at his abba. "They taunted him, and one pulled out a whip and struck Abba with it. Two of them jumped off their horses and I heard him cry out, but I couldn't see!"

The tears that Shim'on tried to hold back escaped and trailed down his cheeks. His voice cracked, requiring him to compose himself. Ashamed, he wiped the tears on his face. "I was hiding and doing nothing! I should have done something, anything! But it was like I was rooted to the earth. When it started to get light, one of the soldiers said that it was time to go. They got back on their horses and left.

"I ran to Abba and found him like this," Shim'on nodded at Yitzchak. "They stabbed him for sport and then left him for dead. He was barely conscious, so I dragged him to these trees. I didn't want to leave him out in the open."

He focused on the faces of Bin-yamin and Yeshua as if seeing them for the first time since beginning his recall. "I knew that I couldn't bring him to town because of the Romans, and the villagers would ask questions even if I could hide him from the soldiers. But what am I going to do?" He looked at Bin-yamin, then back down at Yitzchak.

"Curse the Romans!" he spat. Yeshua grieved for his friend.

Bin-yamin's eyes were filled with concern, but his steady demeanor exuded peace and comfort as he laid a hand on Shim'on's shoulder.

"Shim'on, we will not abandon you or Yitzchak. We will keep this matter to ourselves and help you."

There was silence for a moment and Yeshua could hear birds whistling and chirping in the trees surrounding them. A sparrow fluttered briefly in the branches above the men, before spreading its wings and soaring out over the grassy hill. The beauty and normalcy of life going on about them on such a pain-filled day felt surreal.

Shim'on appeared to return to his blank thoughts, dazed and spent. His abba touched Yeshua's arm and rose, signaling him to follow. Once far enough away that Shim'on couldn't hear them, Bin-yamin faced Yeshua.

"I must go back to town. By now, rumors will be spreading. I am not upset that Shim'on came for us, but he did so in broad daylight and his appearance was certainly—questionable. I need to try and settle people's suspicions and explain to Miriam what has happened to her husband." His face serious, Bin-yamin continued, "Let's hope the soldiers haven't overheard any gossip of Shim'on's appearance."

"But Abba, what about Yitzchak? Will he be all right?"

Bin-yamin sighed and shook his head, "I'm afraid he's lost a lot of blood. I bandaged his wounds as best I could but taking him home is impossible. The Romans would kill him if they found out they didn't finish the job the first time."

"Then what can we do?" Yeshua couldn't imagine any other options.

"We pray. We ask Adonai for wisdom and direction. We pray for mercy for Yitzchak and that he survives his wounds and heals." He looked at Yeshua, "I think that it would be best if you come back to town with me."

He raised a hand when Yeshua began to protest, "I know you want to stay with Shim'on, but Yitzchak needs water, food, and more bandages. Come with me now and return tonight when it's dark. Both you and I returning to town together will look strange, but it will look even stranger if it's only me. We will have to provide a satisfactory explanation. And we must get to the barracks, or there will be even more questions. Let's go tell Shim'on and be on our way."

Bin-yamin explained their plan to Shim'on, and Yeshua promised to return that evening. Shim'on numbly nodded his understanding.

Yitzchak was still unconscious and while he was no longer moaning, Yeshua noticed that the cloths wrapped around his chest and head were darker with blood. He tried not to think about the possibility that the supplies he brought tonight might not be needed by then. With a final look at his friend, Yeshua turned and followed his abba back to Capernaum.

IV

The crescent moon was high in the sky as Yeshua prepared to make his way into the hills that night. While the small amount of light would aid in concealing him, it wouldn't make him altogether invisible. Bin-yamin reminded him of this as he packed the last of the supplies into the sack for Shim'on and Yitzchak.

"Be cautious and try to stay in the shadows," Bin-yamin urged Yeshua, though they both knew that Yeshua already planned to do so. "I'm proud of you son," Bin-yamin's eyes softened, "I don't agree with what Yitzchak did, and it brought him great trouble, but that does not mean we should withhold our help. Adonai sees your courage and watches over you." He wrapped his arms around Yeshua, and his dark beard scratched Yeshua's cheek. "Be careful."

"I will, Abba, I promise," Yeshua said. Gripping Yeshua's shoulders, Bin-yamin squeezed once more and then stepped back, releasing him. Yeshua pulled open the door and slipped into the street. Only steps away from the home, a dark figure stepped out from the shadows.

"Yeshua?" A soft, feminine voice asked.

"Yes? Who is it?"

The figure uncovered her face to reveal the brown-haired girl who caused Shim'on to blush.

"It's me, Lydia." She whispered quietly.

"Does your family know you're here, Lydia? It isn't safe to be alone on the streets this time of night. The soldiers—" Yeshua's words trailed off but both knew the unspoken warning in his words.

"They don't know I'm here, but I have to know if Shim'on is all right." Lydia's voice was filled with worry. "I heard about earlier today."

Yeshua winced. How many others had heard? He quickly pondered how much to tell her. What would Shim'on want him to say?

"He's all right. But pray for his abba. That's all I can tell you right now."

Lydia's eyes filled with relief and concern all at once.

"Thank you, Yeshua." She whispered.

Yeshua nodded, "Be careful." He turned and continued down the street, the darkness enveloping him.

Bin-yamin had created a story that would hopefully provide Yitzchak and Shim'on cover. He told those who asked that Shim'on and Yitzchak were on their way to Bethsaida to obtain fishing supplies when they had come across a poor traveler who had been assaulted by Roman soldiers. The traveler was badly beaten and barely alive when they found him, and Shim'on had run back to town for help. Sadly, by the time Bin-yamin and Yeshua had arrived, the man had died, so they buried him to keep his body from wild animals. Yitzchak and Shim'on then continued on their way to Bethsaida, while Bin-yamin and Yeshua returned to town.

The story was barely strong enough to hold water and Bin-yamin hoped that no one would push to determine the identity of the stranger or his burial location. And, of course, there would be the issue of Yitzchak and Shim'on's whereabouts when they didn't return to town in a couple of days. Yeshua tried not to think about that.

Bin-yamin had learned that several village fishermen saw a group of four Roman soldiers enter town that morning. Apparently, the soldiers had boasted about torturing a man for being a Zealot. It had sounded to the fishermen as though the man had been killed. Sadly, Bin-yamin and Yeshua knew this wasn't far from the truth. They prayed that Yitzchak would survive his injuries and that Adonai would give them the wisdom to know what to do next.

This in mind, Yeshua hoped his exit from town would not be noticed. He stole quietly through the nearly empty streets, thanking Adonai for the limited light provided by the moon.

Rather than leaving town by the main entrance, where he would surely be questioned by soldiers, he took a roundabout way into the hills.

Once he was far enough from Capernaum, he increased his brisk walk to a run, slinging the sack of supplies over one shoulder. The hills looked different in the darkness. Yeshua was forced to pay close attention to landmarks he remembered from when he and Bin-yamin passed through earlier. Soon he saw the silhouette of the olive grove as he drew near. In a rough whisper he called out, "Shim'on, it's me, Yeshua."

He saw a body shift against the trunk of a tree, and a voice responded, "Over here."

Coming nearer, Yeshua saw that Shim'on had moved Yitzchak's body so that his torso was propped against the trunk of one of the olive trees. Shim'on sat beside him. The air held a certain chill due to the departure of the sun hours ago and Shim'on sat with his arms wrapped around himself for warmth. His blood-stained outer tunic lay across Yitzchak for an additional layer of warmth.

"How is he?" Yeshua asked, trying to see the man's face in the darkness.

"I don't know," Shim'on responded wearily, "He woke up late in the evening and seemed to understand what I told him, but since then he's been sleeping."

"That seems good," Yeshua said, trying to encourage his friend, though he knew no more than Shim'on as to what those signs meant. "I brought supplies," he said, lifting the cloth sack he took from his back, "Food, water, blankets, and bandages." He set the pack on the ground and began to take the items out.

"Thank you," Shim'on stood and joined him. "I thought about making a fire, but it didn't seem wise." He paused, lifting his tunic off Yitzchak, and exchanging it for a blanket. He slipped the tunic over his head, "Did your abba talk to my immah? Does anyone else know?"

"Abba told her, and she understands that you and Yitzchak have to stay out here for the time being. Abba said she's scared, but she wants you to know that she is praying for you both. As far as the villagers go, Abba made up a story."

"Your abba, telling a falsehood for us?" Shim'on said in surprise, "That's good of him. Please give him my thanks." He leaned down to the sack to pull out the lehem and goat's milk that Yeshua's immah had sent.

"Lydia asked about you," Yeshua said.

"She did?" Despite the sad circumstances, Shim'on's eyes brightened.

Yeshua nodded, "She wanted to know if you are safe. I told her you are."

Shim'on tried to hide a crooked smile, but Yeshua knew his friend was pleased. In the quietness, Yeshua could hear crickets chirping intermingling with the wind blowing through the grass and leaves. The air, spiced with sage, also held a hint of rain. If they weren't here because of an injured man, it would have been peaceful.

"I'm sorry you were alone all day," he said.

"It's all right," Shim'on responded, "I wouldn't want anyone else to be caught helping us." He looked down at the lehem he held, "We have to go back to town soon anyway. I'm sure Hanoch and the hired men are taking the boat out, but I need to be there. And we have the money owed to the Romans. If they notice Abba and I are missing, they will be suspicious."

Yeshua looked over at Yitzchak. The man's eyes were closed and sweat glistened on his forehead. He was glad the blanket hid the bandages beneath, afraid of how blood-soaked they were. "What is your plan?"

Shim'on reached into the sack and pulled out a flask of water, "I have to bring him back to town at night. I'd like to use your donkey if you can spare him," he looked questioningly at Yeshua.

"Of course, Brother," Yeshua agreed, "But then what? Everyone will know that you have returned but wonder why your abba hasn't. There will be gossip and it will surely get to the soldiers. Your house could be searched, your abba found, questions asked"–

"You think that I don't know that?" Shim'on asked harshly, anger in his eyes. "Of course, I know the risks. I've been sitting up here all day, and all that I can think of are risks! But there is no other option." He knelt on the ground beside Yitzchak and tilted the flask of water into his mouth, allowing the liquid to wet the man's lips. Yitzchak groaned softly but didn't move. Continuing to look into his abba's face, Shim'on spoke, "I prayed all day that Adonai would show me what to do. I cannot think of any other way and I believe that Adonai will protect us. I have to believe this, Yeshua."

Yeshua chided himself. Of course, Shim'on was right. He felt humbled and respected the love and courage in his friend's decision. "I'm sorry, Shim'on. You're right. Please forgive me. Tell me what I can do."

The friends spent another hour sitting on the ground beside Yitzchak and discussing their plans for the following night. When Yeshua left the olive grove hours later, he felt Adonai's peaceful presence with him. But neither of the boys could imagine how much their lives would change due to the events of the following day.

 After returning home, Yeshua shared Shim'on's idea with his abba. The plan was this: Shim'on and Yitzchak would remain in the hills that day. At night, under cover of darkness, Yeshua and Bin-yamin would meet them and bring Yitzchak back to town, drawn on a litter behind a donkey. The man was far too weak to make it back to Capernaum leaning on Shim'on alone, even if he did regain consciousness.

Bin-yamin listened to Yeshua detail the plan, then somberly said he would help. Yeshua knew his abba was risking much by coming alongside Shim'on and Yitzchak. If, and more likely when, the townspeople and Romans discovered Yitzchak's reappearance, there would be many questions. And the rabbi's involvement, if discovered, could be extremely damaging to his reputation and position in the town.

The orange flames of the flickering fire cast alternating shadow and light on Bin-yamin's face as he spoke.

"Yitzchak and Shim'on are our friends. Their family is one of us," He gestured between himself and Yeshua, "And helping one's neighbor is what Adonai commands us to do." His green eyes looked deeply into Yeshua's, "It is not always easy, Son. More wickedness may come of this, but no matter what, Adonai is with us. He will not forget His children." Yeshua's siblings were asleep in bed and his immah sat silently beside Bin-yamin.

"I do not like Shim'on's plan much," Bin-yamin continued, "But I agree with him. I see no other way. We are not going to bring the donkey though, it's too suspicious. We'll have to make a litter and carry him back ourselves. We'll need to be extremely cautious."

"Yes, please be careful," Yeshua's immah reached out to take the hands of her husband and son. Sarai was a strong woman but tonight her voice shook slightly.

"We will, my love," Bin-yamin squeezed her hand in warm reassurance.

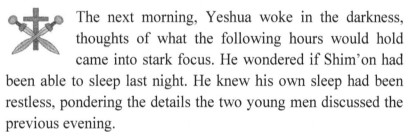 The next morning, Yeshua woke in the darkness, thoughts of what the following hours would hold came into stark focus. He wondered if Shim'on had been able to sleep last night. He knew his own sleep had been restless, pondering the details the two young men discussed the previous evening.

Time at Beth Midrash and the worksite dragged, and Yeshua found it difficult to concentrate. As much as he tried not to ruminate about the night ahead, it seemed he could think of nothing else. Bin-yamin told the story he concocted multiple times, and Yeshua could see the falsehood made his abba uneasy. He hoped Yitzchak would recover quickly so they didn't need to keep misleading their friends.

The Zealots

When the sun finally began to dip toward the horizon, Yeshua was more than ready to leave. Gathering up their things, the men returned home to eat and prepare to join Yitzchak and Shim'on.

Bin-yamin added rope and an axe to a bag of supplies. They would use them to lash branches together and construct a litter. Layers of linen cloth, supplied by Sarai, would pad the litter so that Yitzchak would be as comfortable as possible. Miriam had visited Sarai earlier in the day and brought food for Yeshua to deliver to Yitzchak and Shim'on as well. Yeshua added it to his sack.

Bin-yamin and Yeshua oiled and sharpened their tekton tools as they waited for the agreed upon time. The darkness outside deepened, and the town grew quiet and still. Bin-yamin finally stood, "Ready, Son?"

"Yes," Yeshua nodded and climbed to his feet. He took the sack of supplies and tools and tied it around his shoulders. Bin-yamin kissed Sarai, then pulled the door open. Yeshua followed him into the night.

The town was still and quiet in the darkness. Inside homes, fires dwindled to embers while villagers slept on their mats. Yeshua felt the night enfold him like a black velvet cloth, soft and heavy. He felt a little sick to his stomach and could hear his heartbeat loud in his ears.

He led Bin-yamin quietly and quickly through the streets and into the hills. He was now familiar with the route, grateful for the lack of soldiers on their way. Silent prayers kept cadence with his feet. *Adonai, be with us tonight. Please protect us. Please be with Yitzchak and help him to be all right. Amen.* He could only imagine how anxious and helpless Miriam must feel. He sensed Adonai's comforting presence and felt the tightness in his shoulders loosen.

They would bring Yitzchak back to town and everything would work out. He tried to focus his mind on this positive thought. Nearing the outcropping of olive trees, Yeshua searched for the silhouettes of Shim'on and Yitzchak against the dark tree trunks. Bin-yamin walked to his left and Yeshua could tell he was also trying to see the men in the darkness.

Coming to the tree where Yitzchak had lain the past couple of days, Yeshua was surprised to find no one there. He spied the sack and flask he had previously left with Shim'on lying under a nearby bush. Concerned, Bin-yamin turned to Yeshua and whispered, "Let's split up and look for them."

He began walking south. It was difficult to see in the darkness, and several times Yeshua stumbled over rocks.

The cool night air blew softly against his face, and he stopped every so often to listen for voices or other unusual noises. He was puzzled to hear only a gentle buzzing of cicadas and a rustle of grasses blowing like waves pushed by the wind. He turned back towards the olive trees but saw no one. He couldn't imagine what would cause Shim'on and Yitzchak to leave the area, other than soldiers returning, but he saw no indication of such.

Reaching the copse, his abba gestured to him. As he walked toward Bin-yamin, his abba's face slowly came into focus and Yeshua was concerned to see grief in his eyes. "Did you find them?" he asked, looking past his abba and over the rocky embankment of the hill. He glimpsed Shim'on's dark head, "There's Shim'on!"

"Son…Yitzchak is dead."

The words didn't land fully in his consciousness for a moment, strung out like separate thoughts *Yitzchak-is-dead.* Then they hit him all at once. Yeshua snapped his head back to look at his abba, "What? What happened?"

"Shim'on told me that he slept all day, drifting in and out of consciousness. When he tried to give him water an hour ago, he couldn't wake him up." Bin-yamin looked grief-stricken, "He just lost too much blood. Shim'on is burying him," he gestured to the ravine.

Yeshua stood in shocked disbelief. How could Yitzchak be gone? They had a plan. They had prayed. They were going to get him to safety. But now it was too late?

The more he struggled to comprehend the tragedy, the heavier the weight on his shoulders. The peace he had felt minutes earlier evaporated. All Yeshua knew was that he wanted, he needed, to speak to his friend. He turned from Bin-yamin and made his way down the rocky embankment to where Shim'on stood at the bottom. His friend was hunched over a mound of stones, head down and arms crossed.

"Brother," Yeshua's voice cracked. It was all he could say as he came to stand by him. Shim'on was silent.

"I'm so sorry," Yeshua said. He couldn't think of anything else, and he felt helpless to comfort his friend. The breeze blowing against their faces felt bitter and lonely.

Touching Shim'on's shoulder, he asked, "What can I do? Tell me. I would do anything."

Shim'on shook his head, and spoke in a low wry tone, "He's gone, there's nothing else to do. Now I must go home and tell Immah," He sighed heavily. "I honestly believed he was going to be all right. I thought we could get him back to town and be able to take care of him, make him better."

"I know," Yeshua said softly, his heart heavy, "I believed it too. I'm so sorry."

A resolute look crossed Shim'on's face. "They will pay for this."

Yeshua assumed his friend was referring to the Romans but didn't know what to say. How many similar oaths must have been made by those oppressed by the empire? Yet, Rome stood stronger than ever. The boys stood in silence, Yeshua offering the best he could: his presence to his friend.

It wasn't enough.

At length, Yeshua realized his abba stood behind them.

"Shim'on, we must go," Bin-yamin placed a hand on the boy's shoulder. "The sun will rise soon. People will awaken in town. It's best to get back before then. We will find a way to come back and give your abba a proper burial."

Yeshua knew that like most Hebrews, Shim'on's family had a burial tomb already purchased for the future, and Yitzchak's death deserved the traditional mourning and remembrance. Unfortunately, the man's body would need to be preserved until they could move it, to be kept safe from the elements and discovery by wild beasts and the birds.

Shim'on nodded, looking once more at the mound of stones over his abba's grave. Yeshua could tell that he was still reeling with the shock of the loss. Yeshua was also. They all were.

Weary in heart, the three turned toward Capernaum. Yeshua couldn't help but think of his desperate prayer just a short time before. *Adonai,* he wondered silently, *why did Yitzchak have to die? He was a good man. You gave me peace that we could save him—* his thoughts trailed off into questions.

All of this happened because Yitzchak had met with the Zealots, to stand up against the Romans. Misguided action perhaps, but Yeshua was sure that Yitzchak had a good heart. He had done what he thought best to defend his family and their way of life, the Hebrew way of life. Now what would Shim'on, his immah, and brother do?

He felt the burden settle onto his shoulders again, weighing each step as the men silently reached town and their homes in the early morning darkness. This time Yeshua did not feel Adonai's peace lift the heaviness that wrapped once more around his shoulders and seeped into his heart.

 Days after Yitzchak's death, Yeshua stood among a group of the family's friends on a Galilean hillside and watched Yitzchak's body be placed in the family tomb. As family and friends turned toward home, a heavy rain suddenly descended and drenched everyone. Yeshua knew the weather mirrored everyone's grief.

By the grace of Adonai, the cause of Yitzchak's death remained a secret, but it didn't change the fact that Shim'on's abba was gone. With the loss of his abba, Shim'on took on the role of head of his family.

Often Yeshua and Bin-yamin glimpsed Shim'on and his brother coming to shore after a night of fishing as they walked to the synagogue in the morning. Days and weeks passed and Yeshua barely spoke with Shim'on. This was not for lack of trying. The young man seemed to have built an invisible wall around himself that no efforts Yeshua made could pierce. Yeshua missed him greatly.

One Shabbat morning, Yeshua stopped by Shim'on's home and was greeted by Miriam. "He is here, but he's not himself, Yeshua," she warned quietly, glancing behind her, and gesturing for Shim'on to come. As he waited for his friend, Yeshua couldn't help but think that Miriam was also not herself. Her face was lined with wrinkles and her eyes dulled by pain and sadness. For the hundredth time, he tried to imagine how it would feel to lose his abba. He could not comprehend it.

"Yeshua," Shim'on grunted as he came to the door.

"Brother," Yeshua said, taking in Shim'on's ragged appearance. His friend's eyes were bloodshot from exhaustion and underlined by dark circles. His shoulders sagged in discouragement and grief. His friend had aged years since his abba's death days before.

"I came to see if there is anything I can do," Yeshua asked.

"Not unless you're willing to help me find and kill the soldiers responsible for this," Shim'on tilted his head up defiantly. He spat, an expression of passionate hatred. It was uncharacteristic of the friend that Yeshua knew.

Miriam looked apologetic and scared. Yeshua wished Shim'on could see how his attitude was affecting her.

"We both know that can't be done," Yeshua said solemnly, trying to calm his friend with his tone. "Surely there must be something else I can do. Do you need help mending your nets or on the boat? I could make an excuse to be away from the barracks for a few days."

"I don't need help. We will be fine." Shim'on shook his head, clearly angry. "You know, Yeshua, I thought you were my friend. I thought you had come to your senses after you saw what they did to my abba. You led me to believe that you hated them as much as I do. But I guess you were just saying those things. It's good to know how you really feel. You're a coward who thinks you're better than all of us. Shalom and Adonai be with you," he said sarcastically, and abruptly turned away. With an afterthought, he threw back over his shoulder, "Apparently loyalty to a friend holds no value to you."

The words hit Yeshua as harshly as a physical punch. He stood unsteadily in the doorframe, thinking back to their conversation on the boat, which now seemed a lifetime ago.

That evening was the last time he spoke to his friend. Life moved forward, carrying Yeshua before it like a boat on the Sea of Galilee pushed by the wind.

Over the following months he came to sadly accept that his relationship with Shim'on had changed indelibly. His friend was not the same. Hardness and anger took the place of the laughter and kindness that had once marked Shim'on's personality. The passion remained but was now solely focused on vehement hatred of all things Roman.

When the young men crossed paths, which they did often living in the same town, Shim'on would briefly hold eye contact with Yeshua before nodding a resentful greeting, then continuing on his way.

One particularly frustrating day when Yeshua tried to strike up a conversation with Shim'on and failed, he came home fuming. Sarai was gone and Bin-yamin sat alone.

"It's hopeless!" he cried, throwing off his outer garment and sitting heavily on a mat. "Unless I pledge my promise to hunt down the Romans responsible for Yitzchak's death, Shim'on will never talk to me again." He remembered the conversation on the boat that night months ago and once again felt a pang of regret. He could understand why Shim'on was confused about his change of heart following that night, and once again wished he could have explained it to him. But there hadn't been time. "Am I to forget we ever knew one another?"

Bin-yamin gripped Yeshua's shoulder, looking deep into his eyes. "Are you praying for him, Son?" he asked quietly.

"I am," Yeshua admitted, "though it feels like Adonai isn't listening."

"He is listening even though you may not feel like He is," Bin-yamin smiled sadly, "I have tried to speak with Shim'on too, and I know that his heart seems hard right now. But he's just lost his abba and his emotions are speaking louder than logic. Adonai alone can show Shim'on the truth and soften his heart. We must keep praying for him as well as for Miriam and Hanoch."

Yeshua nodded his agreement, but inside he wondered if the friend he once knew was gone forever.

V

Shim'on couldn't remember the last time he had awakened without the heavy weight pressing down on him. He carried it like a bag of stones, dragging the burden through the streets, onto his fishing vessel, to the market, and back home every day.

The afternoon and evening hours, free of distractions and when he most needed to sleep, were the worst. He could feel the pressure on his chest, crushing the life out of him, and bruising his heart and ribs. If it were a real sack of rocks, the bag would have been torn open by now and the stones inside strewn in his wake. But it wasn't tangible, it only felt so, and he couldn't shake the burden as much as he wished he could.

Shim'on lay in bed wishing he didn't have to get up and go to the sea. In fact, he wished he hadn't woken up at all. Yes, that's exactly how he felt. He glanced over at his immah, who made the evening meal quietly attuned to her sons' much needed sleep. Shim'on watched his immah's habitual movements. Maybe she wanted to keep her thoughts to herself.

He could never tell her his thoughts. The vision haunted him, watching the Romans kill his abba happened over and over. He knew the darkness inside him would scare her, and she was already scared enough. He knew his immah needed him now, but she seemed to be grieving alone. Grief absorbed her not only because of the loss of her husband, but also because of the depression and silence of her eldest son.

Shim'on sighed, the weight heavier than ever on his chest.

Looking back on that night, he cursed his cowardice. He had a dagger; he could have at least tried to save his abba. With Yitzchak gone, Shim'on felt crippled by the guilt and anger he carried. He was letting his immah down. He was letting Hanoch down. Even his abba must be disappointed.

That night, when Shim'on returned to their home without their abba, Hanoch had been furious. Deep in grief, he clutched at Shim'on begging his brother to help him understand why he had gone to Bin-yamin and Yeshua rather than coming to him. Though Shim'on tried to explain, Hanoch refused to accept his answer. Since that day, his brother remained angry and hurt, an invisible wall rising between them. Shim'on couldn't blame him.

Reluctantly, Shim'on pushed himself up from his mat and slid his feet into his leather sandals. His day as a fisherman was just beginning.

He performed netilat yadayim, pouring the water over his hands using a clay basin and cup. He shook the water from his hands and quietly spoke, "amen." He nudged Hanoch awake from where he slept on an adjacent mat and waited as his brother readied himself. The young men ate a hasty meal before leaving.

Closing the door behind them, they began their short walk to the shore. Months ago, Yitzchak, Shim'on, and Hanoch had chattered loudly and happily as they made their way to the sea. Back then, Miriam would tease that they were like the Shabbat shofar, calling the neighborhood's attention to night falling.

Since Yitzchak's death, however, the walk was made in silence.

Reaching the shore, Hanoch commenced unfurling the sails. Shim'on strode down to the water's edge and knelt. He splashed his face with the cold water to wake up. Ears trained, and with a keen eye, he searched out the direction of a steady croaking until his sight landed upon a small frog that looked much like the shoreline rubble. "Why are you still shouting? Go to sleep." He picked up a pebble and lightly tossed it in the direction of the frog, making it leap.

Shim'on climbed back up the shore and into the boat, smoothing his hand over the boat's cedar planking. The vessel was twenty-three-feet long and seven-feet wide. It contained room for twelve to thirteen passengers, though they seldom had any.

With a flat bottom allowing it to be pulled ashore, the men were able to unload a catch quickly and efficiently. He joined his brother and their hired man, Demas, and they deftly prepared the nets and hoisted the sails to take them to the middle and deepest part of the lake.

"Ready?" Hanoch glanced towards Shim'on. He nodded.

"Ready."

Hanoch and Demas jumped from the boat and pushed it back into the water, then pulled themselves over the railing.

The warm wind filled the sails and they moved from shore. Shim'on took a deep breath of fresh air and exhaled. This was truly the one place where the weight lay lightest on his shoulders. He still felt it of course, but the physical demands of fishing distracted him from the constant thoughts battling in his mind. Gusts caused the boat to dip while skipping over the choppy water kicking up spray against his face. Light from the full moon above them glanced off the waves, stark white. His abba had loved it out here too, and Yitzchak had always had the knack for knowing where to find the schools of fish from day to day.

"Adonai told me to fish at the north end today boys," he would say, or "Adonai is good, He sent me a dream that we will fill a net just off the shore." His sons and the other fishermen often teased Yitzchak about his heavenly directives, but often, Yitzchak led the men well, and they would bring in a good night's catch.

Shim'on smiled remembering his abba's boisterous laughter and zest for life. He used to be like that too, he recalled, smile fading. That seemed so long ago. Hanoch directed Demas to lower the sails as he steered the boat into a small cove and dropped the anchor.

The anchor, a large piece of metal attached to a thick rope tied around the boat's frame, was lowered by hand into the water below. Once that was done, Shim'on and Hanoch gathered the linen nets and prepared to throw them into the waters on the east side of the boat. The net was 25 feet around and required no more than two men to cast it into the sea. Once in the water, small pieces of stone affixed to the bottom of the nets would keep them in place and barricade any fish that wandered into them. Fishing was best at night because the bright white nets were more difficult for the fish to see than in the bright daylight.

"The Musht are certainly plentiful here tonight!" Demas pointed to fish jumping near the boat, "I think your abba looks down on us, yes?"

Hanoch smiled, "Let's hope so!" Shim'on simply nodded, he hoped so too. Musht, biny, and sardines were the most common fish in the area. Each was delicious and drew a good price at the market. The nets cast; the three men found places to sit on the cedar planking as they waited.

"I'm exhausted!" Hanoch covered a yawn.

Leaning against the side of the boat, Shim'on couldn't help but emit a low chuckle, "That's not a surprise. You worked in your sleep, Brother. Do you remember?"

"What are you talking about?" Shim'on could see Hanoch feared an embarrassing story was coming but was also reluctantly pleased that his brother's shell was cracking, if only for a moment.

Shim'on sat back a little in his seat as he allowed the peace of the water to wash over him and push his restless thoughts to the background momentarily. His hands flicked in and out of the net by memory, "As we all know, my brother is a quiet sleeper."

Demas snorted and elbowed Hanoch.

"It's not my fault that I inherited Abba's snoring!" he yelped but smiled good-naturedly.

"I had just fallen asleep when I felt *somebody* jabbing me," Shim'on resumed, "I turned over to see what Hanoch was doing and he had part of his blanket in his fist and his other hand was just—"Shim'on pantomimed a hand darning with a needle, mending nets.

The men laughed and Shim'on smiled. Hanoch pretended to scowl but was soon laughing as well. He missed this, Shim'on acknowledged to himself. He wanted to get back to being himself. Why couldn't his effort be enough to pull him out of this darkness, a darkness that had a purpose of its own, determined to rob him of life?

 Eight hours into the smell of the sea and the sweat of labor, Demas appeared to be right. The men pulled in yet another net filled with musht, enough fish to finally necessitate returning to shore to sort and unload."

The anchor rope glistened as Hanoch and Shim'on pulled it hand over hand into the boat. The sky began to brighten with dawn's soft hues. One of the men raised the sail to catch the wind at their backs.

Shim'on manned the tiller as he pointed the vessel back to shore. Twenty feet from the shoreline, Hanoch jumped over the side. The water came to his waist as he guided the boat in with a rope and secured it onshore. Other fishermen were unloading their catches as well, and Shim'on was pleased to see that their own was one of the largest. A full net meant food for his family and a roof over their heads.

Wives, daughters, and young boys not yet old enough to be learning a trade awaited the men on the shore.

After the fishermen unloaded the day's catch, the women and children sorted and loaded them onto carts. From there, donkeys would pull the loads into town to be sold by the women at the market. Since they had been forced to give their donkey to the soldiers before Yitzchak's death, a neighboring family shared the use of theirs until Shim'on could afford to buy one.

Miriam stepped forward from where she waited with the neighbor women and walked toward her sons as they jumped off the boat into the sandy gravel.

"Looks like a good catch last night?" She looked questioningly at Hanoch and Shim'on.

"A very good catch, Immah!" Hanoch grinned at her, "Perhaps good enough to have lamb tonight?" Shim'on could see the joy her youngest son's teasing brought Miriam. "That could be possible," she grinned, and sobered as she looked at her eldest.

She looked from one brother's face to the other, "Yitzchak would be so proud of you both." Her eyes became misty, "He always said you two were going to be better fishermen than him one day."

Shim'on felt her words briefly puncture the hard shell that surrounded his heart, and he could see his abba's smiling eyes and hear his deep voice. The memories flooded him with grief, and he felt tears spring to his eyes. His abba had no reason to be proud of him now. Ashamed, he ducked his head and gathered up a handful of nets.

"Come, Hanoch." he said more harshly than he knew was fair, "There's no time to talk. Your work's not finished."

Glancing at Immah's face, he saw the pain that his dismissal of her kind words had caused, and he felt a wash of guilt.

Hanoch stood awkwardly on the shore between them. Shim'on knew his words cut him as well, a sharp departure from the laughter they had shared a short time before. The other fishermen onshore continued their work, though Shim'on could see some of them watching the scene.

Despair gutted him. Thoughts full of bile returned. Angry and bitter, his chest constricted so that he could hardly breathe. Distracted by this turmoil, he paused his work.

Despite the beautiful pink and purple streaked sky cheerfully making way for the day ahead, darkness hung over Shim'on. Thoughts threaded their way deeper and deeper into the fabric of his being, leading the way to a dark pit. *If only I had done more, he would not have died*, he thought. *But I didn't, and he is dead. What kind of son am I? I'm worthless. Surely Adonai has turned His back on me. I haven't even avenged Abba's death. I should have been the one to die. It would have been better that way for everyone.*

No longer able to keep the gall inside, he felt words bubbling to the surface.

"We won't get to keep the money this catch earns us, Hanoch." He smacked his hand on the side of their boat, "So stop thinking of your stomach. Have you already forgotten the reason Abba died? Have you forgotten the money the soldiers demanded from him and that their gift for his death was demanding even more from us?" He was shouting now, and despite the visible hurt on his immah and Hanoch's faces, he continued.

"I'm doing the best I can, but your laziness is not helping." He directed these words at Hanoch and watched them hit him like a slap in the face. He knew it wasn't true but felt trapped by his pain.

"And I'm sorry I'm not 'myself,' Immah," he aimed these words at Miriam, sarcastically mimicking her comment to Yeshua a few nights before. She flinched. "How do you expect me to be myself? Abba just died." The anger was at its peak, "Or don't you remember?"

With this last comment, Miriam sobbed aloud, and Hanoch stepped forward, hands balled into fists.

"That's enough, Shim'on." He heard a slight tremor in his younger brother's voice. Though two years younger, Hanoch was slightly taller, yet not as muscular. This was the first time Hanoch had dared to oppose him apart from playful roughhousing. Shim'on knew he would beat his brother if it came to it, but he had no real desire to trade blows with him.

"It's enough to disrespect me," Hanoch said in a low voice, "it's another thing to speak against our immah."

Pretending indifference and disdain, Shim'on scooped up an armful of nets and dragged them toward an inlet further up the shore. Hanoch and Demas were left to tend to the fish and load the cart Miriam would take to the market.

The Zealots

As he made his way down the sandy shoreline, he tried to avoid the curious looks of the other fishermen. But one face caught his eye.

Lydia stood a short distance away, her eyes filled with concern and empathy. Another wave of shame rolled over him. Looking away, he continued his way down the shore. Tears pricked Shim'on's eyes, but he refused to let them fall. That would be foolish and weak. No, better to keep his anguish to himself.

He stomped over to where he could watch the Jordan making its way into the sea. Dropping to a large stone, he threw the nets at his feet.

There were only a few other fishermen at the falls, as most of the men were still unloading their catches. In the past, Shim'on, Hanoch, and Yitzchak would have completed their morning prayers standing on the shoreline after unloading the catch. But it had been months since Shim'on had prayed. In place of worship, resentment filled his thoughts. Adonai had abandoned his abba, and though he feared admitting the blasphemous thought aloud, Shim'on's anger was aimed at Him. Hadn't his abba put Adonai above all else? Yet his reward had been a vicious end at the hands of the Romans. Didn't the proverb say, "dishonest scales are an abomination to Adonai?" Why, then, did Adonai continue to allow Romans to cheat and murder His own?

The Jordan poured down a rocky hill, pooling in different areas along its entry into the sea. The quick-moving water made the falls a perfect area to wash the mud from their nets. Often, fishermen remained next to the falls, settling on a rock or a patch of sandy ground to mend or fasten weights to the bottoms of their nets. While they worked, they exchanged news or told stories. Sometimes they sang.

For several minutes Shim'on simply sat, listening to the greenish-blue water bubble like laughter over the rocks and a six-foot drop into the large pool he sat beside. Usually, the sound was familiar and comforting. Today, it grated in his ears. He had sat on this rock beside his abba for the past twelve years, ever since he had begun going out on the boat with him. Yitzchak was always the loudest fisherman around the falls, keeping the other men entertained with jokes and stories. But he had a soft, gentle side too, which had revealed itself just as frequently. People had trusted Yitzchak. He was a safe place to turn to for advice and wisdom or simply a listening ear. Shim'on, his immah, and Hanoch had known this better than anyone.

He glanced toward the boats. Regret colored his thoughts. His immah and Demas must have gone to the market. He saw Hanoch throwing armfuls of nets and other fishing tools to the ground below the boat rather than handling them with care as usual, a sure sign he was angry.

Turning back to the nets at his feet, Shim'on released a sigh. He picked up portions of the linen net, looking for areas where the cloth was unraveling. Using a needle and thread, he set to work mending the tears. Everything needed constant attention. Mending nets was like breathing, and Shim'on's fingers flicked in and out of the linen without conscious thought.

The early morning sun crested the horizon and glinted off the glassy surface of the water. Shim'on squinted at the cloth in his hands.

"*Shalom lekha*, peace to you," One of Abba's best friends approached the falls with a basket piled high with nets and nodded at him. Usually full of loud laughter, Efrayim's quietness was evidence that he had overheard Shim'on's words on the shore.

"Shalom." Shim'on dipped his head in response and tried to ignore the questioning look that Efrayim cast his way. Over the next few minutes, more fishermen joined them. Despite the awkwardness caused by Shim'on's outburst, the air soon filled with conversations about tomorrow's weather, the day's catch, and favorite stories being told for the hundredth time. Relieved not to be the center of attention, Shim'on listened quietly to the chatter around him that was often punctuated with shouts of laughter.

While they worked, many of the men ate lehem and dried fish which their wives, immahs, or sisters brought them. Despite the way he'd hurt her, Shim'on guessed his immah still gave their morning meal to Hanoch. He doubted Hanoch would give him his share based on his angry outburst earlier. He deserved that, he thought.

"Where is Keshir today?" Isaac, one of the fishermen, asked the question of the group. Surprised, Shim'on glanced around the falls, looking for the weathered face and gray hair of the 78-year-old fisherman. Keshir was a quiet man, but kind. He was the oldest fisherman in the group, and one of the oldest in the town of Capernaum. Despite his years, he was still quite fit and had always been the first fisherman on the water since Shim'on had begun fishing with his abba as a child. In fact, Yitzchak often went to Keshir for his wisdom and advice. Shim'on couldn't remember Keshir ever missing a day on the water, but it was true, the old man was not here today.

As he looked around the group, Shim'on glimpsed Hanoch sitting on the other side of the falls. His brother held a piece of pita in one hand and dried Musht in the other. He stared back at Shim'on with a look of defiance and disgust.

"He's home," Eli, one of the younger fishermen and Keshir's grandson spoke.

"Is he all right?" Isaac asked.

"No." Eli looked down at the nets in his hands, "No, he is not. The soldiers were waiting for him yesterday. They demanded twenty shekels."

The shock of the image of what happened to Keshir distracted Shim'on from his preoccupation with his brother. Murmuring filled the air around him. Twenty shekels was a fortune to a fisherman, worth almost twenty days of work. Most fishermen were fortunate if they had one day's earnings saved. Most lived hand to mouth, their earnings sufficient only to meet the daily needs of their families.

"I think, because he is so old, they assumed he had the amount saved." Eli continued, "But, of course, he doesn't. *Saba* uses everything he earns for his family and those in need. You all know that." Eli looked around the group. Heads nodded. Keshir was known for his soft-hearted generosity and kindness.

"They beat him to the ground when he said he couldn't pay. Then they ransacked our home. Only when they'd ripped everything apart were they convinced. And then they took what few things of value we did have." Eli's face was red as he looked up at the men.

"Scum," Efrayim spoke from the rock on which he sat, and several men hushed him.

"Efrayim!" Amos said, "We would all be in trouble if they hear you!"

Shim'on flushed, though the words were not directed at him. Most days, several soldiers walked the coast, taking note of the amount of fish brought to shore and the families with the biggest catches. They would be the families extorted next.

Sometimes the soldiers simply made their demands as the boats were being unloaded.

Shim'on realized there were no soldiers on the shore this morning, which was incredibly fortunate considering his outburst. How could he be so foolish?

"I won't be afraid of those who steal the bread from our wives' and children's mouths!" Efrayim spoke deliberately, angry heat simmering under his words, "And none of you should be either! These soldiers who walk our streets act as if they own us. They were not here first! The Roman scum worship Jupiter while we have *Elohim*, the one true Adonai!" Efrayim slapped a hand against his knee.

"Ah, but He has been silent for quite a long time Efrayim," Shim'on turned to look at another of the fishermen, Erastus. "For hundreds of years, He has not spoken. We keep waiting for the Mashiach, but he does not appear."

"You are right that He has been silent," Efrayim replied, "But I do not believe that gives us cause to submit to our enemies. Perhaps He wants us to fight for ourselves!"

Shim'on wondered if the other men heard the same message he did. Efrayim's words suggested that Adonai's means of justice included the Zealots. He thought back to the night months ago on the boat with Yeshua. Efrayim's words echoed his own from that night. And it was still how he felt. Even more so, now. Glancing across the falls he caught Hanoch's eye again. Although he knew Hanoch was still angry at him, he could also see that they shared the same thought. Was Efrayim a Zealot? He had been a close friend of his abba's.

The men murmured around him, conflicted in opinions on how they ought to handle the foreign presence in their land and city, but united in their anger toward Rome.

The morning burned away into afternoon heat. When the sun finally began its decline to the west, the men separated, slinging their mended fishing nets back into their boats. In just a few hours they would return for the night's work.

Hanoch and Shim'on made their way back to town, their shadows leading the way. The brothers swung themselves over the short rock wall on the outskirts of Capernaum and began walking through the tall grass and the rising chorus of frogs.

Shim'on was spent, emotionally and physically. He looked forward to lying down on his mat and closing his eyes regardless of whether he was able to sleep. Once again, he wished he hadn't been so harsh with his immah earlier that day. As if reading his thoughts, Hanoch shoved him roughly, "Lamb wouldn't have been so bad tonight, don't you think, Brother?"

Suddenly two Roman soldiers stepped from the trees beside Hanoch and blocked their way.

"Halt there!" they commanded harshly. Shim'on guessed them to be in their late twenties. Both were in full armor, one tall and lean and the other shorter and more rotund.

The tall soldier glanced at the other, and turned to Hanoch, "What are your names?"

"Our names are none of your business," Shim'on spat the words and was immediately rewarded with a fist in his side from the shorter soldier. He doubled over coughing.

"We are Hanoch and Shim'on, sons of Yitzchak," Hanoch responded.

"Oh, that's right." The soldier who punched Shim'on uttered a laugh and looked at his companion, "These are the boys whose father we killed."

White-hot anger flooded through Shim'on, and it was all he could do to keep from ripping the ready dagger from the man's side and sinking it into his gut. But he dared not endanger Hanoch.

Looking at his brother, Shim'on saw him also clench his hands at his sides and shake with barely concealed anger. Neither of them dared make a move toward their own concealed blades.

"What do you want?" Shim'on looked at them.

"Oh, we've already claimed your catch today. In addition to your father. I don't think there's much left to take, do you?" The taller soldier shook his head condescendingly, "But just remember," he reached out and clenched the tunic at Shim'on's shoulder, "We know where your Zealots meet and we will do the same to you if you seek to rebel against Rome." He released Shim'on's tunic and shoved him backward. The two soldiers spun on their heels and walked away laughing.

Shim'on turned toward Hanoch, "Are you all right?"

"How could I be all right? Did you hear them? We just stood there while they confessed what they'd done to Abba!"

Shim'on put a hand on his brother's shoulder and Hanoch immediately shrugged it off. Raising both hands in defense, Shim'on leaned toward his brother and spoke quietly.

"Hanoch! Listen to me! What were we to do just now? Attack them in broad daylight? We would be fools! We are surrounded by Romans and mercenaries loyal to Rome! I'm just as angry as you are. I want them to pay for Abba's death too."

"So, what are we going to do?"

"We are going to keep our mouths shut and not speak of what happened tonight to Immah or anyone else." Hanoch tried to speak but Shim'on continued. "You heard what Efrayim said today at the falls. I'm going to pay more attention—see if I can overhear any of the Zealots' plans."

"Take me with you if you go to one of their meetings," Hanoch said. Shim'on shook his head.

"We cannot both risk our lives, Brother. One of us must care for immah, and I am the oldest. Defending our family is my duty."

The late afternoon sun bathed the Galilean hills in harsh golden light and wind rustled in the surrounding olive trees. The throttle of a male grouse drumming for his mate filled the air.

Hanoch fingered the dagger under his tallit and kicked the grass at his feet. "I understand, but I don't like it. Am I to have no part in avenging Abba's death?"

"This is your part," Shim'on assured him, "and equally important. Let's go home."

The young men continued to walk and Shim'on sensed a shift between he and his brother. He knew the hurt from earlier in the day remained, but what had happened between them tonight helped ease the tension. Perhaps it would even usher in Hanoch's forgiveness. Shim'on hoped it would be so.

VI

The remainder of the week dragged on.

Shim'on, Hanoch, and Demas went out on the sea every night as usual. Demas insisted that Adonai's favor rested heavily on them as they brought large catches of fish to shore every morning. Fortunately, their catch was so good early in the week that their debt to the Romans was repaid within days. The soldiers who managed the shoreline continued to collect taxes, but there were no more confrontations like the one earlier in the week.

Silence between Shim'on and Hanoch was still common, but the tension between the brothers lifted. Shim'on no longer took his despair out on those around him, but the conflict inside his own heart was intense. He longed to escape the regret that continued to weigh heavily on his chest, yet it seemed impossible. Over and over, images of his abba trying to escape the Roman soldiers played through his head. Over and over, Shim'on yearned to have done something, anything to save him.

Throughout the week, Shim'on paid close attention to Efrayim's activities and on Friday his efforts finally paid off.

It was morning and the fishermen were back on shore. Shim'on's vessel was pulled alongside Efrayim's on the sandy beach. Hanoch was in town with Miriam and the day's catch, and Demas was at the falls. The soldiers had come and gone, taking their share hours ago. To his disappointment, there had been no sign of Lydia.

Shim'on noticed Efrayim unloading his vessel, his hired men gone. As he watched, he noticed another man join Efrayim. Shim'on threw his handful of nets to the sand below him and jumped lightly over the side of the boat, his bare feet sinking into muddy ground.

He walked carefully, picking his way through sand and mud, avoiding gravel. Quietly, he moved toward the boat's stern. He crept as near as he could without revealing himself, then stopped and listened intently.

"Tomorrow night." Efrayim said.

"Yes, better sooner than later." The other man responded. "Same place?"

"Yes, in the valley to the east. You know the spot."

Shim'on didn't hear the man respond but imagined him nodding.

"All right, I will see you an hour after last light."

"Shalom, Brother."

Shim'on could hear the man's retreating footsteps on broken shells and gravel as he hastened back to the prow of his boat. He scooped up the nets he'd left on the sand and began trudging toward the falls. Excitement coursed through him. He would go to the Zealot's meeting tomorrow night and petition to join them. The idea of grabbing the tall soldier's dagger and plunging it into his chest was satisfying. He envisioned himself surrounded by passionate Zealots, and the thought thrilled him. He would make the Romans pay for what they had done.

The following night, Shim'on stood around the corner from Efrayim's home. He pressed himself against the basalt wall, praying the shadows concealed him. Fortunately, this portion of the street was quiet, and Shim'on didn't have to wait long before he saw Efrayim leave his home.

He waited until the man was half-way down the street before he crept after him, staying in the shadows as much as possible. Efrayim moved quickly. It wasn't long before he and Shim'on left Capernaum behind them. Shim'on released a breath of relief as they entered the foothills, grateful that no soldiers crossed their path.

The warm air was soft and quiet. The moon was only a sliver in the sky. Shim'on struggled to keep his footsteps light, while keeping Efrayim in sight.

Crack. Shim'on tripped over the exposed roots of a tree. Quickly, he ducked down behind the sagebrush, hoping Efrayim wouldn't see him. A muttered curse escaped his lips.

The man stopped and looked around, then began walking toward Shim'on. A rabbit darted in front of Efrayim. The man stopped once again, then turned back toward the valley.

In the dark, Shim'on considered that a leopard could be tracking him, and he'd never know until it was too late.

Shim'on offered up a silent prayer of thanks and continued to follow Efrayim, watching his own steps all-the-more carefully. After some time, they entered the basin. Efrayim paused near a grove of olive trees, and Shim'on halted behind the trunk of a tree. He heard the man whistle softly. Seconds later, the call was returned. Shim'on watched as Efrayim entered the grove of trees and walked quickly after him.

Just steps into the copse, he felt a hand on his shoulder.

"Who are you?" A gruff voice hissed close to his ear. Before he could speak, the hand tightened on his arm and Shim'on was dragged roughly through the trees. He found himself standing in a cave filled with roughly fifty men. The air was smoky due to several lit torches illuminating the space and he coughed.

"Who's this, Thaddeus?" A large bear of a man turned to look at Shim'on.

"I have no idea," The man gripping Shim'on's arm released him with a shove. "He was following Efrayim."

Shim'on saw Efrayim turn to face him, a look of surprise on his face.

"Efrayim, do you know this boy?" the big man asked.

"I do. He's the son of Yitzchak. I thought I heard someone following me tonight, but I didn't see him."

"He's quiet, is he?" The big man stepped closer. Avi was short but muscular, and there was a look of intensity about him.

"Well, Son, my name is Avi Ben Gileon. I'm the leader of this group. I'm sorry about your abba. He was a good man, and we miss him."

Shim'on opened his mouth and shut it without a word. Avi's kindness was unexpected, and he felt tears threaten to fill his eyes. He blinked them away quickly.

"Thank you, Sir," He spoke as confidently as he could. "I am Shim'on, and I would like to become a member of your group."

Several of the men in the cave laughed. Avi just looked at him sympathetically. "How old are you Shim'on?"

"Fifteen." Shim'on stood as straight as he could and puffed out his chest.

"I see," Avi replied. "I appreciate your passion Shim'on, but we fight against Roman soldiers. Men. Look around, do you see anyone your age here?"

Shim'on shook his head. "But I can shoot a bow and arrow, and I'm sure I will learn to wield a sword quickly if someone teaches me." He tried to keep his voice from wavering.

"We don't have time to teach a boy how to fight!" The man who dragged Shim'on into the cave, Thaddeus, stepped forward.

"We risk our lives to defend our families and our land, and to prepare for the Mashiach. Come back when you are a man." He turned and spoke with another Zealot.

Anger burned in Shim'on's chest and before he could think, he stepped after Thaddeus, fist drawn back. When he was steps away, Thaddeus turned and shot a hand out, catching Shim'on in the stomach. Shim'on dropped to his knees, the breath knocked out of him.

"Better be grateful I'm a merciful man. I can tell you, a Roman would have separated your head from your shoulders." Laughter broke out around Shim'on and he felt his face grow hot. When he could breathe again, he stumbled to his feet.

"Just wait," he said to Avi, ignoring the lingering pain in his stomach, "I'll learn how to brandish a sword and I will be back."

He turned and ran from the cave, laughter following his steps.

Y e s h u a: Five Years Later

VII

Yeshua walked toward home with a brace of rabbits swung over his shoulder, salivating at the thought of dinner. When a neighbor passed by, Yeshua nodded a distracted greeting.

With the sun making its final farewell, it ducked behind the nearby hills, and he paused to admire the cast of brilliant colors onto the Sea of Galilee. After a long day of Beth Midrash, tekton work for the Romans, and hunting for Imma's choice dinner, Yeshua's empty stomach twisted in anticipation. Enjoying a tasty meal and then curling up on his mat for a deep night's sleep was the only thing left in Yeshua's heart.

Reaching home, he noticed someone entering the road ahead of him. It was unmistakably Shim'on. Yeshua didn't bother calling out. The last five years had proved Shim'on no longer considered Yeshua his friend. What once caused him deep pain had dulled to a throb. He missed Shim'on's friendship but come to accept the reality.

Turning to step inside, the warm, yeasty scents of fresh-baked lehem assailed Yeshua's nostrils making him salivate all the more.

"Yeshua!" Deborah, his sister, greeted him excitedly. "Look Immah, Yeshua has rabbits!"

66

Smiling, Sarai took the two rabbits from Yeshua's outstretched hand. "Thank you, Son, I'll skin these and get them over the fire right away. Deborah, your help, please?"

"Well done," Bin-yamin smiled up at him from the mat on which he sat. "But where's your brother? Is he not with you?"

Yeshua shook his head, "I haven't seen Tobias since this morning."

"I think I know where he is." Deborah grinned impishly, "Probably flirting with Abigail bat Abel."

"Shush now, there's nothing wrong with that," Sarai replied, "She's a sweet girl and Tobias is old enough to seek a bride."

"What about you, Yeshua?" Deborah turned her teasing eyes toward her older brother. "What girl catches your eye?"

Yeshua chuckled and shook his head, "I'll let you know when I find one." It was true that most young men his age were wed, but Yeshua hadn't found his match yet. He thought of Shim'on and Lydia. As far as he knew, Shim'on had shut everyone out of his life, including Lydia. The thought made him sad for his friend. He took a seat on a mat by Bin-yamin.

"There is something I want to talk to you about," his abba slapped his hands on his knees, signaling a transition of topic. "How do you like the tekton trade?"

Yeshua was surprised by the abrupt question. "I like it well enough, Abba. But I wasn't under the impression that liking our trade was as important as simply having one."

Bin-yamin nodded, "You're right, a trade is certainly necessary, and you have become a well-skilled craftsman."

Yeshua was quickly approaching the age at which he would complete his studies at Beth Midrash. From that point forward he would commit to a trade with which he would provide for a family. The only exception to this path fell to those truly gifted in understanding the Torah and their Judaistic beliefs. In exceptionally rare instances, a rabbi called those especially excelling in their studies to follow him on the path to becoming a rabbi. Even the rabbis had occupational trades to support them and their families, however. While many young men did well in their studies, it was rare for one to be called by the rabbi.

"I plan to be a tekton, like you," he responded.

Bin-yamin smiled. "That's good, but I have another idea. Yeshua, do you enjoy Beth Midrash?"

Yeshua nodded and fingered his tekhelet, thinking. "I do. I enjoy learning how we are set apart as Adonai's people." He thought of the Romans infiltrating their land and disrupting their way of life. "I am proud to be a Hebrew. We serve the one and only God, Adonai with us."

His father nodded encouragingly, and Yeshua realized his voice was strong with passion.

"Son, I'm so proud of you," Bin-yamin said earnestly, "I truly do believe that of all the students I've taught, you have excelled most. You have mastered the Torah, Mishnah, Nevi'im, and read the holy *Ketuvim*, better than any I know. You have a thirst to learn and you help those around you learn. And I do not say this just because I am your abba as well as your rabbi," he winked at Yeshua. "So, I hope you will like my idea," Bin-yamin leaned forward, his forearms resting on his legs.

Yeshua could see Deborah step closer to listen.

"What would you think of following the path to become a rabbi?"

"Me?" Yeshua tried to take in Bin-yamin's words, "A rabbi?"

"Yes, you!" Bin-yamin laughed and pointed at him so there could be no confusion. "What do you think?"

"I don't know." Yeshua fumbled, shocked.

Bin-yamin continued, "Do you remember me speaking of the rabbi I learned under? Phinehas?"

Yeshua nodded.

"He and I have exchanged letters, and he is willing to teach you too, Yeshua!"

Yeshua felt overwhelmed. "Isn't he in Jerusalem?"

"He is." Bin-yamin must have been able to hear the hesitancy in his son's voice. "But imagine it, Yeshua! You would study at the very heart of our people! Zion, the Holy City! Where David ruled and his son Solomon after him. And, of course, Phinehas travels around the region teaching from time-to-time, and you would go with him."

"I-I don't know," Yeshua started, "I have learned the trade of a tekton. I like working with my hands." His mind churned.

"And you can continue doing so!" Bin-yamin inserted quickly, "My friend Stephanas lives in the lower portion of the Holy City, and he and his family have offered to feed and shelter you while you stay there. He too is a tekton and willing to find you work while you are in Jerusalem."

Yeshua was overwhelmed.

"I know it's a lot to think about," Bin-yamin spoke quietly, "But I believe Adonai has called you to this, Son."

"But I'm only twenty-years-old! Don't I need to be extremely wise to be a rabbi?"

His abba smiled. "You have wisdom, Yeshua, more than you know. And you will continue to learn and grow in wisdom throughout your life."

Yeshua's mind spun as he considered his abba's words. He pictured himself standing at the front of synagogues, teaching the Torah and Nevi'im, and answering questions. He knew his abba's role attracted a critical eye. He was looked up to and used as an example of obedience to Adonai and the law. Yeshua liked the idea of others viewing him the same way. But most of all, Yeshua's abba loved Adonai. More than anything or anyone.

"So, what do you think?" Bin-yamin watched Yeshua. Deborah and Sarai stood near the fire, listening.

"I believe I would like to be a rabbi." Yeshua replied slowly. "I trust you."

"I'd hoped so," Bin-yamin leaned back in his seat with a proud smile. "Son, I have been praying for Adonai's direction in your life since you were born. I have faith that pursuing the life of a rabbi is what Adonai has called you to do."

He leaned forward, "There's something I want to impress upon your mind. Yeshua, even rabbis make mistakes and sin. But Adonai is forgiving. Don't ever cease to be humble. Every day submit your will to Adonai and teach others to do the same. To love Him and serve Him."

"I will, Abba." Yeshua nodded his head. "When do I go to Jerusalem?" he asked, unable to keep the excitement out of his voice.

"In just two months!" Bin-yamin clapped his hands together again. "I didn't want to say anything before I was sure plans would align, but they have, praise Adonai!"

"All right, you two. It's time to eat!" Sarai announced and Yeshua could see the pride on her face.

"Yeshua, maybe you'll find a wife in Jerusalem!" Deborah said breathlessly. His abba laughed.

It had fallen into place so quickly that Yeshua's mind spun. For a moment he balked at the limited time left in Capernaum, but those feelings quickly retreated as he thought more. What was here for him aside from his family? His friendship with Shim'on perished long ago and he could just as easily work as a tekton in Jerusalem as Capernaum.

The idea was exciting, and Yeshua could feel it becoming more and more tangible, a longing to purpose his life anew as a rabbi. It was time to move on.

VIII

Shim'on and Efrayim glanced around the small grouping of olive trees. They'd watched the sun slowly dip behind the horizon hours before and a full moon now hung in the blue-black sky above them as frogs croaked in rhythm.

Shim'on cursed under his breath. Though the moon lit the area so that he could see the rugged landscape around him, he knew it also exposed their every movement. He prayed no soldiers watched as they made their way to the valley east of Capernaum. Doing his best to shrug aside his anxious thoughts, Shim'on looked around once more. Seeing no movement, he followed Efrayim from the cover of the trees and continued toward the valley and the meeting of the Zealots.

The wind blew harshly through the sagebrush and olive trees which dotted the hills around them. If he weren't so focused on his feet and avoiding rocks and badger holes, Shim'on would have enjoyed the beautiful landscape. Pinpricks of stars stood out brilliantly against the velvety-black sky, and behind him the moon reflected brightly on the Sea of Galilee. But Shim'on had neither time nor peace to enjoy his surroundings. He pushed forward and soon the men reached the valley.

Once more, they stopped and listened for the snorting of horses, the clanking of a sword against armor, or voices of

72

soldiers as they spoke to one another. Nothing. They entered the valley. The wind carried the pungent scent of sage and pressed Shim'on's linen tunic tightly against his legs with each step he took. Now that he was close to the meeting place, he felt a ripple of anticipation. Tonight was the night.

Since his appearance at the Zealot gathering five years before, he had been preparing. Efrayim had approached him one day soon after the meeting as he unloaded the night's catch. His abba's best friend offered to teach him the use of a sword and dagger. Shim'on eagerly accepted the offer. Over the past five years, he had poured all his anger and bitterness into preparing to fight the enemy. Now he knew he was ready. The fire to avenge his abba's death burned constantly. He prayed that joining the Zealots would bring him freedom from the guilt and anger that still weighed on his shoulders every day.

Soon the men approached a thick copse of olive trees and wild vines covering a cave in the hillside, the perfect meeting place.

As they approached the trees, Efrayim whistled softly, signaling their arrival to the Zealots already gathered. Ten seconds later, they heard a responding whistle. Receiving the approval to approach, the two men pushed through the dense foliage and emerged into the cave. The air was much cooler in the shadows and Shim'on blinked as his eyes adjusted to the dim light. A hundred men crowded into the space, more than the last time Shim'on attended a meeting. He took a deep breath, trying to calm his anxious nerves. Several of the men held lit torches, allowing them to see one another in the yellow light. Avi ben Gileon stepped forward toward Efrayim. "Shalom, Brother."

"Shalom."

"And who is this? You look familiar."

Shim'on smiled, gratified that he had changed enough that the man couldn't remember him.

"I am Shim'on, son of Yitzchak."

"Ah yes," A look of recognition swept over the man's weathered face, "The fisherman's son. How long has it been?"

"Five years." Shim'on replied without hesitation. "And I'm ready now." Shim'on knew he was no longer the lanky youth he'd been. He stood a foot taller now, and time and hard work had caused his frame to fill out. His arms, legs and torso were muscular from lifting heavy blocks of stone as a tekton, and through training with Efrayim.

Shim'on noticed Thaddeus standing several feet away. The man stood close enough to overhear Shim'on and Avi's conversation, and Shim'on saw him watching from the corner of his eye.

"Come, let me introduce you to some of the men." Avi said. Shim'on soon learned that not all the Zealots were from Capernaum. Others hailed from nearby towns such as Gamla, Magdala, Bethsaida, and Korazin. Shim'on knew it would be weeks before he was able to remember all their names and trades.

The men formed a circle of sorts, and Avi stepped into the center of it.

"Let's get started," he said gruffly, glancing around the group.

"We have a new member tonight," he gestured toward Shim'on.

"This is Shim'on from Capernaum, a friend of Efrayim." The men around the circle nodded in greeting. A thrill of excitement filled him. He was finally a Zealot. Shim'on thought he saw recognition cross some of the men's faces. Thaddeus avoided eye contact.

"You've met a few of those here," Avi gestured to the circle around him, "Our goal is to do what we can to dismantle and destroy the Roman presence here in our land and to obey the Torah. The Torah says that there shall be no other deity than Adonai. So, we refuse to see Caesar as such. We believe that Adonai understands our actions and that we act according to His will. We kill those who seek to oppress our people whether they be Romans or those who stand by them. We are cognizant of our number. Nearly a hundred Galilean men against thousands of Romans soldiers occupying our land, but we do what we can. In the end, that is worth more than standing by and doing nothing."

Shim'on couldn't agree more.

"Tova is going to tell us about our new objective," Avi gestured to a rail-thin young man with shoulder-length dark hair. He stepped forward from the circle.

"As you all know, Jerome and I live in Magdala." Tova gestured to another man across the circle, "We have overheard multiple conversations about three Roman contubernium expected in Tiberius in a week." Excited murmuring filled the cave at the prospect of attacking twenty-four soldiers.

"Let's save the talk for after Tova is finished, men," Avi spoke sternly and the voices quieted.

Shim'on had never traveled further south than Magdala, but he knew the road swept along the coastline of the sea. Tova smiled and continued, "We're excited too. As you know, there is only one route for travelers going to Tiberius, the Via Maris. We expect that there will be slaves accompanying the soldiers that will be carrying the supplies. The area is quite lush with lots of trees and bushes behind which to hide. We'll camp in the hills to the west of the road. Our goal will be to attack the soldiers and try not to kill any slaves." He smiled wryly. "Keep in mind that there will likely be other travelers on the road. Hopefully, they will keep their distance once we commence the attack."

Tova shared the plan with obvious anticipation. Shim'on, too, was excited. He had been yearning for this opportunity to do his part for a long time. Some believed that taking the lives of their enemies was wrong. He had been taught such a perspective by his rabbi, Bin-yamin bar Joicha. But his own abba and the Zealots believed differently. Shim'on shared their devout and passionate commitment to Adonai at all costs. Many claimed they must obey the Romans to protect their families. But Shim'on saw their passivity for what it really was. Cowardice. By contrast, the Zealots committed their beliefs to action. He was more than ready to become active as a true soldier in this movement.

"Questions before we hammer down the details?" Avi looked around the circle. The men shook their heads no, obviously eager to move on to planning the logistics of the attack.

"All right then," Avi clapped his hands together. "Tova and Jerome will lead this mission as they know the surrounding area best. Men?"

Jerome spoke, "Though we know that the soldiers are expected in Tiberius in a week, we aren't exactly sure when they will arrive. We will hide in the hills south of the city on Wednesday and that way we'll be sure not to miss them.

"Bring enough food and water for three days and, of course, your weapons. Those of us who have bows and arrows will try to pick off as many as possible from our cover first, but eventually we will engage in hand-to-hand attack."

Over the past five years Shim'on had developed skill with the bow and arrow, sword, and dagger. True, he hadn't grappled with a Roman soldier yet. But Efrayim was an excellent teacher, and Shim'on felt ready for this attack.

"As always, do not travel in groups of more than two: otherwise we might draw unwanted attention."

Tova knelt and began drawing in the dirt.

"Here is Tiberius," he said, drawing an x. "And here is the road leading south out of the city," he drew a squiggly line. "We will hide here," he circled a point on the road, "Half a day's journey from the city."

"The area has excellent cover from boulders and brush. So long as we are careful, they won't suspect anything until it's too late."

Shim'on did the calculation in his head. The place at which they would attack was nearly twenty miles from Capernaum, a full day's travel. He needed to depart the day after tomorrow.

"That's it, men," Jerome said confidently, "Shalom and travel safely."

"Shalom," The men replied and began leaving the cave one by one or in small groups.

Efrayim walked over to Shim'on, "Would you like to travel to the attack point together?"

"Yes," Shim'on replied.

"We will leave in two days," Efrayim nodded. "Do you feel ready?"

"You've taught me well," Shim'on nodded.

Efrayim smiled, "You've been a good student. And I believe you are ready." Shim'on knew he had become like a son to the man. He was fond of Efrayim, but his heart was too wounded to care deeply for anyone since the loss of his abba.

"We'll meet before dawn outside town," Efrayim continued, "I suggest you bring several days' supply of lehem and olives, perhaps a little dried fish as well. Try to keep everything as light as you can, but remember we will likely be gone three, maybe four days."

Shim'on nodded his understanding and turned to leave. Efrayim loitered to speak with Avi.

"Oh, Shim'on," he turned back to face Efrayim. "Whatever you do, don't dare speak of this mission to anyone. Not your immah, not Hanoch, no one. If the Romans catch wind of it, those you told will be the first souls under their sword. Better if no one knows."

IX

Yeshua's head spun as he took in the sights, sounds, and smells of his new home, Jerusalem. He had, of course, been to the Holy City before. Every year since he could remember, he and his family had traveled to Jerusalem for *Pesach*, where families celebrated the faithfulness of Adonai in Egypt. Yeshua clearly remembered his abba explaining the seven-day festival to him as a boy, "when His death angel passed over their marked doorways and saved their firstborn. Pesach is how we remember the faithfulness of Adonai," Bin-yamin had told him, "Adonai led our ancestors who obeyed Him out of captivity in Egypt and to their new land."

Although the exodus from Egypt had occurred over fifteen hundred years prior, the festival rituals kept the memories fresh. Yeshua tried not to fall behind Bin-yamin, though it was challenging with the throngs of people pressing against them on all sides. Capernaum was a thriving town, but it didn't come close to the busy city of Jerusalem.

The air smelled, not unpleasantly, of a combination of fresh-baked bread, sheep dung, roast lamb, and spices.

The sun was at its peak in the blue sky above Yeshua, though the air was still relatively cool. Jerusalem sat atop a hill, and the entire city was surrounded by a formidable limestone wall.

Yeshua was awed by the massive size of each stone block stacked upon another, an engineering feat. The beautiful city was visible for miles, the color of freshly churned butter, a sharp contrast to the brown and green landscape. Once inside the city, limestone paved streets crisscrossed one another. They led to homes and businesses, or to the most important place in all of Judea, the temple. This was the place where Yeshua would study to become a rabbi.

Threading in and out of the masses of people, he stepped quickly to his right as a herd of anxious sheep passed on the street beside him, their shepherd goading them toward the temple market and their sacrificial fate. Booths lined both sides of the narrow streets, and salespeople hawked every product under the sun. They passed a booth where meat of all kinds hung from the ceiling: chicken with feathers still intact, brown-furred rabbit, colorful pheasant, and bloody cuts of lamb and goat. Few merchants sold pork in Jerusalem as it was not *kosher*. According to Hebrew law, only clean food could be eaten for their health and protection. But if a Gentile wanted the meat, he could find it if he wished. Yeshua passed a table covered with bowls filled with brilliantly colored spices. Customers pointed out their selections from a spectrum of flavorful gold, russet, and earth-colored mounds to the shopkeeper. The merchant measured them into small cloth bags with a spoon. Anything one could think of could be found in Jerusalem: bolts of beautifully textured cloth, glass jars filled with dewy olive oil, crates holding downy white doves to be purchased for temple sacrifice. The options were endless.

And the people! Yeshua was amazed at the variety of skin colors, clothing, and different languages being spoken, all at the same time. Brilliant purple and red silks signifying wealth mingled with earthy blue, brown, and tan linen; colors worn by commoners. And of course, the ever-present blood red garments and burnished grey armor distinguished the Romans who stood at their posts and walked stiffly through the streets of the city. There were many more people than Yeshua was accustomed to seeing in Capernaum. This was the heart of Judea, and all walks of life were found together in Jerusalem.

With so many people crowded in one place, Yeshua and Bin-yamin's pace was slow. As they neared an intersecting street, the people packed so densely around them that they were forced to stop. Yeshua craned his neck to see what was happening. For a few moments he saw only Roman soldiers as they walked in tight formation and pushed onlookers to the sides of the streets to make way for centurions on horseback. At first, Yeshua thought the hold-up was simply a show of force by the Romans, but then he saw them. Five men, hands tethered to cedar cross beams, stumbled under the weight of their burdens. They were savagely beaten. Horrified, Yeshua looked away as they approached. He glanced at Bin-yamin and saw sadness etched on his face. Crucifixion. An invention of the Romans to punish those who rebelled against the empire. Yeshua shuddered, glancing at the men as they slowly passed. Their backs and legs bore the marks of the whip and they struggled to remain upright under the burdens they carried. Yeshua knew the agonizing walk was nothing compared to what came next, however. After being sentenced and whipped, criminals were led to Golgotha, just outside of Jerusalem. Ironically for those being led to their deaths, the hill had the form of a skull. Once there, soldiers drove spikes into their hands and feet, pinning them to the crosses. The men were forced to push themselves up on their spiked feet to draw gasping breaths until they eventually suffocated. It was impossible for travelers to miss the gruesome sight on their entry into and exit out of Jerusalem, and it served as a strategic and effective warning by the Romans. Bin-yamin spoke softly, "I fear you will see much of this here."

Yeshua was shocked to hear those in the crowd jeering at the condemned prisoners as if the procession was a show. Others held hands over their children's eyes and ears, trying to protect them from seeing such a horrible spectacle. Many simply watched in silence or conversed quietly with those around them.

Suddenly, loud wailing filled the air and Yeshua turned back toward the noise. Several weeping and screaming women tried to push past the Roman centurions holding them back. Yeshua realized they must be the wives, immahs, or daughters of the condemned men and grieved for them. Unable to reach their loved ones and lost in their grief, they sobbed loudly as they ignored the rough shoves of the centurions. The procession finally passed, and the crowds pressed forward once again. Yeshua and Bin-yamin were swept along in the stream of people. Yeshua's feet moved, but his mind still focused on the scene he had just witnessed. He had never seen so much blood, never watched a crucifixion procession. Certainly, he had seen men on crosses before, but always from a distance. Seeing these men before they met their wretched fate, the fear in their eyes, the women who loved them helpless—it overwhelmed him.

As they neared their destination, Yeshua tried to steer his thoughts back to the reason he was here. They were on their way to the temple, where he would meet Phinehas. For the next few years, he would study under the rabbi with the sole focus of becoming a rabbi himself.

Since the conversation with his abba two months before, Yeshua had only grown more excited about the new adventure before him.

The men walked up a steep portion of the street, and as they reached the top Yeshua stopped in renewed amazement. The temple lay before them, the creamy limestone gleaming in the sunlight.

All who entered the temple courts passed through the "Beautiful Gate." It was so-called because of its Corinthian brass detailing. Yeshua had heard the gate required twenty men to open and seeing it for himself he believed it. Bin-yamin and Yeshua passed through the gates and entered the outer temple courtyard. The area was massive, two hundred and thirty-three feet long on each side.

Yeshua took in the incredible space, noting the four eighty-six-foot-tall lampstands that stood around the edges of the courtyard. Tables surrounded by Hebrews purchasing sacrifices stood inside the courtyard. The people would give their sacrifices to the priests who would kill and offer them as burnt sacrifices to Adonai.

Stacks of crates filled with pigeons, and a corral holding spotless white sheep and bulls stood nearby. Once again, Yeshua recalled his abba teaching him as a young boy. "There are different animals to symbolize the depth of the iniquity. All our sins must be atoned for, through sacrifice. Sometimes a dove, sometimes a lamb. The sacrifice must give rise to a pleasing aroma to Adonai."

The moneychangers at the tables were kept busy, and Yeshua glimpsed bags of coins piled in a basket.

Every Hebrew was required to make atonement for his or her sins by offering sacrifices at the temple. Looking around the courtyard, he noticed several familiar boxes scattered around the area. They were used to collect offerings from the people. Anyone standing nearby when a person dropped a coin into the box could tell what amount was given by the noise it made.

Looking toward the temple, Yeshua could see the entrance to the inner courtyard, where sacrifices were offered to Adonai. Beyond it stood the temple itself, which contained the most sacred place in all of Judea: The Holy Place and The Holy of Holies. Only the priests were allowed the terrifying privilege of entering the temple itself, where Adonai's presence dwelled. The metallic odor of the blood of a thousand sacrifices hung heavily over the courtyard.

"Bin-yamin, is that you?" An elderly Pharisee, clothed in the traditional white robes and blue and white tallit of a rabbi, approached them.

"Shalom, Rabbi!" Bin-yamin warmly greeted the man. "*Ha-shalom lakh*, is all well with you?"

"Shalom, all is well," the rabbi smiled, "It has been a long time. But you can probably tell that by my white hair. I think I had a little less when I last saw you."

Bin-yamin smiled and gestured toward Yeshua, "Do you remember my son, Yeshua? Son, this is the rabbi who taught me all that I know, Phinehas ben Noch."

The rabbi reached out a weathered and wrinkled hand to Yeshua's shoulder, "Yeshua Bar Abba. Of course, I do! And now you're here because he is to become a rabbi, just as his abba before him." Phinehas smiled and Bin-yamin put a hand on Yeshua's shoulder proudly.

"Well, well," Phinehas smiled, "Adonai has a special calling on your family Bin-yamin. And to imagine, I get to instruct your son as well."

"Adonai is good," Bin-yamin agreed.

"I will keep an eye on him," Phinehas assured Bin-yamin. "It was good to see you, my son. My students are coming so I must go." He gestured across the courtyard to a group of young men approaching, "I will see you tomorrow?" He looked at Yeshua questioningly.

"Yes, Rabbi."

"Good," Turning to go Phinehas paused and looked back, "Bin-yamin, by chance, have you heard of the rabbi from Galilee, from the town of Nazareth?"

Bin-yamin shook his head, "I haven't. Who is he?"

"That's what we are all wondering." Phinehas shook his head. "He is stirring up trouble. The people love him though. I am told that large crowds follow him wherever he goes. I'm sure you will hear more of him while you are here." He turned and walked toward the group of young men sitting in a corner of the courtyard.

"Come to think of it," Bin-yamin said, turning to Yeshua, "I did hear some of the tektons in Capernaum speak of a tekton, a rabbi traveling through the towns in the region." He was silent for a moment, then shook his head as if to clear his thoughts.

"Come, Son, let me introduce you to the other rabbis."

For the better part of the next three hours Bin-yamin and Yeshua met and spoke with several different rabbis, fellow Pharisees. There were two distinct religious sects in Jerusalem, Yeshua knew: the Pharisees and the Sadducees. A variety of differences separated them, two of which were their views on the law and afterlife. Yeshua was eager to learn more about each group's beliefs. His abba was the only rabbi in Capernaum, and Yeshua already felt overwhelmed by all he did not know about his new surroundings.

As they said farewell to another rabbi, Bin-yamin seemed to read his son's thoughts. The sun was nearing the horizon and the setting rays turned the limestone of the temple a hazy pink color.

"It's been a long day. It's time for me to introduce you to Stephanas bar Abel."

X

Since Yeshua did not have relatives in Jerusalem, Bin-yamin had reached out to his friend Stephanas and his family. They opened their home to Yeshua and arranged for him to work as a tekton in the Holy City. Stephanas, too, was a craftsman, and Bin-yamin spoke highly of his skill.

Bin-yamin and Yeshua descended to the lower city, where the family lived. Whereas the upper portion of Jerusalem was affluent, and the streets were wide, the lower city was home to the commoners and the poor. The streets were narrower and dustier, and Yeshua felt a ball of anxiety knotting in his stomach as they wound through a honeycomb of residences and streets to the home of Stephanas. The thought of living in this large city filled him with both excitement and fear.

As they walked, his abba joked and told stories about his experiences in Jerusalem when he studied as a young rabbi. Yeshua recognized all the anecdotes from their telling many times before. But he knew his abba was trying to distract him from his anxious thoughts, and he was grateful.

The sun dipped behind the hills in the distance as the men came to a modest limestone home set back slightly from the street. His abba knocked on the wooden door. Moments later, a tall man, similar in age to Bin-yamin, opened it. Yeshua noticed the man had to dip his head so as not to bump it on the doorframe.

"Bin-yamin bar Joicha, shalom!" Stephanas greeted his abba with an embrace.

"And you are Yeshua," he smiled. "We are honored to have you. Please, come in." He gestured inside, and Bin-yamin and

Yeshua entered the home. Yeshua was relieved by how similar this home was to his own in Capernaum. He met Stephanas' family; his quiet wife, Timnah, who was a foot shorter than her husband, and his two adult sons, their spouses, and children. Yeshua soon realized he would never suffer for meals in this home. Timnah was an excellent cook, perhaps even better than his immah, though he knew he would never tell her so. Enjoying the savory lamb, warm pita and garlic hummus set before them, they talked about family, life in Capernaum, and Yeshua's training to be a rabbi. The time passed pleasantly, and eventually Timnah and her daughters-in-law cleared the meal and dishes and brought out sweet date and honey cakes for dessert. After thanking Timnah for the meal and hospitality, Bin-yamin changed the direction of conversation.

"So, how is life in Jerusalem with the Roman occupation?"

Stephanas looked at his daughters-in-law and they rose, stretching out their hands toward their children, "Come, time for bed." The women took their hands and led them to mats in the corner of the room.

Pausing until the women and children moved away, Stephanas spoke quietly, "We try to speak carefully when the children are present. "

"I understand, of course." Bin-yamin apologized to his friend and his sons. Yeshua listened closely, sensing the intensity in Stephanas' tone.

Stephanas glanced over his shoulder and saw that the children were out of earshot.

"Life in the Holy City is—tense." Stephanas searched for the appropriate word. "If you do what the Romans require of you, such as paying your taxes and whatever else they ask, you will be fine. But it grieves me to see the way the Sanhedrin pander to

Governor Pontius Pilate." He looked at Bin-yamin, "Do not misunderstand me, I respect the Sadducees and Pharisees and their interpretations of the written and oral law, but," he continued, "they are blurring the line between pleasing Adonai and man. The Sanhedrin negotiates with Pilate, stroking his ego to get what they want. I believe Pilate sees High Priest Caiphas as a whining child to be satiated as leader of the people."

Yeshua knew the Sanhedrin to be the Hebrew court system. Every city and town in Israel had a Sanhedrin to maintain law and order. The Sanhedrin in the Holy City was the largest, with seventy-one members made up of Pharisees and Sadducees.

"I'm grieved to hear this as well," Bin-yamin said gravely, "What is the attitude of the people in Jerusalem?"

"Some are happy," Stephanas shrugged his shoulders, "Though they tend to be those in the upper city, the wealthy. Rome still demands taxes from them of course, but not much has changed for them. And they can afford it."

"It's those like us who suffer most," he continued, "The less well-off and the poor here in the lower city. Some of the Roman centurions are respectful. They know that this was our land first, and they want a peaceful relationship with us. They pay for their pottery, clothing, food, and so on. But others demand what they want and get it. What are we to do?" Stephanas threw up his hands, "They are our oppressors. We do not want them here. They spoil the beauty and purity of Zion, Adonai's Holy City with their immorality and worldly ways. We cannot overthrow them, though many try." He shook his head sadly. His sons nodded in agreement.

"We saw a crucifixion procession today," Yeshua said, wondering if the men were caught in a rebellion against the occupation.

"Most likely they were," Stephanas answered his question. "There are often reports of Zealot uprisings. They have a presence here, though their attacks are generally small. Two or three Zealots attacking one or two Roman soldiers and the like. Their larger-scale attacks are usually outside the city."

Yeshua knew that he and his abba were thinking of Yitzchak and Shim'on. Bin-yamin did not say anything, so Yeshua held his tongue too.

"Overall, they let us keep our way of life and they maintain theirs," Stephanas conceded reluctantly. "We are grateful for that." He took Timnah's hand as she came to stand beside him. Timnah smiled back.

"Have you heard of the rabbi from Galilee?" Stephanas asked abruptly.

"A friend mentioned him today," Bin-yamin said curiously, "But we do not know much else. Who is he?"

"Well, that is a question many are asking," Stephanas replied. "He is from Nazareth and a tekton by trade. He travels around the towns of Galilee. They say he speaks and teaches with authority unlike that of any other rabbi."

"Have you heard him yourself?" Bin-yamin asked.

Stephanas shook his head, "I have not, but I want to. Hundreds of people follow him."

"To hear a man teach? I have sat under the instruction of great teachers in my lifetime, but none have had hundreds of followers."

"Rumor has it that he also performs miracles."

Yeshua could see the surprise on Bin-yamin's face.

"They say he gives sight to the blind, heals the lame and raises the dead," Stephanas continued, "But, greatest of all, they say he forgives sins."

"What!" Yeshua heard the anger and thinly veiled rebuke in his abba's voice. "Stephanas, you know as well as I that no man has the right, nor the power to forgive sins. Adonai alone can do that, and a sacrifice is required. This man is a blasphemer."

"I hear what you say." Stephanas nodded, unperturbed by Bin-yamin's words, "I felt the same way at first. But the more I hear of him and his words..." Stephanas shook his head in wonder, "Please listen to the reports of this rabbi and his acts for yourself, my friend."

Silence hung in the air for several moments. Yeshua knew his abba was trying to gather his thoughts. Before he could respond, Stephanas continued, "Bin-yamin, you know the prophecies. Isn't the coming of a Mashiach prophesied? One who will deliver us from our enemies and bring peace to all peoples?"

Yeshua knew exactly what Stephanas was referring to. Seven hundred years earlier, the navi Micah spoke about the victorious Mashiach who would bring peace saying,

"He will judge between many peoples and will settle disputes for strong nations far and wide. Everyone will enjoy a time of peace and no one will be afraid, because Adonai has spoken."

Yeshua loved this description of the Anointed One who would bring justice and restore the honor of his people. Around the same time, the navi Isaiah also spoke of a coming Mashiach.

"A descendant will come from King David's family of old. The Spirit of Adonai will be on him. He will delight in obeying Adonai. He will give justice to the poor and make fair decisions for the exploited. His word will cause the earth to shake, and one breath from his mouth will destroy the wicked. He will be clothed in righteousness and truth."

"In that day everyone will be at peace. Nothing will hurt or destroy in all My holy mountain, because the earth will be filled with people who know Me. In that day, the heir to David's throne will be a banner of salvation to all the world. He will be triumphant over all."

Yeshua felt excitement and anticipation just thinking of the prophecies. What a glorious day it would be when the Mashiach came and restored his chosen people!

"Certainly, there are prophecies of the Mashiach," Bin-yamin agreed, "But he is to be a man like us, Stephanas. True, he will likely come from the lineage of King David, but nonetheless, he will be but a man. Certainly not imbued with the power to forgive sins." Bin-yamin spoke solemnly. Yeshua knew his abba thought the man sounded like a heretic, but he didn't want to offend Stephanas who seemed to believe the rabbi they spoke of might be the prophesied Mashiach.

"Well, we have kept you up long enough," Bin-yamin said, signaling an end to the conversation.

"Thank you again so much for the meal and your hospitality." Yeshua echoed his thanks. The men stood.

"Your mats are here," Stephanas walked to a corner of the room. "I hope you rest well. And Bin-yamin," he looked at Yeshua's abba, "Just because the Torah and Nevi'im don't explicitly say the Mashiach will have the power to heal and forgive sins, does that mean he certainly won't? Surely we can't know beyond a doubt." Stephanas' words were respectful but filled with conviction, and Yeshua admired the man's confidence.

Bin-yamin's brow furrowed, but he replied, "It's true, we don't know all things, Brother. That is for Adonai alone."

Smiling, Stephanas turned to go to his mat, "Well, *laila tov*, goodnight."

"Thank you," Bin-yamin said, then paused, "Stephanas, what is the name of the rabbi you spoke of?"

Stephanas smiled, "His name is Jesus."

Yeshua pulled the light blanket over himself as Stephanas blew out the oil lamps lighting the room. Tonight he would go to sleep with more questions than he had answers. He wondered if his abba felt the same way.

XI

"Shim'on?"

Shim'on jerked awake and sat up. His neck and back ached from lying on the hard earth most of the night. The sky above him was tinged in brilliant hues of pink and orange, and the air was fresh and cool.

Lydia bat Jude smiled shyly down at him. Shim'on quickly scrambled to his feet, blinking back surprise.

"I'm sorry," She took a step back. Shim'on's mind raced for a response, while his heart beat quickly just being this close to Lydia. The past five years had changed her from a girl into a woman. Five years younger than himself, Lydia had become even more beautiful. Rarely had he ever been this close to her, and aside from exchanging greetings, they had never conversed.

Lydia laughed softly. "I'm sorry I surprised you."

Shim'on realized that his mouth hung open and he quickly snapped it shut.

"Oh, it's all right," he said quickly, shrugging.

"What are you doing out here?" Lydia glanced around.

"I-ah-what are you doing here? You shouldn't be out here by yourself." Shim'on scrambled to avoid answering the question. He was sincerely curious why Lydia was outside the city alone.

"Now, Shim'on bar Yitzchak," Lydia cocked her head good-naturedly, "Don't go telling me what I can and can't do." She laughed; a sound like the water that flowed over the falls. Shim'on immediately wanted to make her laugh again.

"But, if you must know, I come here often in the mornings. I like to talk to Adonai and be alone while the sun is still rising."

"And your abba lets you?" Shim'on asked in surprise.

"He doesn't have to know." Lydia laughed again.

Shim'on didn't say anything, but inside he liked Lydia's independence and zest. He liked everything about her.

"But you haven't answered my question." Lydia's face sobered. "Shouldn't you be out on the sea with my abba and the other fishermen? I've heard rumors about you, Shim'on. I fear they're true." The twinkle had left her eyes and was replaced by a look of concern.

"What have you heard?" Shim'on meant to sound nonchalant, but the words came out accusatorially.

"That you've joined the Zealots." Lydia looked at him soberly. "Is that true?"

Shim'on was surprised by her directness. Were his actions really this transparent? Or had she been watching him? He considered lying but immediately rejected the idea. He wanted to tell Lydia about his decision.

"The rumor is true." He watched to see how his words would impact her. Being a Zealot was a commitment to violence against their enemies. He doubted a woman could understand or would approve.

"I thought so." Lydia's eyes were sober, but there was compassion in them as well. "I can understand why you'd want to become one of them."

"You do? I mean, it doesn't really matter if you or anyone else understands. It's my decision."

Lydia nodded. "Of course. The Romans killed your abba. You want revenge."

Shim'on didn't like her oversimplified response, though it was partly true. He liked her too much to argue.

"But violence isn't what Adonai wants," She continued matter-of-factly.

"How do you know that?" Shim'on was genuinely interested in her answer.

"I told you I speak with Adonai when I'm out here," Lydia smiled and gestured to the rolling hills surrounding them. "He told me. He wants us to pray for our enemies."

Shim'on snorted before he could catch himself. Lydia looked hurt.

"You're saying Adonai speaks to you directly? And He tells you to love the Romans?"

"Yes, He does." Lydia nodded seriously. "And you could hear Him too, Shim'on, if you spoke to Him and really listened."

"Do you think I haven't done that?" Shim'on answered bluntly. "I begged Adonai to let my abba live!"

"I'm sorry, Shim'on." Lydia's face fell. "I can't imagine how that felt."

"Of course, you can't. Both of your parents are still alive." The guilt was back, the pain of it tumbling out in his words. "If one of your parents were killed by the Romans, do you really think you would pray for their murderers?"

Lydia's eyes held his, but she remained silent.

"I have to go." Shim'on said abruptly. Despite the way her words had affected him, he felt a longing to stay with Lydia. The conflicting emotions confused him, but continuing their conversation seemed impossible.

"I understand. I'm sorry, Shim'on. Please be careful." Lydia said. She took a step back and then turned toward Capernaum.

Shim'on watched her go, resisting the tug to ask her to stay with every step. Once she passed through the city gates, he released a long sigh and looked around him. He had left Capernaum the previous evening while Hanoch slept and his immah washed clothes with the other women.

Since Hanoch was aware of his involvement with the Zealots, he would know the gist of his disappearance, though immah would be concerned. He hoped Hanoch could provide Miriam with a good excuse for his absence. Afraid he would oversleep, and not accustomed to slumbering during the dark hours, he had spent most of the night awake.

Although his body was still, his mind was busy throughout the long hours with thoughts of his abba and the mission before him. He was tired, but he was finally a Zealot.

The early morning air was cool and quiet, save for the cooing of doves in the trees above him. A light breeze rustled the surrounding sagebrush. His campsite lay just past the basalt wall on the edge of Capernaum and the gravel road that led to Tiberius. He and Efrayim had planned to meet on the main road outside the city and travel south together.

It was still hours before the appointed time, but Shim'on was restless after his conversation with Lydia. He looked for people in the area but saw none. Confident he was alone, Shim'on threw the sack filled with food and his bow and arrow over his shoulder. He was quick to gather up the provisions before he left the house the previous evening. He tied his belt around his waist and checked to make sure his dagger and sword were secure. Then he walked toward a narrow path that wound its way uphill between sagebrush and lavender bushes until he could no longer see the main road.

It was a familiar trail to Shim'on, one he and Yeshua traipsed many times before. Thinking of his old friend was like pressure on an improperly healed wound. Shim'on recognized that Yeshua tried often to speak with him following the death of his abba, and that he'd always responded coldly. He knew Yeshua was only trying to help, but Shim'on's pride kept him from being honest about the regret and grief he felt. A part of him yearned to talk to his old friend about his conversation with Lydia, and about his decision to be a Zealot. But he couldn't forget Yeshua's refusal to help him avenge Yitzchak's death. He was not to be trusted.

Shim'on gritted his teeth as he again felt Yeshua's betrayal five years before. Well, no matter, he heard Yeshua left Capernaum months before to pursue becoming a rabbi, following in his abba's footsteps. He wasn't really surprised.

He always knew he and Yeshua were different. His friend acted righteous, but when tragedy befell Shim'on's family– Shim'on spat. He didn't need a so-called friend like that in his life.

Despite his dark thoughts, Shim'on found himself enjoying his surroundings. It was becoming lighter, though he could still see the crescent moon and sweep of glittering stars in the sky above him. It was still a couple of hours before dawn. The air was calm this morning, and Shim'on could hear crickets chirping from the dry grass covering the hillsides. Occasionally, rabbits darted their way across the landscape before him, startled from their sleep by his footsteps.

The ground leveled as Shim'on reached the top of the incline. He was near one of his favorite places. Shim'on loved the view looking out over the Sea of Galilee to the east. The main road was also visible from the hill, and he and Yeshua used to enjoy watching the vast variety of travelers going to and from Capernaum. When they were younger, they pretended to be rulers with vast kingdoms stretching before them, fighting invisible enemies, and protecting their people. Now Shim'on knew better. The rulers of their day did not follow Adonai, and they sought not to protect them, but to oppress them. Recalling the prophecies, Shim'on wondered when their Savior would come to set them free from the Romans. Were they forgotten by Him? Or were the Zealots His instrument to set the Hebrew people free?

Pondering such thoughts, Shim'on stepped out of the shadow of the hilly ravine, then stopped. A man sat on the hill ahead of him, his back to Shim'on. Was it Efrayim? The man looked to be shorter and thinner than him. No, Shim'on decided, it was certainly not Efrayim. But who would be up here this time of morning? And for what purpose?

Suddenly, the man turned and looked directly at Shim'on. He had never seen him before. He looked to be older than Shim'on, but only by three or four years. Behind him, the sky grew brighter, pink and orange hues tinting the Sea of Galilee. A flock of swifts flew over the hills, sweeping their way down to the shore. Still, the man kept eye contact with Shim'on.

He couldn't explain it, but Shim'on suddenly felt completely exposed, his thoughts laid bare. As though the man could see straight through him, something else also came with a jolt. He realized the ever-present anger and bitterness he had felt was gone, replaced by a calming peace.

After what felt like several minutes, the man spoke, "Shalom, Shim'on."

Astounded, Shim'on replied, "How do you know my name?"

99

At this, the man did something completely unexpected. He threw back his head and laughed. It was a deep, joyful laugh that surprised Shim'on, yet he couldn't keep from smiling also.

"I know everything about you, Shim'on." The man said, "Don't be afraid. I'm not here to keep you from your mission."

"Although," he continued, with a sober look in his eyes, "It will bring you sorrow, not the freedom you hope for."

Shim'on's mind reeled.

"Who are you?" he asked.

"My name is Jesus," the man responded.

"Have I met you before? How do you know these things about me?"

"I have known you for a long time," Jesus smiled again. "But you have not known me."

He rose from where he sat on the hill, and Shim'on realized he was leaving.

"Will I see you again?" As the words left his mouth, Shim'on felt foolish. He didn't even know this man, yet he couldn't help himself. Something about Jesus made him want to follow the man wherever he was going.

"Be careful, Shim'on. An eye for an eye and a tooth for a tooth. He who lives by the sword, dies by the sword." Jesus quoted from the Torah.

"But I have come so that you may have life and life abundant!" Jesus clapped his hands together, an excited smile on his face.

Shim'on was baffled. He longed to follow this man, but he was committed to this mission, to avenging his abba's death. He desperately wanted to know what Jesus meant by "life abundant" and what filled him with such joy.

100

"You have great passion," Jesus looked into his eyes. "But is it enough?"

Shim'on stood speechless as he tried to comprehend the man's words.

"Adonai be with you, Shim'on." Jesus walked toward the path down to Capernaum. Before Shim'on could form a response, he was gone.

He realized, with sadness, that Jesus hadn't answered his question of whether he would see him again. His mind spun with questions. In a daze, he made his way to the area where the man sat moments before, and heavily lowered himself to the ground.

He realized then that Jesus wore the traditional white robes of a rabbi. If he was a rabbi, how come Shim'on had never heard of him? Furthermore, it was unusual that a rabbi simply referred to himself by name, forfeiting the due title of authority. And what did he mean by asking Shim'on if his passion was enough? Enough for what? The edge of the sun glimpsed over the horizon; the water below stained with brilliant color.

As he pondered what happened, he sobered. The glorious peace he felt moments before had departed with the rabbi as well.

 Shim'on walked beside Efrayim on the Via Maris. The man arrived at the meeting place less than an hour after Shim'on's unexpected conversation with Jesus. They immediately commenced their trek to Tiberius. Shim'on did not tell him about his conversations with Lydia and the rabbi, however. The encounter with Jesus felt especially personal, almost sacred. How did the man know so much about him? And what did he mean about coming so that Shim'on could have life abundant? One thing was certain, Shim'on felt wonderfully at peace for the few moments he was in the rabbi's presence.

Shim'on felt a pinch of worry. What did the man mean by telling him to be careful? First Lydia, and now the mysterious rabbi. Did he know details about the mission ahead of them that they didn't?

Efrayim and Shim'on continued walking on the dusty road as the sun climbed higher in the sky. The cool of the morning quickly burned off, and the heat intensified. Travelers moved both directions on the road. Many traveled with pack animals laden with goods purchased in Capernaum, or on their way to market there. Heavy scents of surrounding sagebrush and manure intermittently wafted through the air.

The men continued their walk mostly in silence, each alone with his thoughts. At midday, they paused under the shade of an olive grove and ate a meal of dried fish, lehem, and olives; then continued their walk. By late afternoon they reached Tiberius, a town similar in size to Capernaum, situated on the coast of the Sea of Galilee. They traveled through the heavily trafficked city without stopping, although Shim'on was sorely tempted by the scents of freshly baked lehem and roasted lamb sizzling in the market as they passed through. His stomach complained with rumblings, yet his zeal prevented him from giving in to the craving. Most Hebrews considered Tiberius to be unclean by law, as it was built on top of a graveyard. The men passed through the city without stopping.

The sun hung low on the horizon as Efrayim and Shim'on departed the city. The sea lapped at the coastline to their left, reflecting the brilliant purple and pink streaks of sunset. Gulls swooped and spun above the water's surface as they snapped up the occasional fish. The sun was nearly set, and the dusty road they walked was bathed in twilight shadow. The men walked quickly, hastening toward the appointed meeting place. Traffic on the road had decreased. Most travelers had likely set up camp for the night or found lodging in Tiberius.

Shim'on's thoughts filled with tense anticipation. He fingered the dagger strapped under his cloak. What would it feel like to kill a man? he wondered. For three more hours Efrayim and Shim'on continued, their footfalls on the gravel beneath their sandals the only sound they made. The sun continued its downward trajectory until it was fully gone, the orange orb sinking behind the horizon. Then it was dark, and the stars grew brighter until they stood in sharp relief to their backdrop, reflecting like sparkling jewels across the water's surface.

Shim'on wondered how Efrayim would be able to tell when they reached the meeting place. He was even more grateful that he was not trying to find the location alone. Finally, Efrayim slowed and pointed to a faint trace of a trail that wound its way into the hills to their right. The path was barely visible in the weak moonlight. After a thirty-minute climb into the hills, they reached a hidden vista and Shim'on pulled the pack containing his food and bow and arrow over his head.

Ahead of him was a shallow rocky outcropping, and underneath it, Shim'on could see men gathered around a small fire. Whorls of smoke rose in the air. The men approached the group, and Jerome rose to greet them.

"I'm glad you made it, Brothers, how was your travel?"

"Good," Efrayim answered, "We did not draw attention."

"Very good!" Jerome clapped Shim'on on the shoulder. "Already, eighty of us are here. The others will hopefully arrive soon."

"Come," he gestured toward the fire, "join us."

As if guessing at Shim'on's unspoken question he said, "We are far enough above the road that the rocks block the light of the fire."

Shim'on took a seat near the snapping flames and set his pack beside him. After such a long day, he was eager to eat.

"Shalom, Shim'on," Tova greeted him from the boulder where he sat nearby.

"Ready for tomorrow?"

"Of course."

"Good." Tova smiled, "We fight for our families and Adonai! As long as you continue to remind yourself of that, all will be well."

"Also," Tova's face fell, "I meant to tell you personally that I am sorry for the loss of your abba. I didn't know him long before..." his voice trailed off. "He was a good man. I'm sure he would be proud of what you are doing."

"Thank you." Shim'on replied. "And you? Why are you a Zealot?" Shim'on was curious about the motivation behind the young man's decision to join the violent movement. "Did you lose someone?"

"No," Tova shook his head, "But I have known those who have been killed or beaten. All of us are being taken advantage of by the scum that exist in our land."

Shim'on finished his dinner of figs, dried fish, and lehem and excused himself to sleep. Although the band of men were fairly certain their existence was hidden from the road below, voices and their echoes carried easily in the rocky area, and even whispers were a risk.

Using his pack as a pillow, Shim'on tried to get comfortable as best he could. His last thoughts as he lay restlessly looking at the star-studded sky were of Jesus and what the man said about

abundant life. Pondering what the rabbi meant, Shim'on finally
fell asleep.

XII

Shim'on awoke to someone shaking his shoulder. Confused, he glanced around him at his unfamiliar surroundings.

"It's time," Tova whispered and gestured for him to get up.

With a rush of adrenaline, Shim'on remembered where he was. He pulled his tallit tighter around his chilled shoulders.

"Already?" he whispered back to Tova, "I thought they were at least two day's journey from here."

"We thought so too," Tova whispered, strapping a short sword to his side. "But we were wrong. Jerome has been camped a half day's journey ahead of us to keep watch for them, and he just brought word that they are coming now."

Shim'on hastily stood and retrieved his pack. He followed Tova's lead and strapped his dagger to the leather thong tied around his waist.

"How soon will they be here?" he asked Tova.

"Most likely three or four hours," Tova replied, "Jerome saw them set up camp late last night and rushed here to warn us. They have most likely broken camp by now and are on their way."

Shim'on was impressed by Tova's steadiness. He tried to conceal the slight shake in his hands as he tied his sandals and pulled food from his bag.

Tova nodded, "Yes, it's important to eat. You'll need all your energy for what's ahead of us."

Shim'on took a bite. The lehem was dry and flavorless in his mouth. Anticipation and nervousness fought within him. He chided himself inwardly. Today he would avenge his abba by inflicting Adonai's justice on the Roman empire. They stole from him what was not theirs to take, and they would pay. He reminded himself of his training and preparation the past five years. He was ready.

The sky was still dark, but the morning light began to tinge the eastern horizon. Shim'on could see the outlines of the landscape around him and knew the main route would still be in shadow.

He looked around. All the men were awake and girding themselves with their weapons or eating a quick meal, calm and efficient in their preparations.

Efrayim walked over to him.

"They will likely be here within the next couple of hours," he began, omitting any morning pleasantries, "We will move down to the Via Maris soon.

"I would suggest that you start up here, with your bow," he continued. "Once they become aware of our presence, try to hit as many as you can."

Shim'on nodded.

"When you come down to the road, use your sword and dagger," Efrayim continued.

"Be very careful, Shim'on, these are trained soldiers. We have the element of surprise, but even so, they are well practiced with the sword. Stay aware, and do not stay in one place for long."

Shim'on nodded his understanding. Nearly one hundred Zealots against twenty-four Roman soldiers seemed like good odds, but he knew better. Every soldier wore armor and all of them spent countless hours training. They carried swords and daggers and wielded four-foot-tall shields that weighed nearly twenty pounds. They were strong and deadly.

"For your abba," Efrayim put a hand on his shoulder and looked him in the eye, "remember that. Remember your purpose and keep your focus."

"I will," Shim'on nodded.

"Over here," Tova gestured towards them to gather near the now blackened fire pit. They joined the other men, and Jerome stepped into the center.

"They are on their way, men," he spoke so that everyone could hear him, "I expect to see them in no more than two hours. I want half of you to spread yourselves along the road; try to cover at least twenty yards. They will be hemmed in by the sea to the east. The rest of you wait out of sight until I give the signal. There are close to thirty soldiers with slaves carrying supplies."

There was a soft murmur amongst the group, and Jerome motioned for silence.

"I know you are all confident, but don't let your excitement exceed your caution," he whispered, "We have the advantage of surprise. Once they reach the middle of our location, those of you who have bows; use them. Hopefully, we will be able to cut down a few before we engage them on the road."

"Once I give the sign, I want everyone to rush them."

"Any questions?" He glanced around the group. No one spoke.

"All right then. Go ahead and make your way down to the Via Maris. I will stay behind and signal from the heights when they approach. Then I will join you and give the signal when to engage in hand to hand combat. Understood?"

Shim'on could feel the excitement and tense energy in the air. He nodded his understanding along with the other men.

"All right, let's get moving."

The Zealots

Shim'on found cover behind a couple of olive trees where he was concealed from the road but could still see Jerome. The rest of the men fanned out across the landscape, and Shim'on guessed his position to be somewhere in the middle.

The sun finally rose enough to illuminate the landscape around him, and the morning air was quiet save for the carefree chirps and birds that swooped and soared above them.

Since they arrived after dark the previous night, Shim'on hadn't been able to see his surroundings well until now. He looked around. Olive trees, sagebrush, and boulders dotted the foothills where each served to hide a fellow Zealot.

To the south lay the road, already interspersed with early morning travelers. On the other side of the road lay the Sea of Galilee. Fishing boats bobbed on the gentle waves, and sunlight glinted brightly off its surface, causing Shim'on to squint. He thought of Hanoch and his immah wondering how his brother was doing. He wished he could be here, but Shim'on was grateful Hanoch was safe in Capernaum. Losing two sons and a husband would be more than Miriam could bear.

His thoughts turned to memories of his abba. How could Lydia believe that Adonai wanted them to pray for their enemies? The idea was ridiculous. A hot breeze brushed the hair from his sweaty forehead and carried the voices of those traveling on the road below. Anger pressed against his chest and onto his shoulders. He let it seep into his mind and heart. It was fuel for the fire of his hatred toward Rome.

Settling onto one knee, his quiver thrown across his back, he nestled his bow into a flat stone crevice with an arrow notched in preparation. He checked again to make sure his dagger and sword were secured at his waist. They were. Shim'on waited.

Sweat trickled down his face and he grimaced when it dripped into his eyes, causing a burning sensation. His wet tunic clung to his back. Try as he might to remain focused, his thoughts kept drifting to the recent conversation with the rabbi. The man said he had known Shim'on a long time, but that Shim'on had not known him. He wracked his mind to conjure up any memory of meeting Jesus. But there was nothing. He knew that he would have remembered meeting the enigmatic man.

A pebble skittered across the ground in front of him and Shim'on jolted upright. He looked toward its origin and saw the man on his left pointing to the road. Shim'on glanced toward Jerome's location and saw him gesturing to the road as well, warning the men of the soldiers' approach. He cursed himself. He had allowed his thoughts to distract him so that he was no longer focused on the mission at hand.

A cloud of dust rose a quarter mile away and with it, the sound of many voices. Thoughts of anything else but the attack before him fled, and Shim'on focused on the marching steps upon gravel and the clanking of Roman armor. Jerome hastened his way down the hill through the tall grasses toward the Zealots, keeping low to the ground to avoid being seen. He reached Shim'on and hunched behind him, gesturing to the men down the line to watch him for the signal to attack.

The noises came closer and closer. By a miracle of Adonai, no other travelers were visible on the road. Adrenaline coursed through Shim'on's veins. He wiped a hand across his forehead for the hundredth time and noticed that his hand trembled. He hoped he would be able to shoot straight.

The plume of dust came closer and closer, until Shim'on could see the sun glinting off the first soldier's armor. He felt his heart hammering in his chest, his breathing shallow and fast.

110

Jerome waited until half the soldiers passed his position, then Shim'on heard him whisper, "Now!" He gestured to the line of men. Shim'on took aim. One of the legionaries looked to his left just in time for the arrow to bury itself in his neck. He fell to the ground screaming.

The soldiers and slaves surrounding him were confused for a moment, then all hell broke loose. Shim'on aimed another arrow at a soldier but it bounced off his iron armor. In the chaos, it was difficult to hit his mark. Shim'on saw several slaves fall to the ground unconscious or in pain. Though they were innocent, the slaves were unfortunately caught between the Zealots and their enemies.

He notched another arrow and this time it hit its mark, sinking into the leg of a soldier who screamed in pain and fell to the ground. Arrows whistled through the air and Shim'on saw two more soldiers fall, one hit in the forehead and an arrow protruding from the shoulder of another. Despite the element of surprise, the legionaries quickly regained their composure. They formed *testudos*. Eight to ten soldiers formed a unit and put up their shields, creating a 'shell' that the Zealot archers couldn't pierce.

Wide-eyed slaves ran for their lives. Suddenly Shim'on heard a shout as Jerome signaled the rest of the Zealots to attack. They roared in response with a battle cry.

The tremble gone from his hands, Shim'on slung his bow into its quiver and joined the other men as they scrambled from their hiding places toward the road. The Roman soldiers broke from the testudos and prepared for battle. Metal clashed against metal as the swords of the Zealots and Romans connected. The scene was chaos; the soldiers were trapped between the sea and the Zealots.

He watched as Jerome struck down a slave who stood between himself and a Roman soldier. The man moved with intentionality and didn't seem to think twice about removing any obstacles in his path regardless of who they were. Shim'on was quickly distracted by a Roman soldier charging toward him. The man's linen garments were drenched with sweat, and a spray of blood stretched across his iron breastplate. Before Shim'on could pull his dagger, the man was upon him, brandishing a spear. Shim'on ducked and heard the metal tip of the spear scrape against a nearby boulder. He spun around, pulling his short sword from the belt at his waist. The lack of clarity Shim'on felt moments before had disappeared, replaced with passionate hatred for his enemies. With a cry of rage, the centurion sprung toward him and Shim'on bent, sidestepping left. The soldier stumbled, clumsily trying to match his movement to Shimon's. Taking advantage of his window of opportunity, Shim'on thrust his dagger forward, and it sank into the centurion's upper leg. The man howled in pain and fell to his knees. He dropped the spear and clutched at his leg. Blood flowed from the gash and muddied the dust. Shim'on stood, stunned by what he had just done. Suddenly, he felt movement beside him.

Tova swept past him, sword drawn, and sliced the soldier's head from his body in one fast motion. The headless body fell to the ground, and Shim'on jerked away.

"Don't stop until the job is finished," Tova looked at him, then turned as another Roman soldier flung himself forward.

Shim'on looked at the headless corpse and felt a wave of nausea. He was surrounded by soldiers, Zealots, slaves, and animals. Blood was everywhere, on everything.

He saw his dagger protruding from the soldier's side. Instead of retrieving it, he picked up the soldier's spear.

The Zealots

Glancing to his left, he made eye contact with a legionary who appeared to be his age. Shim'on yelled, hoisting the spear to shoulder height, and breaking into a jog. He pushed two slaves out of his way and told them to run. Holding the spear perpendicular in his hands, Shim'on deflected a blow from the centurion and before he could draw his weapon back again, he swung the butt of the spear into the man's armored abdomen. The soldier made a grunting noise, the wind knocked out of him. Before the man could get his breath back, Shim'on pulled the dagger from his waist and plunged it into the man's neck. The soldier's eyes rolled back and Shim'on quickly jerked the spear, dislodging it. The shock of Tova's earlier actions was gone, and Shim'on focused simply on surviving and killing. Suddenly a searing pain ripped through his right shoulder, throwing him forward. Glancing at his shoulder, he saw an arrow protruding from bloody flesh. Behind him, he heard heavy breathing and running footsteps, his attacker almost upon him.

Shim'on let out a cry of pain and anger as he swung around and thrust the spear forward, feeling it hit its mark before he could even register the man's face. Looking up, Shim'on's heart fell. This was not his assailant, but one of the slaves he'd shoved out of the way earlier. The man must have been caught between the Zealots and soldiers as they fought. Shim'on had blindly thrust his weapon, assuming him to be the enemy.

Looking over the man's lifeless body, Shim'on saw a legionary twenty yards away sneer at him. The man turned and maneuvered his way through the men grappling around him, moving away from Shim'on, and down the canyon toward Tiberius.

Shim'on didn't care. He couldn't drag his eyes from the innocent man lying dead at his feet. Slowly, the violence quieted, bodies of men and animals littering the canyon floor. Shim'on felt a hand on his unwounded shoulder and started out of his reverie.

"You all right?" Efrayim stood by his side. "Looks like one of them hit their mark." He nodded at Shim'on's shoulder.

Shim'on dragged his eyes from the body at his feet, willing the man's spirit to return to his blank eyes but knowing it wouldn't.

"He was an obstacle to your survival," Efrayim said quietly. "Don't give it any more thought, Shim'on."

"Well done, men!" Jerome joined the group of Zealots gathering around Efrayim and Shim'on. Jerome's appearance matched that of the rest of the group. Sweat and blood sprayed across many of the men's faces, tunics, and exposed skin. A few, like Shim'on, had injuries. At least thirty were missing. Miraculously, no innocent travelers had been caught up in the action.

"Most of the slaves ran away with the animals when we first attacked, and fifteen of the centurions escaped. I am sorry to say that we lost several of our own." The men dropped their heads as Jerome continued, "But they died fighting for Adonai and our people. Remember them with honor."

"As you know, it is certainly not safe to stay where we camped last night. Those who escaped will take the news to Herod since Galilee is in his jurisdiction, and we will be wanted men by nightfall. I encourage you to split up and camp in the hills tonight. Make your way home carefully tomorrow. Adonai be with you."

Shim'on limped over to a boulder near the canyon wall and sat heavily. Reaching up to the arrow still protruding from his shoulder, he touched it gingerly and grimaced.

"Would you like help?" Efrayim followed him.

"That would be much appreciated," Shim'on gritted his teeth while Efrayim snapped the arrow off as close as he could to the wound. If the arrow was pulled out now, the bleeding would increase and without immediate care and rest, he could bleed out. He would have to wait until he was home in Capernaum, and Lydia could help him.

"Thank you," he choked out gratitude despite the burning pain.

Efrayim nodded, "Let's go."

As they left, Shim'on noticed that a group of Zealots carried bodies of their dead compatriots to the top of the canyon where they would be buried beneath rocks. A memory of himself doing the same with his abba's body flooded his mind. The bloody violence of Tova cutting the head off the Roman soldier, and the moment of burying his own spear in the chest of the innocent slave, dimmed. This was a war against the enemy that stole his abba from him.

He was under no impression that his skill saved him today. The Romans were fierce adversaries, skilled in their form and duties.

Adonai himself had spared his life. He ought to be dead. Shim'on resolved that from this point there would be no regrets, only obstacles to be overcome. Today had served to teach him that his skill was nowhere near that of the legionaries.

He would avenge Rome's murder of his abba. He would train harder. Never again would he bow down to Rome as so many of his countrymen did.

He would silence any thoughts distracting him from his mission, even thoughts of the mysterious rabbi he encountered days before. He recalled Jesus' question and the answer became clear. His passion lay with the Zealot cause.

He would fight for his abba and for Adonai. Surely that would be enough to free him from the fiery anger and heavy guilt he carried within himself every day.

XIII

It had been nearly two years since he arrived and Yeshua loved his new life in Jerusalem. He missed his family, of course, but every day was a new adventure, and Yeshua drank it in.

Each morning he rose before dawn and completed his early morning preparations for the day. Since he arrived in Jerusalem, his passion for righteousness had been kindled into a fire. He felt a fierce ownership and dedication to everything commanded in the Torah. Indeed, he often found himself confronting Stephanas and his family in areas of their lifestyle that did not align with the law. Just days ago, he reminded Stephanas not to carry one of his grandchildren on Shabbat. The night before, he refused to eat the kugel Timnah accidentally made with one non-kosher ingredient. He felt a twinge of guilt when she burst into tears but reminded himself that he was to be a rabbi. Admonishing others to stay committed to the law was his calling. He ignored the small voice in the back of his mind that whispered he was becoming more and more prideful.

After his morning rituals, Yeshua departed to the temple where he sat in the courtyard with five other young men from around the region. For the next four hours, Phinehas riddled them with questions as they listened, memorized, and recited the Torah and Mishnah. At times, he selected a student to teach on a particular subject or portion of the holy writings. Sometimes Phinehas traveled to nearby cities to teach in their synagogues, and in those cases, his students came with him. Phinehas had exceedingly high expectations of the men under his tutelage. Although he chided Yeshua for mistakes, it was obvious to everyone that the young man was his favorite. Yeshua attempted to maintain an appearance of humility under the frequent praise and favoritism showered upon him by his teacher. However, the treatment fed into what was becoming a tower of ego and pride. The fire of his commitment to go to great lengths to observe every stroke of the law grew fiercer.

Afterward, and when in Jerusalem, Yeshua joined Stephanas at a worksite. One week they built a new home for a family. Other weeks they built residential additions or worked on the Roman quarters.

"*Tzaharayim Tovim*, good afternoon, Stephanas," Yeshua greeted the man as he joined him at the worksite for a local family. This week they were building a mikvah, a bath inside the home used for ceremonial washing. A private mikvah was a luxury that not every family could afford. Most in lower Jerusalem needed to use the communal baths.

"Shalom, Yeshua," Stephanas smiled at him from where he sat, eating his midday meal. Yeshua's host was even-keeled, his personality calm and pleasant. Yeshua enjoyed being around him.

"How was your time at the temple?"

Yeshua sat and dug into the meal Timnah had provided for him. Once again, he thanked Adonai for the woman's amazing cooking as he bit into the tangy grape leaves of a dolmade.

"Rabbi Phinehas mentioned that rabbi you spoke of, Jesus," Yeshua said. "He says even the Gentiles speak of him now." Yeshua was still trying to develop his own opinion of the rabbi whose name sparked controversy.

Phinehas believed the man was a heretic, possibly even demon possessed. "No rabbi has the power to forgive sins," he often said with passionate anger. "Yet this rabbi claims to! Blasphemy! Only Adonai can pardon sins. This is why we offer sacrifices and keep the law!"

Yeshua agreed that the rabbi's words were certainly incendiary. But he could not deny the man certainly sounded different than most other rabbis, based on the stories he heard.

"Yes, that is true," Stephanas said, dipping a chunk of lehem in olive oil, "I have even overheard Roman soldiers speaking of him."

"What do you think of him?" Yeshua asked, wiping his forehead with his sleeve. Even in the shade, the heat was stifling.

"What do I think of him, or who do I think he is?" Stephanas smiled, tilting his head. "I'm sure your rabbi has told you his opinion. It matters less what people think of him than what is the truth, isn't that so?"

Yeshua realized that Stephanas had turned the question back to him without answering himself. Though Stephanas was a craftsman without formal education, the man was smart.

Yeshua decided to take the bait, "So you're saying that it doesn't matter what people think of him, but more, who is he really?"

"You tell me," Stephanas shrugged. "People may hate Caesar, but does that make him any less emperor of Rome?"

Yeshua knew where Stephanas was leading, and he felt self-righteous indignation ignite within him. "Rabbi Phinehas and many of the other teachers of the law hate Jesus because he speaks against them. He calls them 'whitewashed tombs' and 'blind guides'. He says they lay burdens on the people they were never meant to carry; laws they created apart from Adonai." Yeshua shook his head angrily, "When he says these things, he speaks against me and my abba as well, Stephanas! Abba is a Pharisee, and I am one too! Who does he think he is to label us so? He doesn't even know us!"

Stephanas finished his meal and began to sharpen his tools.

"Well, maybe you should try to meet him," the man said quietly, "Hear him speak for yourself."

"Maybe I will," Yeshua retorted. The men were quiet as Yeshua watched Stephanas work. The man was an excellent tekton, and Yeshua had learned much from him already. Yeshua knew he was being disrespectful to his host, yet he knew Stephanas would never confront a rabbi. He felt a stab of guilt.

"The navi Isaiah spoke of a cornerstone in Jerusalem," Stephanas continued, sharpening his awl with a stone, "Do you remember what he said?"

"Of course. 'I am placing a cornerstone in Jerusalem, a firm and tested stone. It is a precious cornerstone that is safe to build on. Whoever believes need never be shaken.'" Yeshua recited the words from memory.

"I think of that passage every time we lay a cornerstone in a home." Stephanas gestured towards the dwellings surrounding them.

"Who or what do you think is the cornerstone Isaiah is referring to?" Yeshua knew the man already had the answer but was testing him.

Annoyed, he replied, "The Mashiach, of course."

Stephanas smiled, "Perhaps the prophecy is soon to be fulfilled."

Yeshua scoffed, "By whom, Stephanas? The heretic from Nazareth? Do you really believe the prophecies point to a Nazarene who claims to forgive sins?"

Stephanas smiled, unruffled by Yeshua's protests. "I'm not certain yet. But he is unlike any other teacher I've ever heard."

"If he is as great a teacher as they say, why not spend more time here?" Yeshua asked, "He would have a far greater audience than in Galilee."

"I don't know," Stephanas replied again, shrugging. "His hometown is in Galilee and his disciples are from there as well. He is in Capernaum now I hear. Actually, I was thinking of making a journey to see him myself. Would you like to go together? You could ask Rabbi Phinehas for leave to see your family; you wouldn't have to tell him you want to see the rabbi." He grinned.

Once again Yeshua was impressed by Stephanas' cleverness.

"I suppose that might work," he said, mulling the idea over. "It will take us four or five days to get there and the same to return. I could ask Rabbi Phinehas for a fortnight's leave."

Stephanas nodded, "All right, I will let Timnah know and ask her to prepare food for us."

Yeshua was humbled by the man's thoughtfulness. Whether Stephanas had already planned to see the rabbi or offered to go simply so he wouldn't be alone; Yeshua was grateful he would have Stephanas' company. He was again convicted of his judgmental treatment of Stephanas Bar Abel and his family but shrugged such feelings aside. He was a rabbi's son and soon to be a rabbi himself. It was time he went to see Jesus and form his own opinion.

 Days later, Yeshua and Stephanas departed Jerusalem for Capernaum. Yeshua had told Phinehas that he was homesick and wanted to visit his family. While a young rabbi's request along these lines would usually be denied, Phinehas was fond of his favorite pupil and happily gave his permission. Yeshua felt slightly guilty for not telling the rabbi the real reason behind his trip. However, he rationalized that he needed to see and hear the controversial rabbi for himself to develop his own opinions.

The journey took four days, and the men were surprised by the number of travelers that surrounded them on their route. The name of Jesus was on the lips of nearly every man and woman. On the fourth day, the men reached the outskirts of Capernaum near midday. Yeshua was shocked. Thousands of people camped around his hometown.

"Yeshua!" his immah cried out when Yeshua pushed open the door to his childhood home. She flung her arms around her eldest son. Yeshua breathed in the familiar smell of freshly baked bread that nestled in her hair.

"And Stephanas!" Sarai smiled at him over Yeshua's shoulder. She released Yeshua and gestured for the man to enter. "Welcome to our home!"

"Oh," she smiled at Yeshua, "Your abba is going to be so happy to see you! But" she suddenly stopped, "Is everything all right? Why are you here?"

"All is well, Immah," Yeshua assured her, "We heard that the rabbi everyone is talking about is here. We came to hear him for ourselves."

"Oh yes!" Sarai clasped her hands together, "Jesus is here!"

Yeshua was surprised to hear his immah refer to the rabbi with such familiarity. It struck him as inappropriate.

Suddenly, the door opened and Yeshua's abba entered. His tunic was covered with limestone and basalt dust. Peering around the room, his eyes settled on Yeshua and Stephanas. His face broke into a grin.

"Son! What are you doing here?" He enveloped Yeshua in a hug that caused him to realize how deeply he missed his abba. Bin-yamin released him and crossed the room to throw his arms around his friend. Yeshua answered his abba's question in the same way as he had answered Sarai.

"Yes, the rabbi is here!" Bin-yamin smiled at Sarai and she responded in kind.

In confusion, Yeshua looked back and forth between them, "What's going on? Is there something you need to tell me?"

"Son, Stephanas, you must go see the rabbi!" Bin-yamin's eyes shone, and the smile on his face seemed permanent.

Yeshua couldn't wrap his mind around his parents' demeanor. Just months before, Bin-yamin was critical, even condemning toward the rabbi, Jesus. Now he was urging others to go listen to him speak?

Bin-yamin must have been able to read the confusion on his son's face. He placed a hand on his shoulder.

"I know what you are thinking, Yeshua," he looked into his son's eyes, "I also held reservations, even judgment against Jesus. But then I heard him speak…" His words trailed away, and a smile lit his face.

Yeshua couldn't help but notice that like Sarai, his abba also used the rabbi's name, rather than his formal title.

"You were right, Stephanas," Bin-yamin turned towards the man, "I began to hear reports of what he was teaching, and I couldn't help but be intrigued. He came to Capernaum, and I heard him for myself. He is unlike any other teacher."

"You must go hear him for yourself!" Sarai urged Yeshua and Stephanas again, her face alight in a way that Yeshua couldn't remember seeing before.

"Join us for the midday meal, and then go down to the sea; that is where he is teaching." Bin-yamin urged. "Deborah and Tobias are there now."

Yeshua was perplexed and irritated at the lavish adoration his family seemed to have for this rabbi, but he tried to mask it. The man claimed to forgive sins! That alone made him a dangerous heretic! And yet, his own abba, a rabbi himself, was taken in by him. Maintaining what he hoped was a neutral face, Yeshua agreed to partake in the midday meal, as did Stephanas. One thing was certain; he would not be as gullible as his parents. He planned to listen to the rabbi with a critical ear.

As they ate, Bin-yamin and Sarai asked questions regarding Yeshua's rabbinical studies, Stephanas' family, and tekton work in the Holy City. Throughout the meal, Yeshua was reminded of his love for his family, and theirs for him. He realized that he missed them more than he realized.

After finishing their meal, Bin-yamin departed to his work, and Yeshua and Stephanas to the Sea of Galilee. As they walked the dusty streets, the sea came into view, the midday sun glinting off the water. Memories filled Yeshua's mind-happy thoughts of running through these streets with Shim'on and of his walks with Bin-yamin to Beth Midrash in the early morning cool. There was nothing cool about the weather today, however. The sun beat down upon the men's heads, and Yeshua wiped sweat from his forehead.

Reaching the curve of the road toward the sea, Yeshua paused. The entire shoreline was packed with men, women, and children. Many sat eating their midday meal. Others stood or reclined on the hard earth. Young children scampered among the crowds.

"There must be thousands here!" Stephanas said, equally shocked.

What was even more amazing to Yeshua was that such a large group of people could be so quiet. There was a low hum of voices across the dense crowd, and he could hear children's voices and giggles, but over it all a man's voice could be clearly heard.

"Look over there!" Stephanas pointed to a fishing boat bobbing on the sea's surface, a stone's throw from shore. An olive-skinned young man with dark, curly hair sat at the prow of the ship looking over the mass of people.

"Let's try to get closer," Yeshua said, as he threaded his way through the throngs of people. He listened to the man on the boat as he walked.

"You have heard it said that you have the right to hurt those who hurt you. But I say, do not resist an evil person! If someone slaps you on the right cheek, offer the other cheek also. If someone sues you, go ahead and give them more than they are asking for! If a soldier demands that you carry his gear for a mile, carry it two miles. Give to those who ask."

The words were like salt in a wound. After living in the heavily Roman-occupied and controlled Holy City, Yeshua hated their enemies with an even greater passion than when he had lived in Capernaum. These were the same enemies that stole Shim'on's abba from him. But the rabbi was commanding the people to love the Romans. Yeshua restrained himself from spitting. He would certainly never pursue physical violence against the Romans, but willingly serve them? The idea was repulsive. He could imagine his old friend Shim'on's passionate response to the rabbi's teaching.

The rabbi continued, "You have heard the law that says, 'Love your neighbor' and hate your enemy. But I say, love your enemies! Pray for those who abuse you!" Yeshua could hear the power and conviction in the man's voice. "If you do that, you will be like your Abba in heaven." He gestured to the sky above, "He gives His sunlight to both the evil and the good, and He gives the gift of rain to the just and unjust alike. If you only love those who love you, what reward is there for that? Even corrupt tax collectors do that much."

Yeshua seethed. Now Jesus was saying that serving their enemies was not enough; they must love them too! He looked around and saw hundreds of eyes fixed on the man in the boat, soaking in the rabbi's words. Jesus spoke as if He were the authority on all things. This rabbi was adored by the people, even worshipped. But why? Yeshua couldn't understand why the people didn't hear the idiocy in the man's words, as he could. He spied a couple of boulders ahead of him vacated by a man and his son and moved in that direction. He was already eager to leave but knew Stephanas was following him.

The rabbi's white tunic flapped against his legs in the breeze. Small whitecaps formed on the sea. He stood, balancing himself against the boat's railing.

"And when you pray," he continued, his voice deep and sure, "Don't be like the pretenders who love to pray publicly on street corners and in the synagogues where everyone can see them. I tell you the truth, that is all the reward they will ever get."

Yeshua felt his face flush. He often prayed in prominent places, relishing overhearing passers-by applaud his devoutness. The rabbi's rebuke made him angry because he knew it was true, but Yeshua would never admit as much.

Jesus continued to speak, "Instead when you pray, go pray in private. Then your Abba, who sees everything, will reward you." He looked around the crowd with kindness in his eyes, "You don't need to say a lot of words to be heard by your Abba. He knows what you need before you even ask. Pray like this:

'Abba in heaven,
May your name be kept holy.
May your Kingdom come soon.
May your will be done here,
As it is in heaven.
Give us today the food we need,
And forgive our sins,
As we forgive those who sin against us.
Don't let us give in to temptation,
But rescue us from the evil one.'

And remember this," Jesus' eyes turned somber, "If you forgive those who sin against you, your Heavenly Abba will forgive you. But if you refuse to forgive others, your Abba will not forgive your sins."

Seating himself on a rock, Yeshua seethed inwardly. Who made this man an authority on how to pray? What made him qualified to direct people in how they could commune with

Adonai and how their sins could be forgiven? And referring to
Adonai as Abba! Yeshua shook his head. The way Jesus alluded
to Adonai was sacrilegious! Adonai was their authority, meant to
be feared! He was not a warm, comforting abba that one could
approach with such confidence. To his disappointment, however,
Yeshua could find no signs of arrogance in Jesus' words or
demeanor. The rabbi exuded peace and a steady calm and
humility that was unsettling to him. Glancing to his left, he tried
to gauge Stephanas' reaction to the rabbi's words. To his
frustration, Stephanas' face reflected rapt attention.

"Do not judge others, and you will not be judged," the man
continued. "You will be treated as you treat others. The standard
you use in judging is the standard by which you will be judged."

Easy for you to say. Jesus was challenging the people to do
the impossible! To be perfect! Surely the man knew that he
himself was being judged by many sources. Stephanas' words
from weeks ago came to mind, *"It matters less what people think
of him than what is the truth, isn't that so?"*

"And why worry about something sinful your friend is doing
when you have sins of your own?" The rabbi continued, "First,
repent of your wrong-doing. After that you can help your friend
with his sins."

Once again, the rabbi's words stung Yeshua's heart, but he
resisted their power. All the times that Yeshua made judgments
of Stephanas, his family, and his peers over the past months rose
to the surface of Yeshua's mind. The rabbi was saying that he
was to judge himself before he judged anyone else. For one
horrible moment, Yeshua felt convicted of the depth of his self-

righteousness and pride, but—with effort—he pushed these thoughts back under the surface. It was his duty as a rabbi to make judgments to keep his people in line with the law. Wasn't he supposed to point people to himself as an example of how they ought to live? After all, he was quite righteous. He followed the law more devoutly than most. No, Yeshua concluded, he stood firmly on the law and the beliefs of his forefathers. There was no need to humble himself before the words of this rabbi and their uncertain leading. It was certainly the more logical option. *And the one in which you get to keep your pride.*

"Yeshua?" Stephanas looked at him questioningly, "Did you hear me?"

"I—I'm sorry," Yeshua stuttered.

"I agree, his words are amazing, aren't they?" Stephanas grinned excitedly, mistaking Yeshua's distraction for interest in the rabbi's teaching.

Yeshua had heard enough. Leaning over to Stephanas he said, "I'll see you back in town."

He stood, ignoring the man's look of surprise and disappointment, and threaded his way through the crowds and back toward Capernaum. He could help his abba with his work or study the Torah for the remainder of their time in Capernaum if Stephanas insisted on staying as they had initially planned. Which, based on the man's apparent infatuation with the rabbi, Yeshua assumed he would. But he would not be led astray by the famed rabbi. He had finally made his decision.

XIV

It wasn't working. Shim'on wiped the blood off his dagger with the edge of his tunic, leaving streaks of scarlet on the cream-colored material. He and Efrayim, Jerome, and Tova, along with several other Zealots, had just concluded their attack on a Roman contubernium. This time none had escaped. The past two years had made Shim'on into a practiced fighter, and his skills and abilities had increased with each Zealot attack. But no matter how many Roman lives he took, the depression fueled by the anger and guilt he felt only seemed to dig its claws deeper into his heart.

"Nice work!" Tova clapped Shim'on on the back.

Hanoch and Miriam had become used to Shim'on disappearing for days at a time and returning with bloody garments and sometimes wounds. Out of necessity, Shim'on eventually told his immah about his involvement with the Zealots. Although she kept his secret, she voiced her strong disapproval.

"Let's bury them and go home," Jerome began to drag one of the soldiers by his feet toward a grassy knoll.

Shim'on looked around. Under any other circumstances, the scene would be idyllic. They were two or three miles outside of

Capernaum, in the countryside, surrounded by green trees and wildflowers. The scents of lavender and warm earth drifted in the air.

Shim'on followed Jerome, taking hold of the feet of a soldier. The man was heavy and Shim'on strained to drag him up the slight hill, leaving a trail of bloody grass in his wake.

Shim'on's abilities had set him apart as a natural fighter. Avi took note of the reports of Shim'on's hot temper and passionate hatred of the Romans which drove him to furious action in combat. As a result, he tasked him more frequently with these types of attacks. Shim'on's fiery disposition had already sparked more than one confrontation with others in the group. Many of the other Zealots feared him and gave him a wide berth, so that Shim'on had few friends in the band of fighters.

Although he appreciated Avi's attention, Shim'on refused to take pride in the number of men he killed. As the months went by, however, the number of lives Shim'on took as a Zealot climbed higher and higher. His reputation as a dangerous man garnered him increased attention from the insurrectionists and Romans alike. Shim'on continued to justify his actions as righteous—necessary to avenge his abba, and to protect his people.

The men piled rocks over the bodies and turned toward home, splitting into groups. Efrayim and Shim'on walked toward Capernaum.

"So," Efrayim said as they trudged along the road, "Have you heard the rumors of the rabbi?"

"I'd have to be dead not to," Shim'on replied dryly. While he had heard reports of a rabbi traveling through Galilee, he wasn't particularly interested. As it was, he already had enough demands on his time.

Efrayim laughed, then sobered, "They say that Yohanan the Baptist himself calls him the Mashiach. Did you know that he is the rabbi's cousin?" Both men knew of the prophet who preached in the Judean wilderness. Well respected by the Hebrew people, Yohanan spent his life prophesying the coming of the Mashiach who would baptize them with the Holy Spirit and fire.

"I didn't." Shim'on was surprised.

Efrayim turned to look at Shim'on as they walked. "I heard that Yohanan baptized the rabbi."

"He baptized the one he believes to be the chosen Mashiach?" Shim'on asked, incredulous, "If he really is the Anointed One, it is Yohanan who ought to be baptized!"

"Apparently, he did protest, but the rabbi said that it needed to be done to fulfill prophecy.

"But what's most amazing," Efrayim continued, "is that people say they heard the voice of Adonai as the rabbi came up out of the water."

"What?"

"Yes. They say a dove came and lit on his shoulder, and a voice from the heavens said, 'This is my dearly loved son, who brings me great joy."

"I don't believe it," Shim'on shook his head, "The voice of Adonai, Efrayim, really?"

"I know, I know," Efrayim lifted his hands in defense, "But there were hundreds there as witnesses. How can so many people be wrong?"

Shim'on didn't know, so he didn't answer.

The men continued walking the dirt road toward Capernaum in silence. The morning sunlight cast a beautiful palette of orange, pink, and purple in the sky above them. Crickets drowsily sang from their hiding places in the grass.

"Where is he now?" Shim'on asked, curious.

"The rabbi? Apparently, he disappeared into the wilderness. He hasn't been seen in weeks."

"Well, there you have it then. He's crazy and most likely dead."

"Maybe," Efrayim shrugged.

The men reached the town gates, and Shim'on was grateful he packed an extra tunic. He wouldn't want to risk being seen by soldiers while wearing bloody garments.

Suddenly, he had a thought. "Efrayim, what's the rabbi's name?"

"Jesus," Efrayim said matter-of-factly. "Adonai be with you, Brother," he waved in farewell as he turned towards his home.

"And with you." A jolt of recognition shot through Shim'on. So, this rabbi was the man he had met on the hill years ago. Of course, Jesus was a common name. Still, what were the odds? It had to be the same man. But where was he now? And was he still alive?

The men parted ways just before entering Capernaum, careful not to draw any undue attention. Shim'on entered the town's market area, which already overflowed with residents and travelers purchasing and selling a variety of goods. The air filled with the aroma of freshly-caught fish, sweet and sharp spices, and warm lehem. Though he was hungry, Shim'on was even more tired. His sore muscles ached, and he looked forward to lying down for a while before his night of fishing.

Despite his weariness, a group of three soldiers gathered around a young woman caught his attention. Curiosity redirected his steps to see what was developing more clearly. As he moved closer, his heartbeat quickened. The soldiers were gathered around Lydia.

Shim'on could see that a cluster of her friends stood nearby, clearly frightened but uncertain of what to do. People flowed around the scene, but apparently none were brave enough to confront the soldiers.

"What's going on here?" Shim'on asked, stepping close to the soldiers.

The men glanced toward him and Shim'on thought he saw a flicker of recognition cross their faces. Perhaps they too had heard rumors of the dangerous Zealot from Capernaum. One of the soldiers glared at him and scoffed, "Nothing having to do with you. Keep moving."

Shim'on looked at Lydia and saw the fear in her eyes. Her head covering was askew and dark tendrils of hair had come loose, framing her face. She was beautiful.

Shim'on leaned in and spoke in a low voice. "I'm sure Herod would be happy to hear that three of his soldiers were harassing a young woman rather than performing their duties."

The arrogance in the faces of the soldiers lessened and they looked at one another with uncertainty.

"Fine," the soldier who had told Shim'on to mind his own affairs looked at him darkly. "But don't think I will forget you." The three soldiers left the market, leaving a shaken Lydia.

"Are you all right?" Shim'on looked at her with concern.

Lydia nodded, "Yes, they frightened me. Thank you, Shim'on. I don't know what would have happened if you hadn't come when you did."

Lydia's dark eyes peered into his, making Shim'on uncomfortable. Could she guess his thoughts? Somehow Lydia bat Jude had yet to marry, which roused Shim'on's ire for the injustice. Most women her age were betrothed, and many were already married with children. He was still incredibly attracted to Lydia. Was she drawn to him?

Before he could respond, Lydia's immah approached them and flung her arms around her daughter.

"Lydia! I heard what happened! Are you all right?"

Lydia nodded and looked at Shim'on. "Yes, I'm all right, Immah. Shim'on bar Yitzchak protected me."

"Ah! Shim'on! Thank you so much for looking after my daughter!" Lydia's immah looked at him gratefully, then swept her daughter out of the market, but not before Lydia cast a look back over her shoulder.

Shim'on felt a rush of joy to see her blush when he caught her eye. But how could a young woman who believed in praying for one's enemies be in love with a violent Zealot?

XV

There were no planned attacks for the next several days.

Shim'on's time was devoted to either fishing or sleeping. But his mind was filled with questions. He was tempted to keep replaying the scene with Lydia in the market, but instead he tried to focus on other things. No matter how hard he tried, however, his thoughts kept returning to the rabbi. Where was the man? Could he really be the Mashiach? His conversation with Jesus on the hilltop had certainly been unusual. He remembered the peace he felt while in the man's presence, and how it departed when he left. He recalled the rabbi's words. He wished that he could see the man again and talk to him.

Hanoch noticed that Shim'on was distracted and asked him about it, but Shim'on wasn't willing to share his thoughts. He had developed a toughened facade over his months of involvement with the Zealots. But the problem with a facade was that one strong jab could punch a hole in it, and Shim'on wasn't about to let that happen by sharing his thoughts with Hanoch.

The day before Shabbat, Shim'on, Hanoch, and Demas drifted on the Sea of Galilee. The light from the rising sun began to tinge the sky with color. The boat sat just a stone's throw from shore where Hanoch thought he had seen a large group of musht resting in the shallow water, but the men couldn't see them anymore.

"Let's go to shore," Shim'on decided as Hanoch moved to unfurl the sail. He planned to take part in a Zealot attack that night and wanted to get some rest before the appointed meeting time. After completing their daily routine of unloading the day's catch to be taken to market, Shim'on, Hanoch, and one of the hired men carried their nets to the falls. Shim'on used his needle to mend nets, lost in his thoughts.

The air warmed. The heat released the spicy scents of sage and warm earth. After a while, he lifted his head to stretch, wiping sweat from his forehead. His mouth dropped open.

"Where are all these people going?" Streams of men, women, and children flowed past him, down the shoreline. He looked for Hanoch but didn't see him.

"What's going on?" He asked a fisherman sitting nearby.

"Where have you been?" The man looked at him incredulously. "Have you not been paying attention? Apparently, a rabbi is teaching down there." He nodded further down the shore. "Your brother left to go hear him nearly an hour ago."

Now that he mentioned it, Shim'on recalled Hanoch saying something to him about going to hear a man teach. He'd been too distracted to pay attention. Could it be...? Folding the net, he stood to his feet and joined the stream of people moving south along the coast. He had never seen so many people in Capernaum. There had to be thousands in the crowd. He came within a stone's throw of the boat and could go no farther. People surrounded him in a dense tapestry of humanity. Looking around him, Shim'on realized that men, women, and children from every walk of life had come to hear this rabbi. Rich and poor, Hebrew and Gentile, Galilean, and foreigner. Aside from visiting Jerusalem, which was a melting pot of mankind, he had never seen anything like it. He looked around for Hanoch but knew the futility of finding his brother in the sea of people. Shim'on pushed his way through the crowd, ignoring the protests of those around him until he finally saw the rabbi. The man wore a simple ivory-colored tunic, and suddenly he turned so that Shim'on could see the outline of his face. At once Shim'on was sure. He knew this rabbi. It was the man he had spoken with on the hilltop the morning of his first Zealot attack. Suddenly Shim'on heard shrieks.

"Unclean!"

"Leave here!"

"Get away, scum!"

Shim'on scanned the crowd, trying to see the subject of the disruption. The people parted ahead of him to reveal a man swathed head to toe in dirty white linens, approaching the rabbi. The only uncovered parts of his body were his fingertips and a gap in the head covering where his eyes peered out. Looking at his hands, Shim'on flinched. Instead of healthy pink skin, he saw white deformed stubs. The man had leprosy. Instinctively those surrounding the rabbi stepped back. Instead of moving away from the leper, however, Shim'on watched the rabbi walk toward him! What was the man doing? Leprosy was considered extremely contagious.

Lepers were not permitted in populated towns, but only in leper colonies outside the village. The disease attacked the nerve functioning of those it infected and caused sores to develop all over the body. If ever a leper were to come in proximity to a 'clean' person, one not tainted by the disease, he was required to shout "unclean!" to warn others of his condition. The life of a leper was lonely and filled with shame. This leper was taking a gamble, and Shim'on couldn't decide if he were completely crazy or extremely brave.

Jesus continued walking toward the man until he stood directly in front of him, only a foot or so away. The crowd, which had grown increasingly large, was quiet, holding its breath to see what the rabbi was going to do.

Suddenly, Jesus reached out his hand and set it on the man's shoulder. Shim'on could hear gasps and whispers across the crowd.

"Be healed," Jesus spoke quietly, looking into the man's eyes.

The man began to cry, tears wetting the dirty cloths wrapped around his face. He reached up a hand, and it was then that Shim'on saw that what had been decaying tissue was now healthy skin. The man continued staring at his fingers and then began unwrapping the cloth, revealing a hand, then an arm. The flesh was perfectly healthy; the leprosy was completely gone.

Murmurs spread across the crowd, growing in volume. Everyone was amazed.

"Who is this man?"

"He healed the leper with a word!"

Jesus spoke to the man quietly.

Tears poured down the man's face, and he knelt before Jesus. "Thank you, Rabbi!"

He stood in amazement, and Jesus clapped him on the shoulder, grinning. The man laughed and departed. Shim'on gaped in amazement. How could it be possible? The rabbi had healed the leper with two words! He turned to the man standing beside him.

"How can this be?"

The man beside him shook his head in equal shock. "I don't know. I've never seen such a miracle."

"Do you know the rabbi's name?" Shim'on asked.

"I believe he is called Jesus, from Nazareth." The man replied, his eyes still focused on the rabbi.

So, he had been right. It was the rabbi from the hilltop. Shim'on was surprised to hear that the man was from the town of Nazareth. Nazareth was a small, remote village in Galilee, populated by extremists who were passionately opposed to Roman rule and who deeply adhered to the Hebrew faith. This rabbi was different from most Nazarenes he knew.

Jesus began moving toward the shoreline and the people around him moved to follow. As Shim'on scanned the crowds, his eyes recognized a familiar face. It was Yeshua. His old friend did not see him, and Shim'on had no interest in trying to speak with him. The wounds of the past were still too fresh. But he knew Yeshua now lived in Jerusalem. *I wonder why he's here.*

After observing such a miracle, everyone wanted to get even closer to the rabbi. Shim'on quickly lost sight of Yeshua as the crowds pressed in around Jesus. The scents of sweat, expensive perfumes, and fresh fish commingled in the air in this odd group of humanity. It seemed this rabbi was enigmatic to all walks of

life. He watched as a group of four men, who apparently knew the rabbi, shielded him from the crush of people. To his surprise, four women also appeared to be following Jesus. The religious leaders and societal norms dictated that a woman's place was at home. Shim'on had never seen women follow a rabbi, yet here they were, clearly welcomed by the rabbi. Just then, one of the women turned, and Shim'on was shocked to see the face of Lydia.

The discovery that Jesus could perform miracles spread quickly, and desperate cries sprung up around Shim'on.

"Rabbi, heal my daughter, she is paralyzed!"

"My son is demon-possessed; please help him!"

"Help me!"

Shim'on was overwhelmed by the sheer number of pleas for healing. He couldn't imagine how Jesus felt. What kind of a man was this?

They were close to Shim'on and Hanoch's boat now. Shim'on could see the hired men had unloaded the night's catch. He watched as the rabbi gestured to one of his friends, a fisherman named Shim'on bar Jona that he knew from town. Jesus and his friends climbed into the boat and pushed away from shore. The boat moved a stone's throw from the packed coast and the rabbi's disciples dropped the anchor. The crowd dispersed themselves along the shoreline and Shim'on sat apart on a rocky outcropping that jutted into the water. His view of Lydia was blocked by one of the male disciples.

The rabbi stood at the prow of the boat and began speaking, but it was different from any teaching Shim'on had ever heard.

Unlike most rabbis, Jesus' words weren't lofty and confusing, full of burdensome law and condemnation. Instead, he spoke in terms of things they could understand and identify with, like fishing and farming, pottery, and milling. He talked repeatedly of the 'Kingdom of Heaven' and he often smiled as he taught, a sharp contrast to the often serious and harsh demeanor of the Pharisees and Sadducees.

"You have heard it said that you have the right to hurt those who hurt you. But I say, do not resist an evil person! If someone slaps you on the right cheek, offer the other cheek also. If someone sues you, go ahead and give them more than they are asking for! If a soldier demands that you carry his gear for a mile, carry it two miles. Give to those who ask."

"Rabbi," a man in the crowd nearby spoke, "what of the Zealots? Does this teaching condemn their actions?"

Shim'on listened closely for the rabbi's response.

Jesus said, "You are familiar with the law that says, 'Love your neighbor' and 'hate your enemy.' But I say, love your enemies! Pray for those who abuse you!"

Suddenly Lydia's words from years before flooded into his mind: "Adonai wants us to pray for our enemies." This rabbi was teaching the same thing! Before he could raise his customary wall of defense, Shim'on felt a prick of confusion. The words struck a chord of truth. All the violence and bloodshed that came with his involvement with the Zealots had done nothing to appease the anger and resentment he felt. If anything, his actions had made them worse.

The Zealots

The rabbi called his followers to an impossibly high standard—to love their enemies rather than hurt them. But how could doing that possibly free their people from Rome's rule? It seemed ridiculous. Even so, something about this rabbi intrigued Shim'on. The more he listened to the teacher, the more his inner conflict grew. Jesus told the people to serve one another, to forgive their enemies, to speak to Adonai as their abba. A piece of Shim'on wanted to stand up and shout his arguments with the rabbi while another part resonated with the man's words. What was happening to him?

 Shim'on rose in the early evening before Hanoch woke. Miriam was not home, a fact for which Shim'on was grateful. He ate a quick meal of lehem and dried sardines, then tucked his short sword into the belt around his waist and slung his bow and quiver of arrows over his shoulder. The attack tonight would take place south of Capernaum, on the Via Maris.

As Shim'on left town, he felt the eyes of the Roman soldiers on his back. He knew it was not uncommon for a man armed with a bow and quiver to be seen leaving the city. Most would assume he was going to hunt in the hills surrounding the city. But Shim'on knew the increased Zealot activity in the region had also put a target on the backs of Hebrew men living in Capernaum and the nearby towns.

It wasn't until he was out of sight of Capernaum that he finally breathed deeply.

The plan was to meet Efrayim and two more local Zealots three miles south of Capernaum. It was rumored that an unknown number of Roman soldiers would be passing through Capernaum on their way to cities located further along the Via Maris, and with Adonai's blessing, hopefully they would intercept them. As he walked, Shim'on thought about all that he had seen and heard earlier that day. The rabbi was an incredible teacher, unlike any he had heard before. In addition, he performed miracles. After the healing of the leper, Jesus had gone on to perform many other miracles, such as making the lame walk and giving sight to the blind. He wondered at the rabbi's unorthodox ways of teaching and interacting with the people. It had been more than surprising to see Lydia by the rabbi's side, as well. But then again, she had shown herself to be an independent young woman when he had crossed paths with her outside the city. He smiled, remembering. His thoughts returned to Jesus. A spark of anger rose within him. His people followed this rabbi, who taught peace and loving one's enemies, while he himself risked his own life to defend them. Confusion battled within him.

Soon Shim'on reached the meeting place and found Efrayim and their other two companions already there, hidden behind a grove of trees. The men were roasting a rabbit over a smoldering fire.

"Shim'on! Shalom!" Efrayim greeted him, rising to his feet. The man's dark hair and beard were peppered with gray, but despite the twenty-year difference between the men, Efrayim was remarkably fit. Shim'on knew he couldn't have had a better weaponry instructor. He tucked his thoughts of the rabbi into the back of his mind as the men shared the freshly roasted rabbit and discussed their attack plan.

The sky darkened into dusk and a pale moon climbed into the sky. The four men spread themselves on either side of the road and crouched behind trees, shrubs, and rocky outcroppings, their weapons out and ready. Shim'on was positioned closest to the section of road where the soldiers would first appear, so it was his responsibility to warn the others when they came into view. The fast-approaching darkness made it difficult for him to see clearly, and he squinted at the road when he finally heard the crunch of iron and gravel beneath uniformed feet.

Sure enough, the iron armor and red capes of five Roman soldiers were illuminated by flaming torches two of them held. Shim'on threw a pebble in the direction of the other Zealots behind him, then turned back toward their enemies.

The faces lit by the flickering torch flames appeared weary, and not much older than himself. Shim'on notched an arrow in his bow and held his breath as he took aim. He heard a dull thud as the arrow found its mark. The soldier fell instantly, the arrow embedded in his neck. The sounds of metal swords being drawn from their scabbards rang out in the night air. In the hazy light from the torches, Shim'on could see the soldiers looking around for their hidden assailants.

In the eerie quiet, Shim'on watched Efrayim leap from behind a tree across the road and run toward the soldier closest to him.

The other two Zealots jumped into motion, pulling short swords and daggers from beneath their tallits.

Shim'on prepared to draw his own sword when he heard a rustling to his right, away from the road. He looked toward the noise just in time to see light from a torch reflect off the glittering edge of an iron sword. A fiery pain, worse than any he'd ever felt before, erupted down his left arm. White spots danced in his vision and he gasped for breath.

The soldier had caught him completely by surprise. Shim'on staggered away from his attacker and tried to catch his breath. He glanced down at his arm and saw bone protruding, the appendage barely attached to his shoulder. He vomited and heard the Roman soldier laugh harshly.

"You Zealots," the man spoke. "You think yourselves so much better than us. You serve Adonai? Our god Jupiter has crushed your pitiful god. Why do you waste your energy when you have already lost?"

Shim'on gritted his teeth, anger, and pain coursing through his body.

"You know nothing of Adonai!" He hissed, lifting his sword, and staggering toward the soldier.

The man leapt forward and Shim'on felt an excruciating pain as Roman stabbed his sword into Shim'on's side and then jerked the weapon back out.

"I know He didn't protect you from me." The soldier hissed into his ear, then ran toward the road.

Shim'on gasped in pain and fell to his knees on the hard earth, clutching his side. His hand came away sticky with blood.

I must get back to the road, he thought. He realized that the sounds of hand-to-hand combat had faded.

Gritting his teeth, Shim'on staggered to his feet and stumbled clumsily to the Via Maris. Unlike the Roman soldiers, he had no torch and instead had to rely on the weak light from the moon to see. In the distance, Shim'on heard the faint sounds of footsteps. One of the Zealots lay on the ground a short distance from him, dead.

Efrayim and the other Zealot must have fled, Shim'on realized. Perhaps they assumed he had done the same. He vomited again and then everything went black.

Shim'on's eyes swept open. *Where am I?* Searing pain ripped through his upper body, and the memories from earlier that night came flooding back. He had collapsed on the Via Maris. He sat up and suppressed a cry at the pain. He had to get off the road before it became busy. He staggered to his feet and swayed for a moment, biting back a wave of nausea. Slowly, he began to walk.

Just one foot in front of the other, he told himself. Left foot, right foot, left, right.

The sky above him was still dark, but a faint blue tinge on the horizon signaled the arrival of dawn. Shim'on was so focused on staying upright that he failed to notice the figure that approached. And when he did, it was too late to hide.

"Shim'on?"

Shim'on's vision was hazy with pain, but he blinked it away to peer into the man's face. It was the rabbi, Jesus. Strangely, Shim'on felt guilt wash over him. Hadn't he listened to this man teach about loving his enemies only hours earlier? But he disagreed with the rabbi. Loving the Romans would not bring about the coming of the Mashiach or freedom from these oppressors.

So why did he feel guilty? He hardly knew this man, but something about him made Shim'on long to persuade Jesus of his righteousness. Yet, here he stood, bloodied, and guilty of the very violence the rabbi taught against.

"My friend, please, come sit." The rabbi helped Shim'on over to a nearby boulder and helped him to sit.

The guilt he felt made Shim'on defensive, and despite his pain he mumbled, "Aren't you too holy to be seen with the likes of a Zealot?" He hated himself as soon as the words tumbled from his lips.

"I came for the sick," The man smiled at him, and took a seat on a rock nearby. "Those who think they are well don't look for a healer."

Shim'on looked at him in confusion. Blood continued to flow from the wounds to his arm and side, and he had a difficult time focusing on the rabbi's face.

"I heard you speak today." Shim'on shook his head. "You said we ought to love our enemies and pray for them. I don't believe that. I'm a Zealot." He looked at the rabbi for a reaction, but Jesus sat quietly.

"You are a rabbi. You know the prophecies of the Mashaich and how he will free us from our enemies. We, too, fight for the freedom of our people. How can you say we should love these Gentiles who steal everything from us?"

Shim'on shook with the effort of his passionate words. He wiped blood from the corner of his mouth.

"Oh Shim'on," Jesus' face filled with a kindness and compassion that sliced through Shim'on's hardened defenses. "Have you found the freedom you seek?"

Shim'on looked away. Surely the man already knew the answer to his question. Despite all of the Zealot attacks in which he'd participated, and the Roman lives he'd taken, he was still a slave to guilt and anger.

"Are you the Mashiach?" Shim'on had been pondering the question ever since he heard the rabbi speak.

Jesus looked into Shim'on's eyes for several moments before speaking.

"I am."

The way in which the rabbi spoke the words made Shim'on bow his head.

"Do you believe that I am the promised Mashiach, Shim'on?"

Shim'on hesitated. "If you are the Mashiach, why do you not support our cause? Or join us yourself as our leader? The people love you! If you led the revolt, certainly we could overthrow Rome!"

Jesus smiled sadly. "The way of the Zealots is not the way of Adonai, my friend. There will always be corruption and imperfect governments."

"How can you say that Adonai would not support our cause?"

"Adonai wants His people to love their enemies."

Shim'on snorted.

Jesus' dark eyes investigated Shim'on's. "All men are enemies to Adonai. They sin against Him when they choose their own understanding and lay His commands aside. But Adonai patiently loves them."

A cool, early morning breeze sifted through the grass surrounding the road, ruffling Shim'on's damp hair and cooling his sweaty forehead. "If Adonai still loves you in your sin, how could you not love your enemies?"

"So, I'm supposed to love the men who killed my abba?" The words hissed angrily from his lips. He turned away from the rabbi. "If Adonai loves me so much, why did he allow him to die?"

Shim'on's words hung, suspended, in the air between the men.

"Adonai loves you, Shim'on. He loves your abba, too." Shim'on thought he heard pain in the rabbi's voice, but refused to face him, afraid he would see the tears in his eyes.

His wounds throbbed, and Shim'on closed his eyes against the pain. Suddenly, he felt a hand on his injured shoulder.

"Seek and find, Shim'on," he heard the rabbi say.

Immediately, a sensation like water flowed down his arm, and then his side. The coolness washed away the fiery pain of his injuries.

He blinked and gasped, standing quickly to his feet. He held out his left arm and examined the perfect flesh where moments before bloody skin and bone had protruded. He swung the arm back and forth and above his head-no pain. Then he lifted the blood-soaked tunic from his side. Dried blood stained his otherwise smooth skin. He gasped and looked up at the rabbi. But the man had disappeared.

XVI

"Yeshua!" Phinehas snapped his fingers, "Are you listening to me?"

Startled awake, Yeshua jerked his head up, "I'm sorry, Rabbi," he apologized, "I was up late studying last night." Though it was true, the real reason for Yeshua's distraction lay in the exciting message he had received from Capernaum that morning. His abba was coming to visit him.

Phinehas' demeanor softened, "It's all right, but I expect more from you, Son."

"Yes, Rabbi," Yeshua nodded.

"You are all here," Phinehas continued, gesturing to the young men surrounding him, "because you are Judea's next teachers. Your studies are almost complete, and you will soon travel around the cities of Judea and teach in their synagogues." Yeshua glanced around the courtyard. Already, many were entering the Beautiful Gate. He could hear coins being dropped into the collection boxes. Doves cooed in their cages, waiting to be sold as sacrifices.

"You all bear a heavy mantle of responsibility," he continued sternly, "But I know you are capable of it. Each of you keeps the law. You urge those around you to do the same. If you see any not walking in obedience to the law, you rebuke them and deal with them as the law commands. Now, is all of the law directly from the mouth of Adonai?"

"No, Rabbi, we also have the authority given to us by the Mishnah," a man named Reuben to Yeshua's left answered, referring to interpretations of the laws and Scripture that rabbis made.

"Then why should those laws be followed?"

Yeshua knew the rabbi was referring to laws such as what activities were permissible on Shabbat, or in which cases divorce was justified.

"Because the laws are for their good. They help the people to maintain righteousness."

Yeshua knew that in any particular question of the law, the Sanhedrin would gather, and the strictest view would be adopted by the whole. In this way, they could be sure that Adonai would be pleased by their actions. The system filled him with religious pride and self-righteousness. It was above reproach.

"Exactly," Phinehas confirmed, "And any who criticize such laws as these as apart from Adonai's will?"

Yeshua spoke up, "We rebuke them. If they still refuse to be obedient, they are thrown out of the synagogue."

Phinehas nodded. "We pray that those who rebel against the law will see their sin and return to obedience."

The old rabbi stood shakily, signaling the end of the day's teaching.

"Our time together will end in a month," Phinehas said with a smile. "I am proud of each of you, and I know that Adonai will use you among our people."

Thanking the rabbi, the young men departed and went their separate ways. Yeshua slung his sack of tools over one shoulder and walked toward the Roman quarters in Jerusalem.

"Yeshua, Shalom!" Stephanas greeted him with a smile when he arrived at the Roman barracks. He and a team of tektons were adding on to the dwellings. Unlike others, Stephanas didn't seem to be impressed by Yeshua's position as a rabbi. He simply treated him as a friend. Depending on the day, this both pleased and exasperated Yeshua. Stephanas' hands were white with dust from the limestone blocks he filed to stack one upon another.

"Shalom," Yeshua smiled back, placing his sack of tools beside Stephanas' and pulling out his file to smooth the rough sides of the stones.

"How's the morning been?"

"Aside from being surrounded by Roman soldiers at all times, it's gone well," Stephanas said quietly with a grin.

"What, that bothers you?" Yeshua teased. He knew each of them fiercely preferred working for anyone but the Romans, but work was necessary to provide for their needs, regardless of the source.

"I'm going to be sorry to lose you one day." Stephanas laughed.

"Actually," Yeshua said, "This morning Rabbi Phinehas told us our study will be complete in a month."

"That soon?" Stephanas said. Yeshua was touched by the sincere disappointment in his voice.

The men's relationship had changed for the better since their trip to Capernaum. Although they held different views of the rabbi's teaching, Yeshua tried to be respectful of Stephanas' opinion, and Stephanas did the same for Yeshua.

While hearing the rabbi's words solidified Yeshua's belief that the man was a heretic, Stephanas believed the man to be the Mashiach. Saying such a thing publicly was dangerous, however. Despite the risk, Stephanas spoke to everyone he could about the

'Kingdom of Heaven' the rabbi proclaimed, and of how anyone could be saved if he repented of his sins and believed. Yeshua had never seen a man so transformed by the words of a rabbi. He was fond of his friend and urged Stephanas not to be so bold in his conversations.

"What if the Romans heard you speaking of this 'Kingdom of Heaven'?" he pleaded with Stephanas, "They would think you a rebel, and you could be arrested or even killed! And if the Romans don't get you," he continued, "think of the Pharisees and Sadducees! This rabbi is considered a heretic, and Caiaphas himself holds clout with Pilate, you've said it yourself! They would not hesitate to have you arrested! Please, Stephanas, think of Timnah and your family." But Stephanas always responded the same way. "My friend, you are kind, and I appreciate your concern for me," he would say, "But Jesus has changed my life! Don't you see? The Kingdom of God is eternal! This life is not all there is, Yeshua! If you repent of your sins and believe He will forgive you, you will live with Adonai in eternity! This is a message that everyone must hear!"

Although Yeshua loved his friend, Stephanas' words struck a sour note with him. Could Stephanas not see that Yeshua was already righteous? Yes, perhaps he was not perfect, but Yeshua followed the law to his best ability. Surely Adonai was pleased with him. He felt slightly uneasy when Stephanas reminded him that Jesus said all must repent to receive eternal life, but quickly shrugged the feelings aside. The rabbi was a heretic with no authority to forgive sins.

Timnah and the rest of Stephanas' family also came to believe Jesus to be the Mashiach after Stephanas had shared his experience in Capernaum and the rabbi's words. Although Yeshua continued to criticize the family from time to time when they broke the law, they simply apologized or responded to his judgment with humble smiles. Yeshua could not deny that this change in response seemed due to their newfound faith. Jesus placed emphasis on the condition of a person's heart rather than his or her deeds. He encouraged the people to confess their sins to Adonai for forgiveness first, rather than relying on the sacrifices and insincere obedience to the law. As a rabbi whose primary focus was obtaining righteousness through good works, Yeshua was deeply offended by Jesus' teachings.

"So," Yeshua said, "I received a message from my abba this morning."

"Oh?" Stephanas used his awl to chisel the rough side of a block of limestone. "What did he say?"

Yeshua nodded, "He is coming to Jerusalem."

"That is wonderful news!" Stephanas smiled, "It will be good to see him!"

He nodded at a chunk of limestone, "Can you help me lift this one?" Yeshua took the opposite end of the stone block. Together, the two men lifted the heavy limestone and set it atop the blocks that would become the building's wall. Although Yeshua already had tekton skills when he arrived in Jerusalem, working alongside Stephanas had been invaluable. The man performed excellent work, and Yeshua learned much from him daily. He would miss his friend and mentor.

The following morning, Yeshua left for the temple with eager anticipation. Sparrows flitted from rooftop to rooftop, chirping happily to one another. The sky was a brilliant blue and not even the cadre of Roman soldiers who passed, pushing him roughly to the edge of the road, could dampen his spirits.

The Zealots

Bin-yamin would arrive in Jerusalem soon, and in just a couple of weeks, Yeshua would begin his work as a rabbi.

He looked forward to traveling throughout the nearby regions, teaching in the synagogues, and working as a tekton to meet his needs. He couldn't believe that it was so soon.

Shim'on's face unexpectedly floated into his mind, and he was surprised. His life in Jerusalem was so busy that any thoughts of his old friend were few and far between. He missed the Shim'on he had known as a child. He prayed he had found healing from the loss of his abba and the hatred that blossomed in his heart following his abba's death. He made a mental note to ask his abba about Shim'on when he saw him.

Up ahead, the pedestrian traffic thickened, and Yeshua guessed that it was for another crucifixion procession. He was now used to seeing the horrifying spectacle. This morning was no different.

The swell of murmuring voices from the crowd grew louder as he neared them.

Six bloody men staggered by with cross beams on their backs, as a Roman centurion on horseback yelled out over the crowds, "See what happens to those who rebel against the Emperor! Hail Caesar!" So, it was Zealots again, Yeshua thought. He had to hand it to them, they were a dedicated lot. For every Zealot who was caught, it seemed two more sprouted in his place.

He thought again of Shim'on. Had he become a Zealot like his abba? He hoped not. The procession eventually passed, and Yeshua continued toward the synagogue, thoughts of his old friend departing with the soldiers' footsteps.

XVII

The following days after Jesus healed Shim'on's wounds felt surreal. Multiple times a day, Shim'on looked at his arm and side, still awed that the skin was healthy and smooth.

Only Efrayim and the other surviving Zealot knew he was involved in the attack. And neither of them had seen his wounds prior to the miraculous healing.

He considered telling Efrayim or Hanoch what had happened, but like his conversation with the rabbi years ago, this experience also felt deeply personal. The one person he longed to share it with was Lydia. But they had barely spoken since Shim'on had defended her in the market. Truth be told, Shim'on knew he wasn't a good enough man for Lydia. She deserved a righteous man. Not an angry Zealot. Still, the rabbi's words from that day on the shore, and his conversation with him on the Via Maris, refused to leave his thoughts. Especially his statement concerning loving their enemies.

Seek and find.

In his heart, Shim'on knew that he was an enemy of Adonai Himself because Adonai had commanded His chosen people not to murder, and Shim'on had done that countless times. *The way of the Zealots is not the way of Adonai, my friend.* One thing was certain. None of Shim'on's efforts had brought him the freedom he craved. So, what could?

 The night before Shabbat, Shim'on was supposed to join Efrayim and an entourage of Zealots for an attack. For the first time in years, he felt a deep unsettledness. The words of Jesus echoed profoundly in his mind until he gave up trying to silence them. Shim'on realized he could not take another life. Not tonight. Perhaps not ever. But he couldn't abandon Efrayim without an explanation.

While Hanoch slept and Miriam washed clothing with the other women, Shim'on slipped from the home and into the Galilean hills. The dusky sky draped around him like a cloak, seeping into his thoughts. What was he doing? How could he give up his loyalty to the Zealots? He'd been passionate about killing their enemies for so long. What would his life look like apart from the movement?

Once again, he thought of his conversation with the rabbi. The man had simply touched his shoulder and he was healed. One moment he had been on the verge of death. The next, his body was healthier than it had ever been. If only the rabbi could heal him from the guilt and anger that plagued him as well.

Shim'on shook his head, trying to free his mind of restless thoughts. One thing he knew, he simply couldn't kill another man. That much was clear. He hoped Efrayim would understand.

Shim'on continued his way through the sage and wild grass until he neared a small grove of olive trees nestled against the hillside. His steps slowed.

From experience, he knew to approach a Zealot meeting place with caution lest he was being watched by an enemy. Quietly he crouched, so that most of his body was hidden by the surrounding brush and made his way forward. The loud chirping of crickets surrounded him. Soon he saw the embers of a fire and smelled pungent smoke. A man's figure was outlined by the dying flames. Efrayim. His friend must have seen him too, because he stepped into a small clearing and began to raise his arm in greeting.

Psssssssst. Shim'on heard the arrow before he saw it embed itsclf in Efrayim's chest.

The crickets silenced collectively.

Shim'on dropped to his knees and clapped a hand over his mouth to stifle the cry that sprang from his throat. Efrayim fingered the arrow protruding from his chest in surprise, then fell to the ground. Moments passed and the crickets resumed their singing.

Shim'on remained crouched on the ground, uncertain of how many Roman soldiers were watching. He hoped the other Zealots had either fled or remained hidden. His heart pounded in his ears and he tried to quiet his ragged breaths.

Efrayim remained still and Shim'on knew his friend was dead. Tears filled his eyes and trickled down his face. The man was the reason Shim'on knew how to fight. He had patiently and kindly trained him. He had been a good friend to his abba as well. And now he was gone.

Shim'on dropped his head. Memories of his abba's death washed over him like ocean waves, joining with the fresh grief of Efrayim's loss. Would these Romans take everyone he loved? For the next several hours Shim'on remained rooted to the ground, afraid to move. The smell of the fire dwindled until Shim'on knew it had gone cold.

Finally, in the early morning hours, he decided to take a risk. Slowly, he rose to a squat and surveyed his surroundings. The moon cast enough light to see a short distance, and Shim'on saw no signs of movement. He rose to his full height and began to move slowly through the grass toward Efrayim. He would not leave his friend's body exposed to the animals.

He gathered stones from the hillside and stacked them around Efrayim's still body, then turned and walked heavily toward Capernaum.

 Instead of going home, Shim'on made his way to the sea. When he reached the shoreline, he stood and drew a deep breath. The familiar scents of fish and damp earth filled his nostrils.

"Shalom, Shim'on." The familiar voice came from beneath the olive trees to his right, startling him.

"Rabbi?" He walked toward the voice. The dim light cast by the moon revealed the man sitting on the hillside.

"Would you like to sit?" Jesus gestured to the ground beside him. He brushed his white and blue tallit back from his head so that it rested on his shoulders. Shim'on guessed that he had interrupted the rabbi's prayers.

Shim'on sat. The weight on his chest felt heavier than ever, and anger and grief pressed on his shoulders.

"Would you like to talk about it?" Shim'on turned to see pain in the rabbi's eyes.

"Rabbi"—he paused, trying to decide where to start. "You probably don't remember this, but you spoke with me on the hill outside the city years ago."

"Of course, I remember," Jesus nodded.

"You told me to be careful, and that he who lives by the sword, dies by the sword. Did you know what I was doing there?"

"What did you do, Shim'on?" Jesus asked softly without answering his question.

Here it was, Shim'on thought. His opportunity to tell the rabbi of his deeds. After Yitzchak died, Shim'on refused to talk of him or of his actions as a Zealot to anyone. Now Efrayim too was gone. Something about the rabbi tore down all his walls. Shim'on told Jesus everything: about Yitzchak's involvement with the Zealots and his death, about his own involvement with the Zealots, the men he had killed, and the anger that constantly burned within him. As he spoke, blocks of guilt and regret stacked one atop another. He'd made killing his business. And for what? He still wasn't free of the demons that tormented him. What kind of a life was this? He refused to look at the rabbi as he spoke, sure the loathing he felt for himself was echoed in Jesus' eyes. When he finished, Shim'on was drained. He waited for Jesus to speak. He expected a rebuke. Especially now that the rabbi had heard all the grimy details of his life. Surely, he would hold him in contempt. The night was quiet, and finally Shim'on could bear the silence no longer.

He turned and looked at the rabbi, "You asked me once if my passion was enough. I thought it would be, but no matter how many lives I took, I still felt hate. I want to be free. I want the abundant life that you spoke about." Desperation filled his voice, "Could that ever be possible for me?"

Rather than condemnation and judgment, Shim'on was shocked to see warmth in the man's eyes.

"Shim'on, I already knew all these things. I knew what happened to Yitzchak and what you were going to do that morning when we spoke. I knew of the anger and hate living in your heart. I know that you lost a friend tonight." A look of compassion filled the rabbi's eyes. "I knew everything before I called you to follow me. You are forgiven," He said simply, "Sin no more." He smiled, the weathered skin around his eyes crinkling.

"How can this be true?" Shim'on asked, stunned by the man's response.

"What do you mean?"

"I mean, surely it can't be that simple."

Jesus looked out on the Sea of Galilee. "You expect me to tell you what you must do to be forgiven."

"Isn't that what is necessary?"

Jesus turned back to face him, and Shim'on was surprised to see anger reflected in his eyes. "I do not delight in sacrifice, Shim'on. What I seek is a broken and contrite heart. If my people would give up their stubborn self-reliance, they would be forgiven by simply confessing their sin."

His face softened, "It's truly that simple, Shim'on. You are forgiven." His eyes looked into Shim'on's. "Follow me, Shim'on."

Shim'on felt a flood of relief as he realized that the bricks that had rested on his shoulders and chest were gone. Certainly, this man must be the long-awaited Mashiach. A quiet peace surrounded him, yet he was shocked by the rabbi's invitation. He, a Zealot, was being called by a rabbi? Such an invitation was a high honor, and one given to very few men. It was reserved for those who were exceptionally gifted in the Torah, Mishnah, Nevi'im, and Ketuvim. Shim'on knew he did not deserve the calling. Not only did he lack when it came to his knowledge of the scriptures, but until moments ago, he had been a Zealot, steeped in violence. Why did the rabbi want him as a follower?

"Me, Rabbi?" He asked, incredulous.

"Yes, you, Shim'on." Jesus laughed. "Follow me and I will show you abundant life." Abundant life. The rabbi had spoken of it on the hilltop years ago. Shim'on still couldn't understand why the rabbi would find him worthy to be one of his disciples, but the invitation to follow him was irresistible.

"I will follow you, Rabbi." He agreed. Sorrow and excitement mixed within him. He grieved the loss of Efrayim. But the grace and mercy of Jesus flooded over him, somehow softening the sting of death.

"Thank you, Rabbi!" He dropped his head and cried without shame.

 The sun was on the verge of rising when Shim'on arrived home. Hanoch was on the boat and Miriam was asleep as he quietly made his way to his mat. Sleep proved to be elusive, however. A flood of emotions ebbed and flowed over him. He grieved the loss of Efrayim. The man had been more than a friend. He had been his abba's best friend, and a sort of abba to Shim'on as well. He dreaded having to tell Efrayim's wife of his death the following day. Despite his grief, however, Shim'on felt overwhelming freedom and joy since his conversation with the rabbi.

His first thought after receiving Jesus' forgiveness was of Lydia. He had to speak to her. For the first time since his abba's death, Shim'on wondered if he might have a future with Lydia bat Jude. The rabbi had freed him of his past. Could Lydia do the same?

He tried to rehearse what he would say to her. As he lay on his mat in the early morning darkness, Shim'on recalled his conversation with Lydia outside Capernaum's walls two years before. Now she followed the rabbi. Did she still wake up early to speak with Adonai? He didn't know, but he was willing to find out. Quietly, he pulled on his sandals. Outside, the predawn air was cool, and the sky was tinged pink and purple with the arrival of morning. Shim'on made his way through the quiet streets and out of Capernaum.

He stopped in the place where he had camped prior to the Zealot attack years ago, feeling unsure. This was his plan? To wait outside the city in hopes of seeing Lydia? He glanced around. His mouth was dry, and he felt slightly shaky at the thought of speaking to the woman he had loved from afar for years. Would she laugh at him? Tell him he was too late? Would she hold his involvement with the Zealots against him? She would be entirely justified in doing so, Shim'on knew. But he also knew he had to try.

From over a nearby hill, Shim'on saw a figure approach. Her head was uncovered, and her dark curls spilled over her shoulders and hung to her waist. Shim'on saw Lydia's lips moving, though no one was with her and knew she must be praying. His heartbeat increased, hammering inside his chest. When she saw Shim'on, he saw her hurriedly wrap her hair in the headcovering. It was considered inappropriate for a woman to have her head uncovered in the presence of any man aside from her husband.

"Shim'on?" He was secretly pleased to see Lydia blush when she reached him. "What are you doing out here? Another Zealot attack?"

Shim'on shook his head, trying to steady himself before speaking.

"No, no Zealot attack. I came looking for you."

Lydia stood uncertainly. "Looking for me?"

Shim'on nodded, then plunged ahead. "I saw you yesterday. With the rabbi from Nazareth."

"Oh, yes." Lydia looked confused.

"Well, he spoke to me. Not yesterday. Well, he spoke to me yesterday too, but that's not what I'm talking about."

Lydia smiled at Shim'on's flustered words. He tried again to steady himself.

"That morning we talked years ago; do you remember?"

Lydia nodded, "Of course, I remember."

"Well, after that I met the rabbi. Here in the hills," he gestured. "He knew who I was, though I had never met him before. I didn't know it then, but he knew everything about me. Including that I was a Zealot."

"Was?" Lydia looked at him questioningly.

"Yes." Shim'on looked into Lydia's eyes. "I've decided not to fight with the Zealots anymore. The rabbi has called me to follow him." Shim'on saw joy fill Lydia's face.

"Yesterday when he taught, he talked about loving one's enemies. It made me think of what you said about praying for the Romans."

Lydia listened in silence.

"You were right." Shim'on said quietly, taking a step closer to Lydia. "When I heard Jesus teach yesterday, it was like Adonai told me that His way is not that of the Zealots." He dropped his gaze from Lydia's. "I am not proud of the lives I have taken, and I still feel much anger toward the Romans. But I confessed all of it to the rabbi, and he has forgiven me." Saying the words aloud flooded Shim'on once again with peace. He took another step closer to Lydia and took her hand, lifting his eyes to hers. "I believe the rabbi is the Mashiach. He's different than any man I've ever known." He was surprised to see tears spill from her eyes.

"Did I say something wrong?" He asked, confused.

"No," Lydia shook her head and smiled, wiping the tears away with her other hand. "I've just been praying for you, for this, for so long."

"You have?" Shim'on felt humbled.

Lydia nodded, "When I first heard Jesus speak, I knew he had to be the prophesied Mashiach."

Shim'on felt his heart begin to beat faster, but he plunged forward. Taking Lydia's other hand in his, he looked deeply into her green eyes.

"Lydia bat Jude, I have loved you nearly my whole life. Until yesterday I thought I could never be worthy enough for you. I still don't. But now I believe in mercy. And forgiveness. Lydia, could you forgive me? Do you think you could love me?" The words rushed out and everything in him feared her response.

Lydia laughed and fresh tears sprang from her eyes. "Finally, Shim'on bar Yitzchak!"

"What do you mean?" Shim'on was surprised.

"Why do you think I'm still not married? I've been waiting for you, you fool! I've loved you since I was a girl!"

Shim'on laughed, his heart filled with joy. Though it was customary for a young man to ask his abba to arrange a marriage with Lydia's abba, Yitzchak was gone. Shim'on's conversation with Lydia was certainly unorthodox, but he knew their time together this morning would be a secret shared only between them. He would ask another male family member to make the arrangements. Lydia bat Jude was to be his wife!

Yeshua

XVIII

Yeshua awoke and blinked his eyes in the early morning darkness. Something was different about today, but it took him a moment to remember what it was. Ah, yes! His abba had arrived from Capernaum the day before.

Since he would only be in Jerusalem for a short time, Yeshua and Stephanas had decided not to work today. Yeshua still had his studies with Phinehas this morning, and Stephanas and Bin-yamin planned to meet him on the Temple Mount afterward. Yeshua looked forward to spending the day with the two most influential men in his life.

The three men were up late the previous night, enjoying another feast provided by Timnah. As they ate, Bin-yamin and Stephanas talked excitedly about the rabbi, Jesus. Oil lamps lit the dim room and flickered on the faces of the men.

"He has healed the lame, given sight to the blind and even brought the dead to life, Stephanas!" Bin-yamin told him excitedly.

"But Abba," Yeshua said wearily, "Wasn't it you who first said that a man does not have the authority to forgive sins?"

"I did say that," Bin-yamin agreed, nodding his head, "But Yeshua, I know now, he is not just a man. He is the Son of Adonai!"

"Abba!" Yeshua gestured to him to quiet his voice, "How can you say such a thing! Don't you know it's heresy?"

"It's only heresy if it's not true, Yeshua," Bin-yamin looked at his son solemnly. "Who else but the Son of Adonai has the power to forgive sins and to heal? I know, he cleansed me of my sin."

Yeshua couldn't believe his ears, "What sin, Abba? You are a rabbi; you follow the law better than I do. What could you possibly have done to be forgiven of? And as far as the miracles"– He trailed off, throwing his hands in the air, "He could be demon possessed!"

"Oh Yeshua," his abba studied him. "Do you believe that I am perfect? I too am a sinner in need of Adonai's forgiveness. As are you. Only Adonai can cleanse us from our sin and only the Mashiach was prophesied to be blameless. And Jesus is He." He looked at Yeshua sternly, "Can you truly believe that he is demon possessed when you listen to his teaching or see the kindness with which he speaks?"

Yeshua wanted to cover his ears and run from the house. But love and respect for his abba and Stephanas forced his mouth shut. He listened quietly, still refusing to believe this rabbi was the Mashiach, the long-prophesied one.

He thought back to the first day he arrived in Jerusalem. The things that had overwhelmed him then, now seemed commonplace. He was forever changed after spending the past years in Jerusalem. He was excited to experience this next season of life as a rabbi. He shook off the memories of the conversation the night before and focused on the present. After he completed his morning rituals, Bin-yamin walked outside with him as he prepared to leave for the temple.

"I am so proud of you, Son," Bin-yamin's eyes shone. "I can't believe your studies are almost over and you will be a rabbi!" he hugged Yeshua. "I love you."

Embarrassed by his abba's display of emotion, Yeshua stepped out of the hug quickly. But Bin-yamin's words meant more to him than he knew.

"I'll see you soon!" He bade farewell to Bin-yamin and made his way to the temple. Once he arrived, he was surprised to see a large number of Roman soldiers walking around the mount. Rumors drifted that the Romans suspected Zealot activity and were on the lookout. Yeshua wondered how they would be able to ferret out the insurrectionists from the crowds, but he dismissed the thought. It had nothing to do with him.

Morning studies with Phinehas and the other students went by quickly. Phinehas had just dismissed them when Yeshua caught sight of his abba and Stephanas. The men saw him and walked quickly across the limestone pavers in his direction.

Suddenly, screaming echoed in the temple courtyard. Yeshua looked toward the noise and was shocked to see a Roman soldier who had been standing a stone's throw away slump to the ground, blood streaming from his side. The courtyard erupted in chaos, and people fled in all directions.

Fearing he would be trampled, Yeshua and another student took hold of Phinehas' arms and tried to move him to the shelter of a nearby building. But the slew of people around them wrenched Yeshua's grip loose, and he fell to the ground. A small break in the crowd allowed Yeshua to see across the courtyard. He watched in shock as a man dressed in ordinary garb plunged a knife into the neck of a Roman soldier.

Yeshua scrambled to his feet and tried to see his abba, Stephanas, or Phinehas caught in the surging crowd. Unable to locate them, he struggled against the desperate flow of people. Soldiers on horseback urged their mounts through the crowd, and the people fell back, afraid of being trampled. A woman, her tunic torn and dirtied, limped past him, a bloody gash across her thigh. Yeshua couldn't understand who these attackers were targeting.

As he struggled across the courtyard, he tripped over the stabbed or trampled bodies of both soldiers and civilians. Yeshua tried to avoid looking at their faces. Finally, he reached the area where he last saw Bin-yamin and Stephanas. Desperately, he looked around and yelled out.

"Abba!"

"Yeshua!" Yeshua turned to see Bin-yamin standing ten yards away. Behind him was a burly man Yeshua could only assume was a Zealot, based on the dagger gripped in his fist.

Before Yeshua could signal to his abba, a centurion darted from the crowd to Yeshua's right, his sword drawn and ready. His focus settled on the Zealot behind Bin-yamin.

"Abba, no!" Yeshua tried to warn Bin-yamin, but his abba was already moving toward him.

Yeshua saw the soldier crouch where he stood, on the alert.

"Stop Abba!" Yeshua gestured to Bin-yamin to stop but it was too late. Assuming that Bin-yamin was running to attack him, the soldier slashed his sword across Bin-yamin's chest and then raced toward the Zealot. He removed the man's head from his shoulders in one swift movement.

Bin-yamin fell onto his back on the hot dusty ground. Yeshua rushed to his side and dropped to his knees.

"Abba!" He cried in shock.

Blood poured from his abba's chest and puddled on the ground.

"Yeshua," Bin-yamin panted, lifting his hand. Yeshua grasped it.

"I'm so sorry Abba," he cried tasting the acrid scent of blood rising to his nostrils.

"Yeshua," Bin-yamin groaned and murmured, "You– you must–believe in Jesus. Repent–of your sins. Then we will–see each other–again."

"Abba, no!" Salty tears dripped from Yeshua's chin onto Bin-yamin's chest.

"I love you—Yeshua."

Bin-yamin's hand suddenly went slack and his head fell to the side.

"Yeshua!" Stephanas rushed to the scene, then fell silent, taking in Bin-yamin's lifeless form.

"No!" Yeshua pounded the dirt with his fists, "He wasn't even carrying a weapon, you scum!" he screamed toward the Roman centurion.

"Yeshua, quiet." Stephanas wrenched Yeshua's shoulder so hard that he grunted in pain. "Don't be a fool. Don't give them a reason to kill you too."

Yeshua fell back to his knees beside Bin-yamin.

Stephanas joined him on the ground, "I'm so sorry, Yeshua. We got separated. I couldn't reach you in time."

Yeshua lifted his abba's torso in his arms. How could such a peace-loving man die by such violent means? How could he be gone? Yeshua lifted his head and took in the chaos around him.

More Roman soldiers had joined those on the mount, and they shoved and whipped anyone in their way, asserting their dominance. As he held his abba's lifeless body in his arms,

Yeshua felt anger surge through him. If this was what the path of peace led to, he wanted no part of it.

Shim'on

XIX

Shim'on couldn't remember being happier, or more filled with peace. Jesus, the Mashiach, had forgiven him, giving him a new life. As if that weren't enough, he was to spend his life with Lydia. Shim'on felt more joy than he had ever dreamed possible.

"Shim'on, you are changed." Lydia told him, with love in her eyes.

"I feel different," Shim'on agreed, "I think He's changing me." He realized the anger that burned in his heart toward Adonai was gone. Adonai did not kill his abba. The Romans did. Anger toward Rome still simmered in his heart, but he believed what the rabbi said about violence not being the way to peace or true freedom. But loving the Romans as the rabbi taught still seemed impossible. Shim'on prayed Adonai would change his heart in this regard because he couldn't.

Soon after calling his first four disciples, Jesus called eight other men throughout the regions of Galilee and Judea, from a variety of backgrounds, to follow him.

The past four months had been nothing short of life-changing for Shim'on and the eleven other disciples. A new zeal was awakened in Shim'on's being, for Jesus and the freedom he offered

On a beautiful blue-sky day, Shim'on married the woman he had loved since he was a boy.

Nearly the entire village was invited to the seven-day marriage feast that followed, including Jesus and the disciples. As the tallit was draped over Shim'on and Lydia's heads to symbolize their union in Adonai's sight, Shim'on knew it was a day he would remember forever.

The following days and nights were filled with joy, conversation, and laughter as Shim'on, his bride, and their friends and family reclined around tables heavily laden with wine and delicious food.

Musicians entertained the crowd with harps and singing. By the end of the week-long celebration, Shim'on and Lydia had received gifts enough to provide for their household needs and begin their lives together.

On the final celebratory night, Shim'on gazed at the wife Adonai had brought him. His heart overflowed with love for her. The air was filled with the heady scents of rich oils and delicious foods. Shim'on hoped he would remember everything about this wonderful week for the rest of his life. He looked across the table at the rabbi, who was deep in conversation with Hanoch. Silently, he again thanked the man who had freed him of the guilt and hate he had carried for many years.

Lydia brought balance and calm to Shim'on's characteristic passion. Her sweet spirit was a balm to places in his heart that still ached from the loss of his abba, and now Efrayim. She was good for him.

As was customary, Lydia moved into Shim'on's family home after their marriage. While she still joined Shim'on at the rabbi's side when he was in Capernaum, Lydia had decided to remain home with Sarai after their marriage.

Because her own abba was a fisherman, she was familiar with the responsibilities of the trade.

"Adonai told me to stay here for now," she told Shim'on with a peaceful smile. "I think your immah needs me." Sarai was delighted to have a daughter, and Lydia helped ease Sarai's duties of preparing and selling the fish at market.

Though Shim'on missed her, Lydia's love for his immah endeared her even more to him. His wife enthusiastically encouraged her husband to follow Jesus. Shim'on liked to tease that she already wanted to get rid of him, but he treasured her support.

 The forgiveness he had received from the rabbi had changed Shim'on's life. Now he was one of a disparate group of unlikely followers called by Jesus.

Shim'on smiled as he remembered the day Jesus invited Matthias to follow him. Everyone in Capernaum knew Matthias. Once a corrupt man who collected taxes on behalf of the Romans, he confessed his sin to the rabbi and was forgiven. Hanoch looked at Shim'on with concern that day, wondering if his brother was going to attack a man so clearly aligned with their enemies, but Shim'on was surprised to realize he had no desire to do ill to Matthias. At one time, Shim'on had poured all his energy into hatred and violence against their enemies. Now he served the rabbi, Adonai's Mashiach, with all his being.

Like all the disciples, Matthias' life radically changed the day he confessed his sins to Jesus and was forgiven. Each disciple was an unlikely recruit, yet Jesus called him, nonetheless.

Together, they followed Jesus through Galilee as he taught and performed miracles.

Shim'on had come to know and respect each of the other eleven disciples whom Jesus called to follow him. One disciple in particular shared Shim'on's passionate spirit, trade, and name-Shim'on bar Jona. Though he had not been a Zealot, the other disciple told Shim'on that he had considered it. They were both fishermen, but Shim'on had only been an acquaintance of Shim'on bar Jona prior to the rabbi's invitation.

Though he liked Shim'on bar Jona, Shim'on sometimes envied the disciple's unique relationship with the rabbi. Jesus treated Shim'on bar Jona differently than the other disciples—as if he were preparing him for something.

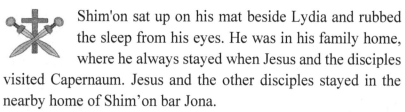 Shim'on sat up on his mat beside Lydia and rubbed the sleep from his eyes. He was in his family home, where he always stayed when Jesus and the disciples visited Capernaum. Jesus and the other disciples stayed in the nearby home of Shim'on bar Jona.

Shim'on knew Jesus rose in the early morning darkness and went to the surrounding hills to pray to Adonai, whom he called his Abba. At first, the men were startled to hear Jesus refer to Adonai so intimately. But as time went on, Shim'on found it more and more easy to believe the man truly could be Adonai's Son made flesh, walking amongst them.

Quietly, Shim'on rose and moved toward the door. He was tired. The crowds that followed the rabbi grew by the day, and Jesus continued to heal the sick, restore sight to the blind, and give movement to the lame. It was incredible to watch, but Shim'on feared for the rabbi. He knew that Jesus must be exhausted. Just days before, he discouraged the rabbi from welcoming a group of children, but Jesus sternly reprimanded him.

"Don't stop the children from coming to me! For the Kingdom of Heaven belongs to those who are like these children." He placed his hands on their heads and blessed them.

Shim'on couldn't understand it. Jesus seemed to be draining himself for the people, and often Shim'on sensed an urgency to his words. But the rabbi was only 32 years old; he had decades of life and ministry ahead of him.

Shim'on slipped out of the home, pulling the door closed behind him. The morning light lit the black basalt dwellings of Capernaum in a coral hue.

When Shim'on began following Jesus, Hanoch became the man of the house, providing for Miriam and Lydia's needs. Thankfully, Hanoch was not bitter. His life, too, had been changed the day he listened to Jesus teach on the seashore. Though Shim'on still harbored some uncertainties, Hanoch had no difficulty believing Jesus was the Son of Adonai. He proudly told friends and family that his brother had been called to follow the rabbi.

Hanoch had insisted that Shim'on rest rather than joining him on the boat the previous night. Shim'on was grateful. He felt more rested than he had in weeks. He meandered through the streets of his hometown, allowing himself to contemplate how different his life was now.

It was strange how quickly and easily the disciples became a sort of family, a brotherhood. Shim'on pondered how twelve men from such diverse backgrounds could get along so well. He concluded, once again, that it was all because of the rabbi. Though they bickered at times about the meaning of the rabbi's teachings and how to apply them, and though they occasionally competed for Jesus' favor, their personal gratefulness and love for Jesus was paramount to anything and everything else. Somehow, he had changed them all for the better as they listened to his words and sought to obey them.

Though it was early, scents of fish, freshly baked lehem, and exotic spices wafted from the marketplace as the merchants set up their wares. He was tempted to walk in the direction of the wonderful smells, but instead Shim'on made his way to Shim'on bar Jona's home.

Shim'on bar Jona stood outside the open door, a look of concern on his face.

"What is it?" Shim'on asked.

"We are leaving." Shim'on bar Jona replied in a low voice. "Yohanan the Baptist's disciples just left. Yohanan is dead."

Shim'on recalled his conversation with Efrayim and remembered the navi was Jesus' cousin.

"Oh no," he murmured. "I will go and tell Lydia. I'll be back."

When he rejoined the disciples, the men made their way to the Sea of Galilee. Already, the crowds had seen Jesus departing the city and they, too, followed the rabbi and his disciples.

"Shim'on bar Jona," Jesus said heavily, as they neared the water, "Let's go to a remote place."

"Of course, Rabbi," Shim'on bar Jona replied.

Shim'on raised a hand in farewell to Hanoch, who was unloading the night's catch several yards down the beach. Small whitecaps peaked on the sea and the water lapped against the shoreline. A seagull whirled and dipped over the water, then snatched an unfortunate fish from beneath the surface. Hanoch grinned and dropped his nets, jogging down the shoreline toward Shim'on.

"Shalom, Brother!" He embraced Shim'on. "Where are you going next?"

"I'm not sure." Shim'on told him about Yohanan's death.

"I'm sorry to hear this." Hanoch's face clouded with concern. "Be careful." Shim'on agreed and said goodbye to his brother. The crowds stood confused as the boat drifted out to sea.

Shim'on raised the boat's sail. A wind from the west began to push them across the water to an isolated area. Soon, the people on the shore were only pinpricks, and then not visible at all. Shim'on raised his face to the sun overhead and let the wind lick at his hair. He missed being on the sea. Glancing at the others, he saw a few equally enjoying this quiet time on the water, while others looked a little green. The rabbi sat on a pile of nets, eyes closed, and face upturned to the sun. Shim'on hoped he slept.

Two hours later, the boat drew near to shore, and Shim'on shook his head in disbelief.

"Are those people?" Jude, one of the disciples asked, pointing to the shore ahead of them.

"They already followed us here?" Shim'on said in frustration, "Don't they know the rabbi needs his rest?"

The sound of the large crowd increased as the boat drew near to land, and when Jesus stepped off the vessel, many came forward with the sick, lame, blind, and demon-possessed. Shim'on watched as the rabbi showed compassion to the people and healed them, despite his grief. The afternoon flew by, and soon it was dusk.

Jude and Shim'on walked over to where Jesus sat.

"Rabbi, this is a remote place, and it's already getting late," Jude said. "Why don't you send the crowds away so they can go to the villages and buy food for themselves?"

Jesus turned to them, "That isn't necessary—you feed them."

185

Shim'on laughed awkwardly, "But we have only five loaves of bread and two fish!" Though the sun had begun its downward trajectory, the air was still hot. Shim'on wiped sweat from his forehead.

"Bring them here," Jesus said.

What was the rabbi going to do? Shim'on wondered. There were thousands of hungry people surrounding them. He was irritated. He and the other disciples were hungry and tired as well. Grumbling under his breath, Shim'on did as the rabbi asked.

When he returned with the loaves and fish, Jesus asked everyone to sit on the grass. He took the food from Shim'on's hands, raised it in the air and blessed it. Then he handed the fish to Kepha and Shim'on and broke the loaves into pieces between the disciples. The men looked at one another in confusion. The brown lehem and fish looked the same as they did moments before.

"Let's just tell the people to tear off a piece until it's gone," Shim'on whispered to Kepha, though the words felt ridiculous. The amount of food split between them would not feed more than ten men. The disciples moved among the people, directing them to tear off a piece of lehem and dried fish. Shim'on allowed the first man to tear off a chunk of lehem and then a piece of fish, then moved to the next person, extending the food to her. He blinked in surprise and glanced behind him at the first man to whom he had offered the food. He was happily enjoying his meal.

"Shim'on!" Ya'aqov called out to him across the crowd, "Is yours still whole, too?"

Behind them, Shim'on could hear Jesus laughing.

"Yes!" Shim'on called back in disbelief.

The disciples continued passing out food among the crowd, as much as each person wanted, and when they were finished, there were twelve baskets left over.

"It's a miracle!" Matthias surrendered his basket of leftovers. "I believe there were more than five thousand here today!"

"We'll trust you with the numbers, Matthias," Kepha teased the former tax collector.

"All right, men," Jesus stood, "Go ahead to Gennesaret. I am going to tell the people to go home."

"But what about you, Rabbi?" Shim'on asked.

"I will meet you there," Jesus replied.

Kepha looked confusedly at Shim'on, "How will he get there?" he whispered, "By foot? That will take at least a half-day!"

"I don't know." Shim'on responded, his brow furrowed.

The disciples made their way from the hills to the boat in the fading evening light and pushed off. It was a dark night with clouds obscuring the moon, and many of the exhausted disciples immediately fell asleep to the gentle rocking of the boat.

"I wish he would have come with us," Shim'on said with concern to Yohanan, who stood beside him at the rudder.

"Yes. Me, too," Yohanan replied, looking at the sky overhead. "We have a good wind now, but I fear these clouds. I don't want the rabbi to get caught in a storm."

An hour later the boat was far from land and the men's fears were justified. "Shim'on!" Shim'on bar Jona shook him awake, "The wind has increased; wake the other men! I fear we are headed into a storm!"

The gentle breeze soon escalated into a gale, and waves slapped against the boat, a number of them cresting over the sides and sending cold water pouring over the men. Andreas and

Shim'on lowered the sail, but the boat was tossed about like a toy in a lake, and the men feared for their lives.

Shim'on clung to the mast, watching the fierce waves helplessly. The wind blew the clouds from before the crescent moon, allowing watery light through. Intermittent flashes of lightning lit both the water's surface and the terrified faces of the disciples. The rain sluiced down from the heavens, followed by booming thunder. Shim'on had been on the sea in a storm, but this was unlike anything he'd experienced before.

With the next flash of lightning, Shim'on thought he saw a form on the water's surface. Taking a risk, he released his grip on the mast to rub the water from his eyes. He squinted again at the sea's roiling surface.

The lightning flashed and Shim'on thought he saw a human shape on the water, perhaps twenty yards from the boat.

"Look!" he yelled to the other disciples, pointing in the direction of the form.

The next time the lightning crackled, Shim'on realized that a man stood on the water. No, he was *walking* on the water! Now he was closer, only fifteen yards from the boat.

"It's a ghost!" Yehudah shouted, and Shim'on certainly agreed that it looked like one.

Tall waves surrounded the boat. The rain pounded down on the disciples' heads, but amazingly the man walking on the water didn't even look wet.

"It's the rabbi!" He realized, with shock.

The next flash of lightning revealed Jesus standing on the water not five yards away.

"Don't be afraid," he said, "Take courage. I am here!"

From beside him, Shim'on bar Jona spoke. "Rabbi, if it's really you, tell me to come to you, walking on the water."

"Are you out of your mind?" Shim'on looked at the disciple incredulously, shouting to be heard above the storm.

"Yes, come," Jesus beckoned him.

Shim'on looked at the waves rolling on the sea's surface and pouring over the boat's side. The rain fell in sheets. The other disciples clung to whatever they could to avoid being swept into the water. And Shim'on bar Jona was asking to leave the safety of the boat to try to walk on water.

"You're crazy, Brother!" Shim'on shouted.

Ignoring him, Shim'on bar Jona swung one leg, and then the other, over the side of the rocking boat.

Shim'on held his breath, sure that the disciple was about to sink beneath the waves. He watched in disbelief as Shim'on bar Jona set one sandaled foot, and then the other, onto the water's churning surface. A blast of cold spray hit Shim'on full in the face and he gasped, then wiped the water from his eyes. Instead of looking down at the water, Shim'on bar Jona kept his eyes fixed on the rabbi. Jesus smiled at him, his hand outstretched.

Envy rippled over Shim'on. Why hadn't he thought to ask the rabbi if he could walk on the water? The idea never even crossed his mind, he reluctantly acknowledged. Shim'on had to admit, Shim'on bar Jona had courage.

Shim'on bar Jona took one step, and then another. The wind blew fiercely. Rain slanted sideways into the water. Suddenly, behind Jesus, Shim'on saw a large wave approach the boat. Somehow it seemed to glide right over the rabbi, but Shim'on watched as Shim'on bar Jona's eyes widened shifting his focus from Jesus onto the oncoming wall of water.

"No!" Andreas cried, as Shim'on bar Jona began to sink, his arms flailing.

"Save me, Rabbi!" Shim'on bar Jona shouted.

Jesus immediately reached out, grabbing Shim'on bar Jona before he was lost under the water's surface.

Shim'on watched as the rabbi spoke to Shim'on bar Jona, the rain still spilling down around them, waves angrily knotting beneath their feet. Envy prickled again. He longed to have the relationship Shim'on bar Jona had with the rabbi. He watched as Jesus and Shim'on bar Jona walked on the water back to the boat and pulled themselves over the side.

As soon as Jesus' hand touched the vessel, the howling wind stopped. The downpour ceased, and the clouds parted and cleared from before the face of the moon. Shim'on and the rest of the disciples stood, soaked through and open-mouthed.

"You really are the Son of Adonai!" Shim'on said, in awe. The other disciples murmured their agreement, equally shocked. Jesus smiled and made his way to the prow of the boat.

The disciples surrounded Shim'on bar Jona.

"What happened out there?" Ya'aqov shouted. "What did he say to you?"

A sheepish grin filled Shim'on bar Jona's face. "It was amazing until I saw the waves, and then I started to sink. I thought that was the end. I called out for the rabbi and then he was there! Pulling me out of the water!"

"What did he say to you?" Yohanan pressed.

"He asked why I doubted him." Shim'on bar Jona shook his head. "Brothers, he really is the Son of Adonai!"

Shim'on looked up again at the clear sky above them. The stars twinkled brilliantly, and the air smelled fresh. It was as though the storm that raged moments before had never happened.

"Will you help me raise the sail?" Shim'on bar Jona asked Shim'on.

Together, they pulled at the water-laden rope attached to the even-heavier linen sail.

"Did you see me out there, Shim'on?" Shim'on bar Jona grunted with the effort, but his face still shone with excitement.

"Did I see you lose your mind over a wave and start sinking in the sea? Yes," Shim'on grinned at him, "I did see that."

"I didn't see you asking to walk on water!" Shim'on bar Jona protested with a laugh.

Shim'on wished the envy in his heart would disappear like the molten storm clouds. He hoped his smile concealed the bitterness beneath. "It was amazing, Brother. I was jealous." He slapped Shim'on bar Jona's shoulder, "Though I wasn't jealous of the sinking part."

Shim'on bar Jona laughed and Shim'on recalled the words the rabbi spoke to his friend on the water.

I'll show the rabbi that I have just as much faith as Shim'on bar Jona, he assured himself.

Yeshua

XX

Yeshua felt the skies were appropriately dark over Capernaum the day of his abba's burial. Hundreds of people walked behind the litter carrying Bin-yamin's shrouded and perfumed body. He was well-loved and respected by many. Sarai sobbed behind Yeshua as he carried a corner of the litter to the family tomb. For whatever reason, Yeshua had no more tears to shed. The anguish of that day in Jerusalem had claimed all his tears, and his grief had turned to fiery anger.

This all happened because of the filthy Romans.

Despite his immah's protests, Yeshua refused to remain in Jerusalem. His excitement over beginning a new stage in life, that of a rabbi, died with his abba. He had no idea what his future now held, aside from avenging Bin-yamin's death. It was ironic, he thought to himself as he set the litter with his abba's body in the tomb cut from the side of a hill. This was how Shim'on felt years ago, but he hadn't understood. Now he would welcome his old friend's company. But it was too late.

Yeshua and three of his abba's friends rolled a large circular stone over the front of the tomb, sealing it. As customary, those who loved and respected the deceased joined them in wailing over the loss and throwing handfuls of dust into the air. Yeshua turned to his immah and siblings. Sarai was still crying, her eyes puffy and bloodshot.

"Immah," Yeshua said gently, "We should go, the women are preparing a funeral meal."

Sarai groaned, "How can I leave him, Yeshua? I need him. How can he be gone?"

"I know, Immah," Yeshua put his arms around his immah and hugged her, "I can't believe he's gone either. But please don't worry. I'll take care of you and Deborah and Tobias."

What Sarai did not know was that Yeshua planned to stay in Capernaum. Since Bin-yamin's death, his dream of being a rabbi was the furthest thought from his mind. For the time being, he would find work as a tekton before deciding what to do next.

"Yeshua?" A woman with a dark head covering walked toward him, "Is that you?"

Yeshua found himself looking into the face of his old friend's immah.

Grief and the loss of her husband had aged Shim'on's immah. But as he looked into her eyes, he was surprised to see warmth and peace.

"I'm so sorry for your loss, Yeshua," she touched his arm, then paused, "Have you heard of the rabbi from Nazareth?"

Yeshua gritted his teeth, annoyed that she would bring up the man today of all days. But he tried to be polite, "I have."

"Your abba loved Him. He believed the rabbi's teaching that if a man repents of his sin and believes that He is the Son of Adonai, he will have eternal life."

She smiled at Yeshua, "I also believe and have repented of my sin."

"And I know," she continued, looking into Yeshua's face, "that you do not believe in the rabbi or his message."

Yeshua startled, "How do you know that?"

"Adonai told me," Miriam smiled simply, "But don't close your heart to Him, Yeshua. He is the prophesied One. I believe that with all my heart. If you believe, you will see your abba again one day, but if you don't"—her eyes filled with sadness, "Don't wait too long, Yeshua."

With those words, Miriam walked away. It was only then that Yeshua realized he had forgotten to ask where Shim'on was.

XXI

Yeshua sat up in the darkness.

His heart raced and his tunic was drenched in sweat. Memories of Bin-yamin's death on the Temple Mount were unrelenting in wakefulness and sleep. He felt for his sandals and slipped them on before tiptoeing around the sleeping forms of his immah, Deborah, and Tobias.

Out on the street, he remained in the shadows as he left the city and entered the hills. Bin-yamin's burial had been three days earlier, and Yeshua felt unmoored, his life direction uncertain. Fortunately, it was easy enough to find work as a tekton, and he already had enough commissioned jobs for weeks of work.

The labor occupied his hands, but not his thoughts. Anger and hatred toward the Romans constantly gnawed at him. Yesterday he was approached by a fisherman named Amos.

The man had pulled him aside and offered him an opportunity to do something with his anger-join the Zealots.

Yeshua wasn't blind to the irony of his situation. At one time, he had been judgmental concerning the insurrectionists' cause. Now he could not deny the appeal of it. Yeshua remained in the hills until the sun hinted at its arrival. Then he turned toward home.

 Months passed, each day fading into the next. When Miriam discovered Yeshua's plans to remain in Capernaum, she begged him not to give up his calling as a rabbi. But Yeshua was determined, and eventually Miriam ceased her protests. He could see that Deborah and Tobias enjoyed having him home and knew that Miriam was thankful to have their needs met through his work. Still, life seemed empty.

Yeshua continued to keep the law and observe all the daily rituals. He pleaded with Adonai to either remove the hate and anger that seemed to permanently live in his heart or show him how to be free of it. But his prayers were met with silence. Amos approached him twice more, inviting him to meetings of the Zealots, and each time Yeshua declined. He knew that Bin-yamin wouldn't have wanted him to become a Zealot, but the temptation to make the Romans pay for what they'd done was more than tempting.

"Shalom," Yeshua raised a hand in farewell to a fellow tekton as he left the worksite for the day. Despite the fading sunlight, the streets of Capernaum still bustled with activity. As he passed a dark alleyway, activity caught his eye. Three soldiers stood over a form cowering against a wall. One of them held a whip.

Yeshua pressed himself into an alcove created by the alley wall and a nearby home.

"Never lie when we ask you a question, boy." One of the soldiers sneered.

Yeshua heard the boy cough and groan. Clearly, they had beaten him.

"Next time, give us the money when we ask for it." The soldier with the whip shoved the boy once more, and then the three moved past him, leaving the alley.

Quickly, Yeshua stepped out of his hiding place and ran to the boy who slumped to the ground.

"Tobias?" He asked in shock, sinking down in front of his fifteen-year-old brother. Tobias' tunic was torn where the whip had cut into the fabric, and Yeshua could see crimson stripes on his brother's chest. His face was dirty and bloodied, and both of his eyes were blackened.

"Yeshua?" His brother wheezed the words. "I'm sorry, Immah sent me to the market, and they demanded money. I told them I didn't have any, but they beat me and found it anyway. I'm sorry," he said again.

Fury made Yeshua's hands shake. He clenched them at his sides. Forcing himself to speak calmly, he said, "It's not your fault, Tobias. You did nothing wrong. Let's get you home."

Tobias groaned in pain as Yeshua helped him to his feet. Passersby gaped as the brothers made their way home, though none stopped to ask questions. Everyone already assumed the cause of Tobias' injuries. Yeshua gritted his teeth as Miriam and Deborah set to work treating Tobias' wounds. His decision was made. Tomorrow, he would speak to Amos and find out when the Zealots met next.

 The crescent moon cast just enough light for Yeshua to see the hills and locate the ravine that would lead to the Zealots' hiding place.

"Oof," Yeshua grunted as he tripped on a rise in the earth. Being in the hills brought back memories of adventures with Shim'on. Hunting for rabbits, target practice, and imaginative battles. Yeshua smiled remembering their escapades. It felt so long ago. Had Shim'on ever actually met with the Zealots? Where was he now? He hadn't seen his old friend or his friend's brother, Hanoch, since his return to Capernaum.

Soon he reached the thicket of olive trees that Amos had directed him to look for and whistled his arrival. Hearing a whistle in return, he pressed forward into the dark foliage and emerged into a small cave. A group of roughly seventy men stood in a loose circle, but the only familiar face to him was Amos'.

"Welcome." A short, but muscular man with a deep voice approached and grasped his forearm in greeting, "I'm Avi, the leader here. I've heard of you from Amos."

He introduced Yeshua to the other men and left him standing beside a tall, lean man named Tova.

"I heard that you are the son of a rabbi, is that true?" Tova looked at him quizzically.

"It is," Yeshua said bluntly.

"That's unusual," Tova said, surprised, "I've never heard of a rabbi's son becoming a Zealot."

"The Romans killed my abba," Yeshua said sharply.

"Oh." Tova said apologetically, "I'm sorry."

"All right, men," Avi raised his arms in a gesture for everyone to cease their talk.

"Our next objective will be sixteen legionaries on their way north."

Yeshua listened intently, paying attention to every detail of the attack plan. Suddenly, a memory from long-ago awakened in his mind.

"Abba, why do the Zealots pursue a path of violence when Adonai tells us not to kill?" His abba thoughtfully responded, *"Sometimes a man feels alone and afraid and wants to make his enemies feel as he does. He tries to justify his violence by saying that he is bringing about Adonai's justice. And this is what the Zealots do. But Adonai does see. He tells us that He does, and that we are not forgotten. And that He is sending the Mashiach soon."*

Yeshua shrugged the memory aside. Did any teaching about seeking peace without violence come from anyone who had experienced real loss? At one time, he believed that maintaining a pacifist coexistence with the Romans was the way of Adonai. But that was before his abba had been killed, and before Tobias was beaten within an inch of his life. He tried to convince himself that based on these events, Bin-yamin would have understood his decision to join the Zealots.

Avi completed his description of the mission and the Zealots disbanded toward their homes.

"I'm glad to have you in the group," Avi said to him after the meeting. "We watch each other's backs here, so I will let you know if you draw attention in town for any reason."

"Thank you," Yeshua said, "I'll do the same. One other thing, was there ever a man named Shim'on with you?"

Avi looked at him with a strange expression, "Why do you ask?"

"He was a friend of mine. At one time."

Avi looked more closely at Yeshua as if suddenly realizing who he was, "You and the fisherman were friends, weren't you? I often saw you together."

Yeshua nodded, "Yes."

"But you haven't spoken in a while, hmmm?" Avi looked as if he were trying to decide what to share with Yeshua. "Yes," he conceded, "Shim'on used to meet with us."

"Used to?" Yeshua wondered.

"Yes, years ago. Until he was called by the rabbi. Now he follows him everywhere."

"The rabbi? You mean the man Jesus?" Yeshua said in disbelief.

"Yes, that's him," Avi said, "They say the rabbi called him while he was fishing, and that he left everything and followed him. His brother too. It must have been a couple of years ago now."

"We miss him every mission," Avi said with a sigh, "Shim'on was the best fighter I've ever seen. It came to him naturally. No one could stand in his way."

Yeshua was stunned. The last time he saw Shim'on, he was filled with hatred and anger. And now he followed the peace-loving Rabbi? He could not reconcile the change in his mind.

He thanked Avi, and said farewell to Amos, then left the cave and made his way through the hills to town. As he lay on his mat that night, thoughts of Shim'on lingered in his mind. What had happened to his friend?

XXII

"Rabbi, there is a messenger here for you," Shim'on gestured toward the man standing nearby.

The men camped in the area where the rabbi had been baptized by Yohanan the Baptist three years before. As always, crowds eager to hear the rabbi and be healed followed them. Though he longed to escape the multitude of people, Shim'on enjoyed the beautiful location. The muddy Jordan River flowed nearby, and verdant trees, bushes, and grass thrived along its banks. Despite the hum of voices surrounding them, it was a peaceful and refreshing place for the rabbi and his disciples.

"Your friends Miryam and Martha send you this message," the messenger said. "Rabbi, your dear friend is very sick."

Shim'on was saddened to hear the news. Miryam, Martha, and their brother, Lazarus, were close friends of Jesus, and he and the disciples often visited their home in Bethany. The siblings loved the rabbi with all their hearts and always welcomed him into their home with open arms and lavish hospitality. Miryam and Martha's kind and compassionate personalities reminded Shim'on of Lydia. The siblings were good friends of many of the disciples as well, including Shim'on. The 'dear friend' Miryam and Martha referred to in the message could only be one person: their brother, Lazarus.

The rabbi was quiet for a moment, then he spoke. "Lazarus' sickness will not end in death. No, it happened for the glory of Adonai, so that the Son of Adonai will receive glory from this."

Shim'on was confused. Every day they were surrounded by strangers who begged Jesus for healing. The rabbi had compassion on them and made them well. So why would he not rush to the side of a close friend in his time of need?

"Rabbi, Lazarus sees you as a brother. Could we not go to him now? You can heal him!" Shim'on spoke impulsively.

Jesus looked hard at Shim'on but didn't answer. Instead, he turned and walked toward the crowds. The messenger left without a response to Miryam and Martha, and Shim'on could only imagine the sisters' bewilderment when they found out the rabbi was not coming. At least the rabbi said that Lazarus would not die. That was encouraging. But why not tell Miryam and Martha?

Two days passed, and Jesus continued to teach and heal the crowds. Though he enjoyed their lovely surroundings, Shim'on could not shake the frustration he'd felt since the messenger's arrival days before. Why were they not hastening to Lazarus?

On the third day, Jesus spoke to the disciples, "Let's go back to Judea. Our friend Lazarus has fallen asleep, but now I will go and wake him up."

Shim'on was confused. "Rabbi, if he is sleeping, doesn't that mean he will get better?"

Jesus paused and looked around the group of disciples. "Lazarus is dead."

The disciples murmured among themselves.

"But you said he wouldn't die!" Shim'on was angry. Lazarus was his friend, and until now, he thought that Jesus considered him one too. How could the rabbi let his friend die?

Jesus continued, "For your sakes, I'm glad I wasn't there, for now you will really believe. Come, let's go see him."

"What, go see a dead man?" Philipos whispered as they packed their mats and followed the rabbi. "I thought he said Lazarus wasn't going to die."

"I thought so too," Shim'on replied, feeling angry. Lazarus was an outgoing, friendly bear of a man, always telling jokes and making his guests feel welcomed. But he was also a man committed to Adonai. He loved Jesus deeply and believed Him to be the Mashiach. Shim'on couldn't bear to think the man had passed away wondering why the Mashiach didn't come to heal him.

As they neared Bethany, villagers informed the men that Lazarus had already been in the grave for four days. Martha met them outside the city and stopped before Jesus. Her dark hair was covered by a headscarf, and her eyes were red-rimmed and bloodshot with grief. When she spoke, her voice was gravelly from sobbing. "Rabbi, if you had only been here, my brother would not have died. But even now I know that Adonai will give you whatever you ask."

"Your brother will rise again, Martha," Jesus replied, and Shim'on couldn't decipher the look He gave to Martha.

Martha nodded, a tear coursing down her cheek. "Yes, he will rise when everyone else rises, on the last day." She spoke the words resignedly.

"I am the resurrection and the life," the rabbi looked tenderly at her, "Anyone who believes in me will live, even after dying. Everyone who lives in me and believes in me will never ever die. Do you believe this, Martha?" Shim'on thought the rabbi's words must be difficult to hear in the wake of such loss. Especially since the rabbi could have healed Lazarus if they had come sooner.

"Yes, Rabbi," Martha looked at Him tearfully, "I believe that you are the Mashiach, the Son of Adonai, the One who has come into the world from Adonai." She turned and retreated slowly in the direction of Bethany.

Minutes later, Shim'on heard wailing approaching. One figure walked ahead of the mourners, and soon he realized it was Miryam, Lazarus' other sister. Miryam too, was crying, and when she reached the men, she fell at the rabbi's feet. She spoke the words that Shim'on knew everyone was thinking.

"Rabbi, if only you had been here, my brother would not have died."

Shim'on saw a look of deep grief, mingled with anger cross the rabbi's face.

"Where have you put him?" Jesus asked.

A mourner who accompanied Miryam replied, "Rabbi, come and see." To Shim'on's surprise, Jesus began to cry. Why was the rabbi crying if he already knew Lazarus had died? Shim'on heard a man standing nearby whisper to another, "This man healed a blind man, couldn't He have kept Lazarus from dying?" Jesus and the disciples followed the sisters and mourners to a sealed tomb.

"Roll the stone aside," Jesus commanded.

"Rabbi, he has been dead for four days. The smell will be terrible," Martha protested.

"Didn't I tell you that you would see Adonai's glory if you believed?" Jesus asked her.

Reluctantly, several men in the crowd stepped forward. Throwing their weight against the heavy chiseled rock, they grunted with effort. The stone rolled from the tomb's entrance with a deep, gravelly groan.

True to Martha's prediction, a stench drifted from the cave. Shim'on pulled the hem of his tallit over his nose.

Jesus looked toward heaven and spoke, "Abba, thank you for hearing me. You always hear me, but I said it out loud for the sake of all these people standing here, so that they will believe You sent me." He lowered his eyes to gaze into the tomb. "Lazarus, come out!" he shouted, authority in his voice.

Shim'on held his breath. For several moments, nothing happened. A flight of pigeons flew from the hills nearby, their flapping wings making crackling noises in the stillness. Suddenly, a figure, clad from head to toe in white burial clothes, emerged from the darkness of the cave.

Gasps and murmurs broke out across the crowd. Shim'on blinked, trying to take in what he saw.

"Unwrap him and let him go!" Jesus said, a smile spreading across his face.

Shim'on watched in shock as Miryam and Martha tremblingly approached their brother and gently unwound the cloths wrapped around his hands, feet, and head. When they could fully see his face, they cried tears of joy and kissed and hugged him repeatedly. Lazarus laughed good-naturedly and insisted they stop. Shim'on couldn't believe his eyes. Jesus had just brought a dead man back to life! When he was fully unwrapped from his burial garments, Lazarus walked over to Jesus and fell to his knees before him. Jesus pulled him to his feet, and the two men embraced. Shim'on stood close enough that he could hear Lazarus' words.

"I understand now, Rabbi. I'll admit that at first, I didn't. I feared you had abandoned me." He shook his head. "But then He showed me and—" Lazarus trailed off and wiped tears from his face.

Jesus leaned close to speak in Lazarus' ear, and Shim'on couldn't hear what he said. When he pulled back, Lazarus' face was bright and peaceful.

Shim'on was awe-struck. What man had power even over death and the grave? In his heart, he heard the whisper of an answer: only the Mashiach.

"Come!" Lazarus gestured to the crowd, "Let's go celebrate! Adonai has brought me back to life!"

 Shim'on feared for the rabbi. Jesus continued to teach and perform miracles everywhere he went. Large crowds followed him, but the Pharisees and Sadduccees were threatened by the rabbi's approval among the people, and even more so following Jesus' miracle of resurrecting Lazarus. After the miracle, many people came to believe Jesus was the Mashiach. As a result, the Pharisees and Sadducees feared their own downfall in power. They frequently sought to manipulate Jesus into saying something that would cause the people to turn their backs on him and return their focus to them. So far, they had been unsuccessful. Jesus had a way of answering their questions with more questions that they could not answer. He also frequently responded with *mashals*. These were the stories that revealed the Pharisees' and Sadducees' self-righteousness, pride, and abuse of power. Shim'on noticed the increased confrontations between the religious leaders and the rabbi, and even heard rumors that the Sanhedrin were plotting to kill Jesus. The reports worried him. Though he was no longer a Zealot, he never ceased to strap his dagger beneath the folds of his tunic. If the rabbi's life were ever to be in danger, Shim'on would be ready.

This morning, the Pharisees once again tried to trap Jesus in His words.

"Show us a sign from Heaven if you are really the Mashiach," a Pharisee pressed Him.

"Why do these people keep demanding a miraculous sign?" Jesus looked at the disciples surrounding him, "I will not give this generation any such sign."

The face of the Pharisee flushed crimson with angry embarrassment, and he signaled his accompanying Pharisees to leave with him. The crowd murmured, and Jesus gestured the disciples toward a boat pulled up on shore a short distance away.

"What other signs do they need?" Jude walked beside Shim'on on the rocky shoreline. "He performs miracles and teaches unlike any other Rabbi. He's clearly the Mashiach. They're just jealous."

Shim'on agreed, but he couldn't shake the vague sense of unease he felt whenever the Pharisees confronted Jesus.

 When they arrived on the other side of the sea, Natanel slapped his forehead.

"What is it?" Ya'aqov asked.

"I forgot to put the lehem in the boat," he grimaced.

"Watch and be on your guard for the yeast of the Pharisees and Sadducees," Jesus said.

Natanel looked confusedly at the other disciples, "Is he saying the lehem was no good?"

"You have so little faith!" Jesus looked at them patiently, "Why are you arguing with each other about having no lehem? Don't you understand yet? Don't you remember the five-thousand that I fed with five loaves, and the baskets of leftovers you picked up? Or the four thousand I fed with seven loaves, and the large baskets of leftovers you picked up? Why can't you understand that I'm not talking about lehem? I'll say it again, 'Beware of the yeast of the Pharisees and Sadducees.'" Jesus began walking inland, and the men fell into step behind him.

"He's right," Shim'on said aloud, "Why would we worry about lehem when he has multiplied loaves before? That's not what he's talking about."

"He's talking about the corrupt teaching of the Pharisees and Sadducees," Matthias said from where he walked in the middle of everyone.

"It is corrupt, there is no doubt about that," Yohanan spoke from behind them. "They just keep creating more and more laws for the people to follow. All in the name of pleasing Adonai. It's impossible to keep them all, and the Pharisees and Sadducees wouldn't think of bending down to help the people carry the burden."

"They walk about as if they are perfect, yet just yesterday I saw a Sadducee in prayer on a street corner, beside a dirty and crying child begging for money," Philipos snorted, "He didn't even open his eyes." He shook his head. "The rabbi doesn't place heavy burdens on the people's backs. He says he has come to fulfill the law and to set us free."

A thought tugged at the edge of Shim'on's mind. He too believed the rabbi was the Son of Adonai, the Mashiach. But, if this were true, it also meant the rest of the prophecies must be true. The words of the navi Isaiah came to his mind, "He was pierced for our rebellion, crushed for our sins. He was beaten so we could be whole. He was whipped so we could be healed. All of us, like sheep, have strayed away. We have left Adonai's paths to follow our own. Yet the Lord laid on him the sins of us all. He was oppressed and treated harshly, yet he never said a word. He was led like a lamb to the slaughter. And as a sheep is silent before the shearers, he did not open his mouth. Unjustly condemned, he was led away. No one cared that he died without descendants, that his life was cut short in midstream."

A ripple of fear spread through Shim'on's heart. The words certainly sounded like a prophecy of death. Did it relate to the rabbi? Once again, he thought of how the crowds worshipped the rabbi. How could these same people turn against him? Shaking his head, he decided that it was impossible.

 Two days later, Jesus and the disciples reached the city of Caesarea Philippi. That evening, as the disciples ate dried fish and lehem around a smoldering fire, Jesus asked them, "Who do people say I am?"

"Some say Yohanan the Baptist," Natanel replied.

"Others say Elijah," said Yehudah.

"And others, Jeremiah or one of the navi," Philipos offered.

Jesus looked around the circle, "But who do you say I am?" The fire crackled and snapped, small sparks wafting upwards.

Shim'on bar Jona stood. "You are the Mashiach, the Son of the living Adonai."

Shim'on felt a familiar pang of envy. He agreed with Shim'on bar Jona, but he wished he had been the first to profess Jesus as the Mashiach. For hundreds of years they had awaited their Mashiach and here he stood before them. The man who would make their people great again and destroy their enemies. He would bring peace to a nation that was thirsty for it. But the Mashiach had never been prophesied to perform miracles or forgive sins. Only Adonai could do such things. The fact that Jesus brought the dead to life and cleansed people from their sins made it clear that he was more than a rabbi. He could only be the Son of Adonai.

Jesus fixed his dark eyes on Shim'on. "You are blessed, Shim'on bar Jona, because my abba in heaven revealed this to you. You did not learn this from any human being. From now on, you will be called *Cephas*, a stone, and on this *petra*, solid rock, I will build my church, and all the powers of hades will not conquer it." Shim'on tried to hide his jealousy. Jesus looked seriously into each face around the fire. "Do not tell anyone that I am the Mashiach. My time has not yet come."

The men around the fire nodded, but Shim'on knew they all shared his confusion. Envy rose like bile in his throat, and he swallowed hard. The rabbi had such a special purpose for Shim'on bar Jona that he had given him a new name. He forced himself to shift focus to Jesus' warning. Why could no one know that Jesus was the Son of Adonai? He tried to comprehend the rabbi's words, but he could not. He remained quiet in hopes that Jesus would provide an explanation. But the rabbi didn't, and Shim'on was left with his puzzled thoughts.

In the following days, Jesus continued to warn the disciples that he must suffer many things and be rejected by the elders, chief priests, and scribes. Once again, he said that he would be killed, and after three days, rise again. Shim'on couldn't understand it. Who would kill the rabbi? The people loved him. Many believed him to be the Mashiach, the chosen One who would triumph over their enemies and lead the Hebrew people to freedom and victory. They would follow Him forever! The religious leaders hated him, but surely, they wouldn't resort to physical violence. Would they?

Confused and saddened, the disciples did not know how to respond.

Much to his frustration, Shim'on's thoughts were frequently clouded by jealousy. He knew it was wrong to feel envious of the disciple they now referred to as Cephas. The disciple was a good man, and nothing he did led Shim'on to believe that he was intentionally seeking the rabbi's attention. For whatever reason, Jesus simply treated Cephas differently than the other disciples. Shim'on knew he ought to go to the rabbi and confess his thoughts. He could ask him about the warnings of his death as well. But pride and shame kept him silent. If he tried hard enough, surely, he could conquer his jealousy. And perhaps Jesus would explain to them the meaning behind his warning without being questioned. But as the days passed, Jesus did not provide any more details of what was to come. And Shim'on's envy settled into the shadowed corners of his mind.

One night after Jesus spoke of forthcoming death again, Cephas stood and asked Jesus to speak with him privately. Though the men stood a distance away, Shim'on and the other disciples could overhear Cephas' passionate words.

"Heaven forbid, Rabbi! We will follow you forever! This will never happen to You!"

Shim'on looked up and studied the two men. A look of resolute strength flickered on Jesus' face, and he turned so that he faced the disciples. "Get behind me, Satan!" He said, his voice deep with authority, "You are thinking of your own needs, and not of Adonai's plan."

Cephas stuttered at the rabbi's rebuke.

"I'm sorry, Rabbi," he said. "I was thinking of what I wanted and nothing else. Please forgive me."

Shim'on felt a fleeting flash of satisfaction at the disciple's embarrassment. *You would have said the same*, a voice whispered in his mind.

Solemnly, Jesus placed a hand on his shoulder, "You are forgiven."

Cephas retreated from the group. Later that night, after Jesus and most of the disciples lay asleep on their mats, Shim'on lay awake in the darkness. It was a cloudy night, and patches of stars gleamed hazily above him. He glanced toward Cephas and noticed the disciple also sat, awake, on his mat.

Shim'on quietly rose and made his way to Cephas. "Are you all right?" he asked in a low voice. Though he often felt envious of the disciple, Cephas was a good man, and Shim'on felt for him after the rabbi's stern rebuke earlier.

Cephas nodded, staring into the smoldering fire. "He was right. I should not have rebuked him."

"Honestly, Brother," Shim'on confessed, lowering himself to the ground, "I would have said the same as you."

Cephas remained quiet. Crickets chirped drowsily from the grass and bushes surrounding them. Shim'on debated how much to confide in Cephas. He desperately needed to share the burden of his concerns for the rabbi.

"Cephas," Shim'on spoke soberly after a short time, "Have you noticed the interactions between Jesus and the Pharisees and Sadducees?"

"Yes," Cephas nodded. "At first, it seemed like the rabbi annoyed them. Now, they hate him."

"Yes, exactly," Shim'on nodded, "They're angry. I fear what they might do to silence Jesus.

"Did you hear him speak to them earlier today? The entire crowd was listening. The rabbi poked holes in their self-righteousness. He's exposing their corruption. For hundreds of years, these men have been the final say. Now he is uncovering their pride and contradictions to everyone."

"Silence him!" Cephas sounded surprised, "I know they're angry, but do you really think they would try to kill him?"

"I've heard rumors—" Shim'on started.

"But rumors are rumors, Brother. Have you seen anything with your own eyes?" Cephas sighed. "I too am worried for him, but so far I haven't seen evidence of a plot to kill him. Have you?"

"No, I have not," Shim'on sighed. "And if they were to do anything to him, the people would riot. I just don't understand why the rabbi keeps prophesying his own death."

"I don't understand it either. But I do agree that we must be careful," Cephas nodded, "There's no harm in telling the others to keep watch."

Shim'on went to sleep that night with an odd combination of soberness and peace. Cephas was right. There wasn't any real evidence of danger to the rabbi. He still didn't understand the prophecies Jesus spoke concerning himself, but he truly believed that he was the Mashiach. And he would protect him from any threat. With his own life if necessary.

XXIII

His involvement with the Zealots had turned him into an efficient, hardened killer. After his first meeting with the Zealots, Yeshua threw himself into training. Now he took pride in his ability to end Roman lives. His fellow Zealots respected him, and due to the number of lives he'd taken, the Romans had labeled him as a wanted, notorious insurrectionist.

"You remember your friend Shim'on?" Amos asked him two nights before, "He was one of our best. But you are even better."

Yeshua revelled in the praise and attention, though he wouldn't show it.

The time Yeshua had spent in Jerusalem studying to be a rabbi now seemed like a lifetime ago. At one time he had taken pride in his righteousness, observance of the law, and calling to become a rabbi. Now he found satisfaction in other things, though he continued to obey the law and offer sacrifices for his sins. Of course, he justified breaking the laws 'do not murder' and 'do not steal', but he had learned to do so relatively well and only felt a twinge of guilt from time to time.

Sarai disliked accepting the food, clothing, and other necessities Yeshua provided her from the Zealots' plunder of the Romans, but what choice did she have? Deborah and Tobias needed to be fed and clothed. Most days he was able to ignore the unsettling reality that violence was doing nothing to ease the anger and hatred he carried.

"They're coming!" Amos hissed to Yeshua and ten other Zealots hidden behind the bend of the road.

The men pressed tightly against the walls of the canyon, their feet scraping harshly on the gravel road. Fortunately, the sound of the approaching Roman centuries and their slaves drowned out any noise they made.

Suddenly, Efrayim raised his arm, signaling the men.

Yeshua jumped forward, simultaneously drawing the sword lashed to his side. The sword once belonged to a centurion, but Yeshua had killed its owner and claimed it for himself. He found a macabre sense of humor in using a Roman's weapon to claim Roman lives.

The small caravan was in an uproar, and Yeshua knew they were surprised by the eleven Zealots who blocked their escape from the rear.

Yeshua waited until a horse, foaming at the mouth with terror, threw its Roman rider to the ground. Yeshua lunged forward onto the dusty road, sinking his sword into the man's neck. The solder grabbed at the wound, sinking to his knees, and then falling forward, dead.

Yeshua continued forward, slashing left and right as he went. While some of his fellow Zealots took care not to wound slaves or non-Romans, Yeshua did not care. In his mind, any person who cooperated with or served the Romans, was as good as aligned with them. His principal focus was the Romans, but he refused to be slowed down by anyone in his way, be they innocent or not.

Thwack. Yeshua heard metal striking a blunt object and turned to look behind him.

"You owe me, Brother!" Jerome grunted from where he had blocked a centurion from stabbing Yeshua in the back. The men grappled, and Jerome twice more deflected blows from the Roman's sword with his crudely-made shield. Yeshua didn't have time to watch his friend's skirmish, however. Turning back to the scene before him, he notched an arrow in his bow and aimed at a soldier standing five yards away, his back turned. The arrow sank into the man's arm, and he cried out in pain as another Zealot sprang forward to finish the job.

The sounds of metal upon metal and grunting, moans, and heavy breathing surrounded him. Dust from the road kicked up by the men's feet hung thickly in the air. Yeshua coughed. He caught sight of a centurion leaning against a boulder, a bloody gash on his head. The man was conscious, but barely. Yeshua swung his sword to finish him.

Pssssttt. Something hissed by his ear and he saw Amos cry out and stumble, an arrow lodged in his thigh.

Yeshua turned to look in the direction of the noise. Five Roman archers stood on the canyon walls above the skirmish.

"There's more above!" Yeshua yelled, "Run!"

Quickly, he ran to Amos and wrapped the man's uninjured arm over his shoulder, "Hold on Brother, let's get out of here!"

Yeshua saw the bodies of five of their number lying lifeless on the ground and cursed. Suddenly, a stinging pain bloomed on his shoulder, and he glanced down to see an arrow protruding from his left arm.

Cursing again, Yeshua shouted to Jerome, "Here, take his arm, get him out of here! Go!" He pushed Jerome and Amos forward and turned, drawing his sword. Thank Adonai the arrow had struck him in the left shoulder and not the right.

The pain burned down his arm and across his back, and Yeshua allowed it to bolster his anger. He followed Amos and Jerome around a bend and then pressed himself tightly against the rugged canyon wall. He could hear the soldiers congratulating one another and cursing the Zealots as they jogged after them. He gritted his teeth as he thought of the five Zealots, his friends, lying dead on the road. He hoped that the rest of their number had escaped before being picked off by the archers above.

Yeshua heard footfalls nearing his position and allowed himself a smile. In their arrogance, the Romans assumed that a couple of soldiers were more than capable of ending the lives of three tired and wounded Zealots.

As the two soldiers rounded the bend, Yeshua pushed himself off the wall and stabbed his sword forward. His blade sunk into the neck of one of the soldiers, killing him instantly. The other soldier roared in anger and swung his sword. Yeshua retrieved his sword from the soldier's neck just in time and dodged the blade. The sword missed its mark by inches and struck the canyon wall, a small avalanche of red stone falling to the ground from the impact.

"Aaaaargggh!" the soldier yelled in anger.

"What," Yeshua taunted him, "You thought this would be easy?"

The men moved in a circle, contemplating their next moves. Quickly, Yeshua sliced his sword downward, ripping a gash in the other man's thigh. The soldier screamed in pain, clutching his leg. Yeshua saw his chance and jumped forward, but the man raised his sword to deflect the blow, catching Yeshua off balance.

Yeshua tripped past the soldier and felt a searing pain as the soldier sliced horizontally down his back. He cursed. His back and shoulder burned as if they were on fire.

"Just die, you Hebrew pig," the centurion spat. "Your companions haven't made it far with one of them wounded. After you die, I'll go and finish them off too." He grinned sardonically.

Yeshua's hatred for the man and his arrogance boiled. But he was so tired. He staggered and put an arm out to balance himself against the canyon wall. The soldier, too, seemed grateful for the reprieve, allowing his sword to hang loosely in his hand. But his arrogant smile remained plastered across his face. Yeshua saw spots and blinked, trying to clear his vision. An image of his abba's face, his broken body lying on the ground of the temple compound, flitted across his mind.

"Damn you!" Yeshua yelled, and the centurion's face showed his surprise as Yeshua pushed himself off the wall and ran at him with renewed fury, sword raised. The man was caught off guard by Yeshua's quick movement, and he raised his arm to shield himself. Yeshua's sword sliced through the man's forearm and into his neck. Blood poured from the wounds, and the man fell to the ground, dead.

"You are the swine," Yeshua spoke to the lifeless body, then wiped his bloody sword on the man's tunic and sheathed it at his side.

Stars danced in Yeshua's vision as he made his way along the canyon wall, stumbling after Amos and Jerome. By now, he hoped they neared Capernaum, but Yeshua feared what would happen when the Romans discovered the two dead soldiers. He tried to run, though it was more of a stumbling jog. Finally, he rounded a bend and could see his friends ahead of him.

"Jerome!" Yeshua called, and the men turned.

"Yeshua?" Amos peered at him, and his eyes widened as Yeshua got closer, "Goodness, man! What happened to you?"

"We must get you help." Jerome said solemnly. "But looking the way you do will get you arrested immediately when we get to town. Let's stop, and I'll bandage the wounds. You can have my extra tunic."

"I'll take care of my wounds later," Yeshua grunted, but resignedly allowed Jerome to lead him to a pile of boulders against the canyon wall.

Jerome patched Yeshua up well enough to escape notice as they entered the city gates under the watchful eyes of the Roman guard. Amos and Yeshua gritted their teeth as they tried not to limp.

The men split up once inside the city gates, and Yeshua walked with effort to his home.

"Yeshua!" Sarai's face turned white as he entered the house. She ran and wrapped one of his arms around her shoulders, leading him to his mat, where he slumped in exhaustion.

"It's my back and shoulder, Immah," he grunted.

"This is going to hurt, Yeshua," Sarai warned, "But try not to make a noise." Sarai quickly tugged off Yeshua's tunic and he could hear her suck in a breath.

"Why do you keep doing this?" Yeshua could hear the anger in his immah's whisper as she dipped a cloth in an urn of water and began cleaning his wounds.

It was a familiar question, and Yeshua was weary of the inevitable conversation that always followed. He gritted his teeth as the cool cloth touched his injured arm, biting back a curse.

"You know why, Immah," he began.

"You always say that it's because of what the Romans did to your abba and Tobias, but I don't believe that, Yeshua. If you really wanted to honor your abba, you would have continued down the path of becoming a rabbi. That was what your abba wanted for you."

Yeshua clenched his teeth against the white-hot pain in his back.

"You weren't there that day, Immah. You didn't see what I did. Abba died because of the Roman occupation of our land. And more of our people will keep dying as long as they are here. Don't you care about Deborah and Tobias?"

"Yes, yes, yes," Sarai dismissed Yeshua's words, "You always say the same thing. But do you really know what I think, Yeshua? I think that you *want* to be angry. Yes, the Romans stole Bin-yamin from us, and they beat Tobias. Those are terrible things. But violence begets violence. When will it end? Have you thought to ask Adonai what He thinks of your actions? Maybe you don't even believe in Adonai anymore, I don't know. You are not who you once were." Her tone softened, "Please return to the man Adonai created you to be, Yeshua," she pleaded.

Yeshua pushed himself up from his mat and spun around, ignoring the searing pain across his back. "Don't you dare tell me what I feel or why I am doing what I am doing," he heard his voice, deep and harsh.

"Sssshhhh!" Sarai gestured to Deborah and Tobias, who were asleep on their mats. Her eyes shone with fear.

"I don't need this," Yeshua snatched up his tunic and mat to leave and then forced himself to turn.

"Immah, I know you believe the rabbi is the Mashiach," he said quietly, "But I don't. The Anointed One is to return our land into our hands. He is to remove our enemies and make Israel a great power again. Do you see your Jesus doing any of these things? The man teaches peace! How could he possibly usher in freedom from the Roman occupation?"

Miriam listened quietly until Yeshua stopped speaking.

"Oh Yeshua," she spoke quietly, but he could hear strength in her voice. "You're forgetting the other prophecies. The ones that speak of our Savior's death and future return. Just because the Mashiach isn't fulfilling your expectations, don't be arrogant in thinking that you know the will of Adonai." Two tears traced their way down Sarai's face, "Please don't harden your heart to Him."

Yeshua turned and closed the door behind him, ignoring Sarai's quiet sobs.

XXIV

The murmuring crowd surrounding Shim'on and Yohanan grew louder.

"See? His own disciples can't heal," a Pharisee nearby ridiculed.

"I don't understand," Yohanan's brow furrowed, "We are commanding it out in the rabbi's name, but nothing is happening."

The boy on the ground shuddered weakly after yet another convulsion.

Shim'on felt his temper flare at the crowd. They were doing the best they could.

Suddenly, Jesus appeared at Shim'on's shoulder. "Why are you arguing with them?"

A man standing nearby stepped forward, "Rabbi, I brought my son so that you could heal him. He is possessed by an evil spirit that won't let him talk. Whenever this spirit takes hold of him, it throws him violently to the ground. Then he foams at the mouth and grinds his teeth and becomes rigid. So, I asked your disciples to cast out the evil spirit, but they couldn't do it."

Jesus looked at the crowd, "You people have no faith! When will you believe? Bring the boy to me." Shim'on saw sadness and compassion in the rabbi's eyes.

His abba put a protective arm around the boy and brought him to stand before Jesus. The rabbi appraised the scars covering the child, his sweat-streaked face, and the heaving of his tired breath. Before the man could explain anything more, the boy convulsed again and fell to the ground, rolling about and foaming at the mouth.

Jesus looked at the boy's abba with sadness. "How long has this been happening to him?"

"Since he was a little boy. The spirit often throws him into the fire or water, trying to kill him." The man raised his arms helplessly, "Have mercy on us, and help us, if you can."

"What do you mean, 'If I can'?" Jesus looked directly into the man's eyes, "Anything is possible when one believes."

Shim'on saw the man's face crumple, "I do believe, but help me overcome my unbelief!"

The boy convulsed on the ground, and Shim'on saw another crowd of people joining those already gathered, everyone clambering to see what was going on.

"Listen, you spirit that makes this boy unable to hear and speak. I command you to come out of this child and never enter him again!" Jesus spoke the words with power, and Shim'on watched as the boy shrieked and convulsed violently, then went terribly still. Moments passed, and Shim'on heard a voice in the crowd say, "He's dead."

Jesus reached a hand down to the child, and everyone was shocked to see the boy grasp it and stand. The astounded abba threw his arms around his son, as tears streamed down his face.

"Thank you, Rabbi!" Keeping his arms around his son, he led him to a house nearby.

Shim'on and Yohanan leaned toward Jesus and asked, "Why could we not cast it out?"

"Only prayer can drive out this kind," Jesus responded. Although Shim'on had watched Jesus perform hundreds, if not thousands, of miracles by now, he never failed to be amazed by the rabbi's power.

Leaving the town, Jesus led the disciples through Galilee. Unlike previous trips through the area, this time Jesus stayed away from the villages as much as possible, and Shim'on sensed that he wanted to spend time with his disciples, unattended by the crowds. Shim'on loved the opportunity to have more time alone with the rabbi. As they walked through open fields and farmland, Jesus continued to speak to the disciples in parables, teaching them about loving their neighbor, serving the poor and not judging one another.

The second day after they left Caesarea Philippi, they passed through a meadow. Shim'on and Yohanan walked on either side of Jesus with the rest of the disciples behind them. All around, the sounds of humming crickets and chattering birds filled the air, and a gentle wind brushed against the branches of the olive trees. It was beautiful and serene, and Shim'on was grateful to be away from the noise of the crowds that perpetually followed the rabbi.

"The Son of Man is going to be delivered into the hands of men, and they will kill him. And when he is killed, after three days he will rise," the rabbi announced.

Shim'on's heart fell. It was as if a dark cloud had passed over the sun. He and the other disciples continued walking. No one asked Jesus about his words.

The Zealots

It's because we don't understand, nor do we want to, Shim'on admitted to himself, falling slightly behind when Jude came alongside them and began conversing with Jesus.

"I don't understand why he keeps saying these things," Ya'aqov spoke from beside Shim'on.

"The people adore him; they don't want to kill him. They want him to be their king. So do I."

"I know," Shim'on responded, "I can't understand it either." He fingered the dagger strapped beneath his tunic.

 Three days later, the men came to Capernaum, where Jesus taught and performed many miracles. All seemed well, and the crowds hung on Jesus' every word. Shim'on savored the visits to his hometown because of the time he got to spend with Lydia. He enjoyed seeing his immah and brother too.

His wife's eyes shone as Shim'on detailed the rabbi's teachings and miracles for her, but her face fell when he told her about the rabbi's warnings regarding his impending death.

"I don't understand." Shim'on heard the emotion in Lydia's voice. "Why would he die? Who would kill him? He is sinless."

"I ask myself the same questions." Shim'on responded. He tried to convince himself that the rabbi's words were not about literal death. Pharisees and Sadducees were often among the crowds following Jesus, and they tried to trap Jesus in his words. As usual, Jesus refused to answer their manipulative questions. Shim'on had never seen a risk of physical violence from the religious leaders, but nevertheless, he and Cephas talked often about the rabbi's safety.

Shim'on watched as Jesus beckoned Cephas and two others of his favorite disciples into a nearby home. The rabbi treated all the disciples as brothers, and sometimes even as sons, but these three disciples, and especially Cephas, had a unique relationship with Jesus. He felt the familiar surge of envy. He, Shim'on bar Yitzchak, would protect Jesus if he was in danger. Perhaps then, Jesus would treat him differently.

 After three days in Capernaum, Jesus announced they would depart for Jerusalem the next day. The festival of Pesach was quickly approaching, and it was customary to arrive early to begin the purification rituals. That night, Shim'on spoke with his family as they ate the evening meal. As usual, his immah and Lydia cooked his favorite things when he was home.

The table was laden with soft rolled grape leaves stuffed with herbed rice and tangy olive oil. They were cooked in a lemony broth, the scent of which he happily inhaled, his mouth watering. He knew these specialties, along with the creamy chickpea sauce and eggplant, took hours for the women to make. Warm brown lehem and anchovies seasoned with salt completed the meal. The family bowed their heads as Shim'on thanked Adonai for the meal before them.

"When will you leave for Jerusalem?" Miriam asked, her eyes bright. Shim'on was thankful that his immah seemed happy again. He knew his immah still felt the loss of her husband, but Miriam had found new life by believing the words of Jesus. Shim'on was thankful his family shared a common faith in the rabbi.

"Tomorrow," he said, trying to hide the tension he felt. He tore a piece from the lehem on the table before him. Miriam, Lydia, and Hanoch would travel to Jerusalem to celebrate Pesach with other family members.

"What's wrong?" Miriam asked, concerned.

"This trip feels different," Shim'on replied hesitantly.

Lydia looked at him meaningfully and Hanoch noticed.

"What? What is it?" His brother asked, glancing between him and Lydia.

Shim'on spoke heavily, "The rabbi has been prophesying his death." Although he had spoken with Lydia of the rabbi's dark warnings, neither his immah nor brother had known until now.

"What!" Miriam was bewildered, "How could this be?"

"I don't understand it any better than you do. But I fear that going to Jerusalem now may not be wise." He continued, "The Pharisees and Sadducees have grown increasingly hostile toward him."

"But surely you can't expect him not to travel to the Holy City for Pesach?" Lydia said. "You must watch him closely, protect him."

Shim'on nodded. He tried to alleviate the anxiety etched on his wife's face. "I pray the rabbi's words are not literal."

"We will be praying, too." Miriam touched her son's arm with concern. Shim'on worried that he should not have shared the rabbi's prophecy with the women.

"It will be all right," Shim'on hugged his immah.

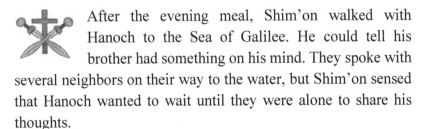 After the evening meal, Shim'on walked with Hanoch to the Sea of Galilee. He could tell his brother had something on his mind. They spoke with several neighbors on their way to the water, but Shim'on sensed that Hanoch wanted to wait until they were alone to share his thoughts.

"So, the rabbi speaks of his death often?" Hanoch asked after a few minutes.

Shim'on nodded. "More than I would like." He pulled himself over the boat's railing.

Hanoch grunted as he pushed the boat into the water, then swung himself aboard. The bow of the vessel dipped under his weight, then bobbed back to the surface.

"I don't like it."

"I don't either. But there's not much I can do. I haven't noticed any obvious threats to him."

"But you're watching closely." Hanoch looked at him. "Do you still carry your dagger with you?"

"Always." Shim'on patted the weapon that he kept hidden under his tallit.

"That's good." Hanoch nodded. "It's hard to believe Jesus has enemies."

"You haven't heard him speak to the Pharisees and Sadducees." Shim'on shook his head. "But even so, I find it hard to believe that they would go so far as to kill him."

The men worked in silence for the next several minutes, preparing the nets and allowing the wind to push the vessel into deeper waters.

"Brother, every day I'm grateful that you are no longer a Zealot." Hanoch said. "And I know the rabbi tells us to love our enemies. But please be careful." He spoke and his voice was gruff. "I don't know what I would do if I lost my brother too."

Shim'on placed a hand on his shoulder. "Don't worry, little brother. I'll be careful. Please take care of Immah and Lydia."

Shim'on knew that Adonai was with them. His son walked in their midst. But as he fished alongside his brother that night he wondered. Would everything really be all right?

XXV

Over time, the anger and hatred that Yeshua constantly felt developed deep, grasping roots. Usually, he could keep his feelings contained, but sometimes they exploded to the surface. Such as tonight.

Yeshua arrived at the Zealot meeting and entered into conversation with a recent recruit, a young man by the name of Erastus. The man had the nerve to ridicule his attack methods.

"I'm sorry," Erastus choked out behind the hand pinning him to the wall by his throat.

"How dare you criticize something you know nothing about?" Yeshua's eyes blazed.

"Let him go," Avi said sternly from behind Yeshua.

"You don't have the faintest idea how to swing a sword to kill a man," Yeshua sneered, his grip tightening on Erastus' throat.

"That's enough!" Avi gestured to Tova and Amos, who stood near Yeshua. The men wrestled Yeshua away from Erastus, who fell to the ground coughing.

Avi strode over to Yeshua and leaned in close to his face. "Don't you *dare* attack one of your brother Zealots again, do you hear me?" His face was low and filled with anger.

"You may be the best fighter we have, but we do not attack our own." He shoved Yeshua back into the circle of men surrounding them.

Yeshua looked at Erastus with contempt, and the young man kept his eyes down.

"Your attention, men," Avi addressed the Zealots. He waited until they grew quiet, then continued, "We have been given an unusual opportunity. We will join the Zealots in Jerusalem and the surrounding towns to mount an attack there during Pesach. I'm sure that almost all of you already plan to travel to the Holy City. We will camp together outside the city and then join the other Zealots to plan the attack. With the amount of people entering the city, the Roman army is bound to be kept busy and we will escape notice until it's too late."

The men murmured excitedly.

One asked, "How large is the Zealot presence in Jerusalem?"

Avi thought for a moment, "I would say that they number close to five-hundred."

Tova whistled.

"My contact in Jerusalem says we will attack at the city gates. That is where the most traffic in and out of the city is, and therefore, the greatest Roman presence aside from the soldiers' quarters themselves. As I said before, with so many people present in the city, I hope that our armed presence will not be as noticeable."

Yeshua's heart hammered in his chest at the news. Striking back at the Romans in the city where they stole his abba from him was almost too good to be true.

Avi continued, "We leave for Jerusalem in two days."

The men nodded and voiced their agreement.

Avi drew the sword hanging by his side, "For Adonai!" He stabbed the weapon in the air.

Yeshua raised his weapon with the others, "For Adonai!" he shouted. *And for you, Abba.*

XXVI

Shim'on arose early the morning they were to depart for Jerusalem. A sense of foreboding overshadowed him. He wanted to speak with the rabbi about it. As usual, Jesus had risen early to go into the hills to pray. Although Shim'on felt guilty interrupting the rabbi's time of prayer, he was desperate to ease the apprehension he felt about traveling to the Holy City.

He found Jesus sitting on a rocky hill overlooking the Sea of Galilee. The early morning dawn cast a soft pink and blue haze over the surrounding hills and water. Shim'on inhaled deeply. The air carried the promise of rain.

"*Boker Tov*, good morning, Shim'on." Jesus looked at him with a gentle smile.

"I'm sorry for interrupting, Rabbi, but I need to speak with you," Shim'on apologized.

"Would you like to sit?" Jesus gestured beside him, and Shim'on lowered himself to the ground. For several minutes, the men sat in silence and looked out over the sea. Fishing boats bobbed on the sea's surface. Seagulls flew across the water, their flight at once graceful and erratic as they occasionally dove for fish under the water's surface seen only by a trained eye.

"Rabbi, I'm concerned for you, about this trip to Jerusalem"–
Shim'on started hesitantly, breaking the silence.

"Do you not remember the prophecies, Shim'on?" Jesus
interrupted, looking out at the sea. "The time has come. I must
fulfill what my Abba wills for me."

"But Rabbi," Shim'on replied in desperation, "What is it that
your Abba wills for you? I don't understand!"

"Do you truly believe that I am who you say I am?" Jesus
looked at him.

"Of course, I do, Rabbi!"

"Shim'on, if you genuinely believed me to be who you say I
am, you would understand why I am going to Jerusalem. You
would understand everything that is to come. And you will," He
looked sadly at Shim'on as he stood.

"Come, it's time for us to go."

XXVII

Two nights after the meeting, the Zealots arrived outside the gates of Jerusalem. Many brought their families, but Sarai decided she and the children would caravan with other family members instead. Yeshua knew she did not trust him. Rather than talk to her, he pretended cool indifference when he left the family home.

The Zealots and their families planned to camp outside the city walls. Hundreds of thousands of pilgrims came to Jerusalem for the Pesach, filling every available lodging inside the city. As they traveled, the Zealots began to hear rumors of the rabbi and his disciples nearing the city as well. Jerusalem perched on a hill that rose above the surrounding valleys, and Avi and his men finally found a patch of available land to set up camp. They began unrolling rugs for tents and sleeping mats. Some collected wood to build fires.

Although most Hebrews traveled to Jerusalem for Pesach every year, for a limited few, this was their first time to see the Holy City. Yeshua remembered the feeling of excitement when he first saw Jerusalem. He felt a sharp pang of grief at the memory of coming here with his abba. For a fleeting moment, he wondered how Stephanas and his family were doing. Surely, they were excited for the rabbi's arrival. He had not spoken to Stephanas since that day in the temple courtyard over a year ago. The memories were still so painful that Yeshua pressed them aside. He tried to maintain focus on their purpose.

"When do we meet with the other Zealots?" Tova asked Avi.

"Once it's dark," Avi said, "So I would suggest eating and getting a few minutes of rest."

Yeshua and the other men complied. They and their families settled into the camp and pitched their tents. The women set out food they had brought from Capernaum, while the children amused themselves or played in groups.

Yeshua couldn't help but wonder what it was like for the Zealots' wives, who certainly knew what their men were planning to do. He was grateful he was not yet married. Yeshua knew his immah was upset by his departure, but despite her disagreement with his actions, she still prepared food for her son to bring. Yeshua was humbled by her kindness in response to his harsh and impatient treatment of her. He knew that she would attribute it to the rabbi. "Jesus says we are to love our enemies and pray for them. He says this is like heaping burning coals on their heads, Yeshua! Do you feel the heat?" She often teased him. He smiled, remembering. Although his actions hurt her, she continued to love him. He regretted leaving so callously.

Even though he didn't believe the man to be who his immah claimed, Yeshua couldn't deny that his impact on his immah's behavior was intriguing.

Hours later, Yeshua woke to Avi shaking him, "It's time to go."

Yeshua sat up and realized he had drifted off. Dusk had faded to darkness, but it wasn't quiet. Around them, the murmur of thousands of voices swelled, and Yeshua was again amazed by the sheer number of people surrounding the Zealots' camp.

The crowds were in a festive mood, enjoying the opportunity to spend time with friends and family and remember the extraordinary event that Pesach marked. For a moment, Yeshua wished that he could join in with them and leave behind the violence and bloodshed. *Don't be so foolish*, he chided himself.

Avi and several of the other men lit torches, and the group of Zealots threaded their way across the valley amongst travelers setting up their tents. Finally, they reached the outskirts of the camps, and Avi led them toward a grove of olive trees at the entrance to a narrow valley.

Yeshua heard the murmur of voices as they neared the copse, and the men were stunned to see an army of more than seven-hundred Zealots seated or standing.

"Welcome," a tall man with a deep voice greeted them, "From where have you come?"

"Capernaum," Avi answered.

The man nodded, "Welcome," he said again, "I am Reuben, the leader of the Zealots in Jerusalem. We are pleased that you are here."

Yeshua remained standing, while most of the others took a seat on the grassy ground.

Reuben clapped his hands once, and the hundreds of men silenced.

"Thank you all for joining us." He looked across the crowd of men and Yeshua saw a diverse range of ages represented.

"We all know why we're here," he said in a strong voice, "To protect our families and defend our homeland against the Romans who seek to destroy us." Yeshua liked the man already. "It is our duty and our honor to do this," he continued, "And I believe this attack will be our greatest achievement yet." He glanced into the faces around him. "I am thankful all of you are here, and your service brings honor to Adonai."

Yeshua could hear the dissenting voice of his immah in the back of his mind. "Some of you have likely never been to Jerusalem before, but that will not inhibit your ability to fight well in this attack. I have tasked thirty of my best fighters," He gestured for the men to rise, "to provide details of our plan and lead you in the attack. You will be divided into groups and the plan will be outlined for you then." He signaled the leaders to divide the men up at will.

"The men from Capernaum," a tall, lean man approached them leading a group of around seventy-five, "Over here. You will join ours from Bethlehem."

The tall man, who introduced himself as Achaicus, explained the plan. The attack would take place in approximately three days at the busiest of the city gates, where the most Roman soldiers would be posted. Achaicus described the position of the guards, protocols the Romans demanded be followed as travelers entered the city, and how the men would know to begin the attack.

"As soon as half of our number are inside the gates, the other half will be about to enter. At that point Reuben will shout, and every man will attack. So be aware of the soldiers and Roman presence around you." Achaicus glanced around him. "I know that you have all been in battle, but this attack will be different for many of you than what you have done before. This will be hand-to-hand combat in a densely packed area."

He continued, "Reuben will shout again when it's time to clear out of the area. Run in different directions. It will be difficult not to run together due to our size but do your best to keep a low profile. The entire Roman guard will be looking for us." He chuckled, "But by then we will have disappeared."

XXVIII

The sense of foreboding Shim'on felt increased as they neared Jerusalem. It was mid-morning as they and the crowd surrounding them neared Bethphage, only hours from Jerusalem.

"I don't feel good about this," Cephas walked beside him.

"Neither do I."

Bethphage was a pretty town on the crest of a hill. To the west of the city lay a valley, and beyond it, Shim'on could see the city walls and surrounding neighborhoods of Jerusalem.

Despite the number of times Shim'on had seen the Holy City, he was still awed by its beauty, crowned by the gleaming limestone temple.

"Yohanan, Yehudah," Jesus called to a couple of the disciples.

"Look at all the people camped outside the city!" Cephas pointed toward the hills that sloped below Jerusalem. "There are so many!"

Yohanan and Yehudah strode by the other disciples as they viewed the city below.

"Where are you going?" Shim'on asked.

"Jesus told us to go into Bethphage. We're to find a donkey and her colt and bring them back."

"You're just supposed to take them?"

Yohanan shrugged, "He said to tell anyone who asks, that 'the rabbi needs them' and they'll give them to us."

Yehudah, who stood nearby, grunted skeptically. "Certainly. I'm sure that any reasonable man would be willing to give up his donkey and colt to such a response."

The men entered the city and returned shortly with the animals. Shim'on couldn't help flashing a grin at Yehudah. The disciple shook his head, incredulous.

Shim'on quickly took off his cloak and spread it on the back of the colt, "Here, Rabbi."

Jesus climbed atop the animal, and suddenly Shim'on remembered the words of the navi Zechariah: "Say to the daughter of Zion, 'Behold, your king is coming to you, humble, and mounted on a donkey, on a colt, the foal of a beast of burden'."

Shim'on was filled with wonder at the prophecy. Jesus was their king. Certainly, he was not crowned as such yet, but clearly it was to come. The people loved him. They expected him to announce his rule any day. Surely the rabbi would give in to their pleas soon and rescue them from the Roman oppression.

Shim'on turned to walk behind Jesus as the colt made its way into Bethphage.

"Cephas!" He turned to his friend, "Perhaps we've had this all wrong!" He reminded Cephas of the prophecy.

"Maybe his purpose in coming to Jerusalem is not just for Pesach. Maybe he has come to the Holy City to be crowned king as well!"

Cephas' face lit with hope and then fell. "But what of the other prophecies Jesus has told us concerning himself?"

Shim'on paused, "I'm not sure about those, but I don't think the navi Zechariah mentions anything about the rabbi being killed. I don't know." He decided not to say anything about the navi Isaiah's prophecies, still hoping they had nothing to do with Jesus.

"Well, I hope you are right. What are the crowds saying?"

The men listened to the swell of voices joining together.

"Blessed is he who comes in the name of the Lord!"

"*Hosanna!*"

Shim'on realized that the ground beneath their feet was littered with the peoples' cloaks and branches from the surrounding date palms they had laid before the rabbi. Their personal tributes lauded the rabbi as the people's Lord above all others. Their belief became an infectious noise, the highest One Who would save them.

"They're worshipping him!" Cephas said, though Shim'on could barely hear his voice over the shouts. He was thankful the rabbi rode the colt as the crowd pressed in around them tightly and he and the others were swept along by the tide of people.

This is incredible, he thought, *I've never before seen so many people. And all of them worship the rabbi! Surely, he will fulfill the prophecies and take his rightful throne as the Mashiach!* Filled with joy, Shim'on joined the crowds shouting, "Hosanna, save us!"

A group of Pharisees pushed their way toward Jesus. Shim'on heard one shout, "Teacher, rebuke your followers for saying things like that!"

Shim'on turned toward them hotly. Before he could retort, the rabbi spoke.

"If they kept quiet, the stones along the road would burst into cheers!" The rabbi's face was stern but did not reveal any pride. The religious leaders muttered to one another in disgust.

He turned to look out upon Jerusalem and Shim'on was surprised to see tears trickle down his cheeks as he continued, "I wish that all of you would understand the way to peace. But it is too late now. Before long, your enemies will crush you and your children into the ground. Nothing will be left because you did not recognize when Adonai visited you."

Shim'on assumed that Jesus was speaking of Jerusalem as a city. The rabbi's words were dark considering the joyous celebration around them.

The river of men, women, and children swept down the hillside and up the road leading to Jerusalem's eastern gate, also known as *Sha'ar Harahamim*, the Gate of Mercy. As they approached the city, Shim'on saw many of those camping outside approach the procession with curiosity.

"Who is this?" Shim'on heard one man ask another.

"The navi Jesus, from Nazareth of Galilee." He heard the man respond.

Soon, Jesus, the disciples, and crowds passed through the gates. The Roman guards looked on in bewilderment. The people continued praising the name of Jesus as he walked along the streets to the temple.

Passing some Pharisees, Shim'on heard one say "You see, all of our attempts have failed. Look," the man gestured toward the crowds, "The world has gone after him."

Soon, the temple rose before them. Though they had all seen it before, the disciples were still awed by the size and beauty of it. Massive blocks of limestone created the walls and pavement around the large building. Masses of people surrounded them.

"This is why Adonai dwells here!" Cephas said in awe, looking up at the magnificent architecture of the building and surrounding courtyard.

Shim'on heard the cooing of doves, braying of goats, and bellowing of calves sold for sacrifice inside the temple courtyard. The characteristic smells of roasting meat and burning grain mixed with the metallic scent of blood drifting in the air around them.

Shim'on stood nearby as Jesus dismounted the colt. He approached the tables of the moneychangers and merchants selling the sacrifices with a look of anger.

"What's wrong?" Toma leaned over to Shim'on.

"I don't know." The disciples followed Jesus.

Goats, sheep, and bulls surrounded the tables of the moneychangers and livestock merchants as they completed transactions with those wishing to offer sacrifices. Many travelers came to Jerusalem from other regions, and they needed to exchange their money for the local currency to purchase sacrifices. It was common knowledge that the moneychangers were less than honest. Most were related to the high priest's family, and corrupt. They over-charged customers for their services and kept generous portions of the profit for themselves rather than distributing them amongst the poorer priests. Unfortunately, however, there was no other option for purchasing sacrificial animals, unless one happened to be a farmer and raised his own offerings. Even then, the sacrificial animals had to pass rigorous standards to be acceptable as offerings. Bags of coins were heaped on the tables, and animal refuse littered the yellowish-white stone ground around them.

The rabbi strode toward the livestock dealers. A leather whip used for goading the animals lay on the table, and Jesus took it in hand and spun toward the crowd pressing in around him to purchase their sacrifices. Suddenly, he cried out, "The Nevi'im declare, 'My Temple will be called a house of prayer for all nations,' but you have turned it into a lair for thieves." Everyone, including the surrounding chief priests and scribes, turned to look at him in surprise.

Jesus strode forward and seized the edge of a table holding bags of money. Wrenching the table upward, he flipped it. Shim'on watched as glittering gold, silver, and bronze coins flew into the air and then fell to the pavement. Those nearby fell to their knees, trying to snatch up what they could. The moneychangers leapt up in shock as Jesus continued to overturn each table. He cracked the leather whip, forcing the merchants and their customers to flee. The goats and sheep bleated in alarm, broke their tethers, and ran from the temple grounds. The doves ruffled their feathers in panic within their wooden cages. The scene fell to chaos, and Shim'on and the other disciples looked on with stunned surprise.

Priests and scribes ran from the temple, their faces hardened in rage as Jesus forced the merchants to pursue their fleeing livestock and evacuate the temple courtyard. Shim'on worried anew what they might do to silence the rabbi. As authorities at the temple, they received a portion of the merchants' profits, and their fury toward the rabbi for interfering in their earnings was evident. Jesus dropped the whip. The rabbi stood boldly before the wreckage of the market, his eyes bright and filled with passion. Shim'on knew that the priests and scribes were incensed by the rabbi's actions, but they had a massive audience and didn't want to risk the rabbi humiliating them further in front of the people.

During the tension, Shim'on heard a voice above the crowd, "Jesus, Son of David, have mercy on me!" A man cried out.

Other voices joined him with their own pleas for healing. They flocked around Jesus, shoving the priests and scribes out of the way. Shim'on knew the rabbi's words and actions were incendiary, but he felt a sense of pride. His rabbi, the Mashiach, had defied the religious leaders in an extremely public manner, exposing their corruption.

But Shim'on knew the Sanhedrin would not passively accept such treatment. Their tempers were being tested, and he worried what would happen when they reached their boiling point.

Yeshua

XXIX

The morning of the attack dawned darkly with a heavy rain descending upon the Holy City.

"Perfect," Yeshua said sarcastically, wringing out his cloak which had collected the rainfall overnight. Still, netilat yadayim and his morning prayer must be attended to, and Yeshua walked in search of a slightly less populated area. After several minutes, he realized his search was pointless. So many people camped around them that finding a quiet area was near to impossible. He gave up and stepped beneath an olive tree, which sheltered him somewhat from the elements. Nearby, several other men stood, their tallits draped over their heads and their eyes closed, deep in prayer.

Despite turning from his training as a rabbi to pursue the life of a Zealot, Yeshua was still committed to keeping the law as best as he could.

Perhaps it was due to the anticipated events of the day, or the gloomy weather, but Yeshua's heart was heavy. Returning to the Holy City prompted fresh memories of his abba and that terrible day on the Temple Mount to spread their icy fingertips over his heart.

"I offer thanks to You, living and eternal King, for You have mercifully restored my soul within me; Your faithfulness is great." Yeshua murmured. He bent his head, so that his tallit shadowed his face. "Adonai forgive me for the sin I commit." He whispered the words, then continued silently outside the lines of his usual morning prayer. *I know that You say not to murder, but You know why I do these things. Are they not justified by our purpose?*

The air was silent but for the murmurs of the men around him.

"I miss him every day. Yeshua allowed the wall around his heart to fissure, *But You let him die. Why?*

The pewter sky above echoed his feelings.

Where are You?

I am not in death or vengeance. Yeshua started, not sure if the words came from within or outside of him. He glanced around, but the other men were engaged in their own prayers. He bent his head again.

Well then, where are you?

I am always with you, Yeshua. I love you. Look to the rabbi from Nazareth.

Once again Yeshua glanced around to see if anyone else had heard the words. Apparently not. The rabbi from Nazareth? Yeshua's defenses rose. Although his abba and immah fully believed Jesus to be the Son of Adonai, Yeshua still believed him to be a heretic.

He pulled the tallit from his head and draped it over his shoulders, walking back toward camp. His heart was deeply troubled and the memories of his last day with his abba saturated his mind like the drizzling rain. He couldn't forget the voice he had heard in his morning prayers, nor could he consider turning back from the mission before him. Never had Adonai spoken to him as He had this morning, however. The mental battle tugged back and forth in his mind, and he was deeply unsettled.

"Yeshua, did you hear me?" Tova looked at him, puzzled.

"What?" Yeshua looked at the man standing in front of him.

"Where were you? I said that we're clearing out in an hour. Eat and get ready."

 The rain did not abate by the time the Zealots broke camp. If anything, it came down harder, soaking the people outside the city and making the roads muddy. Yeshua felt as though Adonai were sending them a sign, and his shoulders sagged under the burden.

I have to follow through with this, Adonai. How could I turn back now? There was no answer to his question, and Yeshua couldn't help but remember the words he had heard earlier. *I am not in death or vengeance.*

The other Zealots noticed the lack of Yeshua's usual bravado and teased him.

"Is this because you're not the only champion here?" Jerome clapped him on the shoulder.

"Don't worry, Brother, all of us know how to fight. We'll make your abba proud."

Yeshua could no longer resist the truth that had pounded on his heart for the past year. Bin-yamin would be anything but proud if he could see him now. He had never advocated for violence. The thought discouraged Yeshua further.

Despite the weather, the crowds flowed up the road before them and into the city gates like floodwaters defying gravity.

"Get ready, men," Reuben said quietly as he slipped through the Zealots toward the front.

Yeshua shook his head to dispel the thoughts burdening his mind and fingered the sword strapped to his side beneath his tunic. His hands and tunic were slick with the rain. Fortunately, the leather strips he wrapped around the sword's hilt for grip were dry. Rain drenched the tallit draped over his head and collected at its peak, dripping into his eyes.

The city gate arched approximately twenty yards in front of him. From the looks of it, he and the Zealots from Capernaum would be among the second group to enter. Achaicus appeared at his elbow and spoke in a low voice to the men gathered around them.

"Listen for Reuben's shout. As soon as you hear it, attack. For Judea! For Adonai!"

"For Judea, for Adonai!" the men repeated in hushed voices.

Yeshua could feel the energy crackling in the air. Hundreds of travelers flowed and merged around him. He hoped they would stay out of the way once the attack started. Previously, he wouldn't have cared about striking down innocent civilians who got in his way, but the actions he'd justified for too long were finally catching up with him. Yeshua craned his neck, straining to see Reuben, but there were too many people to identify him. Ten to fifteen vaguely interested Roman soldiers stood on either side of the gates. Despite their bored looks, Yeshua knew they would come to attention quickly if they noted anything suspicious.

"There's at least three more on horseback," Achaicus whispered, pointing behind the guards, "Probably more that we can't see."

The air was filled with the sound of rain thrumming down on the people and the loud hum of voices. Suddenly, Yeshua heard a shout.

"That's it!" Achaicus yelled, joining the shouts of the other Zealots who pushed their way through the confused people and rushed toward the city gates. Yeshua quickly unsheathed his sword and joined them, the blade ready in his hand. Two Roman soldiers stood confusedly over the bodies of three of their comrades.

"For Judea!" Achaicus shrieked, stabbing his dagger toward the leg of one. The other soldier quickly spun toward him. Yeshua deflected the man's blade with his own. The soldier yelled in frustration and took a step back from Yeshua.

"Filthy rebel!" he shouted, leaning forward, and stabbing expertly at Yeshua with his sword.

Yeshua felt a sting and then warmth spread down his shoulder.

"Ha, you all bleed like pigs!" The man's face twisted in an ugly smile as he raised his sword in front of him.

Yeshua stepped forward, then dodged to the left as the man lunged at him again, throwing him off balance. Quickly he spun and surged forward with his sword, driving it deep into the man's neck. The soldier's face went white and he fell to the ground with a groan. Muscle memory and survival instinct drove Yeshua forward.

All around him, Zealots fought with Roman soldiers. As soon as the attack had begun, the people around them panicked. Yeshua was thrown forward by a terrified group of women trying to flee. Suddenly, Yeshua saw an auxiliary soldier on horseback across the courtyard surrounded by five or six others, all engaged in combat. Auxiliaries were not Roman citizens, but they had sworn their loyalty to the emperor in exchange for Roman benefits. Many of them were even better soldiers than the legionaries and specialized in different types of combat. His heart fell. An auxiliary on horseback was five times more dangerous than a legionary on foot. The soldier on horseback urged the steed toward Yeshua and the other Zealots around him. He sliced back and forth on either side of the animal, not caring whether his blade struck insurrectionist or innocent. Yeshua was sickened to see bloodied bodies of men, women and children littering the stone pavement. Yet he, too, had taken the lives of innocent people if they stood in the way of killing a Roman. How had he never seen the sin in his own actions?

I am not in death or vengeance.

The soldier urged his horse into a trot, baring his teeth in a scowl as he locked eyes with Yeshua. Yeshua also began to run, his sword ready in his hand. The steed drew nearer, until Yeshua could see the whites of its eyes and the foam on its muzzle. He ducked as the auxiliary's sword swung down, and he quickly sliced his own up and across, cutting at the man's exposed leg.

The man screamed in pain, jerking the horse around. Blood dripped from his leg onto the steed's side. Again, he prompted the animal into a trot, and once again, Yeshua ducked, striking now at the man's other leg. Bloodied and in pain, the soldier was enraged. Yeshua was prepared to try to pull the man from his horse, when he heard a cry from behind.

Instead of Reuben, however, Yeshua saw Achaicus.

"Run!" Achaicus' eyes were wide and white-rimmed. "There are too many!"

Before Yeshua could absorb Achaicus' words, two-hundred armored auxiliary soldiers on horseback entered the courtyard. To his dismay, he saw more Roman foot soldiers behind them. The people screamed in fresh panic as the metal clad soldiers began cutting down anyone standing in their way. Yeshua glanced around, shocked to see most of the seven-hundred

Zealots either dead or fleeing. Yeshua recognized many familiar bodies lying under the ashen sky, among them Amos and Tova.

"You, scum!" Yeshua looked up to see a Roman legionary leading three others. The soldiers ran toward him with swords drawn.

He was suddenly terrified. Never had the odds been so stacked against him. Straight ahead lay the main street in Jerusalem, but it was blocked by hordes of soldiers. To his left lay a wet and puddled alleyway, but from previous experience Yeshua knew it led to a dead end. To his right—it was the only option. Yeshua sheathed his sword at his side and dashed across the stone pavement, skidding on the slippery stones. If he could make it to the temple, he stood a chance of blending in with the crowds. If not, well, he would join his abba in death.

The rain made it difficult for Yeshua to stay on his feet and he hoped the soldiers had the same problem, though he could hear their yells behind him, too close for comfort. He rounded a corner. Too late, he saw a merchant pushing a cart filled with produce across the street. Unable to stop, he crashed into the cart, causing it to overturn and fruit and vegetables to spill everywhere.

"Sorry!" he shouted over his shoulder, scrambling to keep from falling. He heard the merchant curse at him and hoped the debris in the road would slow his pursuers down.

It had been a while since he was in the Holy City, and Yeshua tried to get his bearings. He wiped the rain from his eyes. Wasn't there a set of stairs to the temple around the next bend in the street?

Rounding the curve, Yeshua was disheartened to see that he must have remembered incorrectly. The streets in Jerusalem were only wide enough for a donkey-drawn cart and edged with homes and businesses. People were packed tightly into the narrow thoroughfare.

"Stop him!" Yeshua glanced behind in dismay and saw the four soldiers rapidly approaching.

He increased his pace, threading his way through the crowds. Fortunately for him, no one cared about the disheveled and bloody young man in their midst, instead focused on their own business.

There it was! Yeshua could see the stairs to the temple. He had been off by a couple of city blocks. He leapt up the steps, but not before one of the soldiers came into view.

"You! Stop!" the soldier shouted at Yeshua just before he lost sight of him.

He didn't have much time. Yeshua took the stairs in sets of two, trying not to shove those he passed.

"Stop that man!" Yeshua could hear the shouts of the soldiers behind him. He reached the top of the stairs but didn't stop running. The temple courtyard was crowded as he had expected, and Yeshua darted among the people, trying to get close to the courtyard entrance. He didn't know how far the soldiers were behind him, but he didn't dare look. Suddenly, a young girl stepped directly into Yeshua's path, and he skidded on the pavement, trying not to collide with her. His feet scrambled to find traction on the limestone beneath him, but it was no use. Yeshua fell hard, the impact knocking the breath out of him. Dazed, he looked up into the rain.

"Yeshua?" A familiar face floated above him.

"Shim'on?"

Then the soldiers arrived.

Shim'on

XXX

"Wait, where are you taking him? What did he do?" Shim'on protested as two Roman soldiers yanked Yeshua to his feet.

"Shim'on?" Yeshua looked at him bleary-eyed.

"He was part of a Zealot uprising," One of the legionaries said gruffly, tying Yeshua's hands behind him with a rough rope.

Yeshua's eyes looked unfocused and Shim'on saw blood trickle from a wound to his head.

"Walk!" A soldier shoved Yeshua harshly toward the gates leading to the Temple Mount.

"Was that who I thought it was? Yeshua bar Abba?" Cephas appeared at his elbow.

"Yes," Shim'on said, "The soldiers said he is a Zealot."

"What?" Cephas uttered a short laugh, "The son of a rabbi, a Zealot? There must be a mistake."

"My immah told me that Bin-yamin was killed in an attack here over a year ago," Shim'on told him.

"I didn't realize," Cephas murmured. "I'm sorry to hear that." He continued, "It pains me to say it, but if he's been taken to the Roman prison, there's nothing we can do for him."

Shim'on knew he was right. The past had come rushing back as soon as he saw Yeshua. He remembered the anger he had harbored against his old friend and realized that it was no more. Yeshua had tried to help in the wake of his abba's loss, but Shim'on's vision had been clouded by grief. Together, he and Cephas walked toward where the rabbi sat on the temple steps, teaching the people.

Shim'on couldn't stop thinking about Yeshua. If only he could have introduced Yeshua to the rabbi. Perhaps then his friend's life would have been changed as radically as his own and spared death at the hands of Rome.

 It had been six days since Jesus and his disciples first arrived in Jerusalem. The rabbi taught in the temple every day, and each night they returned to Bethany, where they stayed at the home of Miryam, Martha, and Lazarus. The Pharisees and Sadducees continued to find fault with the rabbi, but neither Shim'on nor any of the other disciples noted any particularly alarming developments.

Tonight Jesus spoke to them as they prepared to leave the city. Shim'on noticed that he looked more exhausted of late. Dark shadows underlined his eyes, and Shim'on wished the rabbi would take a day away from the crowds to rest.

"You all know that in two days Pesach is coming. At that time, the Son of Man will be delivered up to be crucified."

Shocked cries sprang up among the disciples, and Shim'on gasped. Again, the men were afraid to ask the rabbi what he meant by these words, but they formed small groups as they followed him out of the city.

"Crucifixion?" Yohanan's face was troubled, "This is the first time he has spoken so specifically about his manner of death."

Shim'on shuddered. Everyone knew what crucifixion was. No traveler or resident of the Holy City could avoid seeing the men hanging on crosses as they entered and exited the city. As a Zealot, he had come to terms with the very real possibility that his life might end by this horrific, Roman-devised punishment. The processions of prisoners labeled as criminals by Rome were commonplace, as they carried their crosses to Golgotha, the hill named after a skull.

"It's the worst invention the Romans can muster," Ya'aqov said, "But why would the rabbi die by crucifixion? What could possibly cause such a thing to happen? He is without sin!"

The men looked at one another in confusion, deeply shaken.

Soon they reached the home of Lazarus, Miryam, and Martha. Time spent with their friends was always a welcome respite for Jesus and the disciples, but tonight Shim'on felt troubled and discouraged. He wished he could talk to Lydia. Her relationship with Adonai was unique, and she always encouraged him by sharing what Adonai revealed to her. He missed his wife. He left the other disciples and walked outside the house.

"My friend! It's good to see you!" Lazarus saw him and smiled, throwing his arms around Shim'on.

"And you too," Shim'on forced himself to smile.

Lazarus sobered. "I sense something is wrong."

"The rabbi has been prophesying his death," Shim'on felt relieved to unburden himself to his friend. "I don't understand him. I don't know what to do."

Lazarus nodded somberly, and Shim'on was surprised the man wasn't taken aback by his words.

"Do you know something?" he asked Lazarus.

"My friend, you know that I died just a few short months ago." He grinned wryly. "But I was in..." he gazed into the distance, then continued, a slight smile on his face, "Paradise.

Before the rabbi brought me back to life here. I saw things while I was there"–He paused. "I saw how it ends."

"What do you mean, 'how it ends'? What did you see, Lazarus?" Shim'on desperately wanted to understand. "What do you know?"

"That I can't tell you, my friend," Lazarus shook his head, "Because he told me not to. But I can tell you not to fear. It is a dark time, but he will make all things perfect."

Shim'on just stared at Lazarus. He felt a mixture of anger and reassurance in response to the man's words. Just then, Martha called out that the evening meal was ready. Lazarus gripped his shoulder and ushered him into the house. "It will be all right, Brother, you'll see."

 Always the entertainer, Lazarus loved to regale whoever would listen with the story of Jesus raising him from the dead. Soon Jesus, the disciples, and the other male friends of the family reclined around the table. They listened to Lazarus' stories while they enjoyed a hearty meal of roast lamb, buttery kugel, and lehem with various dipping sauces and wine. Even Shim'on was enjoying himself, distracted from his worries.

Suddenly, a woman appeared, a scarf draped over her dark hair. In her hands, she held an alabaster flask.

The woman haltingly approached the rabbi. When the light from the oil lamps illuminated her face, Shim'on realized that it was Miryam, Lazarus' sister.

The woman haltingly approached the rabbi with the jar, tears streaming down her cheeks.

"What's going on?" Toma whispered to Shim'on. The other men around the table looked equally confused. It was highly unusual for a woman to appear at such a meal, unless she was serving food.

Miryam stood for a moment before Jesus. Looking into his eyes, she lifted the bottle and brought it back down forcefully against the dirt floor. The flask cracked open. Pure nard, an expensive ointment, trickled into Miryam's hands.

Gasps and judgmental whispers filled the room. Yehudah muttered, "Why was this ointment not sold for three-hundred denarii and given to the poor?"

Quickly, Miryam soaked the ends of her waist-length hair in the rich ointment. She continued to cry as she wiped the rabbi's head and feet with her hair.

The guests watched in shock. The room was soon filled with the oil's spicy, sweet scent.

Interrupting the whispering voices, Jesus looked around the room at the guests lining the table. "Leave her alone." He looked pointedly at the disciples. "Why criticize her for doing such a good thing to me?" Shim'on noticed Jesus' eyes resting on Yehudah. The disciple flushed crimson.

"You will always have the poor among you, and you can help them whenever you want. But you will not always have me. She has done what she could and has anointed my body for burial ahead of time. Wherever the Good News is preached throughout the world, her deed will be remembered and discussed."

Once more, the room filled with murmurs as the rabbi mentioned his burial. Shim'on noticed that Lazarus looked sad, but not surprised.

"This must not happen." Jude looked soberly at Shim'on from across the table.

Cephas leaned in. "The rabbi is clearly the Mashiach. Why does he wait to take his rightful throne as our king? The people want it. We want it. What is he waiting for? And why this talk of death?"

Shim'on agreed with them and yet he, too, could not answer. Clearly, Miryam, like Lazarus, knew something they did not. His heart was heavy with the rabbi's words. The sight of his former best friend being arrested earlier that afternoon also grieved him. Yeshua had looked depleted, empty. That was the only way Shim'on could describe his friend's hopeless eyes and the vulnerability that had surrounded him in the temple courtyard.

He longed to help him, but it was impossible. Now he could only pray that his friend be spared a Roman death, that of crucifixion. But he refused to let such a fate befall the Mashiach.

 The close-knit group spent the next day at the temple, where the rabbi taught the hundreds that surrounded him and healed the sick, lame, and blind. Shim'on kept watch for any threats to the rabbi but saw nothing unusual. Jesus didn't mention his forthcoming death again, and Shim'on observed very few Pharisees and Sadducees in the audience listening to the rabbi. *Maybe they have finally decided to leave him alone*, he thought.

 The morning of the Pesach, Ya'aqov and Yohanan approached the rabbi.

"Where will you have us prepare for you to eat the Pesach meal?" they asked.

The rabbi replied, "As you go into the city, you'll meet a man carrying a pitcher of water. Follow him. At the house he enters, say to the owner, 'The rabbi asks, where is the guest room for me to eat the Pesach meal with my disciples?' He will take you upstairs to a large room that is already set up. That is where you should prepare our meal."

Ya'aqov and Yohanan departed with the message and sent word when they found the house.

Shim'on never ceased to be amazed when the rabbi's words were fulfilled. The disciples spent the day preparing the meal, and later that night they celebrated the beginning of Pesach with the rabbi. Shim'on thought of his immah, Lydia, and Hanoch. Where were they eating the Pesach meal tonight? Oil lamps flickered around the room as Jesus led the disciples in the meal. The men took turns drinking from a cup of red wine after the rabbi performed *kaddesh* for a blessing.

He then led them in eating bitter herbs dipped in salt water, to remember the tears of their forefathers in Egypt as slaves. He spoke of the captivity in Egypt, reminding the disciples of what Adonai had done in freeing them from their captors and bringing them to the Promised Land. After that, the disciples enjoyed a meal consisting of gefilte fish, a tasty fish indiginous to the area, and soup with hearty balls of ground meal and egg bobbing in a steaming, savory broth.

The disciples talked and laughed together, reminiscing how each of them had met and been called by Jesus. Shim'on tried to push his worries to the back of his mind, but he couldn't help noticing that the rabbi seemed heavily burdened. Soon he found out why. Shattering the festive mood, Jesus spoke. "One of you will betray me."

Shim'on looked up from his plate in disbelief. "What?"

The men looked around the table at one another in shock, and Yohanan asked, "Is it I, Rabbi?"

Each of the men echoed Yohanan's question, until the rabbi signaled them to silence.

"It is one of you twelve who is eating from this bowl with me. For the Son of Man must die, as the navi declared long ago. But it will be terrible for the one who betrays him. It would be better for that man if he had never been born."

The rabbi's words stunned the men into silence once more. They were all eating from the same dishes, so it could be any one of them. Shim'on felt his heart pounding. Who here was going to betray Jesus? Everything in him wanted to stand and tell Jesus this would never happen. That he himself would never let such a thing happen. But he remembered when Cephas had said something similar, and how the rabbi had rebuked him. Glancing at Cephas, he remained silent, hands balled into fists with tension.

The rabbi lifted a piece of unleavened *matzah*, a bread to remind the peaceful of past suffering, and blessed it.

When he passed it to the disciples, he told them, "Take, eat; this is my body." The bewildered disciples each broke a piece from the wafer. Jesus then lifted the cup of dark red wine and gave thanks for it.

"This is my blood, which confirms the covenant between Adonai and his people. It is poured out as a sacrifice for many. I tell you the truth, I will not drink wine again until the day I drink it in the Kingdom of Adonai." The disciples were accustomed to the traditional joyous conclusion of the Pesach meal over matzah and wine, and this was not it. Jesus' words were confusing and foreboding.

He passed the cup around the group of disciples and each took a hesitant sip, trying to understand the rabbi's words. The bitter wine ran down Shim'on's throat.

Jesus began singing a familiar hymn, and the music filled the room where they sat. The rabbi's voice was deep and beautiful and Shim'on felt tears come to his eyes as he listened. Slowly, each of the disciples joined in. When the song was finished, the rabbi stood and walked out to a nearby hill, called the Mount of Olives. The twelve disciples somberly followed him, and Shim'on knew they were each contemplating Jesus' words.

The rabbi turned and looked around the group. His voice was sober, and his eyes were filled with sadness.

"You will all fall away because of me this night,"

Gasps of "No! Never, Rabbi!" filled the air.

Jesus continued, "It is written, 'I will strike the shepherd, and the sheep of the flock will be scattered.' But after I am raised up, I will go before you to Galilee."

Shim'on recognized the prophecy quoted from the navi Isaiah, but he refused to accept what the rabbi was saying.

"I will never leave you, Rabbi!" He said passionately.

Cephas stepped forward; his hands clenched into fists. "Though they all fall away because of you, I will never fall away."

The rabbi looked at Cephas with patient compassion. "Cephas, this very night, before the rooster crows twice, you will deny me three times."

Shim'on watched Cephas' face crumple at Jesus' words. He felt a ripple of fear. The men knew that Cephas was one of the rabbi's closest disciples. If Jesus said that even he was powerless against whatever was coming, what hope had any of them?

"Even if I must die with you, I will not deny you!" Cephas cried in desperation. The other disciples echoed the same. The rabbi just smiled sadly and began walking toward the Garden of Gethsemane, a beautiful area at the base of the hill filled with groves of olive trees. The disciples followed him in silence. Shim'on knew they were all reeling from the rabbi's words.

When they arrived at the garden, Jesus told the disciples to wait, but called Cephas, Ya'aqov, and Yohanan to follow him. Shim'on sank to the ground and dropped his head into his hands. A horrible premonition wrapped its dark fingers around his shoulders. Whatever was about to happen, he feared he would not be able to stop it. He felt sick.

The garden was cool and quiet, and a sweet-smelling breeze rustled the leaves of the olive trees. The rest of the disciples found places to sit nearby and immediately fell asleep. Shim'on wished he could join them in slumber, but anxiety kept his mind racing. He fingered the dagger strapped at his waist.

Hours passed and still Jesus did not return. It neared midnight, and Shim'on's eyes burned from exhaustion. Suddenly, his senses came alive. Flickering light from burning torches and murmuring voices approached the garden. He jumped to his feet.

"Wake up!" He hissed at the disciples. He glanced behind him and saw the rabbi.

"Rabbi! Quickly, we must go!"

The rabbi looked at him, and Shim'on would never forget his expression, a combination of fear and love.

"It's all right, Shim'on," he said. "This is the reason for which I have come." He turned to look at the disciples. "It's time. The Son of Man is betrayed into the hands of sinners," the rabbi continued, "Let's be going. My betrayer is here."

Shim'on was dismayed to see a large crowd, armed with swords and clubs, and carrying torches that lit up the cool green darkness of the garden. Why had he not heard them earlier? He cursed. Jesus began walking toward them.

Shim'on felt like screaming. "What is he doing?" He turned to Cephas.

His friend's eyes were bloodshot, and his face was pale. He stared at the mob wordlessly.

As the crowd came closer, Shim'on was shocked to see Yehudah, one of the disciples, at the head of the procession.

"Yehudah?" Shim'on stood, dumbfounded, as the man passed him without a glance and approached the rabbi.

"Greetings, Rabbi!" As was the custom when greeting a friend, Yehudah kissed the rabbi's cheek.

Jesus looked into Yehudah's eyes with sadness, "Friend, do what you came to do." With those words, the crowd sprang to life. Hands reached out for the rabbi, twisting his arms behind his back.

At this, Shim'on awoke from his stupor. He would not allow the rabbi to be taken without a fight. Pulling his dagger from its hiding place under his cloak, he intended to remove the head from the body of a young man gripping the rabbi's arm. But before he could act, Shim'on saw the torch light glance off Cephas' short sword. The man screamed and covered the side of his head with his hands. Cephas had cut the man's ear off.

"Put your sword back into its place." Jesus spoke sharply, and a sudden silence spread over the crowd. "Those who use the sword will die by the sword." Jesus turned to look at his disciples, and his eyes settled on Shim'on.

The familiar words caused him to drop his own dagger to the dirt with a thud. Jesus' voice softened as he continued to speak, his dark eyes filled with pain, yet peace, "Don't you realize that I could ask my Abba for thousands of angels to protect us, and He would send them instantly? But if I did, how would the prophecies be fulfilled that describe what must happen now?" Quietly, he turned to the young man and covered his bloody hand with his own.

The man stopped whimpering and tentatively released the side of his head. Gasps from those closest to the man erupted. The man's ear was fully healed.

Cephas' shoulders slumped. The rabbi looked around the gathering, "Am I some dangerous Zealot, that you come with swords and clubs to arrest me? Why didn't you arrest me in the temple? I was there teaching every day. But this is all happening to fulfill the words of the Nevi'im."

Shim'on stood, rooted in place. This couldn't be happening.

But it was. He noticed people in the crowd pointing at him and the other disciples. They were going to arrest them, too. The mob tightened their grip on Jesus and pushed him toward the city. How could Yehudah betray Jesus, the Mashiach? What was going to happen to the rabbi?

Fear rippled through him as he saw several men leave the crowd running toward him. Without another thought, Shim'on fled.

Yeshua

XXXI

Yeshua awoke, his head pounding. For several moments, he lay still, trying to figure out where he was. What was wrong with his head? He sat up and looked around. He was in a cell constructed of limestone walls. The ground beneath him was dirt. Yeshua put an unsteady hand to the back of his head and felt it come away sticky. He tried to see his hand in the smoky light from the torch flickering in the corridor outside his cell. Blood. He glanced down at his chest and saw streaks of crimson mixed with dirt covering his cream-colored tunic as well. His knees and shins burned, and Yeshua could see dried blood and bits of gravel ground into the skin. Yeshua winced, remembering. So, he was in a Roman prison inside Jerusalem. Well, this was the end, then.

Yeshua knew that any hope of surviving had disappeared the moment the soldiers arrested him at the temple. The Romans never showed mercy. But then, neither had he as a Zealot.

Yeshua thought over the events of the previous day and suddenly remembered Shim'on. Why was he there? Maybe he wasn't, Yeshua realized. He had a head injury; perhaps seeing Shim'on was just a figment of his imagination. He wasn't afraid of dying, but Yeshua wished he could have spoken with his old friend one more time. He would tell him that now he understood why he became a Zealot.

Trying to ignore the pounding in his head, Yeshua rose and walked toward the cell door. *Thunk.* He tripped and looked down at his feet. He was chained to the wall across from where he sat. Yeshua glanced at the ceiling above him. It wasn't stone, but instead looked to be a combination of palm branches and tar, which indicated he was above ground. There were no windows in the room, but Yeshua felt less claustrophobic knowing he wasn't being held underground. He lowered himself to the ground heavily.

His head hurt, so he closed his eyes. The painful throb felt like there was shouting in his head. He squinted his eyes open. Or were those voices?

As the walls around him were stone, whatever noise he heard came through the roof above him. The riotous noise swelled. He winced, the sound pounding his ears. What was going on out there?

XXXII

Shim'on woke behind a cluster of bushes in the Garden of Gethsemane. Immediately, shame—worse than he had ever known prior to meeting the rabbi—enveloped him and made it hard to breathe. He sat up and winced. Last night had been a nightmare.

Though Shim'on fled, two of his pursuers had caught up with him. The men beat him viciously, "a reward for following the heretic from Galilee," they yelled. Bloody and aching, Shim'on had limped his way back to the garden. He fell asleep with the silence of the empty garden echoing accusations.

Images of the rabbi being taken by the Pharisees and an angry mob—while he did nothing to stop them—kept waking him up. Once again, Cephas had proven to be the better disciple.

Shim'on peered about. Above the empty garden, a purple and pink sunrise lit the sky.

He had no idea where the other disciples were, or where the rabbi had been taken. He stood gingerly to his feet, swaying slightly, allowing spots to clear from his vision. Worse than any physical pain was the familiar weight resting on his chest and shoulders. His old friends, Guilt and Anger, were back.

The memory of the crowd grabbing Jesus and forcing the innocent rabbi's arms behind his back kindled in his mind. He

269

must find the rabbi. Shim'on didn't know if there was anything he could do to free him, but he had to try.

He spit on his hands and did his best to rub away the blood on his head and arms. His clothes were another matter. Shim'on could only hope that he would blend into the crowds entering the city and avoid the Roman soldiers' attention. He draped his tallit over his head and walked gingerly up the hill toward the city gates.

To his relief, he entered Jerusalem's walls without being questioned. Shim'on noticed the flow of people moving toward the praetorium, Governor Pontius Pilate's palace.

"Where is everyone going?" Shim'on touched the arm of an old man walking past him.

The man looked irritated but replied, "The rabbi from Nazareth was taken to Pilate to stand trial." Shrugging Shim'on's hand from his arm, the man pushed past him.

Shim'on felt his chest tighten. So, the Sanhedrin had finally found a way to get rid of Jesus, and they were going to let the Romans do their dirty work.

With thousands in and around the city for Pesach, the streets were filled. Limping, Shim'on joined the flood of people and soon arrived at the governor's opulent courtyard. The sight before him made him sick.

Jesus and the chief priests stood atop the stairs to the praetorium. Though he was a distance away, Shim'on could see the rabbi's tunic was stained with dirt and blood. His hands were tied behind his back and he looked as if he could collapse at any moment. But he held his head high, and Shim'on had the overwhelming thought that he was looking at a king.

Hundreds of spectators to Jesus' trial surrounded him. As he watched, Shim'on saw a red object hit Jesus' chest and burst.

More flying objects struck the rabbi and left their mark. The crowd pelted the rabbi with produce, rotten fish, and pebbles from the street. Anger surged through Shim'on. When a man standing nearby threw a rotten piece of fruit at the rabbi, Shim'on shoved him to the ground. The man's companions leapt forward in attack. Shim'on didn't care. It felt good to express his anger with blows.

"Quiet!" A man standing nearby snarled. "Pilate has arrived!" His attackers pushed Shim'on to the ground with a final shove. Shim'on struggled to his feet, wiping blood from his mouth. He strained to see as Pilate approached the rabbi and chief priests.

High Priest Caiphas stepped forward to meet the governor and the men spoke briefly. Shim'on watched as the rabbi was led to face Pilate. Shim'on couldn't see Jesus' face from where he stood. He wished he could hear the words being exchanged. After a few minutes of discussion, Pilate turned from the priests and faced the prisoner. The crowd surrounding Shim'on hushed.

"Are you the King of the Jews?" he asked, using the Gentile word for the Hebrews.

"You have said so," the rabbi responded.

Immediately, the chief priests began to accuse the rabbi of a variety of crimes. Pilate ignored them, keeping his eyes focused on Jesus.

"Have you no answer?" Pilate gestured toward the chief priests, "Do you hear all the charges they have brought against you?"

Once again, Shim'on held his breath and prayed that the rabbi would say something, anything. Instead, he was silent. Pilate looked incredulous.

"Ask Pilate to release a prisoner," Shim'on looked to his left at the voice. A young priest spoke to the crowd, moving from person to person. He said something else, but he was too far away for Shim'on to hear it.

"What is he doing?" Shim'on turned to the man beside him.

"You must not be from here," The man answered, "Every year at Pesach, Pilate releases to us any one prisoner whom we agree upon."

Shim'on's heart filled with hope. "So, they could release the rabbi!" He turned back toward Jesus.

"They could," The man responded, "but the chief priests are telling the people to ask for a man by the name of Barabbas."

Shim'on felt as if he'd been punched in the stomach. "Barabbas? Yeshua Barabbas?" The Romans had altered Yeshua's name to fit their language, but even so it was clearly recognizable.

"Yes, that's the one. A Zealot. He's been wanted for some time, and he was caught in an uprising yesterday. If he's not released, he'll be crucified as they all are. The Sanhedrin want him to go free and the Galilean to die."

Shim'on fought a wave of nausea. He squinted in the harsh morning light as sweat trickled down his back. It seemed wrong that the blue sky should be so beautiful on such a terrible day.

Pilate approached the platform to speak to the people. "Caiaphas has reminded me that it is the custom to release to you any one prisoner whom you want. Who do you want me to release to you? Barabbas the Zealot? Or Jesus who is called the Mashiach?"

All around him, Shim'on heard shouts of "Barabbas!" His throat felt as dry as sandpaper, his words stuck to the roof of his mouth. White spots danced before his eyes.

A woman nearby spoke to her companion, "For a time, I believed the rabbi could be the Mashiach. When he arrived in

Jerusalem for Pesach, I was sure that he was going to announce it. But nothing happened. I'm tired of waiting. If he were the Mashiach, we'd know it by now. He's just another fraud."

"But what of the miracles he's done?" her companion asked, "Surely he must be more than just a man."

The woman shrugged. "I don't know. But from what I see, the prophecies haven't been fulfilled. Death to false prophets. Give us Barabbas!" she joined the shouts of the crowd.

Pilate, too, looked as if he couldn't believe his ears, and Shim'on wondered if they shared the same thoughts. Just days ago, these same crowds had worshipped the rabbi as he entered Jerusalem, proclaiming him the Mashiach. They had thrown their clothing and palm branches before him in honor. Now they cast rotten produce and rocks at him and demanded his death. Bitterness urged him to draw his dagger, and charge the steps to the rabbi, killing whoever stood in his way. It would be a suicide mission, but what did he have to live for now? He had done nothing when the crowd took the Mashiach away. Even Lydia would turn her back on him when she heard what he had done. But he couldn't move. He cursed himself. Even now he was a coward.

"Then what shall I do with Jesus, who is called the Mashiach?" Pilate asked.

"Crucify him!" Shim'on turned in shock toward the voices echoing the chant all around him.

"Why?" Pilate asked, "What evil has he done?"

Instead of a response, the people's cries of "crucify him!" increased.

"Release him!" Shim'on shouted until his voice was hoarse, but he was drowned out by the crowd.

Pilate gestured to his servant boy to bring him a bowl of water. When it arrived, he washed his hands before the crowd.

"I am innocent of this man's blood; do it yourselves."

A woman standing behind Shim'on screamed out, "His blood be on us and on our children!" Others picked up the cry.

Pilate gestured toward a couple of the guards and they disappeared into a limestone building adjacent to the praetorium, returning with Yeshua between them. Shim'on watched them throw his friend to the ground roughly. The people ignored him; their main priority—the rabbi's death—was secured.

"Have the Jews' king scourged!" Pilate commanded. He turned and walked into the praetorium.

Y e s h u a

XXXIII

Yeshua squinted in the bright morning sunlight, disoriented. Two guards dragged him out of the prison and onto a platform. A crowd of people screamed below him, but Yeshua quickly realized he was not the focus of their attention.

"Here's your prisoner!" One of the guards pushed Yeshua roughly so that he tripped down the stairs to the ground. No one in the crowd seemed to care about his presence. Confused, he looked around.

A man stood on the platform above him flanked by Roman guards and Hebrew chief priests. Looking closer, Yeshua realized he knew this man. It was the rabbi from Nazareth. But what was he doing here?

"Have him scourged!" Yeshua heard a tall man in purple robes say.

Yeshua struggled to his feet and looked around the crowd in confusion.

He approached an elderly woman, "What's going on?"

"Get away from me, you, filthy murderer!" the woman shrieked. Those in the crowd looked in disdain.

Yeshua stepped back in shame. He *was* a murderer. He didn't deserve to be free. He had killed Romans, but, more than that, he had killed any innocents who got in his way. He deserved to die. But he had to know what was happening.

A teenage boy approached, and Yeshua reached out in desperation and grasped his arm, "Please, tell me what is happening!"

The boy looked wary, but replied, "They have just condemned the rabbi of Nazareth to death, Sir. To be scourged and crucified."

"But what has he done?" Yeshua asked, confused.

"Nothing. He has done no evil." The boy looked sad, "But my abba says that the chief priests want him dead. It's Pesach. The people chose you to go free instead."

Yeshua dropped his hand from the boy's arm in shock, and the boy turned away. "But but I've killed people," he stuttered aloud. "the rabbi has never sinned. It's not fair that I go free and he dies."

The crowd around him increased their cries and Yeshua looked up to see the cause. He gasped. The rabbi had been chained to a wooden pole in the center of the courtyard. A centurion nearby grasped a cat of nine tails, a Roman whip with bits of metal and bone affixed to the leather strips trailing from it. Yeshua had once faced an attacker with the same weapon and remembered the horrible bite of it.

"Thirty-nine lashes!" A centurion officer commanded.

Yeshua could only watch the first five blows before he had to turn away. Each time the whip bit into the rabbi's body, it tore strips of skin away so that they hung in loose shreds. Each strike produced a spray of blood, and soon the centurion and those watching from the front of the crowd were streaked with it. Yeshua couldn't bear to hear the rabbi's cries with each blow, and he covered his ears, tasting salty tears that he realized were his own. This wasn't right. It wasn't fair. It should be him, not this innocent man.

Finally, the beating stopped, and the rabbi was unshackled from the post. He crumpled to the ground. The thirty-nine lashes he received was the number the Romans deemed a punishment short of death. Several soldiers surrounded him so that Yeshua's view was impaired.

When they stood back, he felt sick. The soldiers had twisted together a crown of thorns and pressed it tightly onto the man's head, drawing blood so that it flowed down his face. They took a purple robe and threw it over the bloodied pulp of his back and legs.

"Hail, King of the Jews!" They mocked, laughing, and jeering at him.

If he hadn't known the man standing before him was the rabbi of Nazareth, Yeshua wasn't sure he would have recognized him.

Near the front of the crowd, a small group of women wailed, tears flowing freely down their faces. One looked to be his own immah's age, and Yeshua wondered if she was the rabbi's immah. A couple of men stood with the women, and they also looked grief-stricken.

Pilate reappeared. He stepped close to Jesus and gestured toward him, "Look, here is the man!"

The crowd started screaming again, "Crucify him! Crucify him!"

"Take him yourselves and crucify him. I find him not guilty," Pilate replied.

One of the chief priests spoke loudly, "By our law, he ought to die because he called himself the Son of Adonai."

Yeshua felt the words pierce his heart like a sword. At one time he would have said the same. He had proclaimed the rabbi to be a heretic, but he knew there was truth in Jesus' words. He just hadn't wanted to listen. His pride and defenses stripped from him now, he could admit as much.

Pilate looked afraid and gestured to the soldiers to follow him inside the praetorium with Jesus. The men left, then reappeared minutes later. Pilate appeared frustrated as he took his place on the judgement seat. The rabbi stood before him, swaying and bloody.

"Look, here is your King!" Pilate exclaimed, pointing toward him.

"Away with him! Away with him! Crucify him!" Yeshua thought the people sounded more and more incensed.

"What? Crucify your King?" Pilate looked toward the chief priests. It was clear that he did not find the rabbi deserving of death. Yet he feared starting a riot by denying the bloodthirsty crowds.

"We have no king but Caesar." The priests responded.

Pilate gestured to the guards. A couple of them disappeared, then returned with a heavy wooden beam balanced between them. Yeshua watched in horror as the soldiers tied Jesus' hands to the arms of the cross, the full weight of it balanced on the rabbi's mangled back. Although he saw the spectacle dozens of times when he lived in the city, never had he considered that it might be his own fate one day. This man was enduring the sentence in his place. A blanket of guilt enveloped him.

"Yeshua," Yeshua looked around him. Had he heard his name?

"Over here." Yeshua turned, stunned to see Shim'on.

His friend looked terrible. Dark circles hung beneath his eyes, and his hair was matted with dirt and sweat. Streaks of blood and dirt laced his clothing, and his eyes were red and distraught with grief.

"Shim'on? I don't understand. What are you doing here? Why are they killing the rabbi?"

"I'm here because I am one of his disciples," Shim'on said tersely, "And they are killing him because they have grown tired of a Mashiach who will not use violence to free them from the Romans. He has done no wrong, but they are going to murder him. It was to be you, but the people called for your release."

"I know." Yeshua avoided looking in Shim'on's eyes. He wondered if his friend hated him for being freed instead of Jesus.

The Romans urged Jesus forward, and he staggered under the weight of the cedar beam, but moved forward, weaving with each step. The crowds shouted and surged around them.

Yeshua watched Shim'on's eyes follow the rabbi. Rather than follow Jesus, Shim'on began to limp the opposite direction.

"Aren't you going to follow him?" Yeshua asked in surprise. "You're one of his disciples."

Shim'on shook his head. "I've failed him. I can't watch them crucify him." Without another word, Shim'on staggered away.

Yeshua watched as his old friend left. He should have felt relief, even joy, at being a free man once more. Instead, a heaviness descended over him. He squinted at the clear sky above him, surprised that it was not dark with clouds. Yeshua didn't know what to do. He hardly knew this man Jesus. Yet the innocent rabbi had taken Yeshua's place of punishment. He joined the hundreds following the rabbi to his death.

XXXIV

Yeshua's head pounded, but he ignored the pain.

Ahead of him, Jesus bent beneath his burden, often collapsing under its weight. Each time he fell, the soldiers beat him mercilessly until he stood again. Yeshua couldn't imagine the pain the man must be enduring. He recalled the first time he saw a crucifixion procession over a year ago. He never imagined that such a fate might be his own.

Finally, the procession exited the city and reached a hill called Golgotha because of the geography of the terrain. Yeshua had heard of the place before but never been there. In the distance, it appeared before the rabbi's followers. Yeshua swallowed hard seeing the rumored rocky surface begin to take shape as the dreaded features looking grotesquely like a human skull. Everyone pressed in as closely as they could to Jesus, but no-one could protect him from his suffering.

Yeshua clung to the outskirts of the crowd. He could still clearly see the form of Jesus ahead of him. The guards nailed the crossbeam to another vertical beam, creating a wooden cross. Then, they positioned the rabbi on it. Others pulled long metal stakes from a nearby bag. Yeshua knew what was coming, but he couldn't look away. The woman whom Yeshua assumed to be the rabbi's imma pleaded with the soldier, tears streaming down her face. The centurions ignored her.

Sweat beaded on Yeshua's forehead and soaked his shirt. His head pounded and mouth was dry with thirst, but he didn't care. He deserved the pain and much worse.

Yeshua watched as the soldiers used a hammer to drive the spikes into the rabbi's wrists and feet, fixing him to the cross. With each blow, Jesus' excruciating screams filled the air.

Yeshua wanted to close his eyes, as though not seeing the gruesome scene would make it less horrifying. But he didn't deserve to be spared from seeing the fate that ought to have been his own. He was free, while this righteous man endured the death he deserved. He tasted salt and realized that he was crying.

Yeshua noticed two other men also being prepared for crucifixion, one on either side of the rabbi. He couldn't block out the agonized cries of the three men, nor the heavy clank of the mallet as the soldiers secured the men to the intersecting pieces of wood. As the centurions pulled the crosses to a vertical position using ropes and pulleys, Yeshua sucked in his breath. He recognized the other two men as Zealots from Jerusalem who had taken part in the insurrection with him.

All three men hung naked from the wooden crosses by their hands and pressed themselves up by their feet to breathe. Yeshua knew the effort was exhausting and horrifically painful. He could no longer bear to watch. He turned, sank to the ground, and dropped his head into his hands.

Adonai, forgive me! I don't know if this is Your Son as many say, but surely, he is righteous! I am guilty, yet he took my place!

"Forgive me, forgive me," Yeshua kept repeating the words, rocking back and forth on the ground. He craved comfort and forgiveness, but all he felt was deep guilt. People moved and spoke around him as if he were not there.

You're no better than these people, a dark voice whispered. *If you were his judge, you would have sentenced him to the same fate.* Yeshua covered his ears against the invisible voice, but he knew it was true. He was selfish. Incredibly selfish. He had been focused on his own desires for self-righteousness, approval, and criminal vengeance. He had placed them above all else, unwilling to hear or see anything else. He had been blinded by his pride.

He glanced up, tears flooding his vision. Already many in the crowd were leaving. He heard some complain about the midday heat and almost threw himself at them. They had demanded an innocent man's death and had the gall to complain about the heat?

The people were satisfied to see the rabbi on the cross but were unwilling to watch the horrible process of death play out. Yeshua knew that death could take hours, but more commonly it was two or three days before crucified men breathed their last. The rabbi's followers remained kneeling as close as they could to the foot of the cross.

"Abba, forgive them, they do not know what they are doing," Jesus groaned. His whole body shook with pain and fatigue. The rabbi spoke the words with effort, and Yeshua listened in awe. How could this man forgive those who had betrayed and killed him? Yeshua would rather have killed than forgiven the man who took the life of his abba, yet this man forgave his own murderers!

"He saved others. Let him save himself if he is really Adonai's Mashiach, the Chosen One!" One of the chief priests said to another.

At one point, a legionary approached the place where Yeshua now lay.

"Don't you know that you've been set free, scum?" he sneered. "But not for long. You can't escape your fate. Soon you'll be like them." He gestured to the Zealots gasping for breath on crosses on either side of Jesus. The other soldiers just laughed. Yeshua remained silent.

Though it was midday, Yeshua felt a shadow come over him. Opening his eyes, he watched as darkness fell over the land. Leaden clouds obscured the sun but brought no rain. Yeshua had an uncanny feeling that creation itself was mourning the rabbi's forthcoming death. A wind began to blow, kicking up gravel so that it bit into the exposed skin of all those on the hill. Yeshua pulled his tallit tighter over his head but didn't move from where he sat, a short distance from the cross.

Three hours later, Yeshua heard the rabbi cry out hoarsely, *"Eloi, Eloi sabachthani?"* Yeshua felt his skin prickle. How could the rabbi's Adonai, the Adonai in Whom he trusted, abandon him? The wretchedness.

A soldier dipped a sponge into a jar of sour wine and jabbed it on a branch, lifting it to Jesus' mouth. The rabbi drank a little, and then cried out again, "Abba, I entrust my spirit into your hands!" He bowed his head.

Yeshua saw one of the rabbi's disciples scramble to his feet and look up into Jesus' face.

"He's dead." He looked at the others in disbelief.

The ground began to shake and split, rock formations around them cracking. Shouts and screams rang out around Yeshua as everyone dropped to the ground, fearing for their lives. After several minutes, however, the earthquake stopped. Yeshua cautiously rose to his feet in the eerie silence.

Nearby, a soldier who had witnessed Jesus' death also climbed to his feet, speaking softly, "This man truly was the Son of God!"

Seemingly nonplussed, two chief priests approached the soldiers and asked them to break the legs of the men on the crosses to quicken the process of death before Shabbat.

With all that had happened, Yeshua had forgotten that tomorrow was Shabbat. He was disgusted that the priests would so callously request that these men's lives be ended in such a terrible way for their own convenience.

The guards complied, but when they came to Jesus and saw that he was already dead, they did not break his legs. Instead, one of the soldiers harshly pierced his side with a spear. A gush of blood and water flowed out, spilling onto the soldier. The man cursed. Yeshua watched in grief and anger as the centurions proceeded to remove each lifeless man from his cross.

Yeshua watched as a man clothed in expensive garments approached the guards. The chief priests left, satisfied that the convicted men were dead and would be buried prior to Shabbat. They could return to their preparations for the day of rest. Yeshua wanted to wipe the smug, self-righteous expressions from their faces. Instantly, he felt conviction stab his own soul. He had been one of those men. If circumstances had been different, it was likely that he would have also been among the judgmental rabbis standing on the hill.

The only people left were the soldiers and the rabbi's followers. Yeshua watched as the wealthy man paid the soldiers an amount of money and spoke with one of the male disciples, who Yeshua heard addressed as Yohanan. Yeshua was surprised to see a priest join the group. The man led a donkey laden with burial spices. Together, the rabbi's followers gently lifted the broken and bloodied body of the rabbi and placed it onto the rich man's cart. The group began to walk slowly back toward Jerusalem.

Yeshua was exhausted physically, emotionally, and mentally. His mind reeled from the events of the day, and the despair he felt pressed heavier and heavier upon his shoulders. What was he going to do now? He was alive while another man, a far better man, was dead.

Yeshua saw Yohanan looking around the hillside. When he spotted Yeshua, he walked his way. Yeshua was tempted to flee, uncertain of the disciple's purpose, but he forced himself to stay. Whatever the disciple had to say, he knew he deserved it.

"We're taking the rabbi's body back to Jerusalem to prepare for burial," Yohanan said heavily. "It's almost Shabbat, so we must hurry so that he can be buried before sundown."

Yeshua wondered why the man was telling him this. "Where will you lay him?" Yeshua asked. Yohanan looked surprised by his interest.

"The man who paid the guards," Yohanan looked toward the group, "he has a new tomb in a garden where the rabbi will be placed."

Yeshua nodded. There were no words for such a terrible loss.

"Look," Yohanan continued, "I don't know why you came here today, but your friend Shim'on bar Yitzchak told me you were once a good man and a friend of his. If you need a place to spend the night, we will be gathering in a room in the city. You are welcome to follow us there."

Yeshua gaped, speechless. He had certainly not expected such an invitation. "Thank you," he stuttered through cracked lips.

The disciple nodded and handed Yeshua a flask of water. He turned and ran to catch up with his companions and the cart with the rabbi's body. Grief and pride fought within Yeshua.

He had no place to spend the night. He could, of course, seek asylum with his friend and mentor, Stephanas. He knew that the man was kind and would never turn him away, but the prospect of seeing him again under such circumstances was too humiliating.

He swallowed all the water left in the flask, then he turned and followed Yohanan down the hill.

S h i m' o n

XXXV

Shim'on could not remember ever feeling such a lack of hope. Jesus, his rabbi, was dead.

He couldn't believe it. He had professed Jesus to be the Mashiach, the Son of Adonai, yet here hc lay. Shim'on stood in front of the roughly hewn stone that covered the rabbi's tomb. He had found the place from rumors circulating around the city. A Roman seal marked the tomb with the words, "King of the Jews."

"Move along!" One of two Roman soldiers guarding the grave stepped forward, stamping the ground with his spear. "Your rabbi is dead."

Shim'on realized the Sanhedrin had heard of Jesus' prophecies of being raised up after death. Though they scoffed at his words, they feared that one of his followers might steal his body to make it look as though he'd risen from the dead. To preempt this possibility, they had requested that Pilate place guards at the tomb.

Shim'on's characteristic fiery passion was gone, defeat taking its place. He had believed the rabbi was the long-awaited Mashiach. Now his only hope lay sealed behind a burial stone.

"I would have followed you forever," He said softly, taking one last look at the tomb. He was grateful that the rabbi's body lay in such a beautiful place. Colorful wildflowers and leafy,

287

green fig and olive trees surrounded him. He couldn't help but think of the time he had stood outside a similar tomb with Jesus. With a word, the rabbi had raised Lazarus from the dead. Yet here he was, laid in a tomb himself. How could the man who resurrected the dead himself die? The shofar signaling the start of Shabbat echoed in the distance, and he turned toward Jerusalem.

 Shim'on walked aimlessly through the crowded city streets. Though it was Shabbat, he had no intention of joining the other Hebrews in the city to worship at the temple. He doubted any of the other disciples would either. Although Jesus was dead and buried, he and the rest of the disciples were still in danger from the Sanhedrin as his followers.

He was startled when a dark-skinned man suddenly grabbed his elbow, his head covered by a tallit.

"Shim'on!" The man hissed.

Shim'on bent slightly to see beneath the man's head covering.

"Toma?"

"Come with me. I know where the others are."

They passed a group of Pharisees and Shim'on noticed one of them nudge his companion and point toward the disciples.

Toma resolutely led the way toward a quiet residential area of the city and looked both ways before knocking on a door.

"Shim'on!" Andreas, Cephas' brother, pulled the door open a little more. Although his face showed the same weariness and grief, they all felt, he smiled. "It's good to see you, Brother." The disciples embraced. Shim'on was drained, but he forced a feeble smile in response.

Shim'on paused when he saw Yeshua.

"Yeshua?"

His old friend stood to his feet awkwardly.

"Wait, is this who I think it is?" Toma stepped forward, his face filled with anger. "What is he doing here?"

Yeshua looked at Toma with a mixture of defiance and exhaustion.

Yohanan stepped between the men. "I know, Toma. I have mixed feelings about him as well. But he followed the rabbi to Golgotha and stayed there until he died. He has no other place to stay."

Yohanan paused, then continued. "And the rabbi told us to love our enemies."

Tomas cut Yohanan with angry glare. "The rabbi is dead, Yohanan. I don't see how loving his enemies helped him."

Yohanan cast a discouraged look at Shim'on.

"And how do you know him?" Toma turned to face Shim'on.

"He was my friend years ago." Yeshua looked at Shim'on, his face inscrutable. "Before he became a Zealot."

Toma snorted in contempt and walked across the room, jostling against Yeshua's shoulder as he passed. "How can you trust a murderer?" Though he knew Toma spoke the words about Yeshua, they pricked Shimon's heart as well. Had Toma forgotten that he'd been a murderer himself?

Yeshua sank back to the ground in a shadowy corner of the room.

There was another knock on the door and Cephas stepped forward. "Who is it?"

"It's me, Ya'aqov. And Thaddeus," A low voice spoke, and Cephas pulled open the door.

"Brothers," Cephas embraced the men, "How did you find us?"

"Friends of the rabbi told us where you were," Thaddeus replied.

"Who is that?" Ya'aqov paused, noticing Yeshua.

"A friend," Shim'on replied simply. He noticed the relief on Yeshua's face and sensed his old friend was grateful that his story would not be told again. He wanted to speak with Yeshua, but the heaviness of so much loss made him long for solitude. He looked around the room. Several of the disciples stood or sat in the small space, though a few were still missing. Two windows faced the street outside. It was dusk and the room was filled with shadows. Several oil lamps cast enough grainy light for the disciples to see one another.

Over the following hours, the disciples reunited, arriving one-by-one or in small groups. They shared their stories, all of them having one common thread: each had abandoned the rabbi. Aside from Yohanan and the women, none of the other disciples had been present for Jesus' trial or crucifixion. Instead, they heard what had happened from rumors in the city, or from those who had been present themselves.

When Philippos arrived, he shared tragic news. In a conversation he overheard between two Pharisees, he learned that Yehudah had been filled with guilt and regret over his actions and tried to return the payment for the rabbi's betrayal to the religious leaders. They rejected his request. Overcome by guilt, Yehudah hung himself. Shim'on was overcome by sadness and anger. Yehudah had been his friend. But he had betrayed the Mashiach, which Shim'on could not comprehend.

All that had happened in the past twenty-four hours was nearly too much for Shim'on to bear.

He mourned his own cowardice that led him to desert the rabbi. He grieved over Yehudah's betrayal and loss of his fellow disciple. Most of all, however, he grieved the death of Jesus. The man had been more than his rabbi, more than the long-awaited Mashiach. He had been his friend. He longed for the comforting presence of Lydia, yet at the same time dreaded seeing her. Would she hate him for his cowardice? The time for the Shabbat meal came and went, but none of the followers or Yeshua felt like eating.

"I cannot believe that Jesus is dead," Matthias spoke slowly, "What do we do now?" No one spoke because no one knew.

As darkness crept over the city, Shim'on noticed Yeshua becoming increasingly uneasy. Finally, Yeshua came over to Shim'on.

"I'm thankful for your hospitality, but I'm going to leave," he spoke quietly.

"What? Where will you go?"

"I'm not sure," Yeshua shrugged, "I'll be fine. It's not right for me to stay here with you all—" He finished without further explanation, but Shim'on understood. Despite Yohanan and Shim'on's willingness for Yeshua to shelter with them, most of the disciples did not feel the same way.

"I'm sorry we had to meet again under such circumstances." Yeshua ducked his head in thanks. "Shalom."

Shim'on grasped the arm of his old friend in farewell. Yeshua returned the gesture, and Shim'on saw grief and hopelessness in his eyes. Then Yeshua turned and left.

 Exhausted and unable to keep his eyes open, Shim'on sat back against the wall and closed his eyes. Within moments, he was asleep.

The next day was filled with dark grief and endless questions to which there were no answers. Why had the rabbi insisted on going to Jerusalem if he had known that his death awaited him there? Who was the rabbi, really? If he was the Son of Adonai, the prophesied Mashiach, wouldn't he still be alive? What were they all to do now?

The questions swirled in his mind; despair, anger, and sadness rising quickly.

When Cephas came and sat beside him late that morning, Shim'on released the torrent he had suppressed for so long.

"Why have you always tried to be better than all of us?" He asked. He kept his voice low so that the other disciples wouldn't hear him, but anger hissed in his words.

Cephas looked surprised. "What?"

"You were obviously the rabbi's favorite. Did you ever think of how we felt?"

"We?" Shim'on could hear the defensiveness in Cephas' voice. "None of the others has ever spoken to me about this. Why don't you speak for yourself?"

Shim'on heard the confidence and truth in the man's words and felt even more irritated.

"Fine then. *You* asked to walk on water in the storm. *You* told the rabbi nothing would happen to him. *You* drew your sword when the crowd came to take him away. You were always the first to show your faith in the rabbi! He treated you differently than he treated me, than he treated us all!" Shim'on gestured to the other disciples, trying to keep his voice low. "I wanted to show him that I loved him just as much as you did, but you never gave me the chance!" He stopped speaking, out of breath. Before he heard the words aloud, the thoughts felt utterly valid. Now he felt foolish and exposed.

Stillness hung in the air like dust, swirling in the late morning sunlight. Then Cephas spoke.

"I'm sorry, Brother. I didn't know you felt this way." He looked directly at Shim'on, and Shim'on knew he was looking into the eyes of a leader. "But I was never trying to be better than you, or any of the others. I loved the rabbi. I believed he was the Mashiach. That's all."

Shim'on could see the man was speaking the truth and shame enveloped him. Cephas spoke again.

"You're right that he treated me differently though. He did, but I never understood why. But he treated each of us differently, didn't he?"

Shim'on considered the disciple's words and realized he was right. In an effort to garner the same treatment as Cephas, he had failed to notice the different ways the rabbi had interacted with each of them. It wasn't as if the rabbi never spoke to him. He did. Countless times. They had fished together on the Sea of Galilee, gone on walks under a tapestry of stars, and laughed as they walked through fields of wheat, picking the heads of grain from their stalks and popping them in their mouths.

They spoke of life, his marriage to Lydia, his abba, and of Adonai. Jesus cared about him, about his life.

He dropped his head, holding back tears. How had he only seen this now, after the rabbi was gone? Jesus had loved each of his disciples equally.

"Forgive me, Brother." Shim'on lifted his head, embarrassed.

"Done." Cephas rubbed his hands together and then pulled them apart, as if releasing something. "He forgave us of much, didn't he?" He looked at Shim'on, his eyes filled with grief.

Shim'on nodded. He was only coming to realize how much.

XXXVI

On the first day of the week, Shim'on woke to excited voices. He saw Miryam, one of the women, speaking excitedly to Cephas and the other disciples.

"I have seen the rabbi!" Miryam's eyes shone, "He told me 'I am ascending to my Abba and your Abba, to my Adonai and your Adonai.'"

Several of the disciples looked away, shaking their heads.

Cephas shook his head. "She's delusional," he whispered. "There was nothing there." Yohanan nodded sadly, "Someone clearly stole the body."

Shim'on sat up with a start. "The rabbi's body is missing?"

Cephas looked over at Shim'on, his face filled with fresh grief. "Yes. The women went to the tomb this morning and the stone was rolled away. The soldiers were gone too. We went to look for ourselves. Miryam is right, his body is gone."

"How could someone steal his body?" Yohanan asked brokenly, "Was it not enough to kill him?"

"Aren't you listening to me?" Miryam stepped between the men, looking back and forth between them. "He's alive! I saw him just now!"

Yohanan looked at Miryam with compassion. "Miryam, I believe you think you saw Jesus. We're all exhausted, and we all miss the rabbi. Don't you think you could have just imagined seeing him?"

"No!" Miryam threw up her hands in frustration. "I really saw him, Yohanan. He stood before me, flesh, and blood. He called me by name."

Shim'on had had enough. Quickly, he tied his sandals and stood. Leaving the others, he ran toward the tomb.

 True to the women's report, the stone was rolled away, and no Roman guards were present. Breathless, Shim'on ducked his head and entered the dark tomb.

Except that it wasn't dark. Shim'on blinked, trying to understand the sight before him. Two men, dressed in brilliant white, sat on the stone where the rabbi's body had lain.

Shim'on gaped, and one of the men rose. "Why are you looking among the dead for someone who is alive? He isn't here!" The man gestured to the stone with a smile. "He is risen from the dead! Remember what he told you back in Galilee, that the Son of Man must be betrayed into the hands of sinful men and be crucified, and that he would rise again on the third day."

Before Shim'on could reply, the men disappeared. Shim'on was alone in the empty tomb. Dank air filled his nostrils, but there was no smell of death. Were the men angels? Surely, they must have been. He rubbed a hand over his eyes. He saw the linens that had enveloped Jesus' body lying on the stone where his body had rested. The cloth that had been wrapped around his head was neatly folded to the side.

"He's gone." Shim'on said aloud. But what was it the angel had said? That Jesus would rise again on the third day? It had been three days since the rabbi's crucifixion. Shim'on rubbed his eyes. He had to be hallucinating. Surely the rabbi's body had been stolen, as Cephas and Yohanan said. But why? Who would take the body of the rabbi? And for what purpose? Shim'on left the tomb, his mind reeling.

When he arrived back at the room, the other disciples questioned him. Shim'on replied that he had wanted to see the empty tomb for himself. He decided to keep the encounter with the two angels to himself, lest he be treated as Miryam had been. But he couldn't shake the thoughts that filled his mind. He was at a loss to understand the empty tomb.

He had failed the rabbi so terribly. Regret and guilt perpetually surrounded him like a dense cloud. He wondered about Yeshua as well. His friend had also suffered the loss of his abba. He wished that he could offer him hope by faith in the rabbi, but all of them-aside from Miryam-wondered if they had been wrong about Jesus being the Mashiach.

He knew Lydia had likely heard news of the rabbi's death by now. What did she think? The foretold Mashiach was to fulfill all the prophecies prior to his death, which included freeing Judea and the Hebrew people from their oppressors. Had he done that? Shim'on struggled to see how. Doubt crept into his heart.

Miryam continued to encourage the rest that Jesus lived, but the group was heartbroken and struggled to believe.

In his most despairing moments, Shim'on wondered if the rabbi had been nothing more than a charismatic teacher. But inevitably he returned to the memory of Jesus forgiving his sins and the sins of many others. Beyond offering forgiveness, the rabbi had healed his shoulder and side with only a touch. He'd performed thousands of miracles for others. He couldn't reconcile the broken pieces. If Jesus was truly the Son of Adonai, how had the Romans been able to kill him? Why had the rabbi let them?

"He said that he must fulfill the words of the nevi'im." Shim'on answered dully during a conversation with Cephas.

"But how?" Cephas asked, voicing similar doubts to his own, "I don't understand how his death fulfilled any of them."

Shim'on shrugged, "Honestly, I don't either. I assumed that he would explain it to me, but he never did." He wished that he had asked the rabbi to clarify his words about His forthcoming death. If he had been willing to ask, perhaps he would have been able to understand at least some of what was happening now.

The men were silent, then Cephas said quietly, "Sometimes I wonder if the way of the Zealots is the way to peace after all."

"No," Shim'on shook his head, "Joining the Zealots is not the answer."

"Did joining the movement ever bring you any peace after your abba's death?" Cephas asked. Shim'on shook his head without speaking.

"I thought not." Shim'on heard the pain in his friend's voice. "Before I met the rabbi, I was desperate for a way to get rid of the anger I felt all the time. I tried many things." He looked at Shim'on with regret. "I was never a Zealot, but I used to be violent. I've been with women..." His voice trailed off and he looked at the ground. "I certainly didn't bring honor to my parents. Just ask Andreas," he gestured toward his brother, who sat on the other side of the room. The men sat in silence for several moments.

"When he called me to follow him, I told him that he needed to hear my sins first," Cephas continued. "I was sure that he would tell me I wasn't righteous enough to follow him." He chuckled.

"What did he say?" Shim'on was curious.

"He told me I was right. I wasn't righteous enough." A slight smile lifted the corners of Cephas's lips. "But he said he wanted

---

me to follow him anyway. He said he would teach me to fish for men."

Shim'on smiled. Cephas' story was like his own.

"Meeting the rabbi changed me," Shim'on said softly. "Until three days ago, I believed that he was the Son of Adonai."

"Do you still believe that?"

Shim'on was quiet. "I don't know," he said soberly.

Cephas was silent, then asked in a whisper, "Did you ever speak with him about the lives you took?"

Shim'on nodded. "I did. Like you, I was sure he was going to reject me. But it was like nothing I've ever felt. One moment I was drowning in anger and hate, the next I was free. Filled with peace." Just remembering the moment when Jesus forgave him brought tears to Shim'on' eyes.

The men were quiet and Shim'on closed his eyes against the pain, leaning his head against the wall. Sometime later, he jolted awake, a bright light bleeding through his eyelids. He realized that he must have slept.

Though it was dusk, a brilliance filled the room. Shim'on, Cephas, and the other disciples jumped to their feet. A form stood in the middle of the chamber.

"Peace to you." Jesus looked around the group, smiling. He was clothed in dazzling white, and his appearance seemed regal to Shim'on.

"Are you seeing what I'm seeing?" Cephas looked at the disciples and back at the rabbi.

"It's a ghost," Matthias took a step back, trembling.

"Why are you afraid? Why do you doubt what you see? Look at my hands and my feet," the rabbi stretched out his hands. "Touch me and see. A ghost doesn't have flesh and bones as you see that I have." Jesus smiled.

Shim'on stepped closer and looked at the rabbi's outstretched hands. At the center of each wrist was a scar, like that caused by a metal stake. Shim'on looked down and saw the same markings on the rabbi's sandaled feet. Jesus lifted his tunic so that the disciples could see a jagged scar indenting his side. Shim'on remembered the soldier who had used his sword to ensure the rabbi's death. Tentatively, he reached out a hand to touch the scar and felt the warmth of Jesus' skin.

"It's really you!" he cried out, falling to his knees.

The disciples around him reached forward, touching the scars in his hands and feet, and shouting in gleeful joy, tears pouring down their faces. Jesus stayed and ate a meal of dried fish and lehem with them. Then, just as suddenly as he had appeared, he was gone.

"Where did he go?" Shim'on gasped.

The disciples looked around the room, but the rabbi had disappeared.

Cephas laughed in wonder. "I don't know where he has gone, but I know that he is alive! We all touched him. We watched him eat. The rabbi has risen from the dead!"

Yeshua

XXXVII

Yeshua clamped his arms tightly over his chest, trying to warm himself in the early morning chill. The sun had not yet reached the alley where he sat, huddled against a rock wall for protection from the wind. He was exhausted from a night spent unsuccessfully trying to stay warm. It had been two days since he left Shim'on and the other disciples. Two days since the crucifixion of the rabbi. When his body had finally surrendered to exhaustion and he slept, his dreams were filled with images of Jesus on the cross, and voices condemning Yeshua for not dying in his rightful place. He wiped a hand across his eyes. He agreed with the voices, but what could he do now? He was alive, and the rabbi was dead.

A crow landed at the top of the wall above him, letting loose a raucous croak. Slowly, people emerged from their homes. Many of them cast judgmental, or even fearful, glances at the dirty, unkempt man sitting against the wall as they passed. Yeshua couldn't blame them. Who would have thought that a rabbi's son would end up here? He certainly had not.

He stood to his feet gingerly, testing to see if his head would pound with the effort. A dull ache spread along the base of his skull, but it was bearable. He made his way slowly down the alley and toward the market. Perhaps there would be a kind shopkeeper who would take pity on him, or maybe he could find some left behind scraps of food. His belly groaned in hunger, and he weaved slightly, lightheaded. The scents of freshly baked lehem and roasted fish assailed his nostrils. What was once a place that enchanted his senses was now a cruel reminder that he had no resources with which to satiate his hunger.

"Please, do you have any to spare?" he asked, his head hung low as he went from stall to stall, barely making eye contact with the merchants. A gruff refusal, a shake of the head, and a threat to report him for harassment were the only responses he received.

In despair, he sunk down against a nearby wall.

"Yeshua? Is that you?" A shadow fell over him, and Yeshua squinted up. The tall, bearded man looked familiar, but he couldn't place him.

"Wait just a moment, I'll be back."

The man returned shortly, a loaf of lehem and dried fish in either hand.

"Here, for you." He handed the food to Yeshua.

"Thank you." Yeshua barely got the words out before biting into the still-warm brown loaf. It was the best lehem he had ever tasted. The salty fish were delicious as well.

The man lowered himself to sit beside Yeshua, and he could finally get a good look at his face.

"Wait, I know who you are. You're the leader of the Zealots in Jerusalem," Yeshua said in a low voice.

Reuben nodded without looking at him. He kept his eyes focused on the increasing traffic filling the market area.

"You remember me?" Yeshua asked.

"I always remember those who fight with us," Reuben nodded, keeping his voice low. "But we shouldn't talk here. It's too dangerous. Follow me."

The bear of a man straightened and walked down a nearby limestone-paved street. Still tightly gripping the bread and fish, Yeshua followed him. He felt stronger already. Reuben led him through a maze of turns, and finally he entered a small home.

A sign hanging above the door read 'Potter.' Yeshua stepped over the threshold behind him, licking the grease from his fingers. A fire burned in a kiln in the corner of the space, and pottery of different shapes and sizes surrounded them. Only one other man was in the room, and he sat at a wheel near the kiln, deftly molding a lump of clay into an urn. The area had a sense of safety to it that immediately set Yeshua at ease.

"Come, sit." Reuben gestured Yeshua toward a mat near the potter.

"This is Amos. He is one of us." The man glanced up briefly from his work to nod at Yeshua in greeting. Yeshua nodded back.

"So, where have you been since the attack?" Reuben asked.

Yeshua shared all that had transpired over the past few days. When he finished, Reuben whistled.

"That is quite a series of events. How is your head now?"

Yeshua touched the back of his skull gingerly. "It's sore, but I'm fine."

"Good." Reuben nodded approvingly. "You've been through much. What are your plans now?"

Yeshua hesitated, then decided against hiding the truth. "Honestly, I'm trying to find the answer to that question myself. I don't want to return to Capernaum. There's not much for me there. The attack here routed our group, and several of my friends were killed."

Reuben nodded, "I know, I'm sorry. I lost many good men as well. We didn't anticipate how quickly the Romans would respond. We will plan better in the future."

"What would you think of joining our group here in Jerusalem for a time? I would value your skill and experience."

Yeshua was surprised. Perhaps he should have seen the conversation going this direction, but he hadn't. He felt a mixture of emotions at Reuben's suggestion. Since the rabbi's crucifixion, he had wondered about the righteousness of the Zealots' cause. The rabbi had preached peace and loving one's enemies, and his life and death seemed to carry far more weight and influence than anything gained or lost by the Zealots' efforts. Yeshua knew beyond a doubt that his abba had agreed with Jesus' teachings and would be staunchly opposed to Yeshua's violent response to their enemies. But returning to Capernaum and his trade was the last thing he wanted to do. He still longed to fight back against their oppressors.

"Why not?" he said in response to Reuben's question.

"I'm glad to hear it." Reuben gripped his shoulder and spoke confidently. "I know the past few days have been difficult for you. In my experience, there is nothing better than channeling anger into action. We have plans to attack a Roman caravan in a week and will discuss the details at our meeting tomorrow night. In the meantime, you are welcome to stay with my family if you have nowhere else to go."

"Thank you," Yeshua replied, humbled by Reuben's kindness. "I would be grateful."

Strengthened by the food Reuben had given him, Yeshua stood. As he bade farewell to Amos and followed Reuben out the door, Yeshua was dismayed to hear the now familiar, quiet whisper. *"This path will not lead where you want to go."* He tried to press the voice back into the shadows of Amos' pottery shop as he stepped into the sunshine.

XXXVIII

It had been a week since Shim'on and the other disciples last saw the rabbi, who appeared to them once more in Jerusalem before disappearing again.

The twelve disciples decided to return to their hometowns following his departure. During the time that they had followed Jesus, their families received support from other family members, but circumstances were different now. Seven of the disciples had returned to the area near Capernaum, including Shim'on and Cephas.

Shim'on felt an increasing sense of dread as they drew closer to Capernaum. Though he knew the rabbi was risen from the dead, it didn't change the fact that he had deserted the Mashiach when it mattered most. He hadn't had the opportunity to speak to Jesus about it either, which weighed heavily on him.

The men arrived in Capernaum in the late afternoon and Shim'on separated from the others. As he approached home, fear and doubt swirled in his mind. Would Lydia even want to speak to him? Would she still love him, or would she regret marrying such a cowardly man?

"Shim'on!" Miriam looked up from the lehem she was kneading. "You're back!" She threw open her arms to embrace her son. Seeming to sense Shim'on's trepidation, she cupped his face in her hands and looked up at him.

"It's so good to have you home, Son." She smiled at him. "Lydia is washing clothes at the falls. She should be home soon."

As she finished saying the words, the door swung open and Lydia entered the house. As soon as she caught sight of Shim'on she dropped the basket full of wet garments and squealed.

"You're safe! You're home!" Before Shim'on could react, his wife flung herself into his arms. "I've missed you!" She smiled up at him. "We heard the good news! The rabbi is alive!" She looked excitedly back and forth between him and Miriam.

"It's true!" Shim'on tried to push the worries from his mind as he shared all that had transpired. Lydia's arms remained wrapped around his waist as she listened to him, her eyes sparkling. Shim'on had assumed Lydia heard of his actions when Jesus was arrested, but her loving reaction to his return home caused him to worry that she hadn't. He dreaded telling her, but he knew it would eat at him if he kept the truth from her.

It wasn't until nightfall that Shim'on and Lydia were finally alone, laying on their mat in darkness in the private room they shared. Hanoch had returned home in the late afternoon and insisted Shim'on share the account of all that had happened again. Shim'on offered to fish with him that night, but Hanoch urged him to rest. He could join him on the boat the following night.

"You've been quiet today," Lydia said, as she nestled into him. "Is something wrong?"

Shim'on turned to face her. "There's something I have to tell you," he spoke heavily. "When the crowd came to arrest the rabbi, I was desperate. I pulled out my knife to kill one of the men that held him, but something happened before I could act.

After that I…" Shim'on paused, the weight of what came next felt crushing.

"You ran." Lydia finished softly.

Shim'on's chest tightened. So, she knew.

"I did." Shim'on nodded in the darkness. "I abandoned the rabbi when he needed me most. I failed him."

Silence filled the room. Shim'on was grateful that the darkness hid the tears of shame threatening to spill from his eyes. He was certain Lydia despised him. He despised himself.

Suddenly he felt Lydia's hand on his face. "You are human, Shim'on. You were afraid. I can't imagine how scared I would have felt if I were there." She paused. "Don't you think the rabbi knew you were going to run? He knew everything about you before you'd even met him. He knew you would leave him. And he asked you to follow him anyway. He chose you."

Lydia's words were a balm to Shim'on's hurting heart. "So, you forgive me for running?"

Shim'on could hear Lydia smile. "It's not for me to forgive you. But I believe Jesus does. And I love you."

Shim'on pulled Lydia close and whispered in her ear, "I love you, too. More than you can possibly imagine."

 Shim'on looked out over the water. Their first night back to fishing in the Sea of Galilee had been wretched, but at least the weather was beautiful. There wasn't a cloud in the sky, and the early morning stars reflected off the dark water.

"It all makes sense now," Cephas said from beside him. "The rabbi reminded us of the many prophecies concerning his death and resurrection many times! But we were too blind to understand."

Shim'on sat on a pile of nets. "We didn't want to try to understand." The five other disciples on the boat nodded in agreement, their faces outlined by the oil lamps that swung from the boat's mast.

"But praise Adonai," Ya'aqov spoke, "He fulfilled the prophecies to show us, to show the world, that he is the Mashiach. In him, there is forgiveness of sins and eternal life!"

"All the miracles that he did," Jude continued, "Giving sight to the blind, making the lame walk, and even raising the dead," He laughed in awe, "Of course, he is the Mashiach!"

"Come and help me, Brother." Shim'on tugged at his end of the net, pulling it into the boat hand over hand.

Hanoch went to the other end of the net. "Still empty," he said, discouraged.

"We've been at it all night, and not a single fish," Yohanan said tiredly. The other men groaned in frustration.

"Morning is coming," Ya'aqov pointed at the thin red line lighting the horizon, "We might as well start back toward shore."

The others agreed, and Shim'on and Hanoch slid the paddles into place since the wind had died overnight. Slowly, they drew near to land.

"Do you have any fish?"

The men squinted, trying to see the man outlined on the rocky shore in the early morning light.

"No!" Shim'on yelled out.

"Cast the net on the right side of the boat, and you will find some." The man called, cupping his hands around his mouth.

"Who does he think he is?" Yohanan muttered, "It's still too dark to see a thing in the water."

"Let's just do it," Shim'on responded. "It can't hurt to try once more."

The men threw out the nets again, this time on the right side of the boat, and waited several minutes before pulling them in.

"I can't even lift it!" Hanoch strained at his side of the net.

"Nor can I!" Ya'aqov cried from the other side.

"It is the rabbi!" Yohanan cried suddenly.

Yeshua

XXXIX

Yeshua stood on the Temple Mount. The area was full of people, as usual. He was not here to worship, however. He fingered the knife strapped beneath his linen tunic. The crowd pressed around him like fast-moving currents in a river. He remained in place, the rock in the center of the stream. Soon he saw his target.

A centurion walked toward him, focused on whatever job he had been tasked with. Yeshua drew his dagger. He moved covertly toward the man, covering the dagger with his hand, and holding it tightly to his thigh. Suddenly, a voice spoke from his right.

"Yeshua, stop."

Bin-yamin stepped out of the crowds flowing around him and directly into his path, separating him from his objective.

Yeshua blinked. "Abba?"

"Stop this, Yeshua." His abba's dark eyes pleaded with him. "This path does not lead to life."

The centurion wove his way through the crowds, closer and closer to where Yeshua stood.

"Abba, I don't understand. How are you here? I watched you die." Yeshua gripped his knife more tightly, but his hands trembled.

Bin-yamin ignored the question. "Yeshua, you must surrender your life to the rabbi. He is the only way that you will ever be free of this hatred."

The centurion was perhaps fifteen yards away now, his movement slow and impeded by the crush of the crowds. The sun glinted off his armor and Yeshua squinted.

"The rabbi preached peace and love towards our enemies." Yeshua spat. "He was not here to free us from the Romans."

The centurion was close now. Yeshua had to focus on the task at hand. He was confused by his abba's appearance, but somehow it did not seem important at the moment.

"Abba, you need to move."

"Yeshua, Son, please, listen to me!" Bin-yamin's hands reached out to Yeshua, resting on his shoulders, but Yeshua felt nothing but numbness.

"I'm serious, Abba, please move."

The centurion approached, just ten feet away. It was perfect. Yeshua would be able to strike him as he passed, then melt into the crowds. No one would see what had caused the Roman to slump over dead on the limestone pavement.

Yeshua tried to sidestep his abba and position himself for the attack, but Bin-yamin pushed himself into his path.

"It isn't worth it!" Yeshua was surprised to see tears flow down his abba's face. But the centurion was too close to wait any longer. Yeshua lifted his dagger from his side and plunged it into his abba's chest, then wrested it free. Bin-yamin's eyes filled with surprise, then pain, then grief. He touched his fingers to the crimson blood flowing from his chest, then looked confusedly at his son.

"I love you, Yeshua."

Yeshua gasped, sitting upright from the mat where he had gone to sleep scarcely two hours before. He was in Reuben's home, in a room that had once belonged to his son. He was relieved to be alone. His hands were slick with sweat and he shook uncontrollably. His heart raced. The dream had felt so real. He had murdered his abba. He raised a trembling hand to his eyes, looking for any signs of blood. There was none, of course. How could he do such a thing, even in a dream? Yeshua felt a cold darkness lurking in his heart. He thought of Bin-yamin's words in the dream, "Yeshua, you must surrender your life to the rabbi. He is the only way that you will ever be free of this hatred." Were anger and hate making him into a monster? He lay back on his mat. He hadn't really killed Bin-yamin. It was only a dream. He wasn't a righteous person, like his abba, but he wasn't evil either. The thought brought no comfort. He repeated the empty mantra to himself until he finally fell into a restless sleep.

 The days spent with Reuben and his family were filled with work and training. Reuben was a tentmaker, and Yeshua assisted him as best he could. At the end of the day, the men often left the city to practice archery or swordplay away from the watchful eyes of the Romans.

Yeshua respected Reuben and suspected that he filled a role similar to that of a son to the man. Reuben's son had been killed in a Zealot skirmish years ago. Though Reuben didn't often speak of him, it was clear the ache of the loss remained fresh.

Yeshua appreciated the structure of life with Reuben and his family, yet he knew it was only temporary.

Dark thoughts protruded into his mind during the daylight hours, and even darker nightmares filled his restless nights. He pondered who Yeshua Bar Abba really was and what would become of him. To his dismay, his hands shook constantly since the nightmare in which he had killed his abba. Reuben never asked him about it, but Yeshua felt shame just the same. He had participated in several attacks since his return to Jerusalem, and the next would be on the following day.

That night, Yeshua fell into a fitful sleep. He stood on a rocky hill. Wind whipped about him, tearing at his tunic. At first, he thought he was alone, but then he turned and saw another man approaching him across the barren ground. As the man drew closer, Yeshua saw the familiar face of the rabbi. The man's dark eyes pierced Yeshua's. He felt completely exposed, every thought he'd had and action he'd done laid bare. He felt an urge to turn and run, but when he tried, he realized that his feet were rooted to the earth. He could do nothing but stand and watch Jesus' approach. Finally, the rabbi stood directly before him.

"Shalom, Yeshua." The word struck Yeshua. *Peace.* He felt anything but peaceful.

"Are you ready?"

"Ready for what?" Yeshua asked, confused.

The rabbi lifted an arm, and Yeshua suddenly noticed that Jesus carried a bucket. He looked closer to see the contents and recoiled. The pail was filled with the nine-inch iron nails that were used for crucifixion.

"No"–He gasped the word.

"You deserve this, don't you?" The rabbi asked him, bluntly.

Yeshua glanced around and noticed a wooden cross lying a short distance from them. Had it been there all along? How had he not noticed?

He mustered his pride. "No. I'm not a very righteous person, but I'm certainly not evil. Everything I've done has been for my family. For our people."

Jesus tilted his head. "Do you harbor anger in your heart?"

"Well, of course, but doesn't everyone?"

The rabbi continued, unhindered. "Have you been resentful or jealous of another?"

"Well, yes." Yeshua was irritated. "But I don't think I'm the only one."

"Have you taken a life?"

The question struck a nerve. Of course, he had. And not just one or two. He had been in the business of killing for the past two years.

"Yes, but I did so to honor Adonai."

Jesus' eyes flashed, and he spoke in a low, solemn voice. "Never do you honor my Abba by taking life. You murder others to justify yourself. Your heart is filled with poison and death."

Yeshua dropped his head, all pride gone. The rabbi was right. He knew as much for a while now but hadn't wanted to accept it.

Jesus continued. "Adonai is perfect. He alone sees and judges the heart. Every motive is laid bare before Him. There are none who is righteous aside from Him. All have sinned and fall short of His glory. And the wages of sin are death." Each sentence fell like the blow of a hammer upon Yeshua's ears.

The sky above them was dark and filled with storm clouds. Lightning flashed in the distance.

"Yeshua Bar Abba, do you deserve death?"

Yeshua looked down at the bucket of nails that Jesus carried in one hand.

"I do." He cried out, tears trailing down his cheeks. It was over. All the denial and lies he had told himself for years fell away to reveal the truth. Strangely, he felt relieved.

"Then come. It's time to pay the consequences of your sins."

The rabbi turned and walked toward the cross. Yeshua found that his feet were free. He followed Jesus. The rabbi's steps were heavy, and his shoulders were bowed under an invisible burden. When they reached the cross, Yeshua expected Jesus to tell him to lay down on it. Instead, the rabbi extended the arm carrying the bucket to Yeshua.

Yeshua took it, confused. He watched as the rabbi laid on the cross himself and stretched his arms and feet along the rough wood.

"It's time." Jesus looked at Yeshua gravely.

"What are you doing?" Yeshua demanded, bewildered. "It's I who deserve to die. Not you."

Jesus spoke, "Surely he took up our pain and carried our suffering. We assumed he was punished by Adonai. But he was pierced for our sins. He was crushed for our wrongdoing. He was punished so that we could be at peace. By his wounds we are healed."

Yeshua recognized the words from the navi Isaiah, speaking about the coming Mashiach. He glanced at the bucket in his hand and felt sick.

"You are he who was prophesied." He spoke the words in revelatory awe.

"I AM." The wind whipped through the surrounding crags and boulders, almost knocking Yeshua to the ground. Lightning cracked the sky, and thunder shook the earth around them.

He looked back at the rabbi. He was shocked to see that the cross was now vertical, and three spikes protruded from the man's wrists and ankles. Blood streamed down the oak cross, pooling among the rocks at its base. Yeshua realized that his hand was heavy, and he looked down to see an iron hammer in one hand. His other hand and arm were covered in blood, and it soaked the front of his tunic as well.

"No!" he screamed, dropping the hammer to the rocks.

He jolted awake, drenched in sweat, heart hammering. He had just seen himself crucify the Mashiach.

XL

"I think it is him!" Cephas cried excitedly.

Shim'on snapped his gaze back to the man on the shoreline. How could he have not known that it was the rabbi?

Shim'on heard a splash. Cephas had jumped from the boat and was swimming as fast as he could to shore.

"Hurry!" Shim'on laughed. He no longer felt envious of the disciple. Cephas loved Jesus as he himself did. He did not need to compete for the affection of the rabbi. Together, he and Hanoch rowed as quickly as they could, dragging the net bursting with fish behind them.

Jesus stood beside a crackling fire, fish and lehem cooking on a stone above it. Shim'on hesitated before walking toward the rabbi. Though he had not vocally denied Jesus, he had abandoned him in the garden. He knew he must ask the rabbi for forgiveness. And if the rabbi rejected him? Well, he deserved it. But he couldn't continue to carry the guilt inside him. Before Shim'on could speak, the rabbi put an arm around his shoulder.

"Shim'on! Come with me." Shim'on felt a burst of fear. Was Jesus going to curse him for fleeing the garden that night? Was he going to tell him he could no longer be his disciple? Afraid, he couldn't bring himself to look into Jesus' eyes. The men walked along the rocky shore. After a while, Jesus spoke.

"What did you want to ask me, Shim'on?"

Of course, the rabbi knew. Every thought was laid bare before the Mashiach. But how would he respond? Shim'on stopped walking and turned to face the rabbi.

"I ran that night. In the garden. I abandoned you."

He forced himself to look at the rabbi, but he saw no sign of judgment or resentment in Jesus' eyes. He continued.

"And I was bitter that you treated Cephas differently than you did me. I was jealous."

"Well done, Shim'on." Jesus spoke softly. He placed a hand on Shim'on's shoulder. "You have put aside your pride and stepped into the light." He looked somber. "The enemy wants you to stay in the darkness. But darkness breeds more darkness. You can only be free of sin by walking in the light."

He looked at Shim'on and the corners of his mouth lifted in a smile. "You are forgiven. Walk in the light, Shim'on."

He embraced Shim'on and the weight on his chest disappeared in a moment. Lydia had been right. The rabbi knew him. He wasn't surprised when Shim'on abandoned him in the garden. But nonetheless he had chosen Shim'on. Shim'on wished they could continue talking, but the rabbi turned back toward the group of the disciples. As they neared the other men, Shim'on felt a wave of sadness wash over him. Somehow, he sensed the end of something was near. Before he could ask the rabbi about it, Yohanan pulled Jesus aside.

Cephas appeared at his side and playfully jostled him.

"What took you so long to get to shore?"

"Thanks for the help, Brother," Shim'on said sarcastically. Cephas grinned as he wrung out his drenched tunic.

The Zealots

The men added more of the fish that they had caught to the fire, and the disciples and Jesus enjoyed an early morning meal, laughing and talking together.

When the rabbi had called him three years ago, Shim'on had never dreamed of the ways that his life would change. And today, the rabbi offered him a new beginning.

XLI

His hands shook worse today than ever.

Yeshua couldn't stop thinking about the nightmare in which he'd killed the rabbi. He wanted to believe it was just a terrible dream, but it felt more significant than that.

Tonight, was the attack, and Yeshua knew he needed to be fully present in the moment. This time, no one would take his place if he were captured by the Romans again. Yet try as he might, his thoughts kept drifting.

In the dream, he had come to believe the rabbi was the long-prophesied Mashiach. But in the light of day, his doubts remained. Jesus didn't fulfill any of the prophecies such as overcoming the Romans or rebuilding the temple prior to his death. So how could he be the Mashiach? Yet everything the rabbi had said in the dream was true. Yeshua was deeply convicted of his sin.

Upon waking this morning, he knew that he could never take another life. He would fight today, but he would not kill. He would stay out of the way as much as possible. Reuben had been exceptionally good to him, and he would not let him down. But after today he would move on—somewhere.

The Zealots

The road below Jerusalem twisted and turned south through a series of valleys. Based on the message from one of Reuben's sources, the Zealots would attack the group of soldiers as they neared Jerusalem tonight.

Yeshua spent the day working with Reuben, trying to hide his anxious thoughts. Still, his friend sensed Yeshua's unease, and asked him about it. Yeshua claimed he was eager for the night's attack, which seemed to satisfy Reuben. Yeshua suffered in silence.

Finally, the sun hung over the horizon, and the men set off toward the meeting point a couple miles away. They joined a group of fifty other Zealots and spread themselves along the valley corridor, hiding behind foliage and boulders.

Yeshua was more than familiar with the attack preparations, but tonight he wanted nothing more than for it all to be over. His hands shook, and sweat drenched the back of his tunic, despite the cool night air. His stomach churned, and he choked back nausea.

Soon the men heard the loud crunch of footfalls on the gravel road, accompanied by the voices of soldiers. The Zealots readied their weapons as the first columns of Romans appeared around the bend, many carrying lit torches to illuminate the dusky surroundings. Reuben shouted, and the Zealots surrounding Yeshua sprang into action. The Romans were surrounded and assaulted by the element of surprise.

Yeshua hung back in the shadows until he could no longer. Tentatively, he stepped into the fray. Yeshua quickly took in the scene around him. Men fought using swords, daggers, and their bare hands. Yeshua drew his own sword, but he knew he wouldn't use it to kill. He hoped it would provide some appearance of intimidation at best. *Adonai, protect me*, he breathed, *I am trying to obey you.*

No sooner had the prayer escaped his lips, than a centurion spotted him from several yards away. The man brandished his sword and jogged toward him. Yeshua sucked in his breath, preparing himself. He was willing to wound the man, but he refused to kill him. The Roman pulled his arm back as he neared Yeshua, then sliced forward with his blade. Yeshua blocked the blow with his sword and pushed forward, knocking the soldier off balance.

The man staggered backward and then regrouped, once more raising his sword, and charging forward. This time, Yeshua swung his blade first, driving downward toward the man's legs. The soldier cleverly sidestepped Yeshua's attempt and stabbed his sword forward. Yeshua barely had time to raise his blade. The steel weapons clashed against one another, and both men stumbled back.

The soldier panted heavily, and Yeshua did not envy him the weighty armor he wore. He began to slowly circle the man, sword outstretched.

"Ha, you are afraid!" The soldier mocked Yeshua's inability to calm the shaking hand that gripped the sword.

Yeshua ignored him. The Roman stretched out his sword, unwavering.

"It's time you die, Jew," He snarled. With renewed energy, he stepped quickly to Yeshua's left and sliced his sword at Yeshua's chest.

Yeshua raised his arm, blocking the blow and pushed it backward. Quickly, he swung his blade down, and the Roman cursed. A trickle of blood dripped from a shallow cut on his thigh.

Frustrated, the soldier stabbed his sword forward, catching Yeshua off guard.

He stepped back quickly, but not before a sharp pain spread down his forearm. The soldier had nicked him. They were even, then.

For several more minutes, the men traded blows. Yeshua had to admit that the Roman was a worthier opponent than many he had faced before. From the corner of his eye, Yeshua noticed movement and glanced away. It was Reuben. The man had failed to deflect a blow from the soldier he was parrying with and fell to the ground. Yeshua watched as the soldier lifted his sword and swung down, stabbing Reuben in the chest.

"No!" He screamed, taking a step forward.

"Yeshua, look out!"

Before he could register the words, a horrible pain tore across his thigh. Screaming, he fell to his knees and dropped his sword. Blood gushed from a deep wound to his leg.

Yeshua looked up to see the soldier he had fought with moments before fall forward, stabbed in the back of the neck by one of the other Zealots. White spots danced before his eyes, and he felt the edges of his vision begin to dim. Around him, the fighting continued.

Yeshua saw the rabbi's face, his dark eyes filled with sorrow. Then his world went black.

 "Yeshua!" He felt someone shake his shoulder roughly. Yeshua blinked, trying to bring the face above him into focus. It was Achaicus, who had led his group of Zealots in the attack during Pesach weeks earlier. A searing pain spread across Yeshua's consciousness, and he gritted his teeth against a wave of nausea.

"Good, you're alive," Achaicus said matter-of-factly. "You've lost a lot of blood. We need to get you to a doctor."

The rest of the night was a patchwork of scenes and memories that Yeshua had difficulty recalling later.

Achaicus and two of the other Zealots had carried him to a doctor in Jerusalem and then left, fearful of drawing unwanted attention. Yeshua remembered hearing the doctor say that one of his main arteries was damaged, and that it was fortunate he was alive at all, considering the amount of blood he'd lost.

After that point, he had slipped back into unconsciousness. He woke up some time later. He lay on a mat on the dirt floor of the doctor's home. His leg was wrapped in clean white cloths, though it still throbbed with pain.

"You're awake." The doctor appeared. The man appeared to be in his sixties, with gray hair and a cream-colored tunic that showed signs of the surgery that he had recently performed on Yeshua's leg.

"I'm glad you pulled through," He smiled kindly at Yeshua. "Do you have family in Jerusalem?"

Yeshua shook his head no.

"Friends then? You will need a place to rest, to heal."

"I'll manage."

The doctor came to stand closer to Yeshua's mat. "Son, you need to realize how serious your wound is. I was able to suture it so that you didn't lose your leg. But I'm afraid it won't be the same."

Yeshua tried to absorb the doctor's words.

"What are you saying? I won't be able to walk?"

The doctor shook his head, "No, you will be able to walk, but you will likely have a limp."

Yeshua looked away.

"I'm sorry." The doctor's voice was filled with compassion, but Yeshua refused to receive any pity.

"So, do you have someone you can stay with in the city?" the doctor ventured again.

Yeshua winced. He knew the answer to the question. The attack had taken more than his leg. It had crushed his pride as well.

 Yeshua limped, painfully, to the pitcher of water in the corner of the room.

"My Brother," Stephanas entered the room at that moment, "Please, let me help you with that."

Yeshua shook his head angrily, "I can do it. This is to be my life, Stephanas. I might as well get used to it."

A stab of conviction tore through him. Stephanas was only trying to help. He was a good friend. Yeshua had not spoken with the tekton since his abba's death on the Temple Mount, and now he had stepped back into Stephanas' life as a burden. It was humiliating.

"I'm going to return to Capernaum," Yeshua turned to face Stephanas. "I've already spoken with a man regarding the purchase of his donkey. I'll be leaving tomorrow."

As if he knew Yeshua was ready for a fight, Stephanas simply nodded, his face passive.

"I see. Are you well enough to travel?"

If Yeshua was honest, the answer was no. His leg still hurt intensely from the wound inflicted just five days earlier. But he couldn't stand being an object of pity, surrounded by those he used to consider less righteous than himself. It was pride, pure and simple. And he guessed Stephanas knew it.

"I'll be fine," he insisted. "Thank you for your hospitality. I'll find a way to repay you."

"There's no need to repay me." Stephanas looked frustrated. "You are my friend, Yeshua." Without another word, he turned and pulled the door shut behind him.

Yeshua didn't know where Timnah and the rest of the family was, but he was grateful to be alone in the home. Painfully, he performed netilat yadayim while balancing on one leg, propped up by the crude staff that Stephanas had fashioned for him. His hands shook so badly that the ritual took him twice the time. Once done, he hobbled back to his mat and sunk to the ground with a groan.

A wave of despair washed over him. Reuben was dead. His abba was dead. He'd lost his best friend. And if the rabbi hadn't taken his place on the cross, Yeshua himself would be dead. A wake of death, loss, and guilt. Well, so be it. He would return to Capernaum and his trade. Certainly, a lame tekton would not be in high demand, but hopefully he could get enough work to feed Sarai and the children. They were his responsibility.

Yeshua turned to lay on his side. Until tomorrow, he would try to lose himself in sleep.

At dawn, Yeshua bade farewell to Stephanas and Timnah. He felt the sadness and compassion in their eyes as he mounted the donkey with effort but couldn't bring himself to say anything more. Yeshua left the city by the main gate, memories of the Zealot attack fresh in his mind. Though it had only been three weeks since his return to the Holy City, it felt like years.

The morning air was fresh and clean, the sky brilliantly blue and cloudless. Yeshua's thoughts cast a shadow on the beauty of the day, however. Surely news of his actions and capture in the Holy City would travel. People would hear of his release in exchange for the Mashiach.

Galilee had been the home and ministry area of the rabbi, and he had been well-loved. Would those who found out about Yeshua's connection to the rabbi's death want his services as a tekton? And a lame tekton at that. Yeshua doubted it, and the thought made him sink into even deeper despair.

Yeshua had so many regrets. He had not brought honor to his abba or his people. *I am not in death or vengeance.*

How had he ever fooled himself into thinking that he was glorifying Adonai by his actions? The nightmare involving the rabbi was never far from his mind.

Yeshua rode slowly along the valley leaving Jerusalem and headed north along the ridges created by the hilly landscape. His leg already ached, but he was not in a hurry to return to his hometown. Wildflowers and groves of olive trees waved at him as playful breezes tousled their foliage. After a while, Yeshua realized he was alone. Although he passed a few travelers bound for Zion, the road was generally quiet.

"Shalom, Yeshua," Yeshua jumped at the voice beside him, a bolt of pain shooting down his leg.

"Sorry for surprising you," A man grinned up at him, wrinkles creasing the olive skin around his eyes. There was no mistaking the rabbi.

"Wh—what, h—how?" Yeshua started, terrified.

"I know where every one of my children is," the rabbi smiled at him, "But sometimes they don't want to be found."

"What do you mean? How are you here?" Yeshua could feel his heart pounding. He kept picturing Jesus nailed to the cross just weeks before. He had watched him die and had seen the soldiers confirm it by stabbing him in the side. But now he stood before him, seemingly flesh and blood.

"I've been calling you for a long time, Yeshua. Your abba knew my voice. Your immah does as well. I love them so much."

Unexpected tears gathered in Yeshua's eyes, but he blinked them away.

"How are you here?" he cautiously asked again. Could the pain in his leg be worse than he thought? Was he hallucinating?

"I am risen as the navi foretold!" Jesus grinned up at him. Yeshua tugged the donkey to a stop, and Jesus also slowed.

"How is this possible?" Yeshua asked skeptically. "I was there. I saw you die!"

"Yes, I know." The rabbi nodded. He reached up a hand. Yeshua sucked in a breath. A jagged, circular scar stood out darkly on the man's wrist. He held up his other hand to show a similar scar. "It's me, Yeshua. Is this really so hard for you to believe?"

Yeshua's dream flooded into his mind.

"What are you afraid of, Yeshua?" asked the rabbi.

Heavy despair, mixed with desperate hope, poured over Yeshua.

"I've killed people, Rabbi," he said in a low voice. "It was I who was supposed to be hanging on the cross, but they let me go and crucified you instead, even though you did no wrong."

"That's true. You are guilty." The rabbi said gently, looking into Yeshua's eyes with a fathomless compassion. Yeshua couldn't help but feel as though he were inside his dream again. But this time he knew the conversation was real.

"Yeshua, I did not come here for those who think they are perfect. I came for the sick, the diseased, the poor, and the outcast. Only those who know that they aren't well can find the Kingdom of Heaven."

"What is it that you want of me?" He looked into Yeshua's eyes.

Yeshua suddenly realized that Jesus already knew everything he'd ever done. But he wanted Yeshua to confess it, to take responsibility for his sins, especially the ones he would rather not bring into the light. Despite knowing this, Yeshua's pride screamed not to do it. Everything in him wanted to stay in the darkness, where his shame could stay in hiding. But something deeper cried out for freedom.

"What of the prophecies?" he delayed.

"What of them?"

"The prophesied Mashiach is supposed to set us free from our enemies. He is supposed to make Judea the authority in all the world. He is to restore the temple."

"Yeshua, have you ever been set free through violence? Or through hatred? Has any earthly power ever been free of its enemies?"

Yeshua thought. "No, but that's what would set the Mashiach apart."

Jesus smiled, "Only when you love your enemies are you free of their power over you."

Yeshua remembered Jesus' words on the cross when he had begged Adonai to forgive his persecutors. What man could forgive his own murderers? Especially if he were without sin?

"I don't want to forgive them, let alone love them," Yeshua spoke the words harshly.

Jesus' eyes looked deep into Yeshua's.

"Yeshua, what gives you the right to condemn others? Do you really believe yourself to be so pure that you can cast judgement on another? Adonai alone is the Judge."

Jesus' words struck Yeshua like a blow, but they carried the sting of truth. He looked away.

"Yeshua, Adonai loved the world so much that He gave His one and only Son, so that everyone who believes in him will not perish but have eternal life."

Jesus' eyes filled with love. "Adonai sent His Son into the world to save it. Not to judge it. If anyone believes in me, he will not be judged. But if anyone does not believe," Jesus' eyes filled with grief, "he has already been judged for not believing in Adonai's one and only Son." Jesus' eyes pierced Yeshua's. "Adonai's light came into the world, but people loved the darkness because they don't want their evil actions to be exposed. But those who do what is right come to the light."

Yeshua felt the words sear his heart like a hot brand. He'd been living in the darkness for so long, knowing that his actions were contrary to Adonai's will, but refusing to step into the light. The years of poison and death suddenly felt too heavy to carry even one step further.

"Rabbi, forgive me!" he cried out, "I don't deserve your mercy and grace, but I beg you for it! I believe that you are Adonai's Son, the Mashiach! Have mercy on me!" He climbed clumsily from the donkey, ignoring the pain.

The rabbi immediately grasped his shoulders, steadying him so that he did not fall. He looked into Yeshua's eyes. "You are forgiven, Yeshua Bar Abba."

Yeshua felt a horrible weight lift from his shoulders, replaced by perfect peace. Tears filled with joy and relief flowed down his face.

"Thank you, Rabbi!"

Jesus' face reflected the same joy that Yeshua felt. He threw his arms around the rabbi in a hug.

"Yeshua, I died and rose again to fulfill Scripture." The rabbi stepped back and looked at him with a joyful expression. "I carried the sins of the world on that cross so that anyone who believes in Me and confesses his sins will find forgiveness and life everlasting."

Yeshua was amazed by the Mashiach's words and soaked them in. Jesus helped him back onto the donkey. Together, they continued to walk the road to Capernaum.

Jesus explained the Torah and Nevi'im to Yeshua, who listened, marveling at the rabbi's words. Though Bin-yamin and Phinehas had been excellent teachers, neither had come close to illuminating the words of Adonai and the prophets as Jesus did. As night fell, they set up camp.

The next morning, Yeshua awoke and found the rabbi gone. Though he was disappointed, he sensed that he would never be alone again. It was then that he realized his hands no longer shook.

XLII

Shim'on hummed to himself as he pulled on his side of the net.

"Time to go to shore?" Hanoch questioned.

Shim'on nodded, "Let's take them in."

It was early morning after a successful night of fishing, and Shim'on took a deep breath of the cool springtime air. He was tired, but it was a good kind of weariness.

The men pulled the boat onto shore and greeted Miriam and Lydia, who stood waiting with the donkey and cart to take the catch to market.

Shim'on was grateful to be back home with his wife. Life had settled into a pleasant cadence, though he had an inkling that it would not remain this way for long. Hanoch left with the women, while Shim'on remained with the boat. He sorted through the nets, setting aside those needing repairs. Soon his stomach growled. He built a fire on the shore, placing two fresh-caught fish over the flames.

Memories of Jesus' appearance days before kindled fresh in his mind. How he missed the rabbi.

He looked up from the flames to see a form limping toward him. As the person drew near, Shim'on was surprised to see a familiar face.

"Yeshua? What are you doing here?"

"Shalom." Yeshua grinned at him. Shim'on noticed the staff that Yeshua leaned on as he walked, and the white bandages wrapped around one of his legs. His face showed signs of cuts and bruising. Despite the obvious physical wounds, Yeshua's eyes held a look of rest and peace. Perhaps even contentment.

"I've decided to come back to Capernaum," Yeshua answered Shim'on's question.

"Are you hungry?" Shim'on gestured to the fish. "I have enough to share."

"Yes, thank you." Yeshua eased his way to the ground.

"Thanks to a Roman," He answered Shim'on's unspoken question as he patted his injured leg lightly. "I'm still healing, but the physician said I'll always have the limp."

"I'm sorry." Shim'on didn't know what else to say. Last time he had seen his friend, Yeshua had been guarded, even defensive. Now he seemed—humble.

"Yeshua, I know it was a long time ago, but I'm sorry for getting angry with you after my abba died."

Yeshua shook his head. "There's nothing to apologize for. I had no idea what losing your abba felt like until I lost my own. I should have tried harder."

He reached out his arm and Shim'on gripped it. Though it was a simple gesture, Shim'on felt the years of tension between them disappear in a moment. They were brothers once more.

"So, what are you doing back in Capernaum?" Yeshua asked.

"Some of the other disciples and I returned here after the rabbi appeared to us. I know, I know, it sounds crazy, but he has risen from the dead, Yeshua!" Shim'on spoke quickly, anticipating Yeshua to scoff at his words.

"I know, I have seen him myself." Yeshua said calmly, but a mischievous twinkle lit his eyes at the effect that he knew his words would have on Shim'on.

"You have?" Shim'on said, incredulous.

"He walked with me on the road to Capernaum. I saw the scars on his hands." Yeshua's eyes filled with joy at the memory of his time with Jesus. "I believe he is the Mashiach, Shim'on. More than that, I believe he is the Son of Adonai."

A smile split Shim'on's face, and he jumped to his feet. "Praise Adonai!"

Yeshua smiled at Shim'on's characteristic loud passion.

"This is wonderful news! What will you do now?"

"I'm not sure," Yeshua laughed. "There was a time when I always had a plan. Now all I want to do is tell others about Jesus!" He smiled, "I trust Adonai will provide tekton work to provide for me and my family. And perhaps He might give a lame man a wife, too." He grinned lopsidedly at Shim'on. "Speaking of which, I hear you finally married Lydia bat Amos. I'm happy for you, Brother."

"Thank you." Shim'on smiled. "I never believed I could be blessed with such a wonderful wife. She is a gift from Adonai."

"And you?" Yeshua asked. "Where is the rabbi now? Will you follow him again?"

Shim'on shook his head. "I will follow him forever, but I get the feeling that he's not staying here." He had spoken with Cephas about this just yesterday. Though he hoped Jesus would remain with them and take his place as their earthly king, somehow, he sensed this would not happen.

"No matter what happens, though, Lydia and I can't stay in Capernaum for long. We must tell people about Jesus. That he has the power to forgive and heal them if they repent and believe in him!"

Yeshua smiled. "The rabbi chose a good man as a disciple. I'm glad that you have a wife who shares the same faith. I will pray for you both." He sobered. "Please be careful, Brother. As we know, the Mashiach has enemies."

"We'll be careful." Shim'on nodded. "But for now, I'll fish until he tells me what to do."

The men continued to talk of the rabbi and his resurrection, and their lives before and after knowing him.

After a while, Yeshua prepared to leave. He pulled himself upright using his staff. Shim'on couldn't help asking a question that weighed on his mind.

"Yeshua, do you ever wonder why the rabbi didn't heal you?"

Yeshua nodded. "After he disappeared, I thought about all the stories I have heard about the miracles he performed. To be honest, I felt a little angry."

Shim'on nodded. He would have felt the same way.

"But then I started thinking about why I wanted to be healed. And really, it's out of pride." He shrugged his shoulders unashamedly. Shim'on marveled again at his friend's humility.

"I think Jesus knew that. If he healed me, I'd have less reason to rely on him. I think that I would try to take care of myself and my pride would grow. So actually," he chuckled, "I think I'm glad he didn't heal me."

Shim'on thought of how the Mashiach had redeemed his own life from death. He thought of his friend Yeshua and smiled. There could not have been any more unlikely believers than the two Zealots whose lives had been forever changed by the rabbi from Nazareth: one the son of a rabbi, the other a fisherman's son. Two killers turned Mashiach followers.

Rabbi, I don't know what's next, he thought, *but whatever it is, I will follow you forever.*

John 21:25 "Jesus also did many other things. If they were all written down, I suppose the whole world could not contain the books that would be written."

THE END

<u>Glossary</u>

Chapter 1

Sea of Galilee–The ancient name for Lake Tiberias, Lake Kinnereth or Kinneret, situated in northeast Israel between the Golan Heights and Galilee in the Jordan Rift Valley. It is the lowest freshwater lake on Earth.
Shabbat-The Hebrew day of rest
Shofar–A ram's horn used to announce religious days or ceremonies
Mikvah–A pool of water used for religious purification
Adonai–Name for God as Lord
Immah–Mother
Abba–Father
Synagogue–The building where Hebrews gather for teaching and prayer
Tekton–Craftsman
Rabbi–A Hebrew teacher, especially one who teaches the Hebrew law
Centurion–The commander of a century in a Roman army
Mercenary–A professional soldier hired to serve in a foreign army
Zealot–A member of a sect committed to overthrowing Rome's rule and establishing a Hebrew theocracy
Shema–Hebrew prayer
Nevi'im–The Prophets
Navi–A prophet (singular)
Torah–The law of Adonai given to Moses
Hebrews–God's chosen people descended from Abraham
Kiddush–Sanctification prayer
Challah–A type of sweet bread
Kugel–A sweet, egg noodle casserole
Mashiach–Messiah or Anointed One
Lehem–Bread

Chapter 2

Modeh Ani–Hebrew morning prayer
Netilat Yadayim–Hebrew hand washing ritual
Beth Sefer–Hebrew equivalent of elementary school
Beth Midrash–Hebrew equivalent of secondary school
Mishnah–Oral interpretation of the Torah
Shalom–Salutation at meeting or parting meaning "peace"
Tallit–Prayer shawl
Tekhelet–Tassels of the tallit

Chapter 3

337

Via Maris–'The Way of the Sea', a road running from Galilee to Samaria

Chapter 5

Shalom Lekha– "Peace to you"
Saba–Grandfather
Elohim–The One True God

Chapter 6

Zion–Name for Jerusalem

Chapter 7

Ketuvim–The Writings

Chapter 8

Caesar–Tiberius Caesar, Emperor of Rome during the majority Jesus' life
Contubernium–A Roman military unit of eight soldiers

Chapter 9

Pesach–Passover
Kosher–Ceremonially clean food according to Hebrew law
Ha-shalom lakh– "Is all well with you?"

Chapter 10

Pontius Pilate–Roman governor of Judea during the time of Jesus
Laila Tov– "Goodnight"
Jesus–The prophesied Mashiach and rabbi from Nazareth

Chapter 12

Testudos–A military battle formation named after a tortoise. Soldiers grouped together and put up their shields to create a 'shell' that was difficult to pierce from the outside.

Chapter 13

The Zealots

Tzaharayim Tovim– "Good Afternoon"

Chapter 14

Musht–The primary fish used for food in Galilee. Recognized by its spiney dorsal fin, it is flat in form easy to fry, with small bones and a simple to remove spine.

Chapter 22

Mashal–Parable

Chapter 26

Boker Tov– "Good Morning"

Chapter 29

Nard–An expensive perfume
Kaddesh–The blessing spoken as part of Pesach
Matzah–Unleavened bread also known as 'bread of suffering'

Chapter 32

Praetorium–The official residence of an ancient Roman governor
Eloi, Eloi sabachthani– "My God, my God, why have You forsaken me?"

Chapter 34

Hosanna– "Praise Adonai!" or "Save us!"
Golgotha–'Hill of the Skull' where Jesus was crucified

Acknowledgments

Ernest Hemingway wrote, "In order to write about life first you must live it."

If there's one thing I've learned about traveling, it's that it widens one's horizons.

At one time in my life, I was content to play it on the safe side. I had traveled to a handful of states, but never been abroad, except for a very brief stay in the Bahamas. After I married my husband (a true adventurer) all of that changed. With him, I explored the historically rich streets of Athens and clung to the back of a scooter in the salty air of the Grecian islands. I soared on a zipline through the Ecuadorian rainforest, an active volcano smoking in the background. In China, I walked on the ancient Great Wall, the stones slick due to the many who had walked it before me. And in South Korea, I stood at the border with the North, looking into the enigmatic country, and the next day sipped tea in beautiful, lush green tea fields.

These experiences and more planted the joy of traveling and exploration deep within me. So, when the opportunity to visit Israel and Jordan in the spring of 2018 presented itself, I was eager to go. For years I had thought about writing a novel based in biblical times. Little did I know that this trip would fan that dream into flame, and, more than that, change my life forever.

First and foremost—Thank you, Jesus, for saving my life. I believe you are the Mashiach. Thank you for giving me the joy of writing and for continuing to teach me about Yourself through the writing of this book.

To my husband, David—aside from Jesus, you have been my rock and greatest encourager. Thank you for believing in me even when I didn't. This book would not have been written without you. I love you.

Samuel—it is one of the greatest joys of my life to be your momma. I will never forget the first time I held you in my arms. I've thought of you many times while writing this book. I pray that you will never doubt God's great, boundless love for you. I love you.

Thanks to my managing editor, Laura Bartnick, for your patience, feedback through the development of my characters and plot, and for your encouragement. Thanks to the talented Capture Books authors and editors: Kathy Joy, Robin Bolton, Sue Summers, Tonya Jewel Blessing, and Lynn Byk who helped to edit and proofread this book. It has been a joy working with you.

Thank you, Susan, Jody, and Julie for your willingness to read my rough drafts! Thank you for investing your time in a novice writer, and for providing invaluable insights. I am thankful for your friendship.

I deeply appreciate the president and faculty of Jerusalem University College who hosted my experience in Israel and Jordan in Spring of 2018. *Read the Land. See the Text. Live the Book.*

To my WATC girlfriends who so sweetly encouraged me along the way-Mary, Christy, Ashlie, and Brooke, I'm so grateful to 'walk in the light' with you ladies!

To Lisa, Claire, Kimberly, Krystal, Trina, Becca, Laura, and Emmanuelle-I am so grateful for your friendship and encouragement. Writing a book is an incredibly vulnerable endeavor, and your confidence in me has been priceless.

Carol, I realize not all daughter-in-laws are blessed with wonderful mother-in-laws, which is why I'm doubly thankful for you. Thank you for encouraging me and babysitting so that I could write.

Thanks to Zachary, a talented artist and the first in my target audience to read the rough draft and give me his perspective.

Ty and Ali—Thank you for graciously and generously helping me with the business side of things. You guys are the best.

And to all my family and friends who encouraged and supported me in this endeavor—your words mean more than you know. Thank you.

About the Author

 G.K. Johnson lives in the Southwest with her husband and son. Always a passionate reader, she has fond memories of frequent bike rides to her local library, where she filled her backpack with books and became well-known to librarians.

G.K. finds fresh writing inspiration on adventures locally and abroad, but until this point, her storylines have been written on the tablet in her mind. *The Zealots* is the first she has put to paper.

G.K. invites you to connect with her on Books for Bonding Hearts website or her personal Facebook page. Find her, also, on Instagram and Twitter and LinkedIn.

THE HIGHEST COMPLIMENT you can give an author, is a recommendation. Thank you for sharing your own recommendation with your book clubs, your reading friends, and on Amazon and social media sites!

G.K. Johnson

CPSIA information can be obtained
at www.ICGtesting.com
Printed in the USA
FSHW010147120121
77575FS